SILVERBLOOD SCION

THE SILVERBLOOD SERIES. 1

SILVERBLOOD SCION

MEGAN MACKIE

Trigger Warning: fade to black depictions of rape and torture, violence against women and children.

DEDICATION

To my teacher Scott, the Lord of Zierath

Acknowledgements

Thank you to my family and friends for their love and support and simply being in my life.

Thank you to Laura and Jen who helped me translate this story so the whole world could understand it.

Thank you to my readers who follow me from book to book and genre to genre, wherever my stories my take me. I treasure you all.

When I let go of what I am,
I become what I might be.

- Lao-Tzu.

Table of Contents

PART 1

CHAPTER 1

MAEVRA RAN THE PEWTER COMB THROUGH ELAINE'S fine, white hair. It was a useless gesture. Elaine's hair had been thoroughly brushed already, but she did nothing to stop the older woman. She only watched her work reflected in the mirror.

"Your hair is so lovely," Maevra said, her voice strong and loving as always, speaking the Anon words because the language of their people, the Ka'in was too dangerous. But Elaine could see the tears trailing from the older woman's eyes. "Yes, so very lovely."

She knew Maevra wished to distract her from what was to come, but no amount of sweet words could mask the sense of doom hanging in the air.

"Is the Silverblood ready?" asked a harsh, hissing voice from the doorway. One of Dakin's wizard-priests, dark men with dark purposes, stood at the doorway. He spoke to one of her guards, but she could feel his eyes bore into her.

Looking up into the mirror, Elaine could not see the face shrouded deep inside a dark purple hood, but she knew it to be Cal, Razal's favorite.

"Is she ready, witch?" he demanded of Maevra, pulling his hood down as he stepped farther into the room.

In the dim candlelight, Elaine could see the lines and whorls that were tattooed over his skin. They were apparently spells etched into his very body that would prolong his life, sweeten his beauty, and maintain his essence. She had no idea if any of it really worked. To her, he just looked sick; his eyes too bright with whatever ceremonial drugs he had already ingested to awaken his majick. She doubted he had a thimbleful of the stuff in his whole body.

Maevra ceased her brushing and rested her hands on Elaine's shoulders, straightening her back. "You were meant to be the One," she said regretfully.

Elaine reached up and clasped one of Maevra's hands. "I am sorry," she said, her throat almost too thick to say the words.

"Oh, for heaven's sake, she is good enough," Cal cursed and gestured at the guard. "Bring her already."

He turned and left in a whirl of robes.

Maevra hurriedly leaned in to kiss Elaine's head. "Remember. You are more precious than sea pearls—" Then she was summarily shoved away.

The guard seized Elaine's arm and hauled her to her feet, knocking over the stool she sat upon in the process.

"Tell Elan I love him," Elaine managed to say as she was hauled into the hallway.

Another guard joined the first, seizing Elaine's other arm roughly.

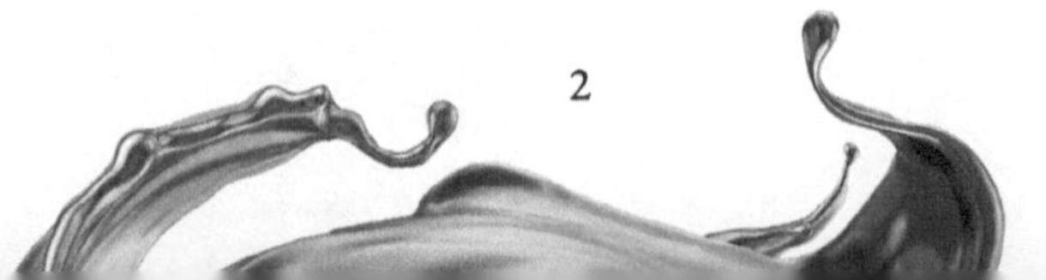

"Be careful!" Cal shouted from where he waited partway down the hall. He glared at her, disgusted as if her treatment was somehow her fault. "Do not bruise her or leave any marks!"

They released her immediately, and she felt a strong temptation to run.

Cal stared her down, waiting.

She reset her shoulders and leveled her head like the princess she was meant to be. Her bare feet made no sound on the freezing cold stone as she walked with poise toward Cal, each guard flanking her. An equally cold wind cut through the thin, silky shift clinging to her otherwise naked body, sending gooseflesh all over her. Shadows danced between the few torches, their blooms of flame whipping hard in the wind.

Once she started moving, Cal spun on his heel to continue down the dusty hallway, turning at the end past the exit full of dark night beyond. As Elaine went past, she could glimpse torches lighting the tents set up in the temple yard for Lord Dakin's warriors and the man himself.

When she hesitated a step before the exit, one of the guards shoved her back into motion.

"Do not even think about it," he articulated coldly and shoved her a second time for good measure. They went down another short hall leading into the temple sanctuary.

The sanctuary was the largest room, occupying most of the temple. Every member of her village could have fit inside with enough space for each of them to swing their arms freely. Large pillars lined each side, creating little alcoves that held broken statuary of long-dead gods. At the far end of the room, stairs led up to a black stone altar. Dakin's warriors stood among the statues and along the wall of the unconsecrated sanctum, focusing on the activity in the center of the room.

Their eyes watched warily as they fingered their bronze swords. Bronze plate glinted occasionally as they moved, winking like fireflies.

Behind the altar stood the sanctum for the long-dead deity, a separate room cut into the wall, which would have been hidden from the worshippers by curtains or lattice woodwork. It was a place where the god or goddess could descend and be with their followers. Now it stood cold and empty. Any sacredness had been long scoured away by time, cold, and dust.

Someone had set up Dakin's camping stool in the space. The man himself occupied it, and he stared at the altar with hungry eyes. Over his immense form hung robes of costly indigo worked with tiny bronze mirrors so he gleamed as he moved in the lamplight. A hood and scarf hung around his shoulders, the inside lined with fur against the chill. It made Elaine think of a marmot preparing to swallow his round head. A rope belted around his generous middle was a bit too high to be his real waist, which had been lost to fat years ago. It should have made him seem beautiful, a symbol of prosperity, yet Elaine felt disgusted to look at him. What she did find beautiful about him was his hair and beard, which gleamed the rich red-gold of the Anon people.

Cal led the way, stopping beside the altar. Other priests still worked, drawing elaborate runes with pigments inside a circle on the stones around the altar. Oil lamps had been placed at the junctures of the ritual space. Two others arranged chains on it, driving them in place at the foot and the head.

At the sight of the chains, Elaine jerked involuntarily away. She did not come to a full stop, but her slowing offended the guards nonetheless. They shoved her hard, and she fell to her hands and knees. The motions caught Lord Dakin's attention.

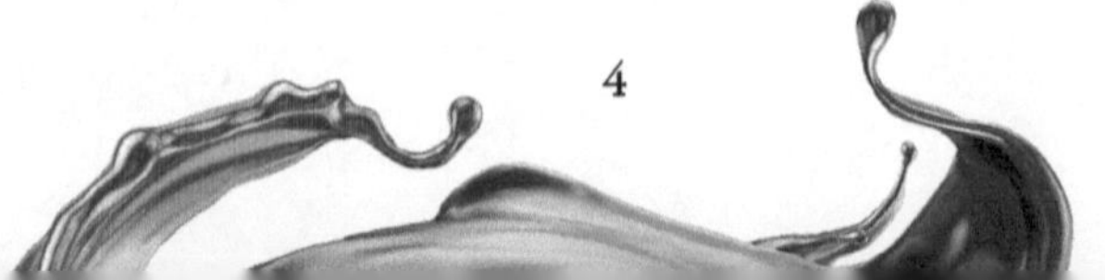

His permanent scowl morphed into a mix of lust and cruelty summed up by his small, closed-mouth smile that said, "I own you."

"Oh, Goddess," Elaine whimpered, losing her composure a moment.

"Your goddess isn't here, Elaine," Lord Dakin answered with a sneer, his voice amplified by the natural acoustics in the room. "She is long, long dead."

"Yes, my Lord. The final seals of her goddess will be broken today, erasing the last traces of her from this world," Razal, the leader of the wizard-priests, said, coming up beside Lord Dakin.

He was a slight man, barely reaching Elaine's chin. When he had his hood down, his bony, gaunt features looked like they could cut glass. Now, he had his hood up over the few scraps of white hair that dusted his head, his eyes wild and liquid green as swamp water.

The guards came to either side of Elaine, lifting her to her feet, barely giving her time to untangle them from the bottom of the twisted shift. "This is wrong. This is a violation of all the gods, not just Isa Kai. You can still stop this, my Lord, for the sake of your people," Elaine pleaded. She had to try, knowing she had so little time left *to try*. Dakin rose from his stool with an animal grunt as they brought her to him.

Dakin's slap whipped her head too fast for her to feel it at first. She tasted blood, coppery and familiar in her mouth. Her hair flew over her face, curtaining it in its flimsy protection so that she could not see his face clearly.

"How dare you, Ka'in animal!" Razal hissed, the old man's voice growling. There were agreeing murmurs from the warriors assembled, their hateful eyes watching the drama playing out before them between Dakin and his unwilling concubine.

Elaine no longer cared for what they thought, if she ever truly did.

"How dare *you!*" Elaine spat back with angry, measured calm, sounding more deadly because of its softness than any of Lord Dakin's shouts. She spat the blood out of her mouth. "You are about to release a horror on the world."

"Oh, Elaine," Lord Dakin said, his Anon accent changing the pronunciation of her name to something that didn't sound like it belonged to her anymore. He stepped closer to his captive. Roughly, he seized her face in his meaty hand and directed it so he could meet her eyes, flaring the sting of her struck cheek. "I think my only regret will be that I didn't break you first like a good bitch."

Then he kissed her, shoving his tongue into her unwilling mouth, only to recoil when he tasted the blood. Elaine felt a little bit of satisfaction at his discomfort, in spite of his last sexual assault on her.

He gestured imperiously, and the guards brought Elaine to the prepared altar. While Dakin had been speaking to her, someone had laid a valuable wine-red cloth over the black stone. The five robed figures, their features now fully obscured by their hoods, assembled themselves to the near side of the slab, ready to take charge of her as she came within reach.

Elaine struggled to hold what was left of her dignity, swallowing her whimpers. They forced her to lie down upon the wine-red cloth that did little to hold back the chill of the black slab. She wondered if she let that cold in if it would numb her to everything else. But it was a child's wondering, and she knew it.

The guards pinned her down hard on the slab as the priests chained her, preempting any struggles she would attempt. She focused on her breathing, trying to stay calm.

She ran the songs through her head: the songs of her people to comfort herself.

It helped to close her eyes. She remembered sitting at Maevra's fire with her twin brother in the time before all of this. With hands clasped together, they listened to the holy priestesses sing, followed by the priests' answering the call, singing from the darkness. It had sent delicious shivers up Elaine's spine under the Harvest moon—a night when the walls between the mortal realm and the Realm of the Gods were the thinnest and people could almost hear the gods answer. It was a prayer for her goddess Isa Kai and her husband Veres Kai, the Harvest God.

Then wizard-priests began to chant, the dark sound breaking her focus. She opened her eyes. The candlelight made the shadows on the broken statues writhe like maddened demons in the throes of a wild dance. A strange cranking sound cut through the chanting, and the chains around her ankles were stretched apart, spreading her legs wide while her hands were pulled straight. Completely helpless, barely able to move, Elaine watched Lord Dakin approach her feet, raising his hands in supplication.

"Great Lord! I come to beg to thee," he declared. "Great Lord, hear me!"

He paused then and looked down at Elaine with a sneer of disgust. "Will someone shut her up?" he hissed.

Elaine stopped the humming on her own and cursed her habit. She hadn't even realized she had started singing Isa Kai's song.

It's alright, she told herself. *It will all be over soon. Isa is with me.*

Razal approached, standing over Elaine's head. Raising both of his hands, he shouted more words dramatically, this time in a foreign tongue. Four other priests chimed a response to each of his stanzas in four-part harmony.

"What do you have to offer the Dark Lord who we summon, the Demon of War, Acies?" Razal asked, this time in Anon, cueing Dakin with a gesture.

"Great Lord," Lord Dakin cried, raising his voice even higher as he stepped around the end of the altar to stop in the midsection, "I humbly beseech your service. I have brought a fine sacrifice for your pleasure, a gift only I can bestow."

Dakin brandished a knife over Elaine's body, and her self-control shattered. She flailed against the taut chains, making them rattle uselessly as animal panic seized control.

It was too late to fight.

Lord Dakin smiled with satisfied pleasure, enjoying her struggles. He raised his eyes again, presenting the knife to the unseen Demon Lord. "She is tamed, Lord, but unbroken. Here is a taste." Quickly, he seized Elaine's wrist to slice the knife across her palm. An unnatural cold-hot fire clicked off her thinking brain with pain, and she cried out, her scream echoing off the once sacred walls.

Blood dripped down the blade, and an acolyte quickly moved forward to catch the drops in a clay chalice. Elaine's silver and red blood immediately began to smoke as it mixed with whatever potion was within.

The warriors gasped and murmured as the room filled quickly with a heady, perfumed scent. The wizard-priest brought the chalice closer, moving it so she was forced to breathe it in. The smoke made her woozy. She blinked hard, struggling to stay awake, but it was no use. The words of her song sat thick and unmanageable on her tongue. A single tear rolled down from her eye.

The knife lifted high over Dakin's head; his eyes rolled back in ecstasy from the deep inhalations of the smoke. The

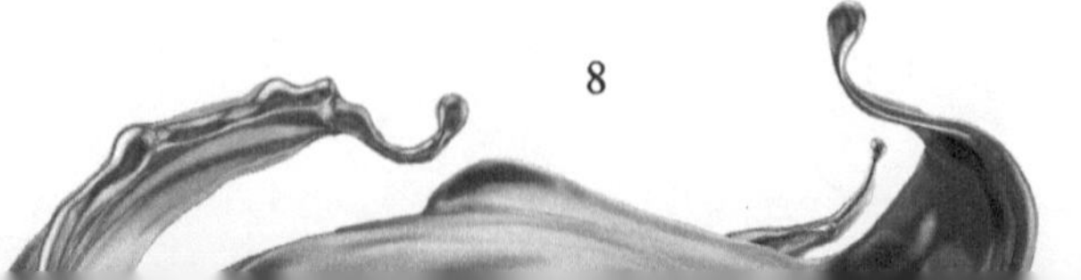

point plunged down. It slammed into Elaine's chest. She felt no pain, only electricity throttling her being. She couldn't breathe, couldn't scream, couldn't move.

Isa had not come.

Dying wasn't like falling asleep exactly; she could still hear Lord Dakin talking. The fat man never shut up, but he was now distant and unimportant.

"<What do you wish of me?>" came another voice. It seemed masculine to Elaine speaking in another language. The sound permeated everything with a clear rumbling.

She realized she was no longer chained.

A sensation of being lifted floats through her.

CHAPTER 2

HER BEING IMMERSES IN SWEET, WARM AIR SO SOFT IT could have been water, yet Elaine can breathe easily and freely.

She no longer wears the diaphanous shift.

She no longer is of her body.

Or maybe she never was.

But she still has a body.

She is simply herself, whole and complete, body and mind, spirit and soul. It feels natural and correct, like lying down in the sun after a hard swim through ice water.

Her hair floats freely. The blonde-white strands waft gently around her.

She slides her hands through the space around, the tingling sensation dancing across her fingers.

She giggles, child-like sounds which become bubbles of euphoria, popping bits of light. The light comes from her. Beyond her is a waiting darkness, melting before her light, welcoming her water to fill its hollowness.

She has a body, but that body is so much more now.

She is a being.

She is not frightened of the darkness at all. Such an idea seems silly.

"Was that it? Is it over?" she asks, the words coming out in her native language, her beloved Ka'in. This is not what she imagined. "Have I died?"

"<What do you wish of me, mortal?>" the voice asks again with more insistence, still in those foreign words that she still understands, though she cannot think of why.

The voice comes from the darkness, but it is not the darkness.

A presence floats beside her, too real to be a dream.

"Who are you?" she asks.

With icy clarity, she realizes it is the demon.

"<I am Acies, Lord of the Battlefield,>" he says.

The demon has found her.

As the idea coalesces in her mind, so too, does he.

He is hideous.

His skin is corpse-like and alien.

Yet it is the body of a warrior, covered in scars, the muscle well-formed over his bones.

He is as naked as she is.

But it is more than that, for she can see all that he is as well.

His spirit and soul lay bare to her gaze, though her mortal mind can barely comprehend all that makes him.

Violence and pain; hatred and fire.

Countless sins scar his essence.

Pain and torment.

He is a force greater than she is.

He is bound by the void, its tendrils piercing his essence.

The void is holding him, the only thing mightier than he is.

It is a terrible sight.

Yet he has a mark of true beauty.

His hair is so black it is almost blue, a coveted color among the Ka'in.

The exact opposite of Elaine's own.

Her own color is white-blonde and is quite common among her people.

Only a couple of Ka'in children in a generation will be born with the illusive black hair, the sign of favor and luck from their goddess.

She can't help staring at the midnight locks as they float, brushing her white. His hair is nearly as long as hers.

He waits patiently for her to finish her scrutiny as if he has eternity.

She supposes he does.

"You are the Demon Lord of War?" she asks.

His feelings change, shifting to red and black.

Echoes of screams and swords accompany memories.

His memories.

"<I am.>"

His gaze sweeps her body and essence.

"<And you are a Silverblooded mortal: god-touched with majick in your veins.>"

"Where are we?" she asks.

"<My hell,>" he says. "<My prison. Torn from the world to live in nothingness—unable to feel or touch anything outside of myself. No other existence—unable to escape even into madness or the dreams of sleep. No sense of time to measure my torment, just eternal existence. Forever trapped between falling asleep or waking up, interrupted by those who come seeking wishes from me in exchange for sustenance to ease my suffering. Their sacrifices are momentary. Fleeting. A drop of time and existence. Yet, a drop of their existence is the finest wine to a creature dying of thirst.>"

Then he shifts, cocking his head to the side as he regards her. "<So beautiful,>" he speaks. "<What do you come to sacrifice? What would you ask of me in return?>"

That's when she finally meets his eyes. She shudders uncontrollably, and her heart speeds up, unpierced, thumping loud in her ears.

They are sky colored.

It is uncanny. No warm browns or greens or yellows of the natural world. Her own eyes are a lovely mix of green and bronze. But his are a bright sky color, deep as wine.

She feels the urge to scream in terror.

The eyes look away hurriedly.

"<Do not stare into the void, beautiful one,>" the demon says, petulantly. "<But know that I suffer since the void cannot look upon your brilliance. Silverblooded child, the only new thing I have seen in an eternity.>"

"Why can't you look at me?" she asks, trembling.

"<Because it offends you so,>" he spits out nastily with deep, utter contempt, but at her or himself, she cannot tell.

Elaine closes her eyes in regret at having caused this creature further harm. "Forgive me, Lord," she whispers reflexively. "I did not mean to offe—"

"<Lord?>" the demon questions. He wraps his arms around his chest, hugging himself, attempting to hide what cannot be hidden in that place. "<Yes. Of course. You come to sacrifice, to make a deal with me and gain my arete.>"

"No, I... I am... I am here against my will. I do not wish..." She trails off, thinking.

Elaine is surprised that her voice seems to be coming from everywhere. She has not actually spoken. The truth of her answer is bleeding out from her entire being. He hears it all. Even with her eyes covered, she knows he can see her down to the core of her very being if he looks, and how can he not? There are no secrets, and she knows that if she wishes it, she may open her eyes and see all of his. The idea terrifies her even more.

"<You wish to keep me here in this realm. In my prison,>" he says slowly. "<To stop me from escaping.>"

"The demon will kill me now." *Her thoughts bleed out with certainty.* "He is a Demon Lord of War."

Yet no blows come, no pain, no tearing, nor rending, though her fears play out for him to see, the various scenarios of what she thought may happen when the demon took her. But none of them come.

"<I will not harm you,>" *the demon says.*

She opens her eyes to regard the creature before her.

"<I do not need to,>" *he says as his eerie eyes drink her in.* "<You are running out of time.>"

He gestures to the soft, warm oblivion around them.

"<It is this place, mortal. It eats your memories, then your body, and then, slowly, anything else that is left. I was once a great being, but now I am barely a portion of what I was. You are a snack for this void. If you wish to survive, best make your deal with me quickly and be gone.>"

"I have no desire to deal with you, demon," *she says, not unkindly. It is only the truth.*

"<There is nothing that you want? Nothing that I can give?>" *he asks despairingly.* "<Why would you come as a sacrifice to me if it were not to deal with me?>"

"Lord Dakin... He is the one offering me as a sacrifice to raise you."

"<You *are* offering the sacrifice; no one else. I will grant you power, beautiful creature. Whatever you wish of me, I will grant in exchange for a gift of equal value.>"

"I don't understand. I am his offering. I'm here to... I want to..." *she replies.*

14

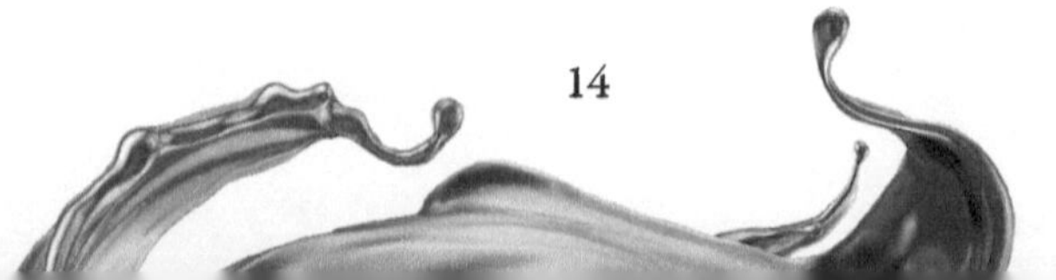

"I want to live. I want to be loved. I want to heal," her too-open soul cries out. She wraps her arms around herself. It does nothing to hide the truth. "I want to fulfill my purpose."

As if in response, the void warps around them.

She is back in the main sanctuary, standing before Lord Dakin. The guards are at her back, and the wizard-priest Razal cackles next to his Lord. Then Lord Dakin slaps her across the face. "How dare you, Ka'in animal!" Then he pauses. They all pause, holding stiffly as statues staring at her.

The demon shudders, his eyes closing as an expression of ecstasy flows over him. "<So long. It has been so long since I have seen anything new.>"

"You see then. He owns me. He is sacrificing me."

"<He does not own your soul. That is impossible. That belongs to you, and only you can share it, Silverblood.>"

The images around her begin to disintegrate, the void sinking into the bodies of the men until nothing remains but itself.

"What is this? What is happening?" she cries, alarmed even as the memory fades into facts with no emotions attached. Soon even those are lost to her.

"<The void. It's sucking your memories out of you. It will consume you the longer you stay here. This is your strongest, most recent memory. If you don't try to hold on to them, the void will suck them all out. Every laugh. Every friend. Everything that makes you ... you—until it takes your name. Then you will be as if you never were, and I will be alone again.>"

The implications of what he says shocks Elaine.

Another memory rises, one far more precious.

Maevra runs the pewter comb through Elaine's fine white hair. Her voice utters soothing words that mean very little and everything in the world to the waiting princess.

"You are more precious than sea pearls," the woman who is like her mother says.

And then the memory is gone, eaten by the void. Elaine feels the loss even though she cannot remember it.

Now she is truly terrified, for this is worse than death. "I do not want this."

"<Neither do I, yet it will one day be my fate,>" the demon says dryly. "<I have only to wait for the void to dissolve me completely. My slow execution.>"

"I want to live," she thinks as her soul cries out. "I want to be more than this."

The demon regards her for a thoughtful moment. Then he moves even closer until he almost touches her.

"<You fear your enemies? With the great power I have, I can slay your enemies. I can protect you. Bind me to your soul and pull me from this oblivion. Set me free from my prison, and I will be your slave.>"

She lifts her head and meets those uncanny eyes. Their intensity burns her, yet her fear of them rolls over and passes away. He is so desperate. She sympathizes with him.

"I have only my mind, body, and soul to offer," she says.

His eyes widen. He twitches as if he desires to grab her, and she can see the reflection of desperate longing emitting from his soul in a language she cannot identify, but she understands it all the same. "<I have only everything I am,>" his soul says.

He licks his lips with hopeful uncertainty. "<Will you give me your mind, body, and soul, Silverblood?>"

She hesitates. She wants to agree. She wants to be convinced. "Why do you not just take it?"

He cocks his head to the side at the question as if what she says is surprising and concerning. "<This place will steal it from me if not given willingly.>"

"How can I give it willingly if my only other choice is oblivion where not even my soul goes to join the God Beyond?" she counters.

Sadness reflects in his essence. He has no answer for that, and he knows it.

"<I can only offer you everything I am,>" he finally says, spreading his arms wide to her so she may see. "<I offer this willingly. My power is yours, my strength, my protection, but I cannot give it unless you offer something in return. Still, I am yours if you want it... if you will take me away from here.>"

"My mortal being is an equal exchange to a Demon Lord's?"

"<God Beyond,>" he whispers, "<you, mortal, are a pearl beyond price.>"

CHAPTER 3

OPENING HER EYES, ELAINE BLINKED SEVERAL TIMES to clear them. She stood in the temple once more but several feet from the altar. Unsteadily, she gripped the back of Dakin's camping stool.

Before her on the altar, a large bonfire danced mightily, reaching toward the high vaulted ceiling.

Elaine's eyebrows shot up in surprise as she realized it *was* the altar where she had been chained. She shivered uncontrollably and forced herself to look away, only to discover a man standing beside her.

A man she knew.

"<Acies, am I dead?>" she asked in Ka'in, forgetting herself, but even as she fought the rising panic in her heart, she laid her hand against her chest and felt it beat. She pinched her skin quickly, and it smarted enough to gasp.

"<Is that him?>" the man she knew to be Acies asked, nodding once, the light reflecting on his renewed face. Elaine flinched at the sound of his voice, clutching at the folds of the

shift she had been sacrificed in, which was now more gray than white. She swore she had just heard Acies speak some foreign language she had never heard before and should not have understood, yet she did.

Acies turned to her, his same sky-colored eyes intense in the darkness. "<Is that him?>" he repeated. "<The one who has harmed you, that you are afraid of?>"

She forced herself to look toward the fire again.

"Yes," she whispered with all her feelings and history loaded into that Anon word.

Acies nodded and Elaine realized he had changed. While within the oblivion, they had both been naked.

Now, when he turned his head, a long braid of black hair swung behind him like a rope laid against a richly woven cloak dyed in a color she had never seen before, pure black. It wrapped around his shoulders, leaving his arms free. The rest of his clothing was the same color, even the leather of his boots, which were also edged with black fur. He looked like a warrior out of legend from the time before the Great War.

"I am the Great and Mighty Dakin!" her former lord cried, pulling her attention back. "Why do you not respond?"

The priests still continued their chanting, gesticulating their hands in strange patterns. The warriors stood focused on the proceedings, gazes transfixed. No one had noticed them.

"The Demon Lord of War has accepted the sacrifice! Behold!" Razal cried. "See, she is gone! The fires have completely consumed her in a matter of seconds."

"We should escape," she whispered, but Acies moved before she could stop him.

As he stepped forward, the light framed his outline, casting her in shadow for a moment. He was easily taller than Dakin, a black shadow menacing toward her once lord and master.

"My Lord! Look! It worked!" Razal shouted suddenly, pointing from across the fire.

Lord Dakin's complaints abruptly stopped, and he turned around in an ungainly swivel. His face twisted into a mask of gleeful reverence, like a child looking upon a winter festival tree.

"It worked!" he repeated, and he scurried forward a few steps toward the demon. "You have come to my call. You are now at my command! I am the greatest man in all the world!"

The demon didn't acknowledge Dakin or even look his way. Instead, he stepped up to the fire. The room went silent, all eyes staring in shock, and the flames died down to half as he approached, like an animal cowering before a greater predator. Dakin's face slipped into a mixture of confusion and indignation with slivers of fear now that the stranger was beside him.

The Demon Lord of War held his hands out toward the waning light and turned them back and forth as if he had never seen hands before. Slowly, he articulated each finger in turn then all of them together.

Then he moved each individually again as fast as he could.

He laughed.

Looking back at Elaine, he held his hands up to her. Strong, vibrant hands.

"<I am alive!>" he said, triumphantly. "<I can feel! Real hands!>"

Dakin exchanged a glance with Razal then took the tiniest step toward the demon. "My Lord..."

"<What do you wish me to do to him?>" the demon asked innocently, his voice carrying well in the acoustically attuned room.

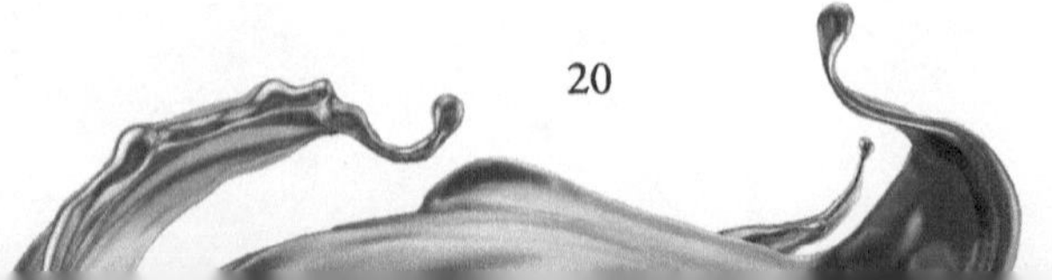

Lord Dakin, obviously not understanding the demon's strange words, looked confused and turned once more to the wizard-priest. Razal came to join him on his left side, the slight old man's eyes bugging out of his head.

"What is he saying?" Lord Dakin demanded, gripping the front of the wizard's robe and shaking him when he didn't respond immediately.

"He... He is speaking in a... a demon tongue, my Lord... I..." Razal stammered like he could not make his brain and his tongue work together. "This is not right; he should have appeared in the circle we prepared."

Elaine could hear frightened whispers from the guards echoing back and forth. "Look at his hair! What color is that? It is a bad sign. It is a dark omen. What have we done?"

"Well, make him talk in Anon. How am I supposed to make him do what I need him to do if I cannot talk to him?!" Dakin fumed.

"My Lord, stop!" Razal hissed, seizing Lord Dakin's arm with claw-like fingers, his eyes showing the whites. "That is not a god but a demon. You cannot command a demon unless you have struck a deal with it, and we have not struck such a deal yet."

"I just gave him my most valuable possession. He is now mine!" Dakin growled.

The demon took a step closer to Dakin, and the man flinched. Then the demon took a long, unsettling sniff. "<He is threatening me, isn't he? Please tell me he is threatening me. Fat pig, ready for slaughter,>" Acies said.

"Razal," Dakin said, his voice trembling, clearly unnerved. "What is he saying, man?"

"Cal!" Razal hissed to one of the younger priests, snapping him out of his frozen rabbit state.

"Uh, my Lords, I... I'm... I'm very certain..." Cal stuttered.

"He's asking if I want to have you all killed," Elaine said, her voice ringing out clearly.

Lord Dakin turned his eyes to her, and they exploded with green fire. "You!" he bellowed, and Elaine involuntarily flinched.

He stepped toward her only to find the demon as a wall. The demon did nothing, only stepped to intercept, yet Dakin flopped backward onto his butt with a startled squawk.

"How dare you!" he screamed.

"My Lord... she has... she has..." Razal stuttered.

"You treacherous bitch! What have you done?" Dakin bellowed. "Kill them! Kill them both!"

Acies's wicked grin matured to a full smile as the warriors drew their weapons and advanced.

The demon turned back to Elaine. "<None shall touch you,>" he assured her and spun with a flourish to face the oncoming horde.

"Kill him! Kill the monster!" Dakin screamed.

Without another word, Acies leapt an impossible distance, clearing the heads of the two guards nearest him, and pounced onto the warrior approaching the other side of the altar. The man died without a shriek. Before anyone could realize what had happened, the demon picked up the fallen man's sword. The bronze flashed as he took the next man's head off in one clean, bloody slice.

Like a spell being broken, chaos took over the room. The guards forgot about Elaine as they turned and rushed toward the fray. All those around Acies dove at him at once, getting in each other's way as much as they got their attacks anywhere near the demon. It did not help that the uneven terrain hampered their charges. Three men died by an ally's blade.

Acies moved with unhurried grace.

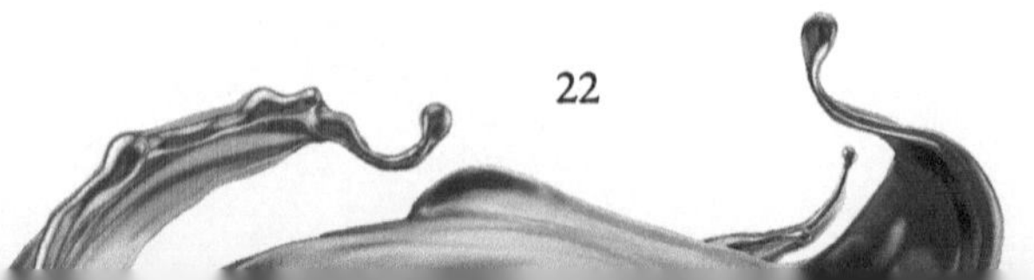

With his newly acquired sword, he blocked an overhead attack. He stepped up on one foot to kick his attacker away. The man tumbled down the stairs.

Spinning around, he placed his foot behind him so that he sidestepped a thrust from behind. While that warrior was overextended, Acies brought the sword around and sliced the man's neck before using the same motion to block a third attack from his blindside.

All of those exchanges happened in a series of seconds. After that, a rhythm set in that Elaine couldn't truly follow. What she saw were body parts and blood spraying through the air accompanied by screams of pain and dying.

Even worse, the demon seemed to be drinking it, licking his lips as he was showered in the blood of the fallen. With each life taken, he seemed to grow faster, stronger, more vital. There was even one whose face he grabbed and crushed, collapsing the skull with just the impossible strength of his hands.

"What have I done?" Elaine choked out loud in horror as she watched.

The Demon Lord of War moved along the stairs, this time engaging in a few passes with another more skilled warrior. The bronze swords clanged and flashed in the near dark as the combatants approached one of the pillars beside the headless statue of a god. Acies forced the warrior back against the statue, dislodging it from its plinth. A warrior hiding behind was crushed and died screaming. The scream distracted the fighting warrior who lost his wrist and with it his sword. Then he lost his life. Laughter echoed off the pillars.

Elaine didn't see the pair of warriors rushing up the stairs at her until it was too late to do more than raise her hands to helplessly shield herself.

Instead of swords piercing her body, the weight of one crashed into her to slam her head against the stone ground. The breath coughed out of her as she took a hit to her stomach. Stars broke in her vision as she fought to inhale. While she struggled, she became vaguely aware of a body scrabbling over her and the feeling of warmth spreading over her stomach.

She was too dazed to do much more than feebly push at the form pinning her down, its rough hands scrambling for purchase. A gleaming knife nipped at her throat with a hot bite, and she went still.

"Don't come near me or I'll kill her!" The warrior bellowed, his sweat-soaked stench washing over her as he tried to lean in and watch his back at the same time. Seizing the front of her shift, he pulled her up, maneuvering her into some sort of shield as he walked them toward the altar. What the warrior hadn't counted on was Elaine fighting back.

"Get off me!" she gasped, her breath struggling to fill her pained lungs. Even as the world around her wavered from semi-dark to dark and back, she slipped away from the warrior's fumbling grasp. Somehow, she got behind him and pushed with a burst of strength. The warrior fell back down the stairs to be skewered on the point of Acies's blade. The warrior died staring at the tip bursting through his chest.

She barely had time to register what she had done when the second warrior appeared at her side, grabbing a handful of her hair.

"Monsters! You're all monsters," he screamed at her, his eyes manic with fear as he slashed with his knife.

Except it was seized before it could break her skin.

The larger hand grasped his wrist. Elaine heard cracking sounds like that of crushed twigs. The second hand let go of her hair, and she shoved away from the altar. With mournful

sobs, her attacker fell back, flung to crash down the stairs with the blood-covered Acies following.

She did not see what more her demon did to the man.

Elaine ran.

Galloping down the stone stairs, she was senseless to everything else except escape. She had no idea where she would go, but she knew she could not stay there any longer as the calls of the dying flooded around her.

She had barely cleared the door when she found herself slammed against the stone wall of the hallway. She tasted her own blood as she bit her tongue. Both of her wrists were being cruelly crushed between both of Lord Dakin's large, meaty fists as his bulk pressed against her, threatening to engulf her.

"I will kill you, you Ka'in bitch!" he screamed in her face. She tried to struggle, but her head rang from being slammed. Her body would not obey her.

He tore her from the wall to force her to the ground, using his bulk to crush her beneath him like he had hundreds of times before. He released her hands to force one of his own hands down on her throat. She pawed at his wrist ineffectually, gasping for air. The other hand brandished a knife, and he pressed it against her cheek.

"I will bleed you dry, Silverblood!" he said. He leaned in then and licked her face, lapping up her blood, probing the cut with the tip of his tongue to bring forth more of her silver-colored blood.

She was going to die.

"No!" Elaine croaked out. Power from her blood snapped, sparking into Dakin's mouth. He bucked back in shock, his whole body shivering as Elaine's majick bit him back. He lost his grip on her throat, and she bucked hard, dislodging the man. Blessed air rushed into Elaine's lungs. In her mad scrabble, her elbow connected with his face, crushing his nose and causing his own blood to spurt everywhere.

Elaine made it to the wall, using it to pull herself to her feet. "I hate you!" she shouted at Dakin. It may have been a simple statement, but it was a truth she had spent so long not saying out loud.

Dakin roared, grasping at his nose, his voice cracking with his outrage. The ponderous Lord looked like an overweight purple beetle as he struggled on the ground.

He was so focused on cursing Elaine, he didn't notice the figure approaching him at a leisurely pace, but Elaine did.

The Demon Lord emerged from the sanctuary, where only the bodies of the dead remained. A fire had ignited from knocked-over lamps. At least one corpse had caught fire, the light flaring behind the figure. Acies stood covered in blood, a pair of swords, one in each hand. Elaine had wanted to run before, but now she could not move.

The figure stopped next to Lord Dakin. Only then did the fallen man notice the boots standing before him. He stared at them groggily before following them all the way up, bringing him to his knees.

"But I don't understand," Dakin said, defeated, in the voice of a small, spoiled child. "What did I do wrong? You were supposed to serve *me*."

Acies said nothing; he only stared down with hooded eyes full of contempt.

Seeing no mercy there, Dakin's pleading eyes flicked to Elaine. "How could you do this to me, Elaine? After everything I've done for you?"

"Do this to *you*?" If Elaine could have spat the words at him, she would have. "You sacrificed me to a demon!"

"Elaine, please, you don't understand. I had to. I had to sacrifice something important. You are my greatest treasure!"

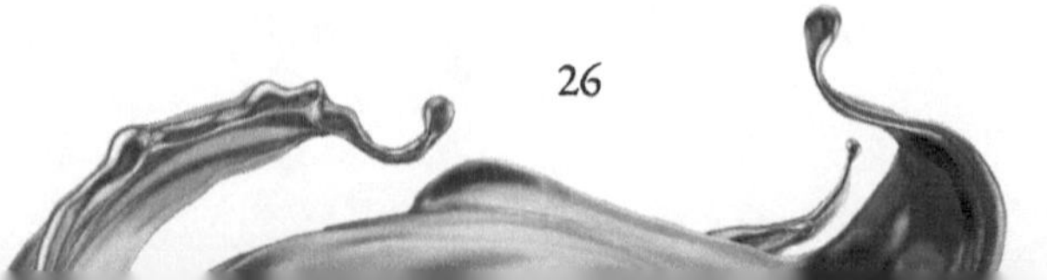

"I'm not a treasure!" she shouted back.

Dakin cowered like a beaten dog. "Please, my sweet Elaine. You don't know what you're doing! I did this for the greater good..." Lord Dakin stopped speaking as the demon moved around the fat man in a slow predatory circle.

"<Order me to end his life.>" He came behind the kneeling man and set the twin swords in an "X," the blades on either side of the fat neck. "<Command me, please.>"

Lord Dakin gave a jittery, squeaky laugh. It was as if failure and impending death had driven him from his wits. He spat a large wad of blood that hit the stones halfway to Elaine's bare, dirty feet. "Ha, the jest is on you, demon. I tricked you. She wasn't even a virgin sacrifice!" he crowed mockingly. "I pawned off damaged goods on you." Then his face twisted toward pleading again. "Is that what I did wrong? She wasn't pure? Is that why you would not serve me? Because of her lack of purity?"

"<What does her body have to do with her soul?>" the demon asked.

Dakin stared at the man. "What... what did he say?"

"He said what does my body have to do with my soul," Elaine repeated.

Dakin whimpered. "Elaine please, please..."

"<Elaine,>" she stated.

He blinked. "What?"

"E-laine. Not I-laine," she spat, finally correcting his pronunciation.

"<E... Elaine.> A-a-after all the kindnesses I've shown you, you cannot murder me! What about your goddess, Isa Kai? What about her mercy?"

By force of will, Elaine pushed herself away from the wall as she stared down at the kneeling man before her.

"You said it yourself. My goddess is not here," Elaine answered.

An arrow bloomed out of Dakin's throat. Whatever else he would have said disappeared into gurgles as blood spurted from his mouth. His eyes widened to perfect circles and his ineffectual fingers clawed at his throat.

Surprised, the demon took a step back, withdrawing his blades.

Dakin's eyes rolled back in his head, and he melted to the floor.

And thus ended Lord Dakin, the would-be king.

Elaine felt heavy. Her tongue lay thick in her mouth as tremors stuttered from her bones.

"Is it over?" she asked, unable or unwilling to look away from the scene before her. "It just doesn't seem like it's over."

"<Get away from her, demon,>" a familiar voice barked in beautiful Ka'in.

Acies paused then raised his dual swords up, ready to continue the fight.

Elaine turned around.

"Elan!" she cried.

CHAPTER 4

ELAINE COULDN'T BELIEVE HER BROTHER STOOD AT the end of the hallway leading out to the front entrance of the temple. Moonlight poured in through the slits in the wall, cutting across his fine, handsome features. His eyes were darkened with charcoal in the manner of her people's warriors. The play of light and shadow made him seem like a gaunt skeletal face with living eyes that burned intensely. Even with the warrior paint, she knew it was him. A dark, shadow line bisected his features, and Elaine realized it was the bowstring of his drawn short bow as he sighted down an arrow at the demon.

"I said back away from my sister, now," Elan ordered, still speaking in their native tongue. He took a step closer, and his white-blond hair flashed in the slice of moonlight.

"Elan, don't," Elaine said, the Ka'in words coming back to her easily after so many years of them being forbidden to her. She struggled to her feet, putting herself between her brother's arrow and her demon. The move made the young

29

Ka'in man hesitate, shifting away from pointing directly at her, but not standing down. Elan was a good shot but not perfect, and the shot would have to *be* perfect with his sister's life on the line.

"Elaine, come to me. It is alright now. I am here," he said as he stepped closer, beckoning with a nod. Outside, there were more shouts and sounds of fighting. He had come with the Ka'in resistance. "Come to me, quickly."

"Elan, you cannot be here!" Elaine tried to beg, but her brother, her twin, continued inching closer.

"We can escape. I have taken care of all of it. We are leaving Dakin's land and returning to the mountains. Just get to the side of the hall and come to me," her brother coaxed.

"<He is your kin?>" Acies asked, the rumble of his deeper voice a sharp contrast to her brother's higher tenor.

"Please, do not hurt him," Elaine begged. She held her hand out to Acies, and he lowered the swords to point them at the ground obediently.

"<As you wish,>" he said, but his eyes continued to follow the arrow pointed in his general direction.

"Who is he?" Elan demanded, nodding his head at Acies.

"I..." Elaine didn't know what to say, or rather, she knew what to say and what the consequences of admitting it could be.

"Who are you, friend?" Elan asked, directing his question at Acies, using the word "friend" as a challenge.

"Friend," the demon repeated, enunciating the Ka'in word carefully. "<No, not his> friend."

Elan's eyes went wide, the tip of his arrow faltering as he studied Acies's face. "His eyes," he whispered hoarsely. "The demon. They released the demon!"

He let loose his arrow.

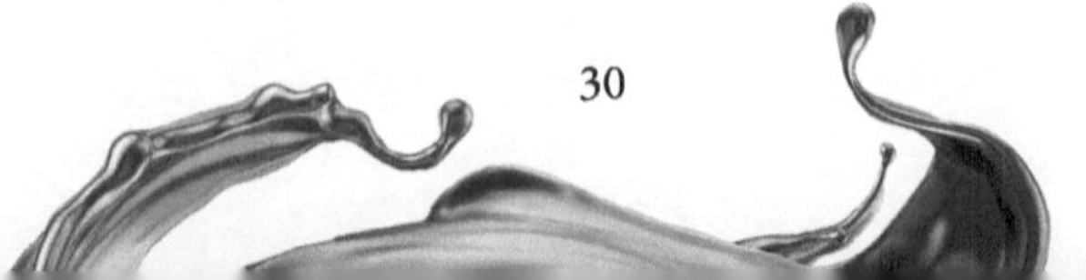

CHAPTER 4

Whether he intended to or not, the missile shot true, buzzing past Elaine's ear. She tried to scream for it to stop, but the forces in motion were already out of anyone's control. As if moving too slowly, she spun, expecting to see the arrow sticking out of Acies's chest.

Instead, Acies blurred into motion. He had stepped aside, and she barely saw him finishing the swing of both swords. A split second later, the arrowhead scrapped along the wall, the arrow sliding harmlessly to the ground. Then, Acies moved, running at Elan with his uncanny speed.

"No, don't!" Elaine cried uselessly, but it didn't stop either man.

She got between them. It was the only thing she could do.

When Elaine awoke, it was not in the cold hall of the dead temple.

Rather, she stared at the mead-colored walls of Lord Dakin's tent. It bounced and rippled as the wind disturbed the fabric as if it wanted to fly from the wood frame. Warmth permeated every part of her, a warmth she had not felt in ages. After the first startle upon waking, she held still, listening for any sounds of Lord Dakin moving about the tent. It was rare that he let her sleep with him through the night, but it did happen. Most of the time, once he had his fill of her "charms," he would kick her out to go to her smaller, adjacent tent, connected by a corridor of cloth to his larger one.

Normally, she wouldn't have minded that. Yet... did that mean she had only dreamed...

She lay in the middle of the bed, taking up as much space as she desired on the overly large, stuffed mattress. She was covered with the softest furs, lying back on one of Dakin's tightly packed, goose feather-stuffed pillows.

As she lay there, she tried desperately to recall what had happened, yet the facts eluded her. Her last memory was of arriving at the long-dead temple and the warriors breaking camp.

Panic threaded through Elaine, and she forced herself to take a deep breath relaxing her clenched muscles. Keeping her breathing even and moving as little as possible, Elaine crawled her fingers over her own flesh. She was naked, but that also was not unprecedented. Otherwise, she felt a general ache throughout her body and a growing urge to relieve herself.

A movement in the tent finally alerted her to the fact that someone *was* there with her. Cautiously, she lifted her head, hoping it would be Maevra coming to take her back to her tent to clean up and dress. She did not see Maevra's sad face or Dakin's round, broad back, but instead, she saw a figure more warrior-like and far taller than either. The appearance of the stranger alarmed her, and she recoiled, pulling the fur against herself.

Has Dakin given me as a gift for the night? she wondered, desperate to remember, but her head only pounded, offering no answers.

Then, the warrior-like man turned toward her.

He was the most beautiful Ki'an she had ever seen: tall with uncanny dark hair that seemed to be slightly damp as if freshly washed. His skin was unmarked, and there was strength in every movement. She marveled as he approached the side of the bed. His head nearly brushed the ceiling of the tent.

She wondered who he was. *Surely such a man would be memorable?* she thought.

Yet she also knew that Lord Dakin would never give away his prize to one such as him. He was clearly a Ka'in with ears that pointed up like hers. Dakin had nothing but contempt for Ka'ins, even if that was belied by his pride in his exotic Ka'in Princess.

Yet the warrior seemed unconcerned about being caught by Lord Dakin or any of his retinue as he sat down on the edge of the bed, bearing Dakin's carved wooden ewer. As he settled, a slip of water escaped from the edge, splashing unheeded onto the muscled thigh of his pants. He fetched a clean cloth from within the water and grasped one of her hands gently. She gasped at his touch.

She expected his eyes to switch to her or startle, yet he simply continued sliding the cloth over her skin, sponging away the blood and dirt covering her. In fact, he had yet to meet her eyes at all.

Surely, he must realize I am awake? she thought.

Yet there was no acknowledgement of that fact; he only washed her gently with the cloth. Scratches and dried blood coated her skin, and soon drips of watery red slipped with each press of the cloth. Neither of them said anything as he worked his way up, checking the scratches as he went. Elaine found herself mesmerized by the care he took with her. Then, he got to a particular cut on her shoulder, one that started to bleed again as soon as he cleaned it. Elaine winced at the small sting. With the same naturalness as his tending of her, he bent over her arm to lick the wound with his tongue.

Elaine yelped, more in shock at the act than pain, yanking her arm away from the stranger. Icy heat burned where the scratch had been. When she looked down at it, all she saw was the bright pink flesh of week-old, healed skin.

The stranger said nothing as Elaine marveled at the miracle. He simply dipped his cloth in the ewer of water to wring it fresh.

As the sensation began to fade, a memory from the dream she had been having came into focus—her slamming into a wall and the sound of Dakin's voice screaming at her, but she couldn't quite make out the words.

"Elaine! Are you alright?" a voice called from beyond the tent in Ka'in, not Anon. The leather flap that lay over the entrance lifted, and Elan, of all people, entered.

"Brother!" she declared, surprised at the sight of her twin.

"Are you alright?" he repeated entering the tent. "What did *he* do to you?!"

The glare Elan gave the stranger evidenced his feelings clearly for Elaine, but he did not unsheathe the sword he had at his hip even as his fingers itched at the pommel.

"She is ... alright," the stranger said, his deep voice sounding familiar. A tingle began in the back of Elaine's mind, a flash of familiarity.

"I see that, but what did you do to my sister, demon?" Elan demanded stopping short of the bed.

"I am..." The stranger stopped, struggling to speak Ka'in words. He glanced at Elaine, showing her his startling blue eyes, except she wasn't startled by them. She had known they were blue. Somehow.

"<How do you say it? 'I am tending her wounds,'>" he finished in another language entirely, looking at Elaine.

Elaine blinked at the strange words, so much *like* Ka'in, yet it sounded like something Maevra's grandmothers would have spoken when talking to their elders... and she understood it.

"Stop speaking gibberish," Elan said darkly, seizing the ewer of water from the stranger's lap, splashing much of it onto the carpets that had been laid over the packed earth beneath.

The stranger smiled darkly at him. "Not my ... concern," he said, this time in Anon, before snatching back the cloth, leaving Elan with the sloshing ewer looking foolish.

The stranger brought the cloth back to her arm as he continued to bathe her. She held still under his ministrations, wishing she could read more of the situation without needing to ask or, even better, wishing she could remember what she had obviously forgotten.

"Acies," Elaine finally said, remembering. "Your name is Acies."

His eyes met hers. "<You remembered.>"

She had to shake her head. "No, I do not actually, but..." That's right. He was a demon.

He nodded. "<You were poisoned by your enemy's dagger. You endured too much and shut down, but you will recover now,>" he assured.

Something about what he said sounded wrong to Elaine, but she could not quite put her finger on what. By contrast, everything felt wrong, so she could not really trust her feelings.

Just then, the flap of the tent opened a crack as someone peered in. The two men turned toward it, and for a heart-leaping moment, Elaine thought she saw Dakin.

"How is she?" another, distinctly not Dakin, voice asked also speaking Ka'in instead of Anon.

"Titama?" Elaine asked, breathlessly. Her heart leapt at the sight of her old suitor, one she thought she would never see again. And then she glanced at Acies, suddenly fearful. Did Titama know? Did the whole camp?

But neither the demon nor the leader of the Ka'in resistance even regarded each other.

Instead, the Ka'in's face smiled as he entered the rest of the way into the tent. "My princess," he said, dropping to one knee before her, crossing his fist over his chest. "I am so grateful we made it in time."

"Barely," Elan grumbled as he glared sourly at the new Ka'in. There was something in the tension between the two childhood friends that Elaine recognized. "And we almost did not—"

"We brought a whole band of us to save you, Elaine," Titama interrupted, rising up to stand before her. "Or avenge you if need be. That is what counts. There were many sins against the Ka'in to repay to that fat pig."

As if a bell had been wrung, memories finally rose like water submerging ground that appeared firm.

She remembered being prepared as Dakin's sacrifice and the ritual itself.

She remembered meeting the imprisoned demon, the man who sat next to her with eerie blue eyes. And she remembered the deal she had struck with him.

Lastly, she remembered the fate of Lord Dakin.

Surprisingly, she felt nothing as she recounted those memories to herself in a matter of moments. She would have expected to feel fear, horror, or a general sadness, but there was nothing. She still had no memories to explain how she returned to Dakin's tent and how she came to be in her current state under the furs, but a small amount of imagination filled that in for her.

"Thank you for coming for me, Titama," Elaine finally said, wishing she had the strength to sit up as she spoke. "You risked much for me."

Titama dropped his gaze to the ground in a show of guilt. Intuitively, she knew what it meant. They had not come to save her; at least, it had not been their primary mission. It explained Elan's ire. He would have prioritized his sister's rescue above everything, but saving the Princess of the Ka'in would not have been worth the terrible risk for the rest.

"Dakin is dead," she said, knowing it was true but needing to hear it out loud all the same.

Titama's lips drew into a line, not at all relieved at what that news should have brought. Elan, by contrast, spat at the floor and crossed his arms. "And may we all piss on his grave," he declared.

"There is more to it than that, is there not?" Elaine asked.

"Dakin's death has created ... complications for us." Titama forced a smile. "This is not something we must discuss tonight. More will be told in the morning. I only came to see that you are well."

"She is well," Acies said clearly in Ka'in. Now Titama looked at Acies, measuring Elaine's other complication with his eyes.

"I am glad of it," he stated, offering his hand. "I am Titama of the Ka'in. You were the warrior who saved our princess?"

Elaine's heart leapt for a moment, but Acies seized his forearm to perform a warrior's shake with a natural ease. "I saved Elaine," Acies agreed.

Elan's expression held stiff, and Elaine realized then that he had not breathed a word of what he had witnessed in the temple. She wished she could ask him what he had or had not said, but she could not risk it.

The man and the demon released the clasp, still eyeing one another, Titama's eyes full of questions.

"From what clan do you hail?" Titama finally asked. Elan cleared his throat, trying to distract from Acies's answer, but all ignored him.

"No clan," Acies said simply.

Titama continued to study him. "Your accent is—"

"Alright, that is enough," Maevra declared as she swept into the tent. Both true Ka'in warriors snapped to attention. "What do you men think you are doing in the tent of a sick woman? Get out now."

Titama immediately yielded to his elder with a solemn, somewhat guilty nod and a repeat of the salute he had given Elaine followed by his quick exit. She felt both sad and relieved to see him go.

Elan looked after him in disgust. "She is my sister," Elan argued.

Maevra set her hands on her hips. "I do not care. You have hot blood right now, and she is too ill to deal with you and your energy. Go tend to the fires with the rest of the warriors."

Elan jutted his jaw. "I am the Prince of the Ka'in—"

"And I am the High Priestess of Isa," Maevra snapped back.

As hot-blooded as Elan could be, he did not have it in him to disobey the older woman for very long, but when he moved to leave, he realized he was the only one.

"Why does he get to stay?" Elan demanded, rudely pointing at Acies who calmly sat on the bed watching the whole scene attentively.

"<Does he believe that he has the ability to make me leave?>" Acies asked in his strange tongue.

Maevra's eyes snapped to the demon sitting on the edge of Elaine's bed. The tremor of fear that painted her features reflected on Elan's as well, though his also were more confused as they both regarded the stranger.

So they both knew.

Then Maevra set a gentle hand on Elan's forearm.

"All will be well, my prince," she assured with a conviction Elaine did not believe she felt. "Keep everyone else away from here ... for Elaine's sake. Rumors are pouring freely from their mouths as it is."

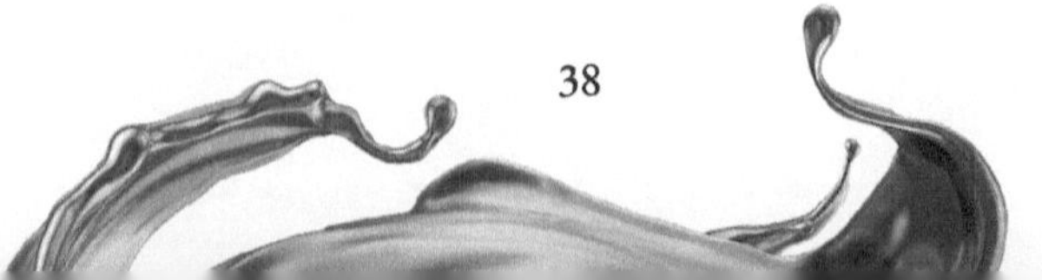

Elan sighed and nodded.

"The water," Acies suddenly said in Ka'in, just before Elan exited. The Ka'in Prince jumped, splashing even more from the ewer he held forgotten in his hands. Acies smiled at him, the predator on display. Maevra interceded, taking the ewer, and went to a small table to refill it from a clay pitcher.

Elan flashed one last look of warning at Acies before he finally left the tent.

Elaine found herself wishing her twin had stayed now that she had to face the high priestess after everything that had happened. She had no idea what she was going to say.

But she didn't have to say anything. When Maevra approached the side of the bed, she immediately bent to lay a kiss on Elaine's hairline, gently stroking her spare hand over her head.

"My precious child," she said, her voice cracking with emotion as she pressed her forehead against Elaine. "I was so sure I had sent you to your death. I thank Isa that you are alive."

"Oh Maevra," Elaine whispered, her own voice cracking with the same emotions.

"<Did you say you were a priestess of Isa?>" Acies asked.

The moment broke as Maevra stiffened. The two regarded each other carefully, Acies's small smile never faltering under her scrutiny.

"<I know who you are,>" Maevra said carefully. She spoke the same language as Acies, but it lacked the musical quality of his, as if she was not a native speaker of it. "<And I saw what you did.>"

More memories bloomed in Elaine's mind: ones that, again, she had no feelings about, but the facts of them brought other fears. A room filled with bodies, covered in blood. Acies's was equally as painted as the walls—then she imagined those same stormy eyes bearing two swords, using them on the people she loved instead of hated. "No wonder your hair is wet," she whispered, drawing the other's attention back to herself.

He glanced at Elaine.

Then Maevra bowed her head to him. "<I must thank you for saving my charge.>"

He narrowed his eyes at her as if he expected treachery. "<You have not answered my question, priestess.>"

"<Much has happened in the time you have been asleep...>"

"<That is *still* not an answer to my question, Priestess of Isa,>" he hissed, standing up, leaving the ewer on the bed. "<If you know who I am as you claim, then you would do well not to play games with me!>"

Maevra backpedaled from his imposing height. Elaine's hand found the strength to snap out to catch his forearm, yet she did not have the strength to hold him back. He broke her grip and grabbed Maevra's arms; she gasped in fear.

"<How soon until your Lady comes to cast me in chains again? What have you told her of me!>"

"<Nothing!>" Maevra shook her head, fighting to keep her voice down and losing it to her terror.

"<Acies, please...>" Elaine begged in godspeech. She hadn't realized she could speak it, but she barely registered that she was. Instead, she attempted and failed to stand or even move her legs. The fur coverings heedlessly fell from her as she grasped the edge of the cot with her hands, forcing her body at least to sitting.

"<I will not go back into the oblivion...>" Acies continued.

"<Isa Kai is dead,>" Elaine said.

His eyes snapped back to her. "<What do you mean, she's dead? She cannot be,>" he said, a tremor of emotion lacing his voice.

"<She is,>" Elaine declared, hoping she was not a fool for rolling these bones. "<I would know better than anyone.>"

"<Why?>" he demanded, narrowing his eyes at her now.

"<Because ... I was to be her Scion,>" she admitted.

He stared at her for several heartbeats. "<Silverblooded,>" he whispered as if he should have known.

Elaine's arms began to tremble from holding her body upright, but she had to will herself to keep holding on. She raised one of her hands in entreaty even though it noticeably shook.

"<Please, I beg you,>" she implored. "<Let her go. No one is coming for you. I promise.>"

When he did, Elaine collapsed.

She barely managed to fall back into the bed instead of out of it. Her torso lay exposed, but she could do nothing about it, not even care. Now freed, Maevra rushed to her side, yanking the furs back up to cover her, then brushed away hair that had fallen into Elaine's face.

Elaine closed her eyes at the touch. She was so tired.

"<She died at the end of the Great War, my Lord,>" Maevra said stiffly.

"<No,>" Acies said.

Elaine forced her eyes open to see him shaking his head. "<She is one of the greatest goddesses that ever walked the world. Such a thing is not possible. You are lying... lying to me!>"

Maevra held up her hands in warning. "<I do not lie to you...>"

"<Shut up!>"

Maevra flinched back from his roar, placing herself between the demon and Elaine. Both women were used to men yelling at them, and she braced herself as if she expected to be struck. Instead, he spun away to snatch the ewer off the ground. He flung it at the tent walls. By some miracle, he missed the post by the merest whiff of air. The ewer bounced off the cloth instead and back to the carpeted floor without breaking.

But Acies broke. His knees buckled, driving him hard into the carpeted dirt floor. He braced himself with a fist, which he then pounded into the ground repeatedly while he screamed so hard that no sound came out.

Grief. It was the sound of *grief*.

Elaine knew it too well to mistake it for anything else. The demon raged against the floor with his fist several more times before he calmed.

Going very still, he panted hard, shaking his head. "<She cannot be dead, old woman,>" he spat. "<Not before I make her answer for all that she did...>" His voice broke again, but he swallowed down whatever he was going to say. He turned to Maevra with eyes that raged like a storm, but his voice was small and earnest as a child's. "<What happened?>"

Maevra found Elaine's hand and squeezed it, pursing her lips together. "<After you were sealed away for your crimes...>"

"<Betrayed,>" Acies growled. "<I was betrayed by your precious Lineage Gods for doing exactly what they wanted me to do, what they themselves were too cowardly and weak to do.>"

"<I cannot speak to any of that, my Lord. I was not there,>" Maevra said in that infuriatingly diplomatic way that consternated lords and lowlifes alike.

It did not deter Acies. "<And the war? What of the war?>"

"<You mean the Great War?>" Elaine asked.

"<Yes!>" he yelled. Outside, Elaine could hear unnerved voices and little else. The camp was listening.

"<The Gods won at great cost,>" Maevra answered for Elaine though he had been asking her.

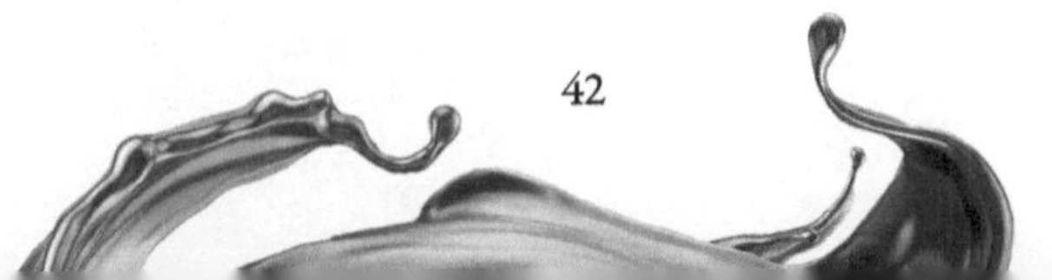

Acies rose, clearly fed up with Maevra. "<Get out, woman!>" Acies ordered.

Maevra jutted out her chin. "<I will not...>"

He turned then and seized her by the throat.

"No!" Elaine pleaded in Ka'in. "No, please, my Lord. Do not hurt her—"

"<I said get out, you old witch,>" Acies growled, heedless of Elaine. "<I will not repeat myself again.>"

Maevra nodded, her expression melting into terrified tears. He released her, turning away to pace at the tent wall in a clear dismissal.

The priestess looked over at Elaine, who made their silent sign for her to obey him and go.

Elaine wanted her away and safe. Outside the tent, she could hear the heavy listening of the camp, thrumming with tension. The Ka'in rescuers had to hear the shouts and had to be wary. Maevra would need to set them at ease if she could ... for all their sakes. However reluctant, Maevra nodded and left.

As soon as the tent flap was secured, Elaine allowed herself to lie back in the bed, no longer able to fight the world spinning around her. It only eased after she closed her eyes, accepting whatever was about to come.

"<I apologize.>"

Elaine forced her eyes open in surprise. Acies still stood with his back to her, his head hanging as he leaned against one of the poles of the tent. She realized he was staring at the cast away ewer. "<She is yours, is she not? Your mother? Your aunt?>"

"<She is the woman who raised me,>" Elaine conceded.

"<Then I shall treat her better in the future,>" he stated.

She studied his back, trying to parse any hidden meanings in a concession he did not need to offer. "<I would appreciate that,>" she said carefully.

At last, he picked up the ewer and moved to the sideboard, plucking another full waterskin that rested on the ground beside it.

"<She cannot be dead,>" he said as he poured more water into it. He came beside her, retrieved the cloth, and returned to washing her.

"<I wish I could say differently,>" Elaine offered. The warm water felt so good; she wished she could relax in it, but such a thing would be a mistake.

"<And you are her Scion.>" He dry-chuckled mirthlessly. "<That figures. The God Beyond plays his games, and we dance.>"

She stared at him as a realization broke over her like a wave, stunning her to her very core. "<You *knew* Isa Kai?>" she asked, breathlessly.

He blinked once at that before his face hardened again as he pulled away the furs over her chest and applied the cloth. She let him; she had learned to desensitize herself to being touched, yet he remained equally detached as he nursed her.

"<It was Isa who bound me away in that prison,>" he said softly.

"<Why?>" she found herself asking.

"<Because I am a demon,>" he answered. It was an obvious answer; it might even be the true answer, but it also felt incomplete. Elaine wanted to ask more questions, but her eyes would not stay open. The warmth of the cloth was lulling her away.

CHAPTER 5

Elan had many troubles. He never thought Dakin being dead would be one of them.

Staring down at the bloated body, his boots stained in the pool of blood underneath, Elan could definitely say he had never imagined this as his fate.

"We are royally fucked," one of the other Ka'in warriors muttered. There were nods and murmurs of agreement. Standing in the hallway of the abandoned temple, now well-lit by a circle of torches, it might as well have been a somber funeral as they all stared at the carnage.

"You had to kill him, Prince of the Ka'in?" Titama said, sneering at his title like it was an insult.

Elan gritted his teeth. "We all accepted that this was a possible outcome."

"And you are saying you had no choice *but* to kill him?" Titama argued, unyielding.

"He was going to murder Elaine," Elan answered, also not giving an inch.

The others shifted on their feet, a couple sighing with exasperation. The band was more than tired; they were bone deep weary. They had all been fighting against their oppressors for a long time with barely little to show for it. This fight for power between their prince and their leader added to it still.

Unfortunately for Elan, most of them saw him only as a symbol and nothing more. A resource to be sacrificed. Apparently Elaine was the same, and that angered Elan more.

Titama stiffened his jaw. "One life does not outweigh our whole people."

That sparked outrage in Elan. "She is our last Silverblood and our princess," he said aghast.

"And if I needed to find water to dig a new well, she would be useful and needful." Titama kicked the corpse. "But we could have traded Dakin *alive* to free our people. Without our people, she is the princess of nothing! I wanted to save her as much as you, but—"

"Spit that lie out of your mouth!" Elan said, snapping the idiom at Titama. More feet shifted uncomfortably. Losing Elaine would have been devastating, but she could have served as a martyr, which was what Titama had counted on.

"We all *wanted* to save Elaine, but we *needed* Dakin alive," Titama restated.

"To trade to the other Anons for what? It's a lot to stake on them keeping true to their word to *us*—*us*, who they think are lower than livestock."

"The Anon will be required to seek retribution for this, you idiot!" Titama stepped forward to throw a punch at Elan, only to have the other warriors nearby restrain him. Elan did not flinch away, though arms barred him from also engaging in a knockdown fight.

The others spun Titama away. He relented and settled himself like a pacing horse. His struggle for control was admirable.

Elan pointed at the body. "Many Anon wanted Dakin as dead as we did. They won't lift a finger to avenge him."

His once-friend, now-rival, placed his hands on his hips. "I had made a deal with one of the Anon merchants."

Grumbled murmurs came from the group. They were as surprised as Elan felt. "What deal?" he asked. "You told us nothing of this."

"It does not matter now. It all hinged on us bringing him to them alive."

"What deal?" Elan insisted.

"She planned to ransom him to his family to the south. In exchange for his life, she intended to extract the governorship from them. She had the leverage to do it," Titama said, defiant in his reluctance to tell all. "With that governorship, she would make it possible for us to free our people. It was all arranged."

"You mean you made a deal with one of the Anon merchants?" Elan spat back, noting Titama's avoidance of saying his co-conspirator's name. The Ka'in Prince had an idea to whom Titama referred, the Anon merchant Amira, a woman who saw herself as a mercantile princess. She was ruthless and intelligent, even for the Anon. If any of them could pull off a coup, it would be her. The fact that she would use a Ka'in warrior band to do her dirty work was proof enough of that.

Elan looked around the group, all wearing bronze breastplates. Though dirty and blood-streaked, the bright sheen of their newness was unmistakable in the torchlight. "She is who provided us with the equipment, is she not?"

The grumbling around them shifted to something more optimistic. The smallest sliver of hope could lead this group, including badly needed equipment and full bellies. They had been following Titama for a while. They trusted him and believed in him, and if it had not been for Elaine, Elan would have too. He was a brilliant strategist and fighter, better than Elan, but his heart was also as cold as the depths of the river.

"The price for all this was a living, breathing Dakin," Titama said, not even trying to deny he had sold them out. "I told you not to rush in, that we would take him together."

Elan could feel the energy of the group shift against him, and it infuriated him. *Are their spirits so weak to be so easily bought off by trinkets and lies? How was Titama able to do this when I am the only one who fights for what we believe in as Ka'in?* Elan thought bitterly.

"Bring him back," a new voice interjected.

The whole group turned to see the stranger standing at the end of the hallway.

None of them had noticed his approach.

Elan narrowed his eyes at him.

The stranger's own eyes were a color Elan could not define; it was like they were of the sky, but the Ka'in Prince could not quite make out what that color really was. It was as if he could see it, yet not perceive it at the same time. Even more disturbing, Elaine's eyes were now the same, as well as her hair, black as coal. Maevra had told the others when questioned about it that the Anon had dyed her hair for their bizarre ceremony to raise... well, this creature that stood before them, looking like a man. A Ka'in man speaking a strange sort of accented Ka'in.

As the stranger straightened from the wall he leaned on, as if he had been listening to their argument for a while, he stepped forward into their circle of light. The stranger was tall, taller than any other Elan had met. The skin prickled on the prince's arms as the thing he knew as a demon came closer. He had kept that information from the others at Maevra's insistence as well. If it had been anyone but Maevra asking him, he would have tried to run the demon through right then and there.

As if they sensed the same danger, the group crowded closer to each other, closing ranks like a deer herd before a wolf.

The stranger said nothing more to the others. He only came forward to look down on the corpse, his arms crossed.

As always, Titama stepped forward. "You did that?" he asked, gesturing at the abandoned sanctuary beyond them.

Almost lazily, the stranger lifted his eyes to the room then nodded. "I did that, yes."

More gasps and mutters from the group, and Elan gritted his teeth. He wanted to tell them what he saw when he had saved Elaine, but...

"What do you mean, 'Bring him back'?" Elan said.

The stranger shifted his eyes to meet Elan's. After a moment, a smile spread across the stranger's face, reading something in Elan that satisfied him.

"I can do it," the stranger said carefully, still unfamiliar with the Ka'in words.

"You can bring him back?" Titama asked, trying to work it out. "From death?"

"You need Dakin alive?" the stranger said. "Without him alive, you are royally fucked."

Elan furrowed his eyebrows.

One of the others spoke up. "Yes, but dead is dead. Not even the gods could bring back the dead."

Titama stepped forward. "Show me."

"No, no!" Elan tried to counter. He stood between Titama and the stranger.

"How can he do it? Are you a sorcerer?" another of the group asked.

"Gods. Sorcerer," the stranger said as if he was tasting the words. "Neither of those. But I can do it if you want me to do it."

"You mean for a price," a third warrior in the group said.

"At this point, I do not care what his price is, only that we succeed," Titama said. "If you can bring Dakin back from the dead, you will have my friendship and thanks."

"Friendship and thanks." The stranger shook his head. "No. I wish to be a Prince of the Ka'in."

Murmurs and furrowed brows passed among the group.

Titama cocked his head. "We do not even know who you are, stranger. We are grateful for what you have done to aid us in saving our princess, but to become one of our—"

"He wants Elaine," Elan stated, not even trying to hide the menace in his voice.

The stranger cocked his head as Titama did. "I want Elaine," he agreed.

"Done," Titama agreed.

Elan whipped his head around. "You cannot give him to her. I am her family—"

"I am the real leader here. I may not be a Prince of the Ka'in in name, but do you think any man here would challenge me? Even you, Elan?" Titama spat. "Besides. What he proposes is impossible, is it not? We risk little to gain much."

There were more nods from the heads of the others, and Elan wanted to scream. "He is a demon," Elan finally said, letting the bones fall where they may.

"I would make a hundred deals with a hundred demons if it drove the Anon from our forests," Titama said with deadly quiet. The others nodded, but Elan realized too late they did not understand what he meant.

The stranger only grinned.

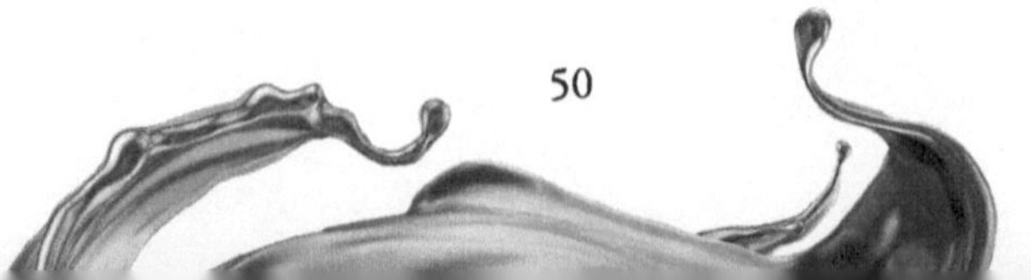

"If you do this thing you claim, then we will make you a Prince of the Ka'in," Titama agreed.

Acies looked over this contingent of warriors as their leader agreed. It had been almost too easy, desperation making them stupid. They did not know that Elaine was his already, given to him by herself willingly. They thought they could bargain with the will of another. From what he could gather, it was a marriage that made one a Prince of the Ka'in, so whatever quaint ritual they had would make her his wife in their eyes. That worked just fine for Acies's purposes. What he needed was for *them* to accept him as such, to be willing to follow him.

With the expectant eyes of the others on him, Acies turned back to the sanctuary room. It stank of death, but it was a perfume Acies remembered. In fact, any smell, taste, sight, or sound was a delight to his starved senses, and it was almost too hard to contain his giddiness at them all. The group was already unsettled enough; they did not need him to be maniacally laughing at inappropriate moments.

Boldly, Acies entered the sanctuary. He gestured for the Ka'in to bring the lights, and they obeyed, chattering to each other quietly. He didn't mind. The more they spoke, the faster he picked up their language. In another time, he would have marveled at how much speech had changed from the source language of all creation, but right then, he was grateful that Elaine at least understood his godspeech.

But she was not here. He had left her sleeping safely, allowing the witch to return to her side and watch over her while he came out to face this new world in which he found himself. He eyed the trappings of armor that both the Ka'in and the dead Anon wore. All bronze. No hint of iron or god-metal among them.

It does not matter, he thought. *Mortals die upon bronze just as easily as any other metal.*

Acies mounted the steps to lay his hands on the altar, feeling the distant warmth in the stone. Nothing, not even ash, covered the stones.

She had bound him to this altar, expending much of her own personal power to cast him into her sanctum, turning the home into a prison. She destroyed the sacred majicks in this temple to feed the new majick she needed to hold someone as powerful as him. One could rely on Isa Kai to come up with something new; no one had trapped a demon like him in such a prison before.

He remembered when he first entered it.

At first, the sanctum showed little damage; it had remained a spacious cave with a beautiful pool and a water-fall at one end. The furniture had been arranged invitingly around it. There had even been a spirit minstrel to tell stories and sing songs. As betrayed as he had felt, he had taken it as a sign that she did not intend to punish him forever. Isa Kai had a temper after all.

But as time passed and the majick that held him needed to be fed, that world faded. The prison began to eat every-thing: the trappings, the world, the minstrel, leaving him hanging in the nothingness. Then it began to eat him. That was when he realized what she had done. She had left him there to die slowly, alone and forgotten by the world he had helped save. Not even an honorable warrior's death.

It was impossible to tell how much of him had been consumed to maintain the prison, but standing there now, in the solid mortal realm, he could feel how little he really

possessed of his old self. Even his memories would be suspect until he found someone to verify them.

And if everyone he had ever known was gone?

He pushed the thought away and focused on the task of the moment. Looking around the room in a slow circle, the prospect of doing what he planned seemed like an undertaking beyond his current power. It would drain what reserves he had taken from these fallen.

"Bring the body … and set him here," Acies said, laying a hand on the altar. He must have said the right words because four of the Ka'in near the door went back obediently. The leader had followed him up, stopping a few steps from the top with Elaine's kin slightly behind him. Both eyed him suspiciously.

"And the others," Acies said. He gestured a circle about the altar. "All around."

The leader, Titama, nodded at the rest, and the rest of his band set about the grisly job of bringing the corpses up to the altar. The fact that these Ka'in did not flinch from the task raised Acies's esteem of them. These were not green farmers who had never held a blade. They were blooded soldiers.

While they worked, Acies took a moment to search around the altar for tools. He could perform his ceremony without them if he had to—he'd done it before—but knew he would rather metaphorically dig with a shovel than his bare hands. Retrieving two of the oil lamps, he managed to light one with the tiniest scrap of his available power. It cast a small glow that threw macabre shadows onto the walls.

The shock on Dakin's face seemed comical to Acies as he was flopped onto the altar like the dead man still waited for someone to come up to him and inform him there had been some mistake.

While the Ka'in who brought the corpse stepped away, gasping from the task, he proceeded to anoint the corpse with the remains of the oil he found in the second lamp, drawing symbols on the forehead and cheeks. If he had done this right away after death, he could have used the blood, but now there was no arete left in the substance to work with; the oil would work just as well, even if it added to the cost.

Once Dakin was anointed, he proceeded to anoint the warriors laid out on their backs in a rough circle around the altar. The Ka'in retreated to the bottom of the stairs. Acies positioned himself at the head of Dakin.

The sound in his throat started low, barely a noise at all as he braced his feet farther than shoulder-width apart, squatting solidly down. With conviction, he slapped his hands against his chest, popping the low sound out in a strong "ha!" He lifted his right arm in a flexed posture and slapped the bicep then repeated the motion with the left, hitting the poses with deliberate care before slapping his chest again. His voice echoed with each strike in a series of guttural cries, calling back to the warrior spirits lost on this very battlefield.

"<Come,>" he shouted, slapping his thighs. "<Rise!>"

The echo deepened, his voice taking on power as he spoke the rites. "<Come, my fallen comrades! The battle is not done, and your strength is needed.>"

He continued the ritual, making fearsome faces, all while maintaining the rhythm of the slaps and cries.

At last, another cry echoed in response. A figure pushed itself to its hands and knees, then to standing.

The Ka'in gasped, but it did not break the rhythm of the spell. The returned soldier took up the same stance as Acies, thumping in echoing rhythm. The other warriors followed suit, a third of the fallen rising back to their feet. The ritual shifted to a call and answer.

"<We are the fallen who rise to your call,>" they answered. "<We fall no more and will stand proud and tall.>"

The bodies reformed, limbs fusing back into place, pulling in what was needed. Grayish light glowed from their eyes as they turned them toward Acies, who continued the ritual. At last, when no more bodies rose, Acies ended the call, hissing and twisting his face in a fearsome mask. The warriors before him hissed and mirrored, their hands reaching upward, twisting even more gruesomely than their blood-covered faces alone.

Acres straightened and turned to the one corpse he hoped would rise, but Dakin's body remained as it had been. Acies circled the altar.

"<So, Dakin the Fallen, you were not a warrior after all, he-who-would-be-king. Even if it were you who made me my deal and freed me from my prison, I could not serve something as weak as you,>" Acies commented to the corpse.

The body didn't respond. He didn't expect it to, and he began stripping off the rings and necklaces adorning it, claiming the spoils of their battle.

"What... What is the meaning of this?" Titama asked. Acies turned to find the Ka'in leader had braved the stairs to come within a short distance of the altar. He stared down at the unmoving corpse.

"He was not warrior ... to come," Acies said, wishing he knew more words to explain what went wrong. "He is not a warrior. Did not come. He is too weak."

He watched the other man calculate, assessing the newly summoned undead warriors. Acies understood his dilemma: it was hard for the man to say Acies failed, but it was also hard to call this a success.

"What... What god do you worship?" Titama asked with the voice of a small child.

Acies had no answer for that.

A different look passed over Titama's face. For a heartbeat, Acies was sure he would draw and attack. And then the man stepped back down the steps.

"We will think of something else," he said to his warriors. "Grab the body."

The warriors swallowed their mettle and obeyed. With a gesture, Acies pulled back his newly made undead warriors so that the Ka'in would feel, if not more comfortable, less threatened.

Soon, only Elan remained in the room, horror painting his face. "What have you done, you demon?" he demanded.

"<I do not think I will be made a Prince of the Ka'in any time soon,>" Acies said. Elan only glared at him uncomprehendingly. "<No matter. There are other ways to power.>"

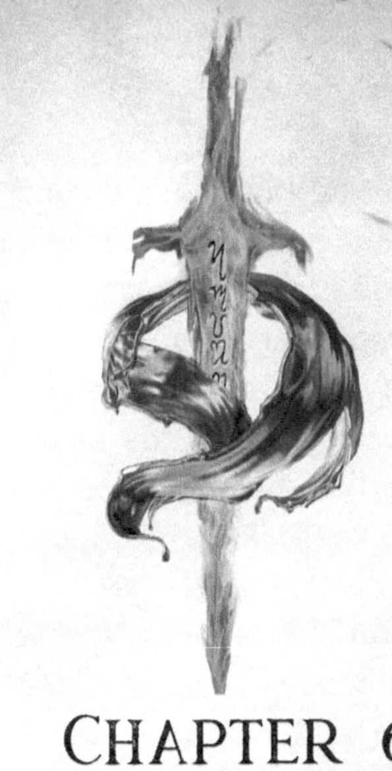

CHAPTER 6

"ELAINE, ELAINE," A VOICE WHISPERED URGENTLY, shaking her awake. Elaine didn't want to waken just yet. Her dreams had been comfortable and safe, and she wanted to climb back into them. Yet the hand on her arm continued its insistent intrusion. "Elaine!"

"I am awake," she muttered, shifting so that she could look blearily up into the face hovering over her. There was scant light in the tent, barely enough for Elaine to make out Maevra's features. Somewhere outside the tent, a few birds were warming up their trills in anticipation of the rising sun. "What is going on?"

"Come with me, child. Hurry," Maevra beckoned, stepping back as she drew her shawl around her shoulders.

Elaine obeyed, sliding to the edge of the bed. As she swung her legs over, Maevra held out a brown tunic for her to don as well as leggings and feet wrappings. She dressed quickly in the dark, taking Maevra's urgency seriously. A million possible thoughts filtered through her mind as she did so, each promising a worse fate than the last. Once she had slipped into the knee-high boots that Maevra set before her, the older woman took Elaine's hand and led her from the warmth of the tent into what remained of the night.

The air bit cold as the gray light brought the other tents into relief. She spotted several of the Ka'in warriors sitting near a fire. Nothing in their postures seemed relaxed, nor did they look rested. Maevra took Elaine's hand and pulled her away from their people.

"What is going on?" Elaine whispered urgently, but Maevra set a finger to her own lips and urged Elaine after her.

Maevra led them to the farthest corner of the temple, away from the entryway that led up into the sanctuary. There they stopped, although Elaine could not see why. Maevra ran her fingers over the carved whorls and sigils, faded and chipped by the frequent forces of weather and time. She whispered softly under her breath as she did so, then she directed her gaze down the back way of the temple.

"This way," she breathed with renewed purpose.

They moved hastily down the wall to turn around the corner. Here the night shadows still clung, but as Elaine's eyes adjusted, they discovered an annex building attached to the main one. A raised walkway connected the two. Maevra did not continue around to the annex, instead heading straight to the walkway. More carvings, deeper and less damaged, decorated the underside.

Maevra knelt on one knee, again running her fingers over the carvings. Elaine knelt beside her as well, wondering if maybe her beloved teacher and adoptive mother had lost her wits after the events of the last few days.

"Maevra, what are we doing here?" she pressed.

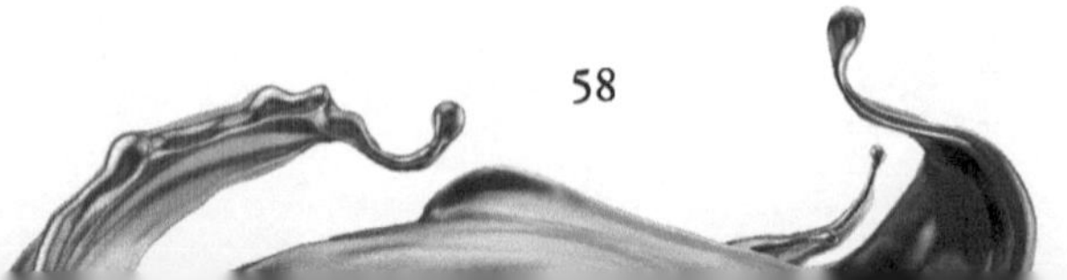

"Elaine." Maevra's voice was low as she grasped her princess's hand with claw-like urgency, making Elaine flinch. "This is it—the way into her secret sanctum."

"What do you mean?"

"I will explain inside. We must hurry. Daughter of Isa, sing the Song of the River."

Elaine's mouth dropped a little at the request. "Song of the River?"

"You must hurry," Maevra insisted.

She didn't want to hurry. She wanted answers.

Furrowing her brows at the older woman, the younger one licked her lips carefully. The priestess's face was so earnest and urgent, Elaine found she really had no choice but to obey.

Softly, she sang, the words whispering out of her on a delicate thread of sound.

> *"The wind will dance when the lady comes,*
> *the trees that bow before her,*
> *may songs of heaven all be sung,*
> *the day the Goddess of the River wanders."*

As she finished the first stanza, there was a thrumming from the carved wall. A silvery glint reflected under the panel, followed by a stony thump and cranking shift. Instinctively, Elaine laid her hand on the panel, using her majick like she did when she dowsed for water. The panel depressed into the wall, then it slid to the side, grinding like a milling wheel too loudly in the early morning quiet. All the birds went eerily silent. Air rushed into the reopened space, sucked inside the gaping darkness.

Maevra's hand landed in the middle of Elaine's back, pushing her forward. "Go!" she urged.

Elaine stumbled forward into the passageway. The ceiling was so low that she had to crouch to clear it. The second she pressed her hand to the wall, more silvery letters flared, casting needed light upon a dust-covered stone floor. They disappeared with the bend of the hallway. Going no farther than was necessary, Elaine waited for Maevra to join her. Once the priestess did, the hidden door slid shut, leaving them in the silvery twilight.

Satisfied, Maevra turned and nodded at Elaine, signaling to proceed. The air was thick with petrichor as Elaine stepped forward. Even with the scant light from the writing on the wall, Elaine kept her hand tracing along the stone.

"Where are we?" she repeated, her voice coming back to her too soon in the confined space.

"A place where we can make it alright again," Maevra said cryptically. "I hope."

Soon enough, the floor dropped down at a steady incline, and she was able to stand fully. They hadn't gone very far when a faint mist of water kissed Elaine's cheek. Surprised, she stopped, touching her cheek.

"Keep going," Maevra said behind her, a new warmth in her voice as if she were very pleased.

Elaine continued down the gentle slope that wove left and right in a series of easy kickbacks. Soon, she heard it: a steady rumbling. The dust of the passage gave way to wetness and growth as her fingers encountered the sponginess of moss on the walls. Many of the glowing words were covered by the stuff.

At last, she emerged from the corridor. As she passed into a vast space, the lights from the corridor pulsed along the walls to outline the room. The light mirrored on the surface of an underground lake.

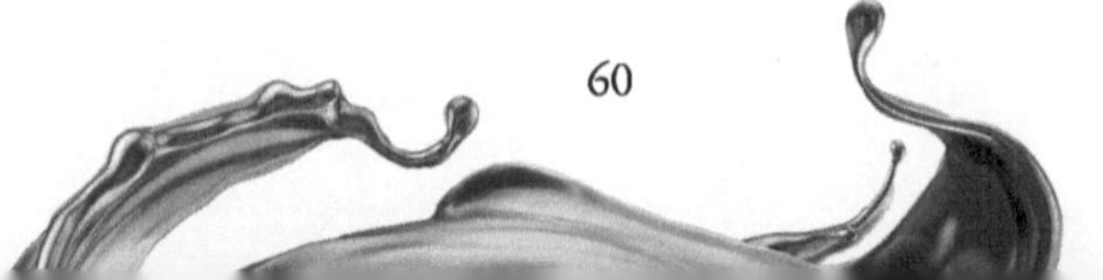

Elaine gasped. All around the edge, statues, mostly of women, were carved out of the living walls themselves. At the far end was a short waterfall, but someone long ago had carved the rock around the opening to look like a pair of arms encircling it, as if an enormous woman with a pot poured the water forth.

"Do you hear it?" Maevra asked, coming up beside Elaine.

"Yes," Elaine breathed. It was the sound of women's voices, chanting words of power and eternal prayer. "To Isa..."

"To Isa, great Goddess of the Ka'in. Goddess of Water, Protector, Giver of Life, Wife of the Harvest God Velas Kai, who together brought prosperity and abundance in their love and joining," Maevra intoned with solemnity.

The words thrummed through Elaine, granting a measure of peace within. "Sacred be Her," Elaine recited, mourning every word of the familiar benediction. For their goddess was dead.

"Sacred be you, Daughter of Isa," Maevra continued, altering the familiar formula. "I, the High Priestess of this Sacred Fount, have brought the Scion of Isa Kai to bathe once more in the waters."

"Maevra? Why are we here?" Elaine asked.

"This is long overdue, and I thought it would never come to pass. It was my duty to take you to the Source, the place where Isa's river comes into being when you became a woman, to see if your silver blood could pass the test, but then the worst happened before I could do so. Every Scion since the Great War has done this, and now at last, this rite can be performed too, to reclaim your power."

"If my silver blood can pass the test?"

"I have no doubt that it will."

Elaine stared at the water. The inscriptions on the wall contained the blessing of perpetual chanting meant to keep this place sacred for such rites. "But this is not the source," Elaine said.

"No, but it's the closest sacred pool to Isa's source. It should be enough."

"You do not know?"

Maevra reluctantly shook her head. "Please, Elaine. Please try."

Elaine sucked in the damp air. "What must I do?"

"Bathe in Isa's water. You will have a vision."

"What will I see?" Elaine asked, already lifting her shirt over her head.

"I do not know. It is a thing only the Scions see, and they never share it, but they are forever changed by it."

That did not sound reassuring to Elaine, but she continued to undress. When she was completely naked, she stepped into the water.

The floor of the lake was slightly rough enough for purchase as it sloped at an easy grade. With each step, Elaine became aware of the water lapping up her body. Once the water reached her middle, she ducked under the darkened surface. Immersed, she felt the drag as the water penetrated her hair, pulling it back. She felt glorious. The water was her home and sanctuary.

Too soon, she needed air, and she returned to the surface, spinning so she floated on her back. She had no idea how far she had gone from the shore; she couldn't really see Maevra anymore in the semi-dark. Instead, she continued to float, waiting for something to happen, for the vision to start and the revelation she'd been promised to be revealed. She could still hear the chanting. Light continued to ripple along the words, not steadily, but as a wave around the lake.

It felt good just to be there, quiet, and floating...

even as thoughts floated into her,

unbidden and undeterrable.

She thinks of Acies.

She sees him in the morning light, among the trees. Snow lies upon the ground.
He hunches in a crouch, furs wrapped around his shoulders. His head snaps up, startled by the sound of her approach.
She has never been so far north before. This is her first winter, and she has ventured out, wrapped in her own furs to explore the cold and see the beauty of the icy snow draped over every branch and rock.
She is just as startled to see this being. His hair is dark and wild as the deep earth, standing with bloody hands over a kill. A short beard covers his chin, so different from Veres's, the Harvest God's, clean face. They have the same blue eyes though.
She thinks of those blue eyes lit by firelight.
His naked body before her, his chest rising and falling with urgency and vulnerability. She traces a finger carefully down the middle of his chest, through the thatch of hair as dark as that on his head, covering the surface of a powerful muscle.
His kiss, his education, as he learns to please her, his trust in her to keep his secret—she holds them all dear to her heart.
The feel of his touch ignites her with relief as she pulls him close.
He stinks of sweat, dirt, and blood.
He has endured so much. His iron sword drives into the ground as if it could help him stand.
Even as he struggles to stand, he draws her close, cursing and praising her in alternating breaths as he kisses her face.
She is safe.
They have turned back the tide for now.
The open wounds of battle lay all around them, torn earth and burned trees.

Bodies of people and animals are strewn among them.

The other warriors move, searching through the dead for the living.

Tears streak her face as she forces herself to hold her head up for the sake of those who look to her for guidance, for protection.

Yet she is unable to process the tragedy that surrounds them.

The war has come so far north.

There is nowhere left that is untouched and safe now. The demons have torn through the land, leaving crushed livestock, lost crops, and dead people in their wake.

Acies's regret is obvious as he drops to his knees before her, his free arm clinging to her legs as he weeps.

The firelight again, Acies's head on her lap as she runs her fingers through his black hair, thinking a hole in the hearth.

Acies stirs, his voice heavy. "<A God of the Hunt is not enough. I have to do something. I cannot just let them destroy everything. I cannot let them.>"

He sits up, staring at the fire. "<I cannot let anyone else die like that.>"

"<What are you going to do?>" she asks. "<What are you prepared to do?>"

"<Whatever it takes. Whatever I have to do, I have to do it.>"

"<Whatever it takes>" echoes through her.

She sees battles and challenges, flashing past too quickly to comprehend.

Foes and darkness and sacrifices, leading through a line of causes and effects.

The thoughts receded.

Elaine opened her eyes. She buzzed from finger to toe. She still floated in the lake, staring up into the darkness above her. The underwater thrum of the waterfall filled her ears. It was so quiet and peaceful; she didn't want to move.

Kicking down, she stood up in the lake, her toes barely touching the bottom, which forced her to tread the water instead. She looked over to the edge of the lake, but Maevra was nowhere to be seen. In fact, Elaine could not tell which way had been the entrance of the underground cave altogether.

She continued to spin in the water. While looking about for Maevra along the edge of the lake, she didn't see the lighted words on the wall, but she could still see just the same. It took a moment to realize the light came from the water, following beneath her as she swam. Without further guidance, Elaine stroked forward, swimming into deeper water, and the light followed her until she reached the edge. There it left the water and trailed up the wall to ignite a carved image in the stone.

It looked like a map.

There was a wide enough pathway for a person to stand, so Elaine pulled herself up.

The carved map of the great continent had been bisected in two with a large wiggling line, reaching from the northernmost mountains to the sacred oceans to the south. Along the line, it was the Ka'in symbol for temple interspersed with what Elaine realized was the representation of Isa's river. With one finger, she reached up to trace the line.

"The Source," she whispered. As her finger traced down the line, however, the second temple lit with the same light as the words on the wall. Her finger continued down the line, and in her mind's eye, she saw slips of a vision, but she couldn't entirely grasp everything that she saw. It was not until the last image that she saw a clear picture of a place she had only heard described in stories: the Ocean Temple, the sacred stone building set on a strip of land, otherwise surrounded by water stretching long into the horizon.

An overwhelming feeling of longing filled Elaine to her very core.

Home. She wanted to go home. To a home she had never been.

"Elaine?" Maevra's voice came timidly from her side. The high priestess had come up beside her, holding out her shawl to wrap around the Scion.

"What is this?" Elaine asked, noting the older woman's awed expression.

"You have seen her," Maevra whispered reverently. "Your eyes are glowing ... and your hair." The high priestess pressed her wrinkled old hand against her own mouth as if that could hold back the joyful, relieved tears from bursting the banks of her eyes.

"I need to go," Elaine said aloud, the idea becoming more sure and solid in her mind as she said it. "I need to find the Ocean Temple."

"You will begin the pilgrimage, at last," Maevra agreed. "Each Scion since the Great War has attempted this, but none have completed it."

"Why?" Elaine asked, tracing her finger once more along the route.

"Each has their story, but it is a choice to walk the path of Isa, and each discovered something about themselves that either turned them back home or forced them to settle where they were. But you, Princess, I know you will succeed."

"Succeed in doing what?"

"Bringing Isa back to us."

"Isa is gone, Maevra."

"No, she is not. I have never believed that. Isa is alive, and you will be the one to find her."

"<Then I was right.>" Acies's deeper godspeech cut the gentle sounds of the sanctuary. Both women whipped around to see the demon standing at the edge of the water.

Maevra stepped in front of Elaine. "How did you—"

"<Do you think there are any secrets of this place that I would not know about, old woman?>" Acies sneered. He bent down and dipped his hand into the water. The light around the room flickered alarmingly. "<I knew it had to be a lie. Isa lives.>"

He stood and began to stroll, walking toward the two women. Elaine wrapped the shawl tighter around herself as he approached, angry and frightened. He had no eyes for Maevra, only Elaine. The reflected light from the water had turned them into twin black pools of their own.

Maevra attempted to block him. "You will not profane her any furth—"

He shoved her aside. She slammed into the wall, crying out in pain.

Elaine yelped and tried to go to her, but Acies blocked her path.

"<Yes,>" he said, lifting his hand to rest along her jaw. She hated herself for flinching away from him, but it did not deter his fingers from lacing into her hair with a gentle caress. "<I will have my revenge, and you will help me get it. We will find that traitorous goddess together and make everything right. Will we not, my Elaine?>"

CHAPTER 7

ELAINE'S HEART WAS HEAVY AS SHE LED THE WAY out of Isa's sacred pool chamber. Acies strolled right behind her, keeping her away from Maevra, who straggled behind. The older woman remained unhurt, just shaken up by the shove, but neither could speak freely with the demon among them.

What am I to do? Elaine thought. Her heart delighted in the idea that Isa still lived, that she only waited for Elaine to fulfill her purpose to come back to the Ka'in, and now, seeking her out could only lead to a confrontation with Acies, who wanted her dead.

These thoughts plagued her as she stepped out of the entrance to stand in the morning light. The sun had risen while she had bathed, and it was cheery and bright, yet unnervingly wrong. Acies emerged out from behind her and immediately set his hand on his sword, his eyes scanning for threats.

"What is it?" Maevra asked, still halfway out of the entryway.

"<Trouble,>" Acies said and marched ahead, leaving behind the two women. Elaine looked to Maevra, whose face reflected her fears. They both knew what trouble could mean.

"Elan," Elaine whispered, fearing for her brother's life, before taking off after Acies.

"Elaine, wait!" Maevra called, but it did no good. Elaine could not wait.

Around the corner, the camp looked much as it had. Even in that short span of time when she lost sight of him, Acies had gotten well into the encampment. He had drawn his sword and spun in place, looking for threats. To her relief, it was Elan she saw first, already rushing over to her.

"Elaine! Get away from her, monster!" he cried as he placed himself between her and Acies. Instead of his usual bow, he was armed with a sword, obviously one taken from the now-dead Anon warriors. He pointed the end of his new weapon at Acies.

"Elan, what are you doing?" Elaine cried, but her brother only threw his other arm out as he backed her away.

Acies whirled toward him, lifting his own blade in response toward Elan.

"<You learn slowly, don't you?>" Acies asked, knowing Elan didn't understand his godspeech.

"Elan!" Elaine pleaded. "Please, you cannot fight him."

"The dead!" Elan stuttered out, still shaking the blade. "The dead rose last night, Elaine. I saw them! He did something!" The young man pointed a finger as well as the sword. "You made the dead rise!"

"Elan, stand down!" Elaine ordered, truly terrified that her twin might have lost his wits, but her brother refused to heed her.

"It is true, Elaine," Titama agreed. He appeared to the left of Acies, his sword set to the level of the demon's neck. Three more of the Ka'in followed suit, surrounding him.

"Oh, Goddess," Elaine breathed as she realized what was happening.

Acies seemed wary but still smirked as he turned his head just enough to note the blades. "Your swords ... are..." He chuckled when he could not find the words.

"Covered in blood," Elaine finished for him.

"We destroyed all your abominations, monster," Titama said. "And now we will deal with you."

"Titama, stop!"

Titama didn't even flinch or look her way. With a grim twist of his features, he thrust his blade, slicing it down and across Acies's neck. Dark blood sprayed.

Elaine couldn't even scream she was so shocked. Acies buckled forward, his hand going to his neck, his sword dropping heedlessly to the ground. There was a horrible gurgling sound as the demon choked. Titama did not even watch him die as he turned, wiping his weapon clean on his sleeve. The other warriors lowered their own swords, staring down at Acies's back as he curled forward.

Titama approached the shocked twins, his gaze cold and resolute. "Move aside, Elan."

Elan jerked, his body still shielding Elaine's as he ripped his attention from the scene to their leader.

It took a second for Elaine to realize what her former lover intended. "Oh, Goddess," she breathed.

Titama raised his blade at her. Elan did the same to meet it.

"Move or I will not hesitate to kill you both." Titama took a ready stance.

"This was not the plan," Elan argued.

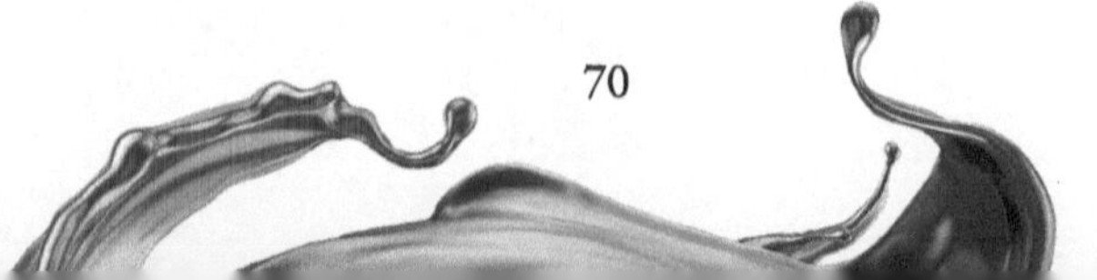

"He was a demon," Titama said simply. "And she is tainted by him. If we do not destroy them both now..." He did not finish the thought, only tightened his jaw.

"Titama," Elaine cried, still not believing what was happening.

"Run, Elaine. Run!" Elan called as Titama moved, their blades ringing out as they met with a clamor.

As if a bell had been rung, the other warriors charged for Elaine even as she took off, blindly running for who knows where. She was not a warrior; she understood the basics of fighting but was better with words and stories. She tried to go back the way she had come, but immediately found herself cut off by several more of Titama's warriors who had flanked them while they had executed Acies.

Except ... Acies wasn't dead yet.

As she spun around like a deer desperately searching for a safe path away, one of the closest warriors found himself pitching forward. Acies had charged him from behind. He then spurred forward, moving uncannily fast as he scooped up the sword the warrior dropped and rammed it into the thigh of the next closest man. That warrior screamed as he went down a mere hand's breadth from Elaine. She startled, her feet sliding and skipping to get away.

Then Acies had her arm, pulling her along toward the edge of the forest.

"<Run! Run!>" he said in a scratchy, strained voice.

There was no time to react or think. Elaine ran.

Just as they broached the edge of the woods, Acies fell back. There were more clangs and cries of pain. She heard Elan screaming.

Elaine stopped her momentum on a tree to look back.

Elan was on a knee, his sword locked with Titama's in a contest of strength. He was losing.

"No!" Elaine cried.

I am here, she thought.

A sensation of certainty washed over Elaine. She extended her hand, which did not feel like her own anymore.

Titama buckled, crying out as she pulled on the water within him and giving Elan a chance to throw him off.

Instead of using his advantage, he disengaged and spun to run toward Elaine, who stared in shock at what she had done.

Acies had fended off several of the warriors from reaching Elaine. Then she spotted Maevra running toward her from the other side of the temple pursued by another Ka'in warrior, his sword raised over his head to cut her down.

"No!" Elaine shouted and gestured again, but this time, whatever she did before didn't happen again. Instead, a sword flew past, skewering the attacker through the chest. Beside her, Acies panted heavily, empty-handed, staring at the way his sword flew. At his feet, all the attacking warriors were dead.

Maevra grasped her arm as she arrived at Elaine's side. "These are our own people!" she cursed.

"I know, and they want us dead," Elaine agreed, taking her matriarch's hand to help pull her along.

Together, they plunged into the woods. Elan came up along the other side of Maevra. Still gripping his sword in one hand, he grasped at Maevra on the other side with his off hand, helping his twin spur the older woman forward.

Yet on that uneven ground it was inevitable that Maevra would trip. She went down between them, her foot caught on a root hidden under the loam. Sweat made their hands slip, and Elaine lost hold of her. While she turned back, Elan kept going a few steps, then took a ready stance with the sword, prepared to protect them from any pursuers... but there was no one.

"Come on, Maevra. Get up!" Elaine urged, but the older woman only seized Elaine's hand.

"Be still!" Maevra coughed, her breath coming in alarming wheezes.

Desperately, Elaine looked about, gasping for her own breath, but she saw nothing—only trees all around them. Her ears strained for any sound of pursuit, yet there was only the wind rustling leaves and a bird or two chirping.

"We lost them," Elan whispered harshly.

"Or everyone is dead," Elaine murmured. She did not want to find out and tugged Maevra to her feet. "We need to keep moving."

"It might be better if we hide," Elan countered.

"Where is your demon?" Maevra asked. Then she moaned in pain as she tried to put weight on her foot. "Damn it to the desert. I think I have twisted my ankle." She began to puff her cheeks to cope, waving the twins away. "Leave me, children. Get away safe."

"That is not happening," Elaine argued with determination. She scooped up Maevra's arm and brought it over her shoulders. That was when she heard sticks crack. Elan shifted position to put himself between the sound and the women just as Acies appeared.

He looked ragged, leaning against a tree with his sword barely in his hand.

"Oh, Goddess!" Elaine cried.

"Go to him. Go," Maevra insisted, pushing Elaine forward.

"Hey!" Elan said, when she sprinted past his guard, but she ignored him.

"<There is no one coming,>" Acies said as Elaine reached him while he curled over, coughing roughly.

"Let me see your wound," she said and pulled away his shirt from his neck. She stared but could not wrap her head around what she was seeing. Covering his neck was drying blackness that leaked from a clean slice where Titama's sword had cut. His shirt was similarly encrusted. She pulled her hands away and stared at the mixture of red and black on them.

"Is this ... demon blood?" she asked, then she ran a finger along the wound again.

He hissed and brought his own hand up to his throat, covering the cut. A low moan rolled out of him, and he bellowed like a sick calf. He panted hard, and Elaine felt wrongness coming from him, making her small hairs stand straight up. Then he dropped back against the tree, and the wrongness disappeared.

"Acies?" she asked. "What... What did you do?"

"<Something very stupid,>" he answered. Then he captured Elaine's fingers and brought them back to his neck. All she found was smooth, unbroken skin under the dried blood. "<See? All healed. I'll be alright.>"

"You healed yourself?" Elaine breathed, marveling.

"He is a demon," Maevra said. "It is not unusual for them to use their power to heal very quickly."

"That wound should have killed you," Elan accused.

Acies growled. "<If only you could have been so fortunate.>" Again he was talking in godspeech, so the Ka'in warrior did not understand.

Elaine shot her brother a dark look, which he ignored. "If it was not for Acies, *I* would be dead now by Dakin's hand."

"If it had not been for your demon, Dakin wouldn't have tried to sacrifice you," Elan argued. "And besides, you would have been fine, Elaine. I came to save you."

"Well, you were too late! I was already dead!" she shouted.

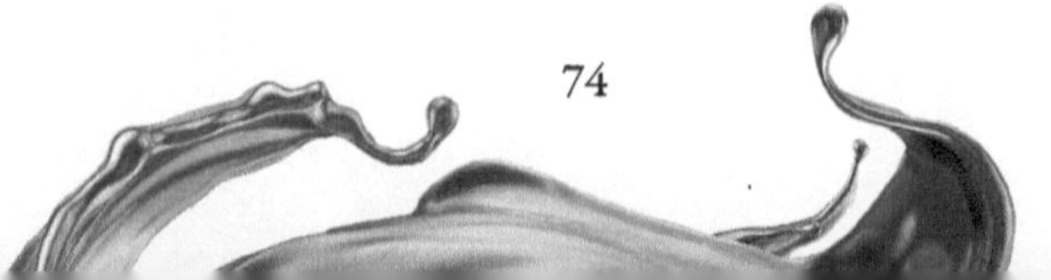

74

At last, Elan stopped fighting and simply stared at her as the horror of that statement penetrated.

It was Maevra who broke the tension. "There will be time for stories later," she said as she hobbled over. She held out her arm to Elan. "Help me, child. We must go."

Elan reluctantly put his sword back in his sheath, grabbing at the excuse to escape the uncomfortable confrontation. Elaine ignored him as well, going to Acies. He wrapped an arm around her shoulders, and together they escaped.

CHAPTER 8

"*<Hmm, a body. A ready body, and the door is open. What an invitation this is.>*"

When Dakin opened his eyes, he could not comprehend what he saw. The world was mostly darkness, but there was motion within it. He wanted to jerk and startle, but his body wouldn't respond. There was an odd silence to him. He expected his heart to be thundering, yet the tattooing beat was absent. This terrified him. He had no choice but to lie there and... then he realized he wasn't breathing either. That panicked him even further.

At last, he pulled air in, making a groaning noise in his throat as he did so, but that too felt wrong. The usual satisfaction from taking a deep breath felt like nothing. Yet he continued to do it, pulling the air in until his chest filled completely then blowing it out, even if it was just to hear the sound of the air whooshing. After a few of these breaths, his sight discriminated the darkness, separating out the tops of darkened trees wavering in the wind from the celestial darkness of the oncoming night consuming the last vestiges of day.

Where am I? he thought.

Whatever was going on, Dakin decided he wasn't dead and took solace in that information.

Yet he still failed to sit up. And despite his immobility, Dakin did feel pain. His chest felt heavy, his gut ached, and a small rock dug into the back of his head.

Then he noticed the steady thump crunch of footfalls in the forest. Losing focus, Dakin ceased his breathing and struggled to will his unresponsive head to turn so he could see who was coming. To his utter relief, two of his warriors, bearing a body between them, did come into view.

With joy, Dakin made a gurgling noise in his throat that was meant to come out as commands to pick him up and help him. The two warriors stopped at the noise, staring down at him from above.

One warrior spoke to the other, and to his horror, Dakin realized they weren't his men. They were Ka'in.

The *Ka'in.* The Ka'in had done this to him.

The warriors exchanged a few more words in harsh whispers before they simply dropped the corpse they carried on top of Dakin and walked away out of his sight.

Dakin gurgled more as the body hit him, but he couldn't escape it nor scrabble away. The body didn't stay put but slid sideways off him, leaving only a blood-covered arm pressing against his face. Dakin whimpered, closing his eyes and willing himself to be back at his fortress, warm in his bed, Elaine naked at his side and waiting for him. None of that manifested.

Then he remembered.

That whore! he thought, though he would have spoken it if only his tongue would work. *It was Elaine who did this to me. Elaine betrayed me! Even after I granted her the favor of sparing her brother in exchange for her compliance! I didn't have to do that, and it ended up costing me greatly. How dare she! She was mine, and I could dispose of her how I chose. That ungrateful cow!*

Even as he silently raged about it, the warriors returned bearing another body, which they dumped unceremoniously on top of him again. The second body pressed the bloody arm harder into his face, forcing the still-warm blood into his mouth.

Dakin's attention suddenly zeroed in on the taste. He had tasted blood before, but this was not merely the metallic tang he'd known all his life. A shiver accompanied it, invigorating his tongue. In fact, his tongue moved! Life returned to it, and he licked hard at the bloodied arm, sweet nectar coating the inside of his mouth. Soon he could swallow, and he even chuckled as he licked away the blood from every part of the hand and wrist. He needed more, demanded more.

So he bit down.

What filled his mouth was cloying, but he couldn't stop. A thumping sound filled his skull, and he realized the heart had still been beating in the body of the arm he now feasted on. He pulled and guzzled like it was the finest wine, and he didn't even notice when his hand moved to grasp the wrist in order to drink down more.

The heartbeat faded away.

Dakin's whole body felt re-invigorated enough for him to get that damn rock out from under his head. Despite his triumph, he still felt weaker than a newborn kitten overall. Just as he thought to attempt sitting up, a third body thumped against the small pile. The warriors hurried away without looking back, disappearing into the forest.

Dakin stared at the newest body to join them. This fellow had been split from groin to one of his shoulders, like spitted boar. Dakin plunged his face into the gap, drinking down the fluids within. Though as he drank and drank, he only felt marginally stronger. There was none of that shivering life within the liquid. It was only cloying blood and foul viscera. This body was truly dead.

At last, when he could take in no more, he found he had the strength to crawl out of the hole and away among the trees. He barely made three body lengths when the two warriors returned bearing a pair of torches aloft. Others followed them, dragging wood and bits of a tent. One had gathered up an armful of dried leaves.

They are going to burn the remains. And they would have burned me with them, he thought, horrified.

There weren't many of the Ka'in, barely a handful, but they still outnumbered him. Luckily, they did not notice his absence and only continued to pile up the kindling around the bodies.

"What ... is ... hap-pening?" he managed to say out loud, but no one, neither god nor demon, answered him.

Lacking other choices, he decided to continue to crawl. By luck or fate, he found himself on the edge of his encampment. He managed to pull himself to his feet with a tent pole as he peered among the rustling canvas for the sight or sound of anybody living who could help him. But Dakin had never been a patient man, and when no one challenged him or presented themselves to him, he took it upon himself to stumble toward his tent. All he wanted was to lie down and sleep. He didn't even pause as soft lamp light edged the bottom of the tent. His chunky fingers fumbled at the ties to the entrance, and he cursed louder than was prudent at the defiant strips of leather, finally tearing one to gain entrance. He plunged through into the warmer light of the tent, stumbling to a stop as he stared down at his bed.

She had been there.

He could smell it, her scent thick in the air.

He laid his fingers on the surface of the mattress, seeking out the lingering warmth of her. Pressing his face into the surface of the mattress, he inhaled and inhaled. It was like the sweetest perfume. It was like the deadliest wine. It was... it was... it was...

Calls came from outside the tent. Dakin froze. Crouching down beside the bed, he hissed through his teeth.

The Ka'in, they were everywhere.

What was he doing here? This was foolish.

They were coming for him.

They had *her*.

She belonged to him.

They will pay, he thought.

The flap over his doorway pulled back as two Ka'in warriors appeared, talking their inane language to each other. They didn't see him until it was too late. They didn't see him until he attacked, fastening his teeth into a glorious throat, drinking deeply. Light snapped on his tongue as it poured down his throat. He drove his victim to the ground, the screams drowning out as he crushed the windpipe. Power flowed through him.

The Ka'in's companion shouted.

More shouts responded.

The warrior shoved hard against Dakin, dislodging him from his victim. Flopping onto his back, the fat man's limbs wobbled aimlessly for a moment before he managed to roll over. By then, feet surrounded him with swords drawn. He hissed and snapped at their ankles. He did not care if he seemed like a wounded animal.

He was an animal.

A powerful one.

He felt the strength ignite his limbs, and he leapt up with more speed than he had ever known. He batted away his next victim's sword, which cut into his palm, but he didn't care. More blood. More light. More power.

The Ka'in around him were stunned as they watched him drink away their companion's life.

Sheep, all of them.

The butt of a sword slammed into Dakin's temple, igniting the darkening world with early stars. He fell to the ground then swiped at his attacker's leg. His ragged nails scored the other warrior's calf, buckling him to the ground.

Dakin did not waste the opportunity. With a lightness that belied his bulk, he scrambled back to his feet and ran, plunging himself into the darkness.

Razal battled his way through the brush, cursing every deity he had ever prayed to, every person he had ever known, and every object he ran into as he fought his way out of the forest. The wizard-priest hadn't stopped running since he'd escaped the temple. Even when he paused to catch his breath, his thoughts went back to the slaughter of his followers, and it spurred him on again.

What have I done? What have we released unto the world! The thought repeated over and over again.

Razal's sense of time had been consumed with his utter terror. When he plunged into the night forest, some part of him had been aware that he was likely to be consumed by an animal or a lesser demon of the forest. Yet he had not cared, wishing only to put as much distance between himself and the terrible thing behind him. As the dark night progressed, his many crashes and bruises had finally slowed him to a walk. In the morning sun, he had walked for miles and was completely lost in the endless forest. Bone-weary and aching in every part of his body, Razal finally thumped against the side of a large tree and remained there.

He had no memory of sleeping, for his dreams were only another endless series of running away while his arguments and justifications plagued him.

I made a poor choice in Dakin. I should have courted the whore. Who could have thought that she had any intelligence at all? She seemed so demure and well-trained. To betray us like that. Dakin, the fool!

It was these thoughts that woke him with a snort and a start. He found himself on the ground before the tree, every part of him screaming from his body to his voice. Immediately, he ceased, swallowing back his terror.

It was full day, the sun streaming through the trees. He was alive, which was a miracle. Maybe the animals and demons of the forest saw no value in the frail body of an old man, but he would have thought to have woken up dead.

He cursed himself for such irrational thoughts, even while he laughed out loud. It was a maniacal laugh, even to his own ears.

Leaning back, cradling his aching arm against his body, he continued to laugh. "At least I am alive," he said aloud as if it were the greatest joke of his life. And maybe it was.

Soon, even the laughter abandoned him. Utterly exhausted, Razal let the cold wind sink into his sweat-stiff clothes. Another rational part of him was aware that he was still very much in trouble, in danger of fever and death by continued exposure. What was left of his luck would run out. He needed to keep moving, but he had never felt more exhausted. Getting to his feet again seemed impossible.

"How did she do it?" he asked himself. He had watched Dakin plunge the knife into her chest. The act should have killed her. Replaying the memory though, he remembered something not looking right, something striking him as unexpected. For one thing, there had been no blood. Dakin had plunged the blade into her chest, but when he yanked it out again, the woman's silver blood should have pooled from the wound, but then her body disappeared, presumably taken by the...

Instead, there had been flames, and the sacrifice had survived unblemished.

His years of research had made the wizard-priest confident that he had the ritual to unlock the prison correctly. He had cross-checked with various former Ka'in high clergy; he was the foremost expert on the dead gods. He knew the legends and stories about the Demon Lord of the Great War and had parsed out the facts from the tales. None of this should have happened.

Razal had not realized he had fallen asleep again until he jerked with a start. Twilight was already coloring the sky, inviting bright colors to salute the Great Chariot's passing. Panicked, the old man leaned forward, his body one great ache. He pulled his fingers out before him and was horrified to see the tips dark as death. Had the demon poisoned him after all? Stiffly, he tore at his shoes and saw similar signs on his toes. It was so hard to move and so hard to think that he almost didn't see the forester until the younger man had practically tripped over him. Razal squealed at the young man's appearance but was unable to move away.

"Whoa! Whoa, there old man," the forester said in blessed, wonderful Anon, raising a placating hand as he came forward. "I will not hurt ya. What happened to ya?"

The forester got down onto Razal's level, and his soothing words had their effect on the once great wizard-priest.

The forester was obviously from the village, dressed in warm leathers, his breath billowing out in puffy clouds from his red, round cheeks. A cap of leather covered his head, tied under his chin, making him look like a creature more than a man at first glance.

Like a child, Razal held out his shaking hands. The forester came closer, setting the bundle of wood and twigs from his back onto the ground before taking the delicate hands in his large bear-like ones. The heat from them felt like hot pokers as Razal's fingers were prodded painfully. He almost yanked them back. The forester nodded knowingly. "You got frostbite, but if you feel that, there might be hope yet. Come on with me. My home is close, and we can get you some help. My mother will know what to do. She's a healer."

The forester came to Razal's side, pulling the wizard-priest's arm over his shoulders while lacing his own arm around the frailer man's waist. "Don't worry. You're safe now," he assured soothingly, and Razal burst into child-like tears.

"Thank you, thank you, thank you," he repeated as he was lifted back up to his feet.

Then the forester abruptly jerked.

At first, Razal didn't register what had happened as he turned to see a hand plunged into the forester's chest. He made a sucking breathy sound, his grip losing its hold on Razal, who landed awkwardly over the uneven ground churned up by great tree roots.

Above him, the forester was thrust back against the great tree as a monster shaped like a man latched its mouth on the exposed neck. Spurting sounds garbled any other cries the young man would have made, yet his eyes moved, full of fear and shock to stare down at Razal, pleading with him for help.

All the wizard-priest did was scream with wild, mad abandon as the forester died. Desperate, Razal crawled, grasping at the roots like they were handholds on a wall, trying to pull himself away. He barely got to the next tree when the demon dropped the newly made corpse to the ground.

It turned; its face was directed toward the darkening sky.

Razal's irrational panic froze him in place as he stared up at the blood-coated face of Lord Dakin.

The Lord's eyes were closed, an expression of pure ecstasy washing over him, as if he was savoring a fine wine. The red washed thickly down his chin and throat, outlining the round jowls, making the man look closer to a pig than anything human.

Then Dakin opened those eyes.

They blazed with their own inner light, a hazy purplish-red pulsing. They were the eyes of a true demon that stared through Razal's soul. A greasy smile halved the face.

"Razal," the voice of Lord Dakin purred, and he sauntered forward, walking with an ease and grace the ungainly Anon lord had never displayed when he had been alive.

"My-My L-L-Lord," Razal stammered out.

The demon moved closer. Razal moaned pitifully.

Then Dakin jerked back in surprise. He narrowed his eyes. "What is wrong?" the Demon Lord asked.

"You-you-you..." Razal kept repeating, senselessly, his eyes flitting back and forth to the dead forester lying only a few feet away.

Then Dakin squatted down next to Razal and patted him on the head. "You bastard," the demon said, his eyes blazing with anger. "You lied to me."

Razal's clever mind began working again. "H-how can you say that my Lord? Look at you," he stammered. "You... my Lord. Look at you!"

"Yes, I am covered in filth. I have crawled out from a pit of corpses after you left me for dead." Dakin seized Razal's face in a shockingly powerful grip. Razal tried to paw at the attacking arm, but his grasp was feeble in comparison. "You lied to me! You said the demon would make me powerful. I do not *feel* very powerful."

"But look at you!" Razal said, muffled but clear through Dakin's filth encrusted hand. "You... You did it, my Lord!"

The squeezing lessened. "Did what?" Dakin's brow furrowed above unsure eyes with that same stupid look that Razal had mocked behind his back countless times. "The demon did what you asked. He empowered you. Look," Razal gestured feebly toward the forester. "You killed a full-grown man with your bare hands!"

Dakin did look, blinking at it as if it was the first time he ever saw a body.

Razal dug into the tiny crack of doubt. His life literally depended on it. "You... You will be the greatest warrior of your age! Look, my Lord. Take a good look! See? I did not lead you astray."

Razal's gamble paid off, and Dakin let go of his face to look at his hands, which had always resembled overstuffed sausages to Razal. Yet those sausages had nearly torn his face off.

"She betrayed me," Dakin said, rolling a pinch of dried filth between his sticky fingers.

Razal knew who he meant. "And we will make her pay for her betrayal, but she's still the fool because look at what you have become."

"You knew this would happen?" Dakin questioned.

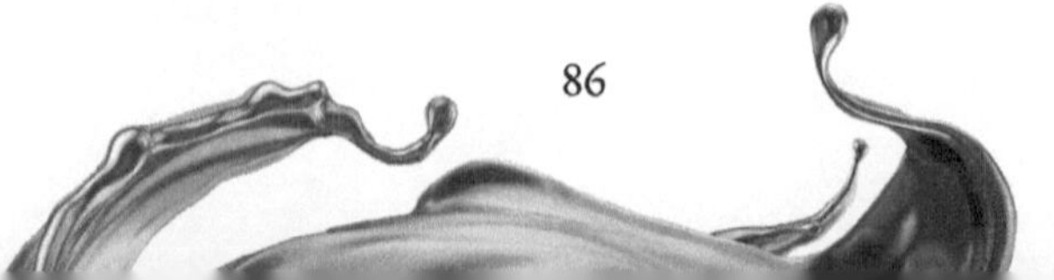

Razal pushed himself back up to sitting. "I knew that some great blessing from the gods would be placed upon you," he said. "And it has, my Lord! It has. I am so grateful I lived to see our great work accomplished!"

Dakin stood up. "Our great work has only just begun." The piggy eyes turned thoughtful. "Yes, yes. I feel power within me. It sings in my veins. But... But what can I do with it?"

"We must discover this, together," Razal said, struggling to bring himself up to his feet. "Now that it has happened, I can consult my writings. Once we learn the full extent of your abilities..."

"I can have my revenge on that woman," Dakin said delightedly.

"Yes, yes, my Lord," Razal said, even as a sick shiver coursed through his guts.

"Very good, Razal. Very good," Dakin said, wiping the blood across his chin with the back of his hand. "I will let you live after all."

The demon turned away then and marched toward the tree line. Darkness had fully fallen. With a painful groan, Razal pushed himself back to his feet and hobbled after the demon. He would live one more day.

CHAPTER 9

"I AM SO HUNGRY!" ELAN COMPLAINED FOR THE dozenth time.

They had been walking, or what qualified as walking, all day.

Elaine ignored her brother's complaints as she headed over to a section of bushes. They were not the right ones for finding berries, but she looked anyway in case there was something hidden within. Elan was doing the same even as he grumbled every other word. As she moved around the bush, she did find some edible mushrooms clinging to the dark side of a tree. She immediately popped one into her mouth, savoring the nutty flavor with a hint of dirt.

She could do this; they would survive. They had before.

"Elan!" she called as she gathered up the rest of the mushrooms into the bottom of her tunic. When he appeared beside her, she handed him half of the mushrooms.

He downed them all ravenously, barely tasting them.

"If I had a bow, I could have shot us a deer twice over," he said, scanning the forest around them.

"We will make it," Elaine answered.

"I highly doubt that," Elan sneered. "Not with that demon dogging our every step."

"You leave Acies alone, Elan."

"Elaine, he is a danger to all of us. He is a *demon* for Goddess's sake."

"Which is why I want you to leave him be. I am aware, better than you, how dangerous he is."

"Yes, and while he may need to protect you since you seem to be his anchor in this world, Maevra and I aren't, and he will kill us the first chance he gets. You just wait and see." Elan abused his sword on a tree branch, cracking it off and shaving away its branches to make a staff, probably for Maevra.

"So do not antagonize him."

Elan leaned on his new staff to test its ability to bear weight, which brought him closer to his sister. "What is your deal with him anyway?" he asked just above a whisper.

"I... I do not really know," she admitted. "He needed me to get out of the prison he was kept in, and in exchange, he has kept me safe."

Elan furrowed his brow at that, thinking. "So you *did* make some sort of deal with him?"

"Yes, but the terms of it were incredibly vague. I do not really know what they mean, and I am frankly scared to ask. I know it is unwise, but we have honestly been through a lot in only a day, and we are far from safe yet."

"I would feel better if I knew what he wanted," Elan said, straightening to shoulder the staff.

"He wants revenge on Isa for betraying him. Possibly on the other gods as well," Elaine told him.

"Betrayed him?" Elan snorted. "I know nothing of this story."

"There is much we do not know about the deities that walked the Earth ages ago, okay Elan?" Elaine snapped, irritated at her brother's derision and questions.

Instead of snapping back, Elan grabbed her hand. "Hey, sister," he said, holding her hand gently, even as she didn't take it because it was holding the mushrooms in her shirt. "I swear to you, I will free you from whatever agreement you have made with this demon. I swear it on my heart and bow."

"A bow which you no longer have," Elaine noted, but his words had cooled her ire a bit. "Do not swear to do the impossible, Elan. Just swear to me that you will do everything you can to keep Maevra and yourself safe, and that will be enough."

She turned back to head where Maevra sat on a fallen log, waiting for them.

Elaine was more worried about the older woman's ankle, which had doubled in size since they had escaped. If they had been near the river, she would have plunged it into the cold water. Maevra sat up straight on the log, her eyes closed, her face in perfect repose as if she was doing nothing more than enjoying the warmth of the day and the sounds of the forest.

"Here," Elaine said, when she came up beside her, offering the mushrooms within the dip of her tunic.

Maevra opened her eyes and took one to pop in her mouth. "Did you eat any?" she asked Elaine pointedly.

"I had some," Elaine hedged.

Maevra sniffed at that, took another, then said, "You have the rest." Elaine didn't argue but went to the lee side of one of the large trees a few lengths away.

"How are you doing?" she asked Acies. He squatted against the tree, a dark shadow in the late afternoon, his arms wrapped around his knees, his head buried within.

When he did not answer her, she held up the remaining mushrooms. "I found something to eat. It's not much, but it will help."

"<I do not eat food,>" he growled, still favoring godspeech even as she spoke in Ka'in.

Elaine stood next to him unsure of what to do. "What do you eat then?"

His eyes appeared over the bar of his arm. She squatted down next to him, waiting patiently for an answer.

"<I eat like all demons eat,>" he said reluctantly.

She furrowed her brow as she remembered what he had done to the warriors in the temple. "You need blood," she said.

"<No, I need the arete within the blood.>"

Elaine blinked at the unfamiliar term. "Arete? I do not know what that is."

He growled in his throat, but Elaine did not flinch away from the warning.

"You will have to teach me how to help you," she continued. He shifted in place, reminding her of a little boy. She dared to place a hand on his arm. "Are you ... ashamed?"

"No," he barked in Ka'in, which sounded more like a lie.

She withdrew her hand, nibbling on her lower lip. Arete? What could be this arete?

"Do you..." Elaine licked her lips. "Do you mean the silver in my blood? Is arete majick?"

"<It is the spark of the God Beyond that lives in all things. The pure power of creation,>" he finally answered.

Elaine smiled. "So yes, arete is majick."

"<As you like,>" Acies snapped. "<Your words are strange.>"

"And this arete is what you need to eat."

"<It is not like with mortals. It is not food exactly.>"

She finally sighed. "Look, Acies. I am trying to help you, but you are going to have to help me to do that."

But he said nothing more.

"Elaine!" Elan called, and she got up, leaving her demon there to frankly wallow in self-whatever. She couldn't quite call it pity, but it was certainly a problem of pride and possibly a mixture of something she did not understand.

When she returned to Maevra's side, Elan proudly presented her with a handful of berries to go with her mushrooms. Accepting the gift, Elaine sat down on the log next to Maevra and slowly ate everything, making sure she tasted each thing in order to feel fuller. Content with his actions, Elan returned to his foraging.

"What is wrong, my child?" Maevra asked. Elaine blinked, having fallen into a thoughtful stare.

"Maevra, what is arete?" she asked.

The older woman licked her lips. "It is a term they use in the south for what we would call majick."

"Then I was right." Elaine nodded. But she furrowed her brow even further.

"Why do you ask?"

"Acies seems to be suffering, but he will not let me help him. He says he needs arete."

"I see," Maevra said neutrally.

"So how do I give it to him?" Elaine lifted up her hand to look at the veins of her wrist. "I have majick in my blood. When I was in the temple..." Elaine swallowed back the lump in her throat. "When Acies ... saved me, I saw him drink the blood of Dakin's warriors."

Maevra inhaled, leaning back slightly as she understood.

"But ... they were just normal people," Elaine said. "How could he drink majick from normal people's blood?"

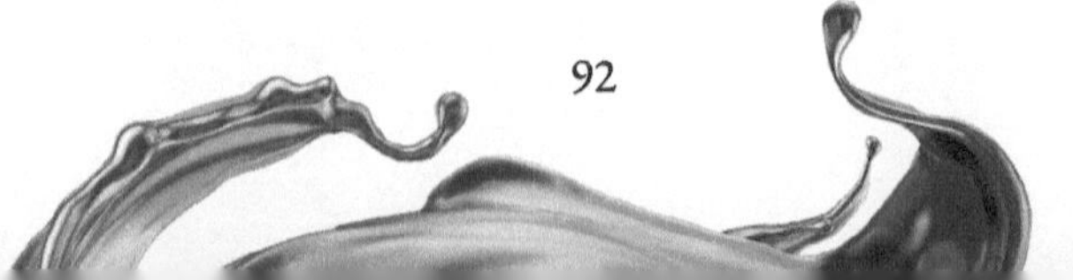

"There is majick in all of us, Elaine. I have taught you that," Maevra said.

"Yes, but not like there is within me," Elaine argued. She gestured with her hand, opening the palm to the sky. After a moment of concentration, water appeared in her palm. She had done this trick a million times, but this time her palm overflowed with liquid. Much of it pattered to the ground before she managed to slurp what remained into her mouth, easing away the dryness.

"You are correct, Elaine. There are very few who can command majick as you do. I believe that is why your demon chose you."

Elaine snorted. "He did not have much of a choice. Neither of us did."

"Be that as it may, you are very special. You have always known this."

"Which means it may not take as much of my blood to renew him as ... anyone else."

"I do not know very much about the matter of demons, child. My realm was the gods and how to destroy or protect *against* demons. What I do know is all things have a degree of inherent majick to them, from the plants to the trees to—"

"To the mountains and seas, yes," Elaine finished. "I know this, Maevra. It does not help me."

"And the gods," Maevra added, finishing her sentence despite Elaine's interruption.

Elaine pressed her lips together. "Yes."

The older woman patted her knee as Elan returned. "We better get moving. If we do not find shelter soon, we are going to be a meal for the forest soon."

"Elan, I do not think Maevra can go any farther," Elaine argued, but the priestess forced herself slowly up to her feet.

"I will do what must be done, and if it is to walk a little farther, then I will walk," she declared in a tone of voice that would not tolerate any argument.

Yet, Elaine argued. "Just wait a minute," she said, gently pressing the older woman back to her seat. "Let me go to the privy quick before we head out again." Maevra capitulated to that suggestion, though Elan gave her a dirty look, which she returned.

Elaine took herself a few feet away, finding a decent-sized tree to squat next to take care of her needs. Just as she finished up, a whistled melody, so different from the calls of the birds, twittered on the wind. She stood up, looking around her in through the woods, but all was quiet and still.

Again, the whistle called, shifting its melody as if continuing with a familiar song Elaine could almost remember. Spontaneously, Elaine sang back the notes, answering the call with a repetition of the initial notes. Her voice echoed ethereally through the empty hall of trees carpeted with dead leaves. The whistle trilled joyfully in response, now coming so close that she thought it was in the next tree over.

Just as Elaine thought she saw something peering down from the darkness of the branches a movement zipped away, leaping from branch to branch too fast for her to follow. Then it was gone.

After she waited a few breathless moments for whatever it was to reappear, she decided it was time to go back. Then a branch cracked.

"Hello?" she called.

"Elaine?" she heard Elan call from a few steps away.

But he wasn't the source of the crack.

She whirled again toward the sound and yelped as she almost tripped over a small creature no higher than her knee looking up at her.

It was covered in long bright yellow feathers with a crest laid straight back over its head. A piece of impossibly white cloth edged with dark gold laid across its back, fastened under its chin, or rather beneath an enormous beak of equally bright gold. The creature stood as still as a statue and regarded her with inky black eyes that didn't blink.

After a heavy moment of regarding each other, the bird-like thing cocked its head to one side and opened its broad beakish mouth with a sort of duck-like grin.

"Are you my mistress?" the bird-thing asked in Ka'in with a high-pitched trill. Elaine cringed a bit at the sharp sound.

"Are you a demon?" she asked in return.

The creature slid its eyes sideways in a clear guilty look. "No," it said.

Wary, Elaine remembered the tales of demons that would appear innocent in order to lure prey. "Who *are* you?" Elaine asked, taking a step sideways, so as not to turn her back on it.

"I..." the creature hesitated. "I am... I was..." Its feathers shivered, shaking with fury. "You must be!" the creature declared excitedly, throwing its feathered limbs at her. "You must know what I am. You are favored of the Lady Isa. I can see it! You can tell me!"

"Tell you what?" Elaine asked, getting more anxious by the creature's strange display.

"No! I am doing this all improperly! First, we must be introduced!" The bird creature then bent forward, extending a feather-covered, three-fingered hand into a sort of courtly bow, dipping its head low.

"A deep pleasure to meet you, my mistress," it said formally. "What is your name that I may address you?"

"<Elaine, are you there?>" Acies called from a distance.

At the sound of the deeper voice echoing through the trees, the little creature's crest stood straight up, revealing bright red feathers under the layer of sun-bright yellow. The black eyes brightened, and it scurried over faster than Elaine could backpedal to stand in front of her, placing itself between her and the sound of Acies crashing through the woods.

"He is freed! The Demon Lord! I will not let him hurt you mistress!" the bird creature declared with all the righteous fury the little being could muster.

That righteous fury translated to a trembling in its wings, which inadvertently battered at Elaine, and she stumbled back to land hard on her backside. Acies must have heard the whooshing *oomph* she made because he flew straight for them, appearing out of the woods to halt a few feet before the little bird creature, his sword upraised.

"It is! It is you! How did you get free!?" the little creature demanded of Acies, who stood there staring down the little challenger.

The larger man lowered his weapon in an obvious show of relief and dismissal. "<Oh, it's a temple guardian. This is all we needed,>" he muttered. "<Elaine, are you alright?>"

"Uh, yes," she replied, pushing herself back up to sitting, then she promptly pulled a feather that had somehow gotten in her mouth.

The little temple guardian did not like being ignored. "How dare you insult me! I am a gelic spirt of the highest order! Slanderer! Betrayer! Indeed, betrayer worst of all!" the gelic said, crest ruffling with indignation. "I will keep you from harming the mistress with every last ounce of spirit within me!"

"<And I have had my fill of this,>" Acies declared as he strode forward. Without breaking step, he punted the bird creature like a leather ball out of the way. It flew sideways, feathers and all, squawking in surprise as it arched away into a pile of loam. Acies then offered his hand to Elaine to help her to her feet.

"Why did you do that?" she protested, even as she accepted his aid to her feet.

"<I heard you cry out. Are you alright? Did the old temple spirit startle you?>" he mocked. She grinned unwillingly as she brushed away the dead leaves clinging to her backside.

"But what is a temple guardian doing out here?" Elaine asked.

"<Gelic,>" Acies snapped. "<Is there a temple nearby?>"

With a maximum amount of indignity, the gelic reappeared, swiping and thrashing out of the loam.

"How dare... How dare you!" it trumpeted.

Before things continued to escalate, Elaine came forward and knelt down before the little gelic.

Demurely she bowed her head, setting her hands folded in her lap. "Please forgive me and my companion for his rudeness to you."

The gelic stood stunned at her apology, wings stopped in mid-flap as the beak opened and closed with slow, methodic clicks. Then it dropped its face to the ground, curling over in a perfect show of contrition.

"No! Please mistress, forgive me. I did not know this foul demon is your companion. I am so ashamed to have disgraced myself in front of one such as you."

Elaine raised her head, smiling down on it. "Then let us agree to let this issue go and continue in our new friendship."

"Yes! Yes, thank you mistress!" it squawked, lifting its head to look up at her adoringly.

"But Acies is right. I too would like to know if there is a village or temple nearby?"

"A temple? Yes. Yes, my temple. The temple of Isa, if it please you, mistress."

"Yes, yes, that would please me very much," Elaine said, growing her smile. "Is it far?"

"No, no, not at all. This way! This way!" The creature leapt to its feet and immediately disappeared into the brush. Elaine and Acies exchanged a look just as the gelic came back. "This way?"

"We have two other companions that need to come with us," Elaine said standing up.

"Oh! Of course! Of course!"

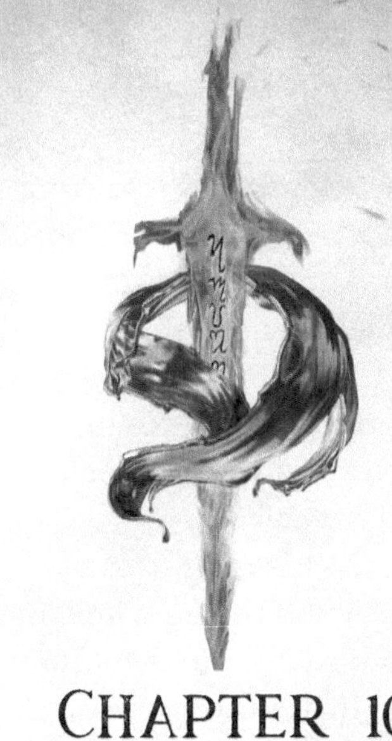

CHAPTER 10

"Where is Elaine?"

Elan started at the question, having nodded off himself. "She went to…" His words trailed away as he scanned the trees but caught no sight of Elaine.

"She went where?" Maevra asked, her voice darkening as she folded her arms over her chest.

"Dammit." Elan gritted his teeth as he jumped to his feet. "You were supposed to be watching for her too."

"Go see if she is near those trees," Maevra instructed.

"I already am!" Elan snapped, though he had to adjust his trajectory a bit to accommodate Maevra's instructions.

"Elan! Take your sword!" Maevra called.

Cursing, he wheeled back and quickly scooped up the naked weapon where he had dropped it.

Dammit, Elaine. Why are you making this so difficult? he thought as he lifted the blade to ready height, all the while scanning the trees furiously.

Off in the distance, darkness had crept up to swallow the sky, small flashes hinting at an oncoming storm. *Dammit twice over!*

"Elaine!" he shouted, his heart thumping hard against his rib cage.

"She must be nearby," Maevra continued to call after, as if her instructions were really of any help.

"Hello?" he heard her call out.

"Elaine!" Elan shouted, leaping over a large fallen branch like a deer as he spun about the trees looking for his sister.

A high-pitched whistling sound cut through the air. He froze in place, the hairs on the back of Elan's neck rising. Listening to his instincts, the archer lifted the sword higher. Swords were not Elan's favored weapon, but he could use them.

A twig snapped.

He spun.

A flash of movement pulled back behind a tree.

Elan cursed under his breath as he shifted to another stance, keeping his focus on that spot.

"I saw you, creature!" he shouted. "You do not frighten me!"

As he took another cautious step closer, an equally high-pitched whine buzzed his ear. He only had second to turn and attack, not even registering what dove straight for him. His aim was true, and he swung the blade straight into the creature, knocking its trajectory away to crash mere feet from him.

The crash did not end the thing though. Instead, it thrashed on the ground, tearing up clods of earth. It was a horrible creature, made of scales and feathers the color of dried blood, with too many appendages whipping around it as it struggled to right itself. Finally, the creature showed its face, glaring with ink-black eyes out of a bird-like face. Its fury burned Elan straight to his core.

Before he could lift his blade to attack again, he pitched forward, having been knocked down to the ground from behind. He rolled onto his back to stare up into the slack-jawed face of the demon standing over him, his own sword raised.

Elan realized his last thought would be, *I told you so,* to Elaine, even if it was only in his head. Then a second creature that had dived above him skewered itself on Acies's sword under the force of its own momentum. The weight of the thing overwhelmed the demon, and he dropped onto his knees, flopping the creature to Elan's side, its grotesque face inches from his own.

Elan rolled up to his feet with a yelp. By some miracle, his hands seized on his dropped sword. With a fluid motion, he swept it around and took the creature's head off as it tried to make a leap for Acies. It collapsed in a pile of ichor-covered feathers. The smell made Elan gag, and his eyes burn.

More whines and whistles cut through the air like fine wire. The discordant harmony they created forced Elan to grab at his ears.

He dropped his weapon heedlessly.

A wave of nausea flowed over and through him.

The noise increased.

Elan cried out in pain.

He could barely force his eyes open as he managed to turn his head skyward enough to see. Above, three more of the creatures hovered, their scaly tails whipping under them. They were strange malformations of bird and lizard, entirely something from a nightmare. Whorls of wind spun up dirt from the flap of their mighty wings. Yet he swore he saw one of them simply hover in the air without flapping its spread wings.

Demons. They had to be demons.

That was all Elan managed to see before he lost his battle with his guts. He couldn't care. What little he had in there spilled onto the grass. His head rang so badly, he just wanted to fall to his side and die. Then, at least, it would stop. He felt the rough grab of a creature as it attacked and dug its talons into his upper arm, dragging him along the ground. It felt like a distant thing, and he barely registered the pain with it. He felt floaty and disconnected. Maybe he had already left his body and was now journeying on the path toward the Beyond.

He became disabused of that idea when he dropped painfully onto the ground. It had not been the demon in the sky but the one on the ground that had grabbed him.

"Elan!" He thought he heard his sister call through the discordant noise, which was abating at last. Stunned, he managed to sit up a little and touched an itch by his ears. His fingers came away red with blood, which he stared at, trying to comprehend what that could possibly mean. Thinking was still so hard. Lying back on the ground again, he closed his eyes. It was better that way. If only he would die.

Except Elaine wasn't letting that happen. "Come on, Elan. Move!" she shouted in his ear, bringing fresh pain to his head. She seized his shoulders, hauling with all her might back into some sort of shelter. He couldn't really register where he was or how he got there. A movement caught his attention again. A leg and foot skidding up the turf and dirt to press against his leg. He distantly heard the grunting of a man exerting against a huge force.

Elaine's demon.

He stood like a wall of warriors, holding back one of the alien bird-creatures with the bar of his now-damaged bronze sword. The demon won the contest of strength, throwing the creature back while it screamed in rage. Then he surged forward again, bronze blade swinging to keep them back.

The three creatures cried and spat at him, whipping their tails angrily, but none of them dared to get closer. For each attempt, they were met with bronze, no matter how fast or how coordinated they tried to be.

At last, frustrated, one made a swing at him with its whiplike tail. Reacting, he sliced his blade through the air and tail easily. It dropped to the ground, twitching like a snake while the three bird-creatures screamed again, backing way off.

Using the space he had made, the demon spun on his heels. Without slowing, he seized Elan's upper arm in a familiar tight grip and helped Elaine haul him into the safety of a half-collapsed shelter, more like a cave than a proper house.

"Oh, crap," Elan said, or thought—he couldn't tell. "He just saved my life, did he not?"

Elaine gripped her brother against her, his head lolling drunkenly as he continued to talk in nonsensical sounds. If she didn't know better, she would have thought he had been possessed and was speaking tongues. Blood trickled from his ears, but he seemed to have no other wounds that she could see. She felt helpless as she watched Acies stand between them and the danger.

The bird-like creature, the gelic, waddled up beside her. Gently, it set its feathered hand on Elaine's arm. She could feel it trembling. "Oh, oh, oh," it kept whispering in tiny squeaks. "I am so sorry, my lady. I am so, so sorry."

Not knowing what else to do, Elaine hugged the small one's shoulders, pulling it to her like a child. It complied, hiding its face in her shawl. "This is not right. This is not right," it moaned.

"Nothing has been right for a very long time," Elaine muttered. "What are they?"

"My kin!" the bird-creature moaned. "They have fallen and become demons. I am so sorry."

"The gelic is right," Maevra said, appearing beside her. The older woman looked like she was about to drop, leaning hard on the staff Elan made her as she gulped back air. Their escape to this shelter, which they wouldn't have even seen if not for the gelic's aid, had taken its toll on the injured older woman. "Those demons were once temple guardians, driven mad with hunger and rage. They can never be redeemed again."

Dirt erupted outside as one of the demons plummeted to the ground, attempting to dive-bomb Acies, who leapt impossibly out of the way.

"Can we stop them?" Elaine asked, having to shout over the noise.

Maevra rolled her lips. "Possibly. You must call to them. You are now a Scion of Isa with the last splinter of her power in this world. They may be too far gone to save, but there is always a chance they may still answer if you call. It is at least worth a try, I think."

"Call how?"

"Sing to them, Elaine. We hid our words of power in our songs. You must sing to them. Sing 'The Lady Faire.'"

Elaine swallowed the lump in her throat. She watched Acies fight, moving with grace and deadly force, even as he was thrown about like a leather ball, only to land in a crouch on his feet. Blue light flashed from his eyes; he was fighting with everything he had. She had to try something.

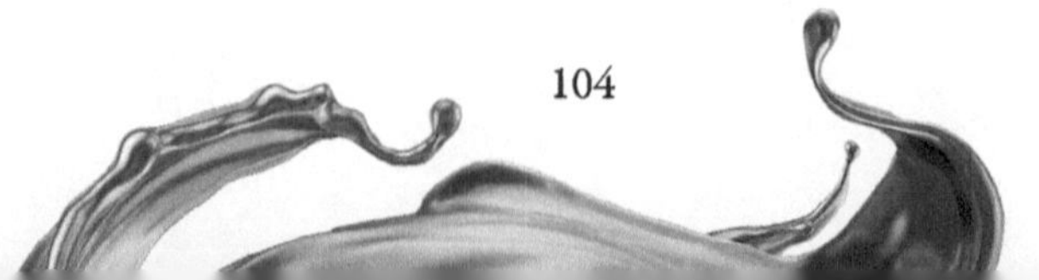

Shifting Elan's weight over to Maevra, Elaine stood. The dark shawl wrapped around her shoulders slipped, draping down her one side more like a cloak, and she clung to its edge with shaking but resolute hands.

Acies would have enjoyed this fight, except it was a terrible mess. The demonic gelics fought with animalistic abandon, their reason long deteriorated along with their supply of divine energy. Whatever intelligence the divine had granted them was long used up, and their desperate hunger for arete had forced them to turn to other, lesser foods. All they understood was hate and anger and need, a combination that could bring down the most skilled of warriors just by the chaos of it alone. Their discordant noises were affecting him too, although he hadn't succumbed as fully as Elan had. His only advantage against it was how each of his attacks interrupted the noise, keeping it from building to a point where it liquefied his brain. Still, it inhibited his ability to think, creating a pounding headache he had to contend with mentally as much as he fought physically.

Acies was not in as good of shape as he wanted to believe. Though none of his skills had left him, the imprisonment had taken a toll on his being all the same. He had consumed arete from Elaine to escape the prison, her silver blood carrying so much potent power that he had needed very little. That combined with the last of his own had been enough to help him break them free through the fragile walls of what remained of his self-consuming prison. It had also left him with very little left of his divine life force, and if the mortal warriors had realized that, it would have been a simple thing to end him there and then. But they hadn't and didn't, which had allowed him to drink up their arete and renew himself.

They had been a poor substitute to the fine wine that had been Elaine, yet it had done the job. He had to be careful with her; she was the only anchor that kept him from the pull of his prison. No matter how far he escaped, if she should die, he would be called right back to it, and that really would be the end of him. If only he had not had to fight so soon after.

Even worse, the body he now inhabited, templated off of Elaine's genetics and combined with what made him uniquely him, was inherently strong and fit, but there was no muscle memory, no endurance or stressing that only came from taking and giving beatings. He needed time to retrain; he was as soft as any new being would be. The creatures were catching lucky blows against him, nothing fatal yet, but it was costing him more and more of what little of his personal arete he had remaining.

For every sword swipe he managed, he had to dodge or parry three attacks. The warriors weren't even accomplishing that much, being only temporary distractions for these things, barely getting any viable hits in. The math of this fight was against him.

What would Isa think of him now?

His luck turned when a tail caught him in the middle, throwing him ten feet to land hard on his back. The wind knocked out of him as his sword was knocked out of his hand. The world went too bright then too dark for a moment. He could hear the fight, and he realized he was going to lose if he didn't move.

Taking on men had been one thing, but battling demons such as these?

They were the least of the arcane world. These had been temple *servants* turned into demons. They should have been the least of demonkind. Yet they were pulverizing him into dust. He'd die of the shame of it if nothing else.

He tapped more of his arete to clear his sight and push back the concussion he otherwise would have. Before him, three of the demonic birds had landed, waddling over toward him on their wings tipped with clawing hands more like bats than birds. Their monstrous maws were split open, those long, tentacle-like tongues flicking in and out, swiping the air to search for him. Their ink-black eyes yawned, seeing very little, he realized. Still, they would find him soon. He struggled to a crouch.

"<Pi was right,>" he said out loud, remembering his old friend and blood brother from the war long ago. "<Time alone is Lord of All. You pathetic spirits have become so powerful because you have had more time to build yourselves up. Glutting yourselves on the weaker until you are nothing but pure monsters. What would your lady think of you now?>"

A hiss rose up from the lot as they understood his godspeech.

Acies cracked a smile.

One of the demons feinted to his right, and he stepped back in his low crouch, moving toward his damaged sword, while preparing for an attack. He didn't really believe he had a chance to get to it but damned if he didn't die trying.

He chuffed a dry laugh. "<So, this is how it ultimately ends for me? Not in a glorious battle,>" he continued, keeping all three in sight, even as two split to come along the sides, trying to flank him. He had to keep moving, so he kept talking, "<but here, strung out, centuries later in the maws of lesser beings who have forsaken their purpose. My only remaining question is, how can such creatures like you even be *allowed* to get this bad?>"

Like a thick string plucked inside, he felt understanding thunk into place, the truth that he had been denying since first being told. But it was the only explanation for this to be allowed to occur, and he could not deny it any longer.

The gods and goddesses who would have come to stop these atrocities from becoming ... were gone.

Isa was gone.

Night had truly fallen, wrapping them all in darkness as his death came for him.

That's when he saw *her*.

Behind the bird-bat demons, Elaine stood in the entrance of the collapsed building's cave-like entrance. Only her pale face showed visible between her black clothing and the darkness within, as if she were a shrouded corpse exiting a tomb. Above, thunder rumbled.

A memory cut through Acies as he stared up at the Scion of the goddess he hated. She was much as Isa had been, that same expression, sad and resolute, full of true power and prepared to do what she must.

"No," he croaked out, though whether to the memory or to Elaine, he was not sure.

Then Elaine sang. Her voice rang out, thrumming with power, tasting like Isa in the back of his throat.

The creatures froze at the beautiful note. They didn't turn to her but held perfectly still as they listened. More notes—a calling as the voice rose and fell off to rise again. Goosebumps skittered down Acies's skin, and within his heart, he wanted to answer that call with his own.

Then one of the demons began to keen a low, discordant noise. It was the same sound that had made Elan's ears bleed and Acies's head ache. Yet as the sound touched her song, the keening changed, mellowed as it blended, then corrected. The other demons added their own keens to the sound, finding a place in the chorus until it was one unified harmony. The demons turned at last toward her, waddling forward on their monstrous hand-tipped wings.

Elaine emerged from the cave of ruins, walking boldly toward them. Acies wanted to yell for her to stop and stay back. However, doing so would disrupt the song, the only thing holding them in check. He dared not risk it.

She approached the first one and held out her hand toward its beak. At first, the demon stared hard at her, and Acies imagined it wrapping its whip tongue around her wrist and tearing her arm off. Mournfully, its head dropped hard onto her hand. It closed its black eyes, like a mastiff adoring its master. Soon, they were all crowding around her, pressing their heads against her sides and legs, begging to be petted, or setting their heads against the ground at her feet, continuing the pitiful keen, lower than before so that only her voice soared.

He knew the song. Normally, the song would inspire and strengthen, but in this context with her lone voice ringing out, it sounded somber and mournful, encapsulating everything that had been lost to these creatures.

Then, as peacefully as a dream, the demons broke apart into tiny shards of light, bright and clear as stars. The darkness of the storm rumbled overhead, making them glisten all the more as their lights swirled together around Elaine, dancing in her hair and tugging on her shawl.

She smiled, tears streaming from her eyes.

Gaining speed, the lights whipped and whirled, lifting her off her feet a moment as the spirits of the gelics burst away. They spread out to the farthest reaches of the forest and sky, winking out like fireflies.

Elaine stood there, watching them go long after they disappeared. Then she turned to Acies, her eyes shining as she squatted down beside him. "<Are you alright?>" she asked, apparently not realizing she was still speaking in godspeech.

"Aye," he responded in Ka'in, not yet truly sure if it was true or not.

"Can I help you?" she asked, and he pulled away, not wanting her to touch him.

He would never admit it to her, nor did he think he had the words to explain it, but his whole body felt stunned and distant from him, and it even hurt to breathe. "No," he said.

She accepted his answer, stood serenely, and moved back toward the shelter where her kin hid.

When he got the will for it, he probed his ribs. "<Two broken,>" he muttered to himself. And the cost to heal them would be too high.

His head swam. If anything else cared to attack at that moment, he would be in a lot of trouble.

"<You have seen this before,>" the high priestess—the witch—stated as she appeared next to him. She hobbled closer, the end of her walking stick digging into the dampened dirt as she gave it too much weight.

"<I have battled other demons before,>" he conceded. "<The gods must truly be dead to allow such abominations to grow so powerful unchecked.>"

"<You believe me now?>" the hag asked.

"<Aye!>" he barked, which was a mistake as it set his head off again. He pitched his voice down. "<Isa would not let this sort of thing happen if she were able to do something about it.>"

Maevra nodded toward Elaine. "<Now you understand why Elaine is so precious to us. She is all we have left. I have taught her everything I could, but my knowledge is poor in comparison to those before me. We are a dying people.>"

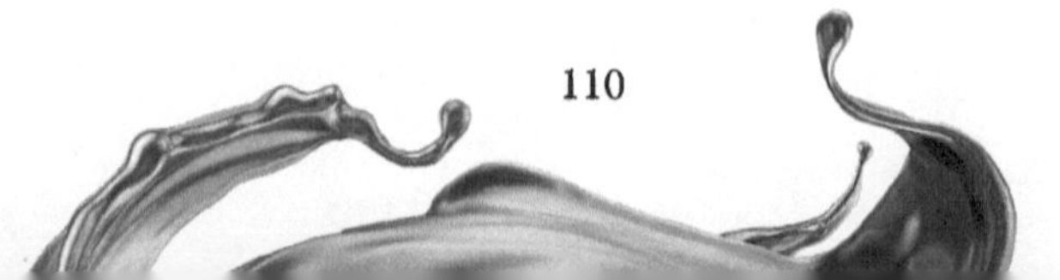

"<Yet it should not be possible, if what is said is true, that Isa is gone,>" he mused. "<Isa was the source of all this, the gelics, your Scion, even the boundaries of my prison, which has held for years. It was the only sign I had that she still lived. If she is dead, how is this so?>"

"<I have no answers for you, and I would not impart them if I did.>"

He glared at the hag, and she took a step back from it. "<Then I will find them for myself. Be assured of that,>" he added.

"<Your revenge will not bring you the peace you seek, demon,>" she said, a touch of chill in her voice. "<You see for yourself what the gods' absence has wrought upon the world.>"

"<You desire a force to fight for you, and I desire revenge against those who betrayed me. Those two desires are not mutually exclusive at all, are they?>"

Clutching her staff, she jutted out her chin defiantly. "<A demon cannot take the place of a god. You will consume all to try to sate your unending thirst, and we will all suffer greatly for it.>"

"<There is always another battle,>" Acies said, pressing himself to his feet while holding his ribs with other arm. "<And unfortunately for you, a demon is the only one who will answer your prayers.>"

CHAPTER 11

ELAINE FELT BONE TIRED WHEN THE RAIN FINALLY broke free from the clouds above, pregnant with their watery burden. She had returned to the ruins where Elan lay but had been unable to keep him awake. Now, she could only watch and pray that he stayed alive. A kitten had more strength than Elan right then.

"We need to get him warm," Maevra said, returning herself to the cave, hobbling with her stick in a slow uneven shuffle. A pang of guilt shot through Elaine, and she stood up to help the older woman but was waved away when she came too close. "Do not worry about me. We must do what we can to survive this night."

"What is wrong with him?" Elaine asked, brushing away at the dried blood coming from her brother's ears.

"<The sound attacks from the demons have made him sick,>" Acies said, coming up on the other side of Elan. He started patting along her twin's body, checking his limbs and inside his shirt. "<He does not seem to have any other serious injuries.>"

"Does that mean he will be deaf?" Elaine fretted. "The blood coming from his ears..."

"<No, that is temporary. Sound very rarely bursts your eardrums without long-term exposure. The high frequency of the sound made him sick, but it will fade with a bit of time.>"

"I understand very little of what you just said," Elaine admitted, hovering her hands over her brother's face as Acies picked him up.

"<It is knowledge of the gods then. Trust me. He is going to be fine if this cold and rain don't kill him,>" Acies said.

"Elaine," Maevra's voice cut through the discussion.

The older woman stood holding her staff before her, staring out as the rain poured like a waterfall now. Standing in it was the remaining temple guardian. The water poured around it, dampening its feathers like it would any other bird, yet this spiritual creature glowed down the filaments of each of its feathers with an internal light as if a tiny shard of sun lived within. It worried its hands before it, very unsure of what to say or do, but its eyes pleaded, focusing on Elaine.

Acies stepped up beside her. Then he snapped his fingers at it and spoke in Ka'in. "You. Make fire?"

The gelic raised its head, looking at Elaine as if she were the one who had spoken. "Yes, mistress! I can! I can make anything burn, if it please you?"

"<Order it to come in and start a fire for us,>" Acies instructed, taking off his cloak to tuck into the cracks around and over the door, creating a half curtain with it.

Yet she didn't have to order the little gelic to do anything as it already had scurried in. It jumped about in the dark space, pulling and yanking while making little grumbling noises. It moved so fast, the light it cast streaked about with after-light. Soon enough it had a small pile of dead leaves, twigs, and other unnamable detritus placed into a depression in the floor to make a fire pit. Then it held out its hand. The glow within its feathers gathered, leaking away until it pooled. Once all the concentrated light was focused, a spark leapt out onto the pile of kindling which *fwoosh*ed with a burst of flames.

With the fire glowing merrily, the gelic, now as dark as the other mortals in the space, rushed back out into the storm, disappearing from sight.

"Where is it going?" Elaine asked as she tried to follow where it went.

"<To fetch more wood if we are lucky,>" Acies said, turning back to Elan. "<We need to move him closer to the fire.>"

Just as Acies lifted the Ka'in Prince up into his arms, both men groaned with pain. Elan twisted, murmuring incoherently.

"<Curses,>" Acies muttered, but it was too late to put Elan back down. Instead, Elaine's brother turned his head to the side just in time to throw up, or rather, dry heave, onto the floor.

"Oh, Elan," Elaine said, coming to help, but Maevra grasped her arm instead. She thrust an old, dried-out hollow gourd at her.

"Take this and fill it," she ordered Elaine then pointed from Acies to the fire. "Take him to the other side."

Elaine did not argue but went to the front of the cave where a steady stream of water splattered onto the ground. After rinsing it out, she filled the gourd from that and brought it back. By then, Elan had stopped dry heaving. Acies plopped him against the wall nearest the fire and backed away in disgust. Elan stared at the glow of the fire as he breathed through his nose.

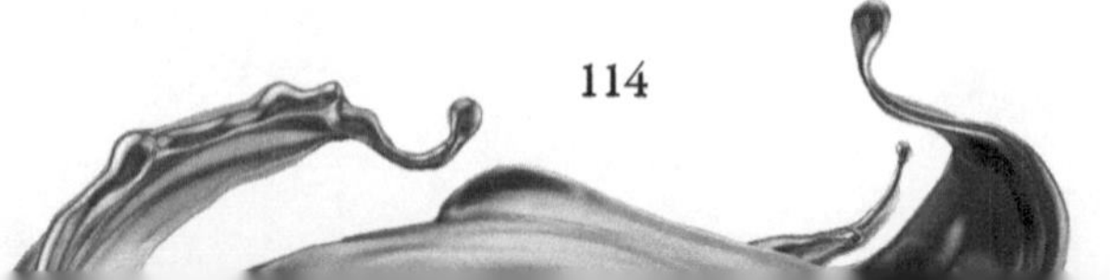

114

"Am I dead?" he asked.

"Not yet, my prince," Maevra answered gently. She took the gourd from Elaine and offered the narrow end toward Elan's mouth. "Please, Elan. Drink," she whispered softly.

"Yes, brother. Drink," Acies said, mockingly with his thick Ka'in words. He had moved to the entrance of the cave, rinsing off what little had come out of Elan's stomach from his boots in the small stream of water.

Elan emitted a sound between a groan and a growl at Acies before closing his eyes and drinking down the water in slow, steady gulps. While he drank, the gelic returned, arms filled with broken branches and chunks of wood piled twice as high as it was tall.

"That is not going to do us much good if it is wet," Acies said as it waddled past, but the gelic ignored him. Once it cleared out of the rain, its hands glowed the same golden color as before. Steam popped and *whooshed* from the wood so suddenly, there was a distinct singe smell in the air. Then the gelic dropped the load before feeding a few sticks into the scant fire. Soon enough, a proper blaze lit the room, throwing heat over them all.

Elaine brushed back her twin's hair from his face. "Feel better?" Elaine asked.

"Aye, more or less," he answered, covering his already closed eyes with his hand. "Maybe it would have been better if I'd died."

"Curb that tongue!" Maevra scolded as she slapped at his hand. "You are alive and whole. You mock the gods with your complaints."

"What gods?" Acies asked. He seemed to only be speaking Ka'in now.

Maevra speared a glance at the demon but settled in front of the fire to arrange it better with a stick. As soon as she did, the light increased in the room.

"Where are we? Are we safe now?" Elan asked.

"Safer. Not fully safe," Acies said, crossing his arms as he stood by the entrance of the cave.

"We can stay here for the night. It will be alright," Elaine assured. She slipped off her shawl and hung it next to Acies's cloak to fill in the remainder of the doorway. It wasn't much, but it would help. It also placed Acies on the outside of the group in the small space between the outside of the cave and the wall of rain. Then she stepped out to join him there.

"But *it* cannot," Acies said, nodding toward the gelic in Ka'in.

The creature squawked in surprise. "No, please mistress, do not cast me out!" it begged as it waddled out past the cloaks.

"<What is it that concerns you?>" Elaine asked in god-speech, stepping out to join him in the threshold.

Acies huffed once, his eyes searching the rain for answers. "<Those demons that attacked us? Those were once temple guardians like them, turned demon by breaking the forbidden law, consuming the life force of another. For temple guardians to turn demonic, there have to be no worshipers, no god or goddess, no arete given to them freely.>" He tucked the hand back under. "<So, they stole that power from wherever they could. Hundreds of years have passed; the gelics either could become demons or die, so how is it this one...>" Acies gestured at the trembling creature, "<survived unchanged?>"

"<It ... is a fair point,>" she said, then regarded the spirit. "<Well? What is your answer, gelic?>" Elaine asked, acknowledging that it had been listening. The gelic looked between Elaine and Acies.

"I do not speak the language of the gods, mistress, only the speech of the people of Ka'in, for gelics are closer to the Ka'in than to the gods," it answered.

"I see," Elaine said, switching back to her mother tongue as she knelt down beside the small spirit so that she was on the same level as it. "He asked how it is you can be as you are when your kin have become demons," she repeated gently.

"My kin..." A big, bright tear, like a drop of real gold, broke from the gelic's eye to cascade down around its beak. "When the mistress Isa left ... we swore to watch over the temple."

"What do you mean by 'she left'?" Acies demanded also having switched to Ka'in, his eyes reflecting the storm. "Where did she go?"

"We did not know her fate," the little gelic continued. "We are only made to serve the temple and the temple is all that we know. The Lady of the River left, her heart broken and body weak, and did not return. My kin continued to serve the temple and serve those who honored her, the priests and priestesses. Then fewer and fewer came to honor the Lady Isa. The priests and priestesses died, and none came to replace them. We grew weaker and weaker. My kin grew ... hungrier and more frightened. Still Lady Isa did not return. We stayed faithful until..."

The gelic shuddered its feathers and swallowed. "The last of the worshippers... They came for her festival, to honor us, and we received them, but then... Stone, my kin, could not resist any longer. They gave in to the hunger and... and..."

More tears slipped down the small gelic's face. "The worshippers screamed and screamed. We tried to stop Stone, but then others of my kin succumbed, drinking blood and stealing the life of the faithful against the edicts of Lady Isa. They devoured them all."

The little gelic trembled uncontrollably, and Elaine wanted to wrap her arms around the creature, but it held up its wings to stop her. "Please, I must finish..." it peeked up with eyes full of guilt. "It is not all."

"Finish it then; I grow tired of this," Acies snapped. "You drank the blood of the Ka'in too, didn't you? But maybe not as deeply? Did you break the edicts of *Lady Isa*?" he asked, giving the name of the goddess a nasty twist as he spoke.

The gelic hung its head. "Most of us were horrified by what Stone had done, but then Stone and those that followed it returned and enticed the others. One by one they fell until only I, Flame, remained. I clung to my duty to Isa, but I was so hungry and weak. Then Flame became Flicker, a shadow of what I was before. I knew I was dying. Then Stone came and brought with them a mortal—not a Ka'in, an Anon youth. Stone said that I would not betray Isa if I consumed one of the mortals from the south." Flicker stared into the long distance, reliving the memory as it spoke. "Stone spoke so compellingly, so convincingly, so kindly. Stone wished only to help me, and I *hungered* so badly... So, I did as Stone bid me. I drank from the Anon."

Flicker laid its hands against its eyes, shuddering from the horror only it could see and would never be able to unsee. "It tasted... It... The hunger eased, but I felt—"

"You *are* a demon," Acies stated.

The little gelic, Flicker, looked up with wide, wet eyes. "Am I, mistress? Can you tell me? Am I still unworthy? I sought penance for what I did. But the lady has not returned. I do not know what to do. Please, mistress. I do not want to be a demon."

The gelic bowed its head, weeping as it continued to plead, its voice diminishing with each fruitless entreaty.

It hurt Elaine's heart.

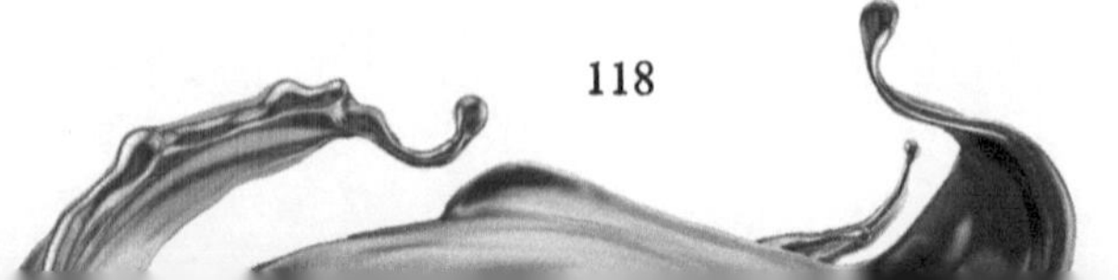

118

Gently, she laid one of her hands over the small spirit's head. The feathers were so soft. They burst with little waves of light where her fingers touched. The little pristine white cloak on its back trembled as it wept.

How could such a creature be considered a demon? she thought.

"I forgive you," Elaine said.

The gelic's head shot up, eyes wide with hope.

Elaine smiled down, nodding. "You are forgiven," she assured.

Flicker wiped its eyes with the back of one feathered hand. "Truly? Truly, mistress?"

"I do not see anything about you that is tainted or evil. You made a mistake. That does not make you a demon."

"It does," Acies argued, first in Ka'in before he switched to godspeech. "<They consumed the arete from another. Even if it is the smallest drop, that makes them a demon!>"

Elaine shook her head. "I forgive you," she continued to say to the gelic. "You only have to forgive yourself now."

A burst of light enveloped the little spirit as it cried in joy so bright it almost hurt. Then it rushed to her, burying its body against Elaine as she returned the embrace. The tears were now joyful, relieved ones, wetting Elaine's already damp sleeves with stains of gold. She tried not to glance at Acies, who regarded all this with black hostility.

Her smile fell, but she renewed it when the gelic lifted its head.

"Thank you, mistress," Flicker said, wiping at its gold-encrusted eyes. "Thank you. Thank you."

Elaine nodded again, receiving the thanks. "You said your name is Flame?"

The gelic shook its head with a sniff, which was a strange sight to see with a beak. "No, mistress. I am Flame no longer; I am only a Flicker of myself."

"Is that what we should call you then? Flicker?" Elaine asked.

"Yes, mistress, please! I will be your Flicker and serve you as if you were my Lady if it pleases you?" Elaine was pretty sure those ducky eyes were going to be the end of her with their adorableness.

"Do you not have to stay with the temple?" Elaine asked.

"<That which binds it to the temple is gone,>" Acies grumbled. "<It is free to do as it wishes. I still would not let it travel with us, but like it said, it is your decision.>"

"Then thank you, Flicker. I would be honored," Elaine assured.

"I promise to serve you faithfully for the rest of my days," Flicker declared proudly.

A peculiar feeling washed over Elaine, her skin prickling as a wave of goosebumps flooded across her arms, and then the sensation was gone. Majick had passed between them, but the little creature didn't seem to notice.

Then Acies muttered a low growl in his throat, his gaze promising violence.

She eyed him cautiously, aware that she had just crossed him. "Flicker, would you go tend the fire?" she asked tactfully. She needed to get the little gelic away from them, so she could deal with whatever price she would have to pay for her actions.

"Yes, please." Flicker smiled a ducky smile as it waddled back in.

Elaine stood up and turned, prepared for whatever punishment her demon would bestow on her. She had been struck before; she knew she could take it.

"<That was very foolish,>" Acies muttered, then he whirled to walk straight out into the storm, leaving a surprised Elaine to stand there and watch him go.

CHAPTER 12

"Oh for Goddess's sake, what is taking so long? It has been days since Lord Dakin left," Amira complained as the Anon woman paced.

She stopped near the window of her apartment with its view of the fortress of Icathor, turning the goblet of undrunk wine in her hand. She had been sipping on the well-made stuff all night, but it had done nothing to ease her nerves.

"No new reports as of yet," her house scribe Carmol said from his place at the writing desk. He was imprinting her personal seal on all the important documents as fast and as efficiently as only he could while the world went about its day in the fortress city beyond them, the common people oblivious to the machinations of their betters. The sound of the market filtered in through the window, the music of Icathor, as if it was another ordinary day. Usually, such sounds calmed Amira's nerves. But now, too many things were in motion, too many risks that she could not necessarily rig the game on, and she did not like it.

"My brother is a fool," she muttered as she abandoned her wine on the windowsill. She touched the statue base of the patron Goddess of Icathor nearby, a silent prayer that did not ease her heart. "We were not ready to make this move on Dakin's stronghold without the fat man in hand. Now it will be a bloodbath out there."

"The dice are already cast," Carmol said simply, and she hated that he was right. When the Ka'in scum had not appeared with Dakin in tow, her brother Elio decided to take his warriors and go seize the granaries from Dakin's remaining generals despite Amira's objections. The fact that no one in the greater world had noticed was not a good sign.

"It is hard to say if this was a bad move or not. These sort of games do not have a set of rules," Carmol said, picking out drying clay from the seal so it did not corrupt the next impression.

"The alliances I have painstakingly built will crumble if I do not have the bloated pig to lynchpin it!" Amira growled.

"Yes, I am aware," Carmol said with a touch of the conde-scending annoyance all the men of her father's household affected. She found it very irritating, like dumping oil on her already raging fire. She thought about dumping him into a fire, but most houses could not afford their own personal scribe, and replacing the man came with its own challenges.

Carmol continued to talk, completely oblivious to her murderous intentions. "But your ruffians are late, and if we wait much longer for them to bring his esteemed lordship, the game may still be lost if generals decide to play their own gambit and replace him with one of them. Or one of the other families. There has been talk. The granaries are the key to everything."

"The granaries," Amira sneered. "Even if another family managed to grab them from Dakin's generals, any one of them would be willing to negotiate pretty heavily for legitimacy if they have half a brain cell. He did not need to go over there and risk everything himself. We could still have made a favorable deal with whomever—"

"Or you might get forced into brokering a deal you do not want," Carmol sneered again.

"You watch your tongue, scribe," Amira snapped, finally having enough of his condescension. She seized her goblet and slapped its contents over his careful work. The scribe stilled, staring at the splotch of wine besmirching his damp clay tablets.

Making a deliberate choice, he pushed away from the desk and bowed his head. "I apologize, mistress," he said obediently.

That was good. He still knew where his bread came from. Not from Elio, her brother, who wouldn't even remember to feed himself if there was a fight to be had anywhere. Not from her father, who had not come back to Icathor from the Southern Capital City and her family's ancestral home in almost ten years. It was Amira who ran the household. Amira who ran the family trade in Icathor. Through Amira, all things flowed.

After a long moment of letting him stew, she heaved a theatrical sigh and uttered, "You are forgiven."

He raised his head and reassessed her face. "Your concerns are valid, mistress."

She sighed again. "It is hard when I do not control every piece on the board."

"We have a very good chance of winning this with the stones we have..."

Just then a noise from within the house alerted both of them. Angry voices drifted through the door, and both people in the room looked at each other with equal, palatable alarm.

Carmol bolted to his feet, gesturing for Amira to hide while he went toward the door, but instead, Amira drew her father's bronze sword, kept clean and sharp for exactly this reason.

Her scribe approached the expensively carved wood door, warily pulling it by the ring to peak through the crack into the short hallway. When he saw nothing, he went farther out to stand at the narrow flight of stairs. Amira followed him, sword at the ready.

Carmol hissed when he saw the blade. "What are you doing here?"

"Who is it?" Amira demanded as she came up beside him, but she saw the answer for herself. Standing at the bottom of the steps was the Ka'in rebel Titama, being blocked by one of the house slaves from coming up the stairs. He glared up at the two Anons above him.

"I must speak to you," he said in his crude use of their language.

Amira pursed her lips together, then handed the sword to Carmol. "Let him up," she conceded.

The belabored house slave shot the Ka'in a cursed look, but he ignored it and brushed past to mount the stairs. The Ka'in rebel leader's limp was not lost on Amira, but she said nothing as she passed Carmol the sword before turning back to her room and her abandoned goblet. She refreshed it as the Ka'in followed her in, Carmol staring daggers at the rebel leader's back as he brought up the rear.

Amira poured a second goblet of wine and turned with it. Predictably, the Ka'in saw it and reached out a hand to take it, and just as predictably, he frowned almost to a scowl when she gave the goblet to Carmol instead. Having established clear lines of alliance with that small gesture, she sat on the stool in front of the writing desk and crossed her linen-covered legs.

The Ka'in continued to stare his own daggers at her, waiting for her to speak first. She played the staring game for a few breaths, then gestured impatiently at him to start speaking.

Titama huffed through his nose, shifting his feet a moment in that way warriors had when they were delivering bad news as if they still thought they could fight or flee their way out of it.

Amira's heart sank.

"Dakin is dead," he said.

She tightened her grip on her folded hands but otherwise did not react. "What happened?" she asked evenly.

The Ka'in shifted his feet again. "There was a fight. He was killed. These things happen in battle."

"You were given strict instructions to not let *this* thing happen," Amira said coolly.

"He is gone," but there was something in the way he said it that sounded like a lie to Amira. Men were often so very terrible at lying, especially ones that communicated through action instead of words.

"I told you," Carmol said unhelpfully, "there are things that we cannot predict in these sorts of games. It is a good thing now that your brother made a move to take the granary. It is the only move we have at this stage."

Amira glanced out at the window at the building that towered over the city: the great granary, the symbol of Icathor. She wished she could see through the walls to know what was happening within.

"Fine, you failed," she said to the Ka'in, standing to go to that window to hide her expression. "Now leave. Do not let anyone see you, or we will have to kill you."

Not taking the dismissal, Titama continued to stand there even as Carmol tried to usher him away. "I am not leaving until I am paid," he said, his voice thick with emotion and stubbornness.

Amira looked over her shoulder at him.

"Paid for what?" she asked, shocked at his boldness. "You have not done a thing for me that is worth paying for."

"I lost warriors in this—"

"And these things happen in battle," she replied snidely.

Carmol pulled on the Ka'in's shoulder, but he shrugged it off. When Carmol insisted harder, the scribe found himself flung backward and landing violently on his ass.

"My people!" the Ka'in shouted, spitting as he said the words. "We eliminated Dakin for you. That is worth something."

"It means nothing if I cannot seize control of the granaries," she shouted back, gesturing at the far-off building. "So you better hope that we do manage to take them, or I can give you nothing, even if I was inclined to. You are not the only one risking warriors this day."

Titama's face did not shift; it was fixed with determination.

Amira sighed, desperately trying to think of what would appease this warrior and get him out of her house. Titama's grip on his pommel was certainly a clear and present threat, and she had handed over her only defense to the idiot on the floor.

"Carmol," she said, looking down on her fragile scribe, who was taking his dear sweet time getting off the floor. "Give Kanni and Tyra to the Ka'in."

Carmol shot her an objecting look, but she didn't meet it. She was too busy locking wills with the Ka'in. "Yes, mistress," he said and hauled himself downstairs.

"Will that satisfy?" Elaine asked. "I have let free those I can control."

Still, his face was fixed, staring at her.

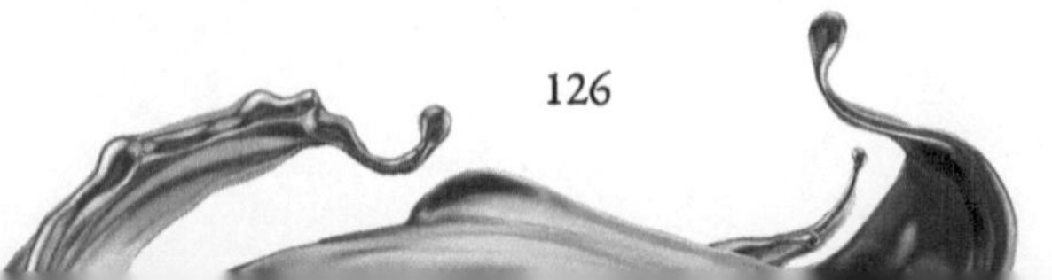

"It is all I can currently do, so if you wish to live to fight for your people once more, you need to leave and pray," she argued, though she didn't even know if she spoke the truth or not. Even if Elio did succeed that night, honoring her promise to this Ka'in would be dangerous.

She took in the man before her, his strange, pointed ears and the way he spoke aside, she could see that he had been through a hard fight. He had bruises on his face that hadn't even purpled yet and a scrape at the corner of his mouth. He wavered on his feet too.

She held out a hand toward the door. "Take what food and drink you need from the kitchen. I will contact you."

His whole body shifted toward the door, signaling that he truly wanted to leave, but he forced himself to stay, not yet willing to give up yet.

"I will contact you." Then Amira set her hand on the base of the patron goddess statue. "I swear it by Nymphaea who watches over Icathor."

At last, those broad shoulders dropped. He gave her the tiniest of nods, but she saved her smirk for when he turned his back to go to the door. Even if it had been a small battle, it was always a pleasure to win.

Before the door could be opened, however, Carmol reappeared frantic. "Mistress! Mistress!" he cried, but it was all he got out before a bronze tip appeared through his chest, coated in his blood. He made a final strangled noise while his fingers tried to grasp at the point, to comprehend it, then the sword was withdrawn back inside him. He dropped to the floor. If not dead, he would be very soon.

Amira couldn't move as she stared. Behind her scribe stood a nightmare of a man. "The Sword," she choked out in terror. Dakin's right hand general stepped the rest of the way through the door, walking heedlessly over the body before him as if it were an exotic rug she had brought in from the south.

"What is this?" he asked, gesturing with the tip of his sunset-colored sword at Titama, the only one now standing between her and certain death. She had the insane thought pass through her mind that she really should have offered the Ka'in a goblet of wine.

Carmol had been right. One really could not always predict how these games were going to play out.

"So, Amira of Icathor, your treachery extended all the way to the Ka'in," Lorab said, and he spun his sword around in a showy circle beside him, flicking off blood. Some of it splattered on Amira's face at the same time Titama drew his sword with desperate speed.

She screamed as the two men clashed, the Ka'in and the Sword, exchanging blows heedlessly in the too-small space. Amira ducked desperately, trying to find a path through the grunts of the fighters to escape out the door. Just as she tried to make her move, Lorab thrust his blade through the stomach of the Ka'in, driving him back to pin him to the wall right in front of her, effectively blocking her escape.

The Ka—Titama made a gasping noise, his eyes wide. Then he turned his head toward her, his dying gaze meeting hers, pleading with her, but she had no idea for what. Hot burning empathy spread across Amira's chest, and she choked out a sob.

She stretched her hand to the Ka'in's face—she had no idea why. They meant nothing to each other.

"D-demon," Titama gasped out with a final reedy breath with so little voice that Amira could not be sure of what she heard. "D-d-dakin..."

Lorab jerked his sword from Titama's chest, letting the dead man drop next to her scribe. Amira took a step back as the point redirected toward her own chest.

"Oh, Goddess!" she cried, stumbling back against the small family altar. Desperately, she clung to the carved woman's feet.

Lorab chuckled as he advanced closer.

Any desperate attempts to run were pre-thwarted as other warriors filled the doorway of her room.

"You got her?" one of them growled, his own blade shining blood-coated bronze.

"Caught in the act and everything. Conspiring with this Ka'in here." Lorab kicked at the body on the ground.

"Shall we take her?" another of the warriors asked, one who was still hyped up from the fighting, dancing on his toes with eagerness.

"Dakin will want her alive, but we will take our spoils first," Lorab agreed, setting his sword aside and stepping forward with a hungry grin.

The fourth warrior turned to exit the room, her slighter frame marking her a female. The second one went to say something to her, but the third only hit his shoulder and muttered about leaving her alone. The three men advanced on Amira.

"Dakin is dead!" Amira squealed.

That made all the warriors in the room pause. "Who told you that?" Lorab asked, arching an eyebrow at her.

She glanced at Titama's body.

The warriors encroached again. Lorab grabbed her arm to tear her from the shrine.

Amira cried, "My brother—"

"Is dead," Lorab finished, and he pulled her closer, kissing her neck while slipping his blood-coated fingers into her hair.

Amira wanted to be stunned. Her brother was dead? But there was no time to feel anything else for anyone else. She screamed again as she fell to the floor, trying to push Lorab off of her, but the other two men grabbed her arms, then helped their leader pin her legs open. She screamed and thrashed, but all their strength overpowered her own. She was helpless.

"My father!!" she screamed.

"Is not here, and I doubt he cares anymore," Lorab commented.

All Amira had left was to look up at the statue of the patron goddess.

"Nympha," she sobbed. "Save me, please."

The goddess did not answer.

CHAPTER 13

ELAINE AWOKE WITH A START. SHE WAS FAIRLY warm. The small shelter they had created in the ruins actually held the warmth in admirably. Without a blanket, she felt cozy, even if the ground was fairly hard. Sitting up, she realized Flicker sat next to her, the radiant heat from its little body contributing to her warmth.

Realizing she was awake, it turned to look at her with alert black eyes. "Everything is well, mistress," it said softly.

She nodded but sat up all the same. Elan and Maevra slept nearby, Maevra in a sitting position leaning against the wall, and Elan with his face turned toward the fire. He always hated his nose getting cold.

Elaine got up and came alongside him. He looked a lot better; his color was the right shade and his breathing peacefully even.

"Have you been watching all night?" Elaine asked Flicker just as softly, who nodded emphatically.

"I do not sleep like the Ka'in do. I cannot fight, but I can watch over you and alert you all to danger, or even lead it away before it comes," Flicker said, puffing up its chest.

Elaine smiled, then rose to peek past the cloth wall. Outside, the rain had stopped, but the dark and wet hung as heavy as a shroud.

"What time is it?" she asked, though there was no way to tell.

"The sun will rise soon," Flicker informed her, flapping up to look out the cloth barrier with her. "Your bound demon has not returned."

"I see that," she murmured, concerned.

Elaine emerged to stand closer to the entryway. She could feel him, like a tug in her chest or pressing on a wound that hadn't healed yet. Direction or distance or state of being, however, eluded her. It was a strange sensation.

"Do you know where he is?" she asked the gelic as it stepped up beside her, its natural glow casting a small bit of light into the wet darkness.

"Yes, mistress. Do you wish me to fetch him?" Flicker offered.

"No, just ... tell me which way and how far," Elaine said.

"That way, mistress," Flicker said, pointing off into the dark. "Several steps down the hill."

"What is he doing out there?" Elaine murmured as she tried to peer through the early morning dark. "I'll only be a moment. Please shine your light for me so that we can find our way back to you."

Flicker bowed formally at the waist. "Yes, my mistress, but I should come with you."

"No, please stay here and keep guard over Elan and Maevra. Acies will keep me safe out there," Elaine assured. She plunged into the dark, picking her way carefully over the wet roots and forest floor detritus in the direction that Flicker had indicated.

Drops danced on her head, Most of the wet coming more from the trees themselves than the sky. She tried to keep a sense of the distance she had traveled, but too soon realized what a bad idea this was. Her only way to navigate was to look back frequently to keep Flicker's light a beacon in sight.

"Acies?" she called out into the night.

No one answered her.

After a few more steps, she tripped over a large ... something on the ground. She hissed as she scraped her hands, catching herself. "What the hell am I doing?" she asked herself as she gingerly rubbed them together. They stung where her fall had drawn blood, but there was also something more coating her palms.

I couldn't have bled that much? she thought as she rubbed her palms together. Alarmed, she brought her palms to her nose, breathing in the distinct smell of death.

"Oh, Goddess," she cried as she felt around behind her to find a cooling body in the loam of the forest.

To her relief, the body was covered in short fur; it was not Acies. Then her hands slid up a graceful neck and encountered antlers: a young deer. Some predator had made a kill, then abandoned it, possibly because it had heard her coming.

A stick broke somewhere, and Elaine realized that it might be coming back, or a bigger predator may attack her for it. Best to get out of there before then.

As she got back to her feet, an arm wrapped around her waist, pulling her back against a tree. Immediately, she bucked, screaming a choked yelp as the body pressed against her. A man's nose pressed into her throat, and she felt wet lips brush her skin.

"No! Stop!" she cried, shocked.

Dakin had found her. His men had found her. "No!"

The man pushing against her backed away, dropping her breathlessly to the ground. "<I am sorry,>" a rough voice speaking godspeech came from the darkness.

The sound of his voice cut through Elaine's panic, allowing her to take a breath in.

"Acies?" she asked, her voice wobbling as her hands shook.

She felt rather than saw the figure of her demon. She could hear his breathing in the dark, labored, almost wheezing.

"<What are...>" He started but stopped as his voice quivered. "<It is dangerous out here. I will ... lead you back ... to the others...>" She felt his hand come to grab her arm in the dark, but then it hesitated and retreated. "<Come... Come this way...>"

"<What is wrong with you!?>" The question came out harsh and demanding. Its sharpness stopped Acies.

"<Just stay back,>" he growled.

She disobeyed, this time seizing him in return. To her surprise, he was searing hot to the touch, burning through the cloth of his shirt. At her touch, a shiver tore through his body.

"<You will tell me what is wrong. Now,>" Elaine commanded. There was a break in the clouds above, and the moon cut through, bringing its soft ethereal light to the water-rich world below its gaze.

"<I... I do not know, Elaine,>" he said, sounding genuinely scared. "<I can feel it. It is calling me back. I am hungry. I can't...>" He pulled away from her hand again. "<Do not touch me. I cannot hold back.>"

"<From what?>"

"<From taking from you.>" He retreated from her, his moon shadow pulling away to reveal the dead animal between them.

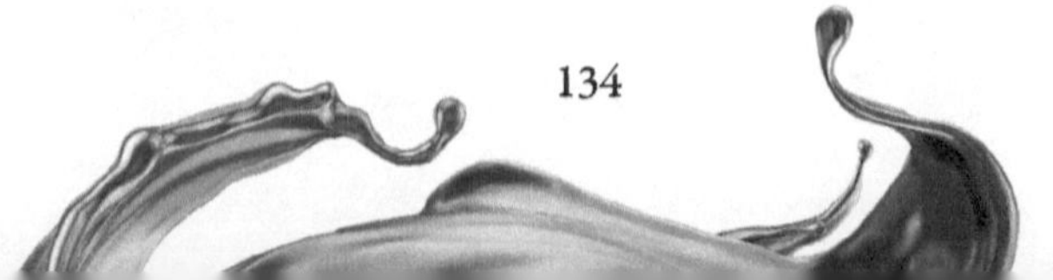

"<You killed the deer,>" she stated, letting him disappear completely around the tree.

"<Yes,>" came the small answer.

"<And drank its blood.>"

"<It did not work,>" he said.

Strangely, these facts did not frighten her. Maybe it was the fact that he kept retreating from her. Elaine furrowed her eyebrows. "<What do you mean?>"

Slowly, she followed him around the tree, moving an inch at a time so that she wouldn't startle the large man on the other side.

His face and chin were covered in blood as dark as ichor, its color washed away by the moonlight.

"<I could not... I could not draw energy from it,>" he admitted.

"<You were trying to consume its majick... I mean, arete?>" she said, willing to him see that she understood.

"<Yes, it did not work. It should have worked. I have done it before.>"

"<I see,>" she said, looking back at the deer, putting the pieces together. "<But my blood would help you, but you are afraid that you will lose control and hurt me?>"

"<If you should die, then I will return to my prison. I cannot risk you...>" He moaned in pain. "<I don't know what is wrong. I should be able to pull arete from any form of life.>" He curled against a nearby tree, bracing his hand against the trunk.

"<How much do you need?>" she asked, daring to step closer to him. In the pale light, he looked up at her from under his arm, wary and hungry, pleading and angry.

He is a soldier, she realized. *He needs to be commanded.*

And she was a princess. She knew something of this. With an imperious finger, she pointed at the wet, torn-up ground before her. "Kneel before me, demon," she said in Ka'in, not unkindly but with a supreme confidence that he would comply because she had asked.

And he did. He came, albeit reluctantly, sinking to the ground onto one knee, the muscles of his body outlined under the black of his shirt.

He pressed one fist into the ground, the other elbow braced into his knee.

Elaine held up her wrist. "Is this what you desire?" she asked. She squeezed her palm where she had scraped her hands, forcing it to ooze her silvery blood into the cup of her hand. It glinted like liquid moonlight.

Acies's eyes went wide, the hungry look passing over his face as he leapt up to seize her hand. He meant to force himself on her like Dakin would and the familiar panic seized her. Immediately, she whipped it away, bringing it close to her body. "No! Stop!" she barked.

He did, seized by her will, despite his own desire. The wild, manic eyes went to her, filling with such rage it took Elaine's breath away. Yet he did not move, doing as she commanded as he returned to kneeling. This time, his fingers sank into the loam, gripping the ground itself to hold himself back.

"N-not like that," she said, hating herself for trembling but unable to do anything different. She swallowed. *I'm going to do this,* she told herself. *I want to do this. He needs my help. We need him to survive.*

"I know it is hard, but please be gentle," she pleaded softly. Slowly, she lowered her hand, offering it to the demon at her feet.

"<Take what you need, but don't grab me,>" she said, granting permission.

He growled in his throat, his eyes locked on the silver blood in her palm. She held her hand out again.

This time he lifted his own hands, stained with damp earth. She set hers delicately in his, and he simply held it there tenderly. A warmth overwhelmed her, and she laced the fingers of her other hand through his dark, long hair. He pressed into her palm, closing his eyes as he savored her touch. And yielded when she pressed his head forward until his lips touched her palm.

Cold and hot flashed into her wounds, shooting spikes up her arm as his mouth locked on, his tongue darting into the abrasions. She yelped and had to brace on his shoulder to keep from falling over. His other arm snapped around her waist to support her, pulling her against him as he rose on both knees, still drinking in her blood. The intensity of the feeling forced her eyes closed. The hot-cold sensation continued to roll up her arm, burning its way into her chest, stretching from her temples to her groin. She whimpered again as he consumed her from the inside. She couldn't tell whether it was pleasure or pain. It was just intense.

"Stop, stop!" she gasped when she couldn't take it anymore.

The sensation ceased, and her legs gave out. Her body slid down his. He caught her in his arms, cradling her to his chest. His breathing labored against her, and her head swam. She felt so groggy and weak, all she could do was let her head flop onto his shoulder as he held her, still in the kneeling position with only each other to cling to.

"Oh, Goddess," she cried, and she wept. She tried to hold it back, but the wave of pain and sadness that she kept bundled up in her chest broke free and flooded, overwhelming her being. She pressed her tingling hands against her eyes, seeking sensation as she cried. "I'm sorry. I'm sorry," she repeated.

"Don't be … sorry to me," he said in Ka'in, though his lack of knowledge of the language made his words stilted.

"I didn't like it. I don't like…" she said, shaking her head. "I tried but…"

"Of course not," he assured gently.

She pressed her hands to her face. "Why do I always have to be the one to give?" she cried, knowing they were words she wasn't supposed to say, but feeling too broken to hold them back.

Acies growled in his throat, and he cupped her head with his hand as if to shield her. "I will never do that to you again. I swear. I *swear*."

"No," she whispered, shaking her head. "I told you that you could. I permitted it…" Then her breath caught as warmth slid into her from his fingers.

"Go to sleep," he whispered as his fingers brushed over her scalp, easing her pain. "Go to sleep and forget. Nothing will hurt you anymore."

"<This was a mistake,>" Acies whispered as he held his most precious prize in his arms. She slept heavily and had long enough for the sun to fully rise over the horizon. The clouds still hung heavy, so it was not too bright but plenty light now for him to see.

He had combed his fingers through her hair all the while, marveling in its softness. She hadn't said anything about it having been turned as black as his own, but then, it wasn't like they had been near any reflective surfaces. Nor had she noticed her eyes were now blue.

"<Strange that none of the Ka'in said anything to her about it,>" he wondered. It felt so good to speak again, to feel the speech of the gods in his mouth and on his tongue. And he had all this because of her.

Yet he couldn't get her words out of his mind, now that it was calm from the ravenous need for arete. *Why do I have to always be the one to give?*

Acies stiffened, but she slept completely insensate to him. He wanted to argue with her words, tell she was wrong, that she was the one who had told him to do it.

He had told her to leave.

She was the one who offered.

This wasn't his fault; it was hers.

"<Coward,>" he cursed himself.

The one whose fault this was had left him to die. *She* had abandoned this princess in his arms.

The one whose fault this was could not answer for her crimes.

He wanted to tell Elaine he was sorry, but he knew himself. He knew those words would never leave his lips. If he hadn't been able to say them to a goddess, how could this princess expect to hear them from him?

"<She doesn't,>" he answered himself. "<I am a coward.>"

He understood what he had just done to her.

She would be terrified of him now, and she would be right to hate him.

She would never forget.

Not unless he made her.

"Shhhh," he breathed softly, pressing his head against hers. In her sleep, she flinched to pull away, but he cupped his hand around her head to hold it in place and she did not resist further. Whatever her previous lord had done to her, he had trained her well in obedience.

She was a princess. She should have been a queen.

"<I can make you one,>" he promised.

A queen bound to a demon. It sickened him to his being. She had been tethered to a monster, and he was simply another one.

It is for her own good, he lied to himself. *She swore to me her mind, body, and soul. She chose this.*

They were all lies. What choice did she really have?

He set his forehead to hers, pressing in like a lover would, but he was not a lover. He slipped himself into her mind.

She breathed in sharply, but he was already inside, using their connection to perform this task. He could only do this to those who were bound to him, and this would hurt in its own way, but she would have no idea where it came from.

The recent memory of his feeding on her sat on the top of her mind, still fresh, still being formed in the dendrites and myelin of the brain. He stopped those impulses intuitively, taking the memory of what he had done with him as he consumed the slip of arete that supported it. It was foul, full of her pain and misery, layered over echoes of other similar suffering, the countless violations she had suffered at her previous lord's hands and body. Even looking at this small fraction of the depth of it, he could not imagine how she bore it and remained as strong and assured as she was. He was tempted to take all of it, erase her pain entirely, but such an act could drive him mad to suffer all that she had all at once. He was already risking enough.

Once the memory was pulled from her completely, her whole body relaxed, melting unconscious into his arms. She would sleep now, and when she woke, she would not remember.

He could not admit to himself that what he was doing was wrong. He could not admit to himself that these acts made him the monster Isa believed he was. He could not admit...

He could not admit...

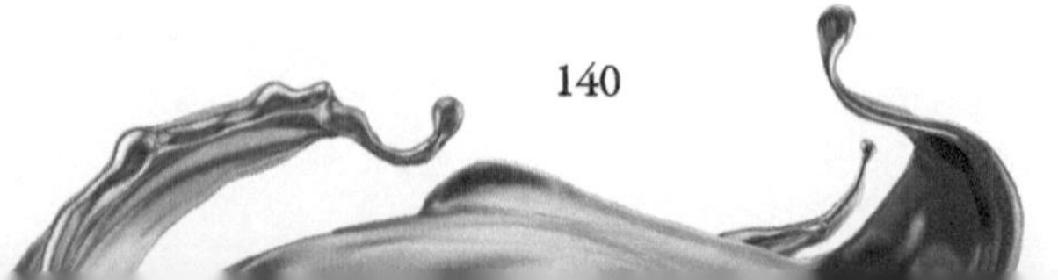

He could not admit...

Elan's fist clenched against the tree he leaned on. His whole body shook. He had watched his sister be violated by that demon and had done nothing to stop it.

He had woken to find her gone, and when he had gone out to search for her, he had found the demon, feasting on her.

Freezing in place, he had simply stood there, shocked at the sight. Even as she cried out, he had done nothing. Simply stood there.

Coward. You fucking coward! He cursed himself as he watched, but nothing he did or said made his feet move or his hand raise.

He was terrified.

It was only when it was over that the spell on him seemed to break. He stumbled back, running blindly in the woods until he collapsed between a pair of trees, cowering beneath it, hiding his head as a child would under a bed for fear of a scary dream.

After an eternity, he was sure the demon had heard him and was coming for him. It had to be creeping up slowly to the tree, ready to pounce the second he fled. It became impossible to hold still. He had to know when death was upon him. He pivoted out as slowly as he dared, his whole body shaking as he tried to peer around the trunk.

To his shock, there was nothing there.

"He's eaten her," he whispered aloud. "What would he need to eat you for?"

Again, the mantra of *coward* echoed over and over until the words spilled out of his mouth. "You coward, you useless fucking coward!" Then he saw it in the graying light. A large rock. It wasn't much of a weapon, but if the creature had his back to him while he feasted on his sister, then Elan would be able to get the drop on it. And if he failed, then the creature would kill him too. A fitting atonement for his cowardice.

His thoughts went no further than that as he tore the rock free from the tree roots, and he made his way back.

To his surprise, he had only gone a few steps in his haste and found the demon and his sister exactly where he had left them.

The demon was indeed curled over his sister, but he wasn't eating her. He held her, even rocking her like a small child with a doll. He could see Elaine's eyes were closed, and a moan nearly escaped his lips as he thought that she might be dead. Then Elaine moved, shifting in the demon's arms while she continued to sleep, smacking her lips together innocently.

She is alive! Elan realized. Sickening relief washed down him like the rain, and the rock fell from his limp fingers to thump on the ground. For a horrifying moment, Elan thought he saw the demon stiffen at the sound. Any moment, he would turn his head and look straight at Elan.

The demon leaned forward and stood up, lifting Elaine in his arms. She settled there peacefully, and he turned, walking away with her through the woods.

And Elan just watched them go.

He had to do something. He had to find a way to save his sister.

But as soon as they were both out of sight, his legs gave out from beneath him, and he crouched down, clutching his head and weeping.

I am not a coward; I am a mere mortal man. What can a man do against a monster like that? he reasoned with himself.

If only the gods *did* still exist.

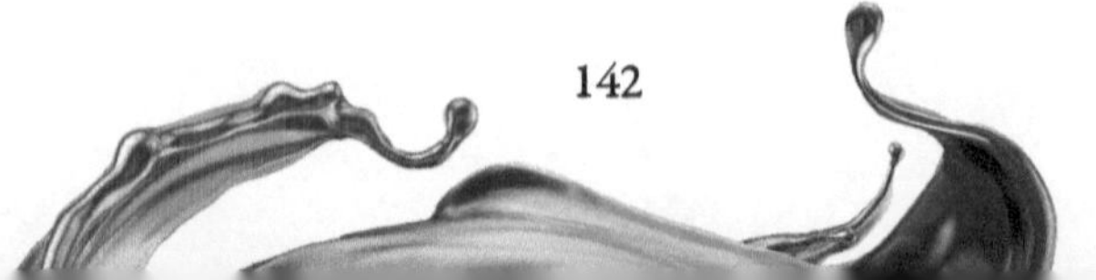

CHAPTER 14

"You almost had me, Amira." Dakin sneered as he stared out the doorway to his balcony, overlooking the houses of his people clinging to the sides of his fortress like moss from a tree. The darkness of the sky flashed periodically, illuminating them all, making the light of the torches and lamps near the doorway pale in comparison. He could feel the dawn coming over the horizon, but the storm was not letting up to allow the rays to shine.

So much had happened in such a short amount of time. Dakin marveled at it.

"Getting back to *my* fortress was more difficult than I expected," Dakin stated, turning back to the woman forced to kneel before him by two of his most loyal, and more importantly, alive men.

Barus, his general, held the ties that bound her arms behind her back to her ankles, making sure she didn't thrash, while the other, Lorab, held her head so her throat lay exposed to him. The painful angle of her neck created an exquisite portrait. That combined with her beautiful eyes, wide as a maddened horse's, and the way she panted as if in the throes of sex, he found himself quite hard.

Razal sat nearby, nursing a goblet of wine and watching with large wary eyes.

"Your brother was a fool, Amira," Dakin stated, relishing her name in his mouth. He came back into the room as the storm wind followed him inside, making the torches and lamps dance violently. "Poor Elio. His timing was decent. My absence and the subsequent mayhem it unleashed on all you merchants grasping for power... it makes me think that almost none of you expected me to come back alive."

The woman before him said nothing, but he didn't need her to speak, protest, or even cry. His only requirement was that she listen, and she was doing that admirably. "By the accounts of my warriors, or rather my remaining warriors, he did well. Killed his way in here quite efficiently, achieving his goal. Truth be told, if I had known his ability in this regard, I would have used him in the upcoming campaign. It is a real pity. His plan did not go past taking my fortress, did it? He had no idea how to hold what he had won. But your plan, however..."

Dakin slid one of his pudgy, blood-damp fingers along Amira's throat, leaving a line of red. She whimpered, and a shiver rolled through him. He almost came right there, but he swallowed it down. He wanted this to last as long as possible.

"Traitoress, both to me and your brother. How much work was it to unite the other merchants behind you? Was it just a matter of spreading your legs, or did you have to throw money in as well? Promises? Gifts? How far did this conspiracy go? Or did you just let them fight it out over your brother's corpse and then you planned to pick up the pieces?"

He strolled through the bodies in his council room, a mix of fresh and old corpses, testifying to the chaos that had reigned over the past couple of days. With agility his body had not had in years, Dakin squatted next to the corpse of Elio, the one who would have won it all. His surprised face stared eternally at the ceiling above, a fly making a home across the eyeball. While Elio's face was clearly unmarked, the rest of him was a mess of stab wounds. It was impossible to pick which injury had killed him. Dakin found the fly's progress fascinating.

Dakin regarded the nearest body, that of old Jossum, the advisor his family had insisted on sending to "assist" in his administration of Icathor. The man had been his glorified jailor whose ambitions obviously extended beyond simply serving his family. Jossum's face was also stricken in a permanent look of surprise. But then Dakin had been equally surprised at how easy it had been to plunge his own hand into the old man's chest to tear his heart out. He had only intended to punch the wind out of the old coot. Razal had been correct... He was quite blessed indeed.

"I suppose it does not matter, does it?" he continued. "Whatever you planned, Amira, you failed, and I succeeded." He stood up and turned to her. "I have become a god, and you will soon be a corpse."

"P-please," Amira begged before Lorab shook her back to silence. She recoiled from his Sword but was unable to escape.

"Oh!" Dakin said gleefully. "Are you going to beg? Oh, yes, I suppose that is only proper. You would beg for mercy from the gods now that you are actually in the presence of one. It seems only proper. Lorab, let the woman speak." Dakin gestured imperiously with his blood-covered hands, which were now turning tacky and uncomfortable.

Lorab obeyed, releasing Amira's head.

Dakin gestured a dismissal at him. "Go and order me a slave to bring me some water to wash."

His man only hesitated a moment then bowed his head reverently, which pleased Dakin, and the man went to obey.

"Please, my Lord..." Amira started, but Dakin gestured again.

"No, no, no, this will not do. Penitents must come before their gods, naked and on their knees. You have the knees part."

An understanding look passed between Dakin and his general Barus, who pulled a knife. The ripping sound was delightful as Amira's body was bared before Dakin, his lust growing more urgent.

"Come to me," he gestured. "Kiss my feet and tell me how regretful you are."

She obeyed, crawling toward him with her arms still bound by the ropes, her tears flowing freely with every inch. At last, her lips wrapped around his toe, dirty from the loss of his shoes, the muddy refuse of the forest then the streets of his city. The kiss was so dainty, he barely felt it. It wasn't enough.

"Lick it," he growled, and she did so. He groaned in his throat as the pressure, and pleasure erupted throughout his body. He nearly buckled from it. The sweet release of the moment shivered through him.

"Please, Great Lord," she whispered, her voice a tentative reedy whisper. "Please, show mercy." She turned up her tearful face to him.

"Yes, little one. Yes, I forgive you," he said magnanimously. He gestured toward Barus as Lorab returned, leading a terrified slave bearing an ewer of water in a bowl for his washing. He stepped away from Amira, now collapsed on the floor, the haughty woman who had told him she would never fuck him in a thousand years finally put in her proper place.

The slave set up the bowl on the table, and Dakin held out his blood-covered hands over it, waiting as the slave poured the warmed water, sluicing the blood and viscera slime into the bowl below. Razal moved to refill his goblet from the bottle before also filling a second one which he brought to Dakin, bowing his head as if the great wizard-priest was a slave himself.

Dakin leaned his head forward, indicating that Razal should assist him to drink from the cup. The wizard-priest flinched when he met Dakin's eyes but complied. The wine tasted wrong to Dakin, but he took a healthy gulp all the same. He had always loved wine.

The wine doesn't taste different. It is just the blood coating in the inside of my mouth, he lied to himself.

"Barus, what remains of our forces?" Dakin asked, returning to the business at hand.

"We have roughly a third left, and the demons press in on us from the outside. I am concerned that the short-sightedness of the merchants has doomed us all," he said. Frank and to the point—a feature Dakin had not always loved about Barus but had always been necessary since Barus also had always stood between Dakin and mortal danger. Ever since they had been children, the once-slave warrior had placed himself between danger and the many attempts on Dakin's life. Dakin never felt safe without his shield beside him, even if the shield never learned to tell him what he wanted to hear.

"Do not present me with problems; give me solutions. How are you going to fix your mess?"

"We confiscate the slave market and press them into service," Barus said, unperturbed by Dakin's accusation that this was somehow his fault.

"The merchants will not like that," Razal commented.

Barus leveled a cool gaze toward the wizard-priest. "The merchants are dead. And those who are not soon will be," he said as if it were a promise.

Dakin knew that Barus had survived the insurrection by his skill and through a handful of men in the granary holding back the other forces from taking it. If it had not been for Dakin's timely arrival with his new god powers, Barus would have been dead eventually. The desire for revenge glistened in Barus's eyes. "We should confiscate everything from the merchants for that matter. With their own households decimated by recent events, that matter should be easy enough."

Lorab sneered. "Arming slaves? Have you not always warned me of the folly of that?"

"Letting the fortress fall to the demons would be far worse, and they do not care for lesser or greater status, only for blood and bone. That will be enough to inspire the masses to turn their weapons outward instead of inward," Barus said confidently.

"Especially, my Lord," Razal interjected, speaking at last, "if the promise that the best of them will find a place among your men, the chance at a better life will inspire the loyalty we need to reaffirm your power."

"Hmm," Dakin said, thinking it over as the house slave worked meticulously to cleanse his hands and nails. "Would you do such a thing, slave?"

The youth looked up at him with wide, dark eyes.

Dakin continued, "Would you fight for me, your new god, for a chance to be one of mine?"

"Yes, my Lord," the youth said with awe and excitement at the idea.

"Hmm," Dakin said again, assessing the youth up and down. "Then take him with you, Barus. Blood him and prepare him to stand by my side."

"Yes, sir."

"I would say, my Lord," Razal continued, "you may not even need to force the people to do anything at all. As your high priest—" Dakin eyed Razal suspiciously. The wizard-priest hesitated a breath but could not stop once he had begun. "To be named your high priest would be an honor I would humbly accept if you so sought to lay that burden on my shoulders. I would make it my first mission to preach to the people about your rise, telling the story of your becoming and all that I witnessed. Already you have accomplished many great deeds, liberating them from the evils of the unworthy who sought to keep them enslaved. You are their liberator! They owe their existence to your mercy!" Razal finished his pretty speech with such passion and fury, he upset the remaining contents of Dakin's goblet onto the floor. He didn't mind, the wine had obviously gone off anyway.

Dakin waved a bored hand. "Fine, fine. Take what warriors you need with this high priest of mine and make it so. How long until we can be ready with an army?"

Barus blinked at that. "Three months."

"I want it sooner!" Dakin whined. "I have the power now; I will be king!"

"Yes, my Lord," Barus said, hesitating. "But the demons—"

"My Lord," Razal said, bowing his head. "You must remember that we are just mortal men. You have been touched by the power of a god." Razal and Barus exchanged glances.

Dakin sighed. "Very well. Raise me an army, Barus. Come up with a plan to prosecute a proper war."

That was all the dismissal Barus needed, and he exited immediately.

"As for my Sword," Dakin said, gesturing for Lorab to come closer now that Barus was gone, "I have a task for you.

Take a handful of warriors you trust and meet me down in my courtyard. I will be with you soon."

Lorab held his silence, the other feature Dakin loved most about the man outside of his efficient killing ability, and left.

At last, Dakin returned to gaze down on Amira.

"Slaves!" he bellowed and a pair of Ka'in women appeared at the door, peeking in terrified and cowed. He gestured at Amira. "Have her taken to Ela—my mistress's rooms. I want her bathed and perfumed. Maybe feed her too."

Dakin left then, heading to his own chambers to finish cleansing himself and changing his clothes, his ponderous belly full and satisfied from the traitors he had devoured. So much was going right for him. He had never been so happy in his life.

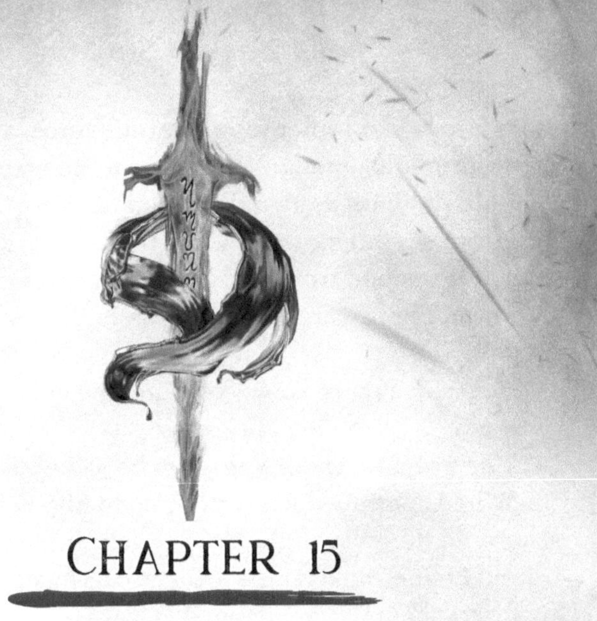

CHAPTER 15

As the day progressed, Elaine had still not awoken.

Acies sat next to her, staring down her brother across the space. He did not see Elan awaken, but the twin looked much better—although still a little unsteady on his feet from the assault on his inner ear.

Acies was not a true healer and knew very little outside of the common injuries sustained in battle, but he was fairly certain the night of sleep solved whatever physically bothered the Ka'in Prince.

The demon didn't expect gratitude or anything so trite from Elaine's brother, even if he did save the idiot's life yesterday, but he had hoped that there would be a cease in hostilities. No such luck. If anything, Elan's passive aggression and naked glares were even worse.

It was the least of his worries, though. Every time he checked on Elaine, he cursed himself for having lost control like that. It had been bad timing; she hadn't recovered enough to take another hit on her life force, and he hadn't been disciplined enough to ration out the arete he had. Yet it should not have mattered. He had not known that taking arete from any other source would be insignificant compared to what he gained from her. There was some other pull on his power. There were too many possibilities, and he feared all of them.

He needed more knowledge, and the only one who may know more was the high priestess.

Maevra had said nothing when he had returned carrying Elaine and continued to say nothing to him now while they sat around the gelic's little fire. The gelic fretted between the fire and Elaine, but did little to disturb its mistress's sleep. He was aware that neither intended to leave her alone with him.

As if any of them could stop me if I chose to... But he did not finish that thought.

At last, Acies couldn't take it anymore. He pulled down her shawl from the entrance of their cave and laid it over Elaine.

"Watch over her," he muttered at the two beings in Ka'in, just to make sure they knew who was really in charge, and took himself out.

Despite the gloom inside the cave, the day after the rainstorm was radiant with color and fresh smells. The sun beamed down, creating beautiful leaf patterns on the forest floor, and nothing seemed to deter the birds from crying hail to it. Its beauty stopped him in his tracks. Tears beaded at the bottoms of his eyes at a sight that he never thought he would see again. It overwhelmed his every sense: touch, taste, sound. It was almost too much.

"What are you doing, monster?" Elan asked, bringing him back to the moment.

The Ka'in Prince leaned against the outer cave wall, so harshly sullen it told Acies that he was actually quite afraid.

Good. He had reason to be.

Acies didn't answer him. Instead, he strolled farther into the forest, seeking a bit of flat space between the trees. When he found one decent enough for his purposes, he stripped off his blood-stiffened shirt, and tossed it against the roots of a tree. He stretched, loosening his muscles and joints, whirling his arms and legs about until he had engaged every part of himself.

This body felt glorious as he slid into an old training routine, enjoying the feel of existing again, of being alive and real in a world that was alive and real.

He started with the basics, going through patterns and footwork, fighting routines developed by the gods themselves. Once complete, he found a decent-sized stick and began again. His body protested as the routines increased, but still, he pushed until he ran slick with sweat.

It was about halfway through when he became aware of Elan's eyes watching him once more from the shadow of a nearby tree.

Acies didn't stop or acknowledge him, only shifted back to earlier footwork, slowing his pace down so that the young man could observe what he was doing.

While Acies usually preferred the Pi-Bunkite style of fighting, the Ka'in style was designed with the Ka'ins in mind, complete with attacks and retreats, favoring speed and swiftness over raw power. He could feel the Ka'in Prince's eyes on him the whole time, but he did not engage or ask to work on anything, which was fine as they had plenty of time.

Once he had finished, Acies tossed away his stick and plucked up his shirt. Both he and it needed rinsing, so he decided to look around and see if he could stumble on a stream or creek nearby. Sure enough, his "shadow" followed him, moving deftly through the forest so that Acies actually lost sight of the Ka'in Prince a few times. Instead of finding the creek though, Acies stumbled over the carcass of the deer he had killed last night. Staring down at the corpse, it looked like it had been gnawed on by a few animals but was otherwise intact.

"Did you do this?" Elan accused, his voice coming from the trees.

He still couldn't see him, so Acies ignored the question. He didn't know the right words in Ka'in to explain it anyway. He cast about for a strong enough tree branch instead, finding one tangled up in some tree climbing vines. He yanked the whole mess down and started working to plait the vine into a rope that would be suitable enough for the task.

He could feel the Ka'in Prince seething at him, but neither said anything to the other for the time it took for Acies to prepare his materials. Once he had, he tied the deer's feet to the pole. It wasn't the strongest rope he had ever made, but it seemed like it would work getting it back to the shelter.

"Grab the other end," Acies said to the forest once things were ready, his dirty shirt tucked into his pants like a rag to keep his hands free.

"What? No!" Elan said, giving away his position beside a tree to Acies's right. Applying a little arete, Acies knew he could move fast enough to be behind that tree and on Elan before he had time to react.

Of course, applying a little arete would make it possible to lift and carry this deer back by himself as well. Yet Acies did not want to waste his limited resources like that. Elaine would need more time.

Still, he wondered again at his inability to draw sustenance from the life force of the deer.

"You would rather waste deer?" Acies asked in his broken Ka'in, lifting up his end. "Sister is hungry."

"My sister would be better off having nothing to do with you at all," Elan snapped.

Acies sighed. This was getting tedious.

"What did you do to her? Last night?" Elan continued, now that the seal on his mouth had been broken.

"That is … between me and her."

"I am going to kill you, by the way. I am going to find a way to set her free of you, and then I am going to kill you," the Ka'in Prince challenged.

"Is that … going to be now?" Acies asked, affecting a bored air. "Because if not, then help. Look, I will take…." Then Acies's words failed him, forcing him to indicate the nearest end of the pole with inadequate gestures. Elan looked at him as if he were an idiot.

"You mean you will take the front?" Elan finally said.

"Yes, I will take the front. You take…" He pointed at the other end.

"Back?"

Acies clapped, then saluted him with open palms as if he were a merchant at a market, and they had just reached an understanding. "Yes, yes. I take front. You take back. My…" Then he slapped himself on the rear of his shoulder, showing his vulnerability to the Ka'in.

"Your … backside?" Elan supplied.

"Yes, my backside to your front side. So, you feel safe."

Elan furrowed his eyebrows at that, and Acies wondered if he got something wrong. Then the prince closed his eyes and shook his head. "You mean: you are going to turn your back on me. That's how you would say it."

"Turn my back on you. Back and back? It is the same word?" Acies questioned, secretly delighting that they had engaged in something more than idle threats.

"Yes, back and back is the same word. I mean, anything behind you."

"Yes, then, you grab the back, and I grab the front. We take it for your sister."

He plucked the front end of the pole, making a show of displaying his back to the other end. For a long moment, Acies considered that he might have to drag the thing back to their camp himself, but at last, the other end levered up. Both men set the deer pole on their shoulders and set off up the rise to the shelter. It took a few silent steps to find a rhythm they could agree on, but Acies considered it a first victory toward bringing Elan to his side.

Just before they got to the shelter, an odd sound hit Acies's ear. Elan must have heard it too because both men stopped in unison, holding still to listen better. Then it cracked again, a creaky pop and whisper much like a giggle coming from up in the branches.

"It is not the gelic demons," Elan whispered.

Acies shook his head in agreement, scanning the branches. He noted that Elan did not even consider that it was an animal stalking him. He wondered if the Ka'in sensed the darker presence just as he did.

Then all at once, the forest came alive with screeches. They were terrible sounds echoing off the trees, which began to shake and shiver. Leaves and twigs fell from above.

"We need to get out of here," Elan said.

Acies shook his head and gestured with his finger in a circle, conveying the idea "We are surrounded."

Elan cursed in Ka'in.

"<That's enough!>" Acies shouted in godspeech, his voice echoing preternaturally loud, and the screeching immediately abated. Acies set his end of the deer pole down, freeing his hands as he continued to scan for the threat. "Stay," Acies said, then leapt climbing up the nearest tree at an impossible speed. Elan's cry of surprise followed him up.

As he broke through the first layer of branches, he caught sight of what had made the horrible noise.

Round, little faces made up of mostly large, glowing-yellow eyes stared down at him as he appeared out of nowhere from their perspective. The majority of the small demonic creatures startled and scattered. Only a couple of the largest monkey-shaped monsters continued to cling to their branches with too many fingers. The larger bogins displayed their overly sharp teeth in a display of force.

As one, they started to screech again, but Acies only grinned and leapt higher, jumping up the next set of branches and startling the whole lot of them again into the trees. "<Oh, is that all you got, cowards! Petty screeches and no claws!>" Acies yelled after them.

"<We see you, Demon Lord. We have no quarrel with you,>" the largest of the bogins said. He moved like a sloth, curling his claws one at a time along his branch, but Acies wasn't fooled by the show. Bogins were lower-class demons, more dangerous in groups than individually, but for any single one to grow large like that, they had to have cunning and strength.

"<Is that true now?>" Acies asked, cocking an eyebrow at the bogins' de facto leader. "<Then why have you gotten my attention?>"

The bogin leader shifted on its perch. "<The guardians are gone. They kept us in check. Kept away the bigger things. There is a hole in our world. We came to see what that was about. We see a new demon in its place. We see you but do not know you.>"

"<Continue not to know me,>" Acies said. "<To know me is your death.>"

The bogin leader hissed at that, and Acies leapt to grab its skinny neck.

He missed as they all scattered away to other trees, the bogin leader showing its true speed in its escape. Acies did not pursue, choosing instead to drop back to the ground. This had the added bonus of startling Elan, who had been peering hard into the trees. At least he had kept his end of the pole up so the deer had been mostly off the ground.

"What was that?" Elan demanded.

"<Bogins,>" Acies said, picking up his end of the pole. "Nothing to worry about. <Lesser demons.>"

"<Bogins?>" Elan asked, butchering the godspeech word.

"I do not know what Ka'ins call them. They are small demons. Nothing to worry about. They will leave us alone."

"I see," Elan said, unconvinced.

And he was right not to be because the bogins didn't really leave them alone. As they walked, the bogins continued to screech and call, some even throwing things like sticks and small stones. Acies kept ignoring them, treating such behavior as beneath him, but Elan struggled to hold his temper.

"<Is that offering for us?>" one of the creatures called.

"<You should leave it here,>" another agreed.

"<Give us an offering, or we will rip your face off!>" shouted a third, and the rest took up that echo.

"What the hell do they want?" Elan demanded.

"Nothing we will give. Keep walking. Ignore," Acies said, already planning to come back later with his sword to clean the tribe out.

Then something slimy and stinking slapped Elan in the face. "To the Goddess!" he barked, dropping his pole to whirl about, wiping the gunk off his face. "What the fuck is this stuff?"

"<You do not wish to know,>" Acies said in godspeech, unable to suppress his smile.

"What?" Elan asked, looking to Acies, but then understood much to his horror. "Oh, my Goddess, gross! Disgusting!" He continued to wipe at his face, getting the mess all over his hands before grabbing several large leaves from a bush to continue his futile clean-up job.

The bogins laughed and laughed.

Having enough of this, Elan picked up a rock from the ground.

"No, wait—" Acies tried to say, but Elan had already thrown. It shot straight into the trees, scattering the bogins. Then one dropped to the ground, black blood oozing from its cracked head.

With a bit of a strut, Elan walked over to the creature and kicked it. The thing cried out, curling around itself in pain.

"Damn, I did not kill it," Elan muttered, staring down at the pitiful creature.

Acies came up beside him, pulling out the jeweled knife on Elan's belt. The Ka'in man flinched and stepped back at the action as if he expected a sneak attack, but Acies simply held the knife out to him, handle first.

"Kill it then," he said, gravely.

Elan hesitated, but before he could take the handle, the demon's wound closed up. With enough haste, the thing went for the trees and disappeared.

"Stupid," Acies commented, his eyes still watching where it had disappeared.

"How did it do that?" Elan asked, shocked. "I cracked its skull open."

"First mistake," Acies said. "Remove weapon—demon can heal. Demon does not die from wounds. Demons die when all their *arete* is gone." He pointed after the creature.

"That demon has less arete now, easier to kill, unless it takes another's arete. More likely another will take that one."

Elan furrowed his brows as he looked at the ichor-encrusted splotch on the ground, then up toward the tree. "So even if I were to mortally wound you, you would not die?" he asked.

Acies shrugged. "I am a strong demon. Be really hard for you." He cracked a smile at Elan, but the Ka'in Prince didn't laugh or get upset. Instead, he looked pensive.

"Especially after you consumed my sister."

Ah, Acies thought, *that explains it.* Acies did not let any guilt or remorse cross his features. Instead, he shrugged. "She will recover. You can make new arete, given time. I cannot. She shares hers with me; I protect her. And you."

The reminder did not seem to affect Elan's mood. Still, he picked up his end of the pole, and they walked back in thoughtful silence. After Elan's attack, the bogins left them alone, and the remaining walk went quick enough.

Before they approached the shelter, Acies steered them to the side of what remained of the ruined walls, not intending to clean their kill so close to the entrance. To his surprise, they found a rock slab he hadn't seen before. The rock looked worked and shaped by someone who knew something of stone carving to create a table. The two men set the deer on it. It was the perfect size.

"We do not really have time to butcher this," Elan said, more thoughtful and less hostile now, "We need to get moving."

"We go tomorrow. Elaine sleeps today. We have time to butcher this," Acies said and indicated Elan's knife. "You know how?"

Elan gripped the handle and glared. "Yes."

"Good," Acies said and tromped away back into the woods.

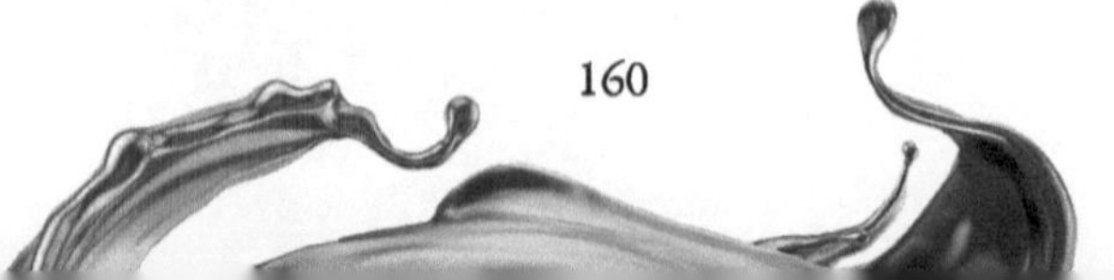

"Hey! Where are you going?"

"To find more wood," Acies said then turned back. "Unless you give me the knife. I clean; you go wood."

Elan's face gave him his answer, and Acies tromped off to collect logs. He could hear the bogins up above, leaping through the trees, following him. When he bent down to pick up a promising thick stick, a rock came flying toward his head, which he caught in mid-air. The small feat excited the creatures, who all ran away with more skittering cries.

"<Why do you follow me, little demons?>" Acies asked, tossing and catching the rock casually with a couple of passes.

When they didn't answer, he flung it back into the trees. He got a tiny screech as his reward. Chuckling to himself, he returned to his scavenge.

Once he had a decent armful under one arm, he turned back toward the shelter. Above him, the bogins still chattered, but something had changed in the tone of it. Acies stopped and continued to listen. At last, he had to close his eyes to really focus on what they were saying.

"<The Protector of the Forest is coming.>"

"<Yes, he is coming.>"

"<The Protector of the Forest.>"

"<We must flee.>"

"<No, we must stay. Great bounty. Great bounty indeed.>"

"<This forest is protected.>"

Acies snapped his eyes open to stare down the bogin leader who had appeared and now clung to the trunk of a tree. Its eyes had changed from an eerie yellow to a deep red as it stared at him with naked hate.

"<You brought the Protector upon us!>" it declared, lifting an accusing claw to stab at the air in Acies's direction. "<We demand compensation!>"

"<Who is the Protector?>" Acies asked instead.

The bogin leader sniffed. "<We will not tell you if you do not know.>"

"<I will compensate you for information,>" Acies stated with no preamble.

The bogin leader eyed Acies as it weighed his offer.

"<What would that be then?>" it asked.

Acies dropped his gathered sticks and held out his hand. "<A mouthful.>"

The bogin's eyes went wider before it grinned, revealing too many sharp, sharp teeth.

"<Each?>" it asked.

"<No. Just you. The bravest of the bogins who would treat with a Demon Lord and even call him friend,>" Acies said, grinning back in his own display, even though his teeth were more mortal looking. The bogin began to chuckle, delighting in the idea as much as the offer.

"<Ask your questions then,>" it said.

"<What is the Protector of the Forest?>"

"<A demon. Greater than you.>"

"<How do you figure?>"

The bogin furrowed its ponderous, fleshy brow. "<It's large. Larger than you. Larger than a horse,>" it sniffed, turning away.

"<Is it a horse?>"

The bogin slid its eyes sideways. "<No.>"

"<Then what is it other than a demon?>"

"<You already asked three questions. Deal is done. Give me my reward,>" it said smugly as if it had won a game.

Acies retracted his hand, holding it up at his shoulder. "<We never specified a number.>"

"<Yes, we did. Answers to three questions in exchange for a mouthful.>"

"<A mouthful in exchange for answers to my questions, and you know it. You don't answer all of my questions, you don't get your mouthful, and I dare you to try to take it from me.>"

The bogin laid down its ears. "<Three answers is more than fair payment for a mouthful.>"

"<Then you should have bargained for that. Do you want it or not?>"

"<Fine! Fine!>" it snapped. "<I do not know what the Protector is, only that if you hear him coming, you hide quickly.>"

"<Him?>" Now it was Acies's turn to raise his eyebrows. Not "it." A "him." "<Interesting. And why do you fear him? Why is he coming here?>"

"<The guardians are gone,>" the bogin leader said as if it were obvious.

"<The temple guardians. The gelics,>" Acies stated.

"<Yes, they were the only things that could collectively hold the Protector back. Now they are gone, and the Protector heard the call.>"

A stone dropped in Acies's stomach. "<The call?>"

"<Yes, we all heard it. The call,>" the bogin leader shuddered just at the memory of it, a look of twisted ecstasy passing over its face. "<It was beautiful.>"

Acies knew exactly what that meant. Every demon within range of that song, possibly the whole forest, would have heard the call within it. How many more would come seeking Elaine and the prize she was? This was a much bigger problem. They needed to leave these woods by tomorrow morning at the latest.

"<Any more questions?>" the bogin leader demanded.

"<No, you did well,>" Acies said and extended his hand. "<A mouthful only.>"

The bogin moved, flashing its speed, though Acies hardly knew why it was necessary. He had no intention of running. The bogin leader grasped his arm in its claws and bit down hard on Acies's hand. Icy fire shot through his arm, eliciting a grunt from Acies as he was pulled forward by the creature's weight. Black blood poured into the thing's mouth, and it swallowed gleefully.

It disconnected then, keeping the agreement. But the hot-cold sensation of another being eating his life force, albeit a small portion, still had a toll on Acies. The thing continued to hold onto his arm as it licked its lips and caressed its stained teeth with its tongue. He could practically hear the creature debating the risk/reward of taking another bite.

"<Let go,>" Acies said darkly.

The bogin met his eyes for a too long, pregnant moment.

Then a fire spark flashed near the bogin leader. He yelped, letting go of Acies's arm and scurrying back to the trees.

"Begone, foul demon!" Flicker howled, blasting another of its tongues of fire after the bogin, igniting some of the leaves for a moment even though they were too wet and only smoked for a few seconds.

Once the demon was out of sight, Flicker sniffed at it as if to say, "That showed it," before turning back to Acies.

"You are wounded," it remarked.

"I am fine," Acies answered, cupping his hand around the serrated flesh. It hurt terribly, but it was nothing he hadn't felt before and couldn't heal quickly. "Why did you defend me?"

"You belong to the mistress, and therefore, it is in my business to defend what belongs to my mistress," Flicker answered haughtily, eyes still on Acies's hand. Acies recognized the hungry glint in the tainted gelic's eyes, and he opened the hand, flashing the black blood within at the creature.

"<You do not have much arete left. If you are to survive, you cannot waste it like that.>"

"What?" the gelic asked, blinking once to tear its gaze away from Acie's hand. Even though he did not speak god-speech, Acies was pretty sure it understood anyway. Still the demon switched back to his broken Ka'in.

"The fire. It was ... waste of *arete*."

"N-nothing is wasted if it is in the service of my mistress," Flicker countered, his large, black eyes widened, returning its focus to Acies's hand.

Acies lowered it, offering toward the gelic. "Let me repay you for your kindness," Acies said softly.

For a long moment, Flicker stood there, staring, bill slightly parted. Acies thought it would go for it, but instead, the gelic closed its mouth and stepped back.

"Thank you for your generous offer," Flicker said, then turned and stalked away as if its ducky feet were cast in bronze.

Acies had to admit to himself that he was impressed by the little spirit's inner strength, especially one who had already tasted the raw life force of another. Licking his own hand, the wounds fully closed in less than a minute, the burning of the speedy healing dissipating along with any marks that otherwise would have been left behind if the wounds had healed mortally.

Acies plucked up his pile of forgotten branches and turned to head back to the shelter.

They would be able to smoke much of what they would be carrying before tomorrow, and he could tend it all night while the others slept. He hoped Elaine would be awake soon. He would give her a feast.

CHAPTER 16

RAZAL ENTERED HIS STUDY, ONE OF THE THREE chambers Dakin had granted him upon his entering the Lord's service. It was a luxury that the Lord had reserved only for himself, who occupied three rooms in the fortress himself. It was an honor that raised him even above the Sword and the Shield.

It was far better than bunking at Icathor's only temple, barely a shrine really, to the fortress city's patron goddess, Nymphaea. Like all the other deities, she did little actual service for her people, and her temple had fallen more or less into ruin.

Razal had risen high from an abandoned child eating scraps in the slums, to being used by the priests in the south city, to becoming a respected priest himself whose understanding and comprehension of the ways of the gods were second to none. Yet few had recognized his genius, and then they feared it when he began to study the demons that plagued the lands, unraveling their secrets to understand their true potential. They had called him sorcerer and demon himself in whispers behind hands and closed doors. This fear had led to his being passed over for the honor of being the high priest to the Ocean Gods.

He had not taken his defeat lightly.

Instead, he had found a persuadable patron in Lord Dakin, one with another power to muscle up the resources he needed and greedy enough to risk much in the endeavor. And most importantly, he had a silverblood in his power. It had seemed a sure sign of Destiny, the only deity that Razal still whispered any prayers to.

Razal was *destined* for greatness and power. He was *destined* for respect and riches. He would return to the Temple of the Ocean Gods and flaunt his victories.

But now, he sat in his lab with the view of the open bedroom and the receiving room across from his lab, and he saw them for what they truly were. His prison. His tomb, dedicated to his failures.

Once the door was shut, the old man began to weep unashamedly. He crumpled to the ground into a pile of bones with meat barely clinging to them, hiding his face in his long-fingered hands with their broken nails.

All of his acolytes murdered, all of his prestige, everything he had worked for... they would curse his name now forever, once the world learned of what he had done.

Power was to be his. All it was supposed to have cost was the life of one insignificant slave, whose only value was her special blood, the correct sacrifice to ensnare the power of a demon.

"Where did I go wrong?" he asked himself, or maybe he was waiting for a god to come and tell him and explain all this. Yet Destiny did not appear with an explanation.

Even with his eyes covered, he saw the faces twisted in pain. He saw his beloved Cal's guts twisted as the meaty coils fell from him after the bronze sword sliced through his middle. Cal had shielded Razal with his own body, saving him from imminent death. Razal had held him as he gasped for breath that wouldn't come, his eyes begging for Razal to save him. There had been nothing the great wizard-priest could do. He couldn't even think to try something, a prayer, an incantation, anything. All his knowledge had left him in that moment.

He had failed.

He wanted to die; he wanted to escape it all.

That idea spurred him forward. With trembling hands, he went to his supply shelf, pulling at bottles of distilled unctions, dropping anything and everything that he thought he might need, painkillers and sleep potions that were lethal when taken whole. He combined them together. He didn't want to feel any more pain. He wanted the screaming to stop. He wanted to sleep and never wake up and escape... oh finally, escape. Escape the monster he had created, the thing wearing Dakin's face, wielding Dakin's power. The sight of Dakin's face covered in blood, the way he had devoured the poor forester who was only trying to help him, offering him succor in a world gone mad. Even he had been destroyed before the demonic powers Razal had unleashed.

"My Lord, is all well?" a voice called from the hallway. One of the slaves opened the door to cautiously peek in.

"Get out! Stay out!" Razal shouted as he shoved his potion behind him, terrified that anyone would see what he was doing. Rationality had no place within him anymore.

"M-may the goddess watch over you tonight," the slave called through the door. Then they were gone, leaving him alone in the darkness of his room.

How soon? How soon until the whole fortress is consumed by this darkness? Until the whole world? The gods would not return to save them or stop it. Had he not proven that the gods no longer exist, that they had destroyed themselves in the Great War? The demons had truly won. Every god or goddess in the world gone, sacrificed to save it, leaving the world to honor them with empty words of prayer and praise. All useless. All forgotten.

"We mortals have followed our makers."

He laughed so maniacally, it hurt, but he couldn't stop. He didn't want to stop; he wanted it to last. He wanted to be mad.

Pouring his strange concoctions into a drinking bowl, he shifted it back and forth.

Death in a bowl.

It smelled awful. He left it on his worktable, needing, desperately needing, to find some wine to mix with it. The search became his mission, and he tore through his receiving room until found a half-opened bottle. His last toast with acolytes before setting out. His last night with Cal. He moaned as he held the ceramic bottle, pressing it against his chest so hard he might break it.

He returned to the concoction in his lab and stared down at the potion, looking like a greasy mess in the bowl. It seemed like a foul thing to add what remained of his wine to, but the prospect of turning away was an equal yawn of impossibility. Still, he imbibed a swallow of the unadulterated alcohol, its luscious burn slipping down his throat, but doing this did nothing to touch the hard stone in his chest.

Instead, there was a burning in the back of his throat which became bile. Dropping everything, he went to a chamber pot and threw up into it, wasting his wine. It was several minutes before the cramping inside him eased.

A knock came from the door. He froze in shock at the sound.

"Who—Who is it?" he demanded, his voice reedy and weak even to his own ears.

"Open up," the brusque voice of a man Razal barely knew ordered on the other side.

Razal stared at the door as if he couldn't comprehend such a thing. But the banging came again, more demanding, and Razal rushed over to open the door. "It is not locked..." he said lamely.

Barus entered bearing a lamp in one hand, his face stiff and all business as he shut the door firmly behind himself. Light filled the darkened room, reflecting back in on shining bronze armor plate. The only hint to Razal's eye that anything was wrong with the illustrious general was the pallor of his face, now more ghostly than tan.

"What happened?" the general demanded of the wizard-priest as if they had a close relationship. Razal almost found it insulting.

"I..." Razal stammered, but his throat went dry, and his tongue felt too thick. He grasped the wine and poured too much into his mouth, desperate to get some wetness within. The action tried Barus's patience.

"Stop it, you charlatan," he barked, slapping the bottle out of Razal's mouth. "You have brought this on us all, and now you will tell me WHAT HAPPENED?!"

"It is as I have foretold," Razal said, slipping into his priestly speech as naturally as pissing himself. "We unlocked the great power held within the Temple of Isa and Veras."

"And all hell broke loose," Barus spat. He set his lantern on the worktable and wrinkled his nose in disgust at Razal's concoction still waiting for him there. "That thing that is down there, it talks like Dakin, it walks like Dakin, but it does not act like Dakin. What he did to those ... insurrectionists—"

"Saved your life," Razal interrupted, even as he wondered why he was even bothering to defend their actions when he was in the middle of escaping the consequences.

Barus did not concede the point. "I told him! I warned Dakin not to go. Not to listen to a priest of no god!" Barus launched into pacing back and forth through the room. Normally, Razal would have been even further insulted and indignant at the slur to his priestly qualifications, but there was nothing left in him to even give a token resistance. This was what it meant to be truly broken.

Razal lifted the bottle and drank down the dregs of his wine, only to remember too late that he had meant to add it to his potion.

Unfortunately, Barus stopped at the bowl on his work-table again. He looked from the bowl to Razal's sorry state. "You are seeking the coward's way out."

"It is too late," Razal said, tears renewing down his face. "The demon has been released; Dakin is..."

Barus began pacing again like an anxious horse in a stable stall. "So he is a demon?!"

"Yes," Razal coughed out. "Yes, Lord Dakin has become a demon, and we are all doomed."

"No, I refuse to accept that," Barus said, slashing the air with his hand. "I have been fighting back the demons all of my life. Dakin is now something more than simply a demon. What I saw was a single man defeat an entire force, an insurrection force, all by himself. He destroyed them all. A power truly like that of the gods." He stopped and nodded. "*You* were the one who was right. You have made Dakin more than a mere man. For that I... I apologize."

Razal laughed bitterly. "The world has truly turned upside down when Barus the Great Shield apologizes to a lowly priest of no god." He continued to laugh, and Barus's face got redder, which only made it worse. Razal began choking on the laughter.

He didn't even see the hand come until it had snapped his face to the side.

It had done the trick, sobering Razal immediately, the sweet sting on his gaunt cheek. His head cleared immediately, and a sense of deep calm settled into him.

"If it were up to me, I would leave you to your madness and poisons and never look back," Barus said, picking up the poison bowl. With one powerful throw, he chucked it out the window toward the rising sun. Razal watched it go, swallowed up by the sunlight like a miracle.

"But I need you, wizard," Barus continued. "I need you now more than ever to make sense of this madness. We must control this power, channel it where it is needed."

"What makes you think Dakin can be channeled?" Razal asked, sneering.

"Because despite all his newfound power, that thing wearing his skin thinks it is still Dakin. Dakin was an idiot."

Razal blinked. "If I am to be honest, I agree with you," he stated plainly. "It was what brought me here to Icathor. I found it his most attractive quality."

Barus grasped Razal's shoulder. "I have no doubt you had your own machinations, priest, but now you have to help me."

"Or what? You will kill me?" Razal sniggered then lifted the bottle to his lips only to remember after he tried to drink that it was empty.

Barus's face shifted. "Dakin has already declared you his one and only high priest. Everything you have worked for, I imagine, is in your grasp, and you want to end it all here? This.

Can. Be. Managed," Barus said. "We make this monster a god. Or are you just going to let all of the sacrifices be in vain?"

At the word sacrifices, Cal's face rose again in Razal's mind's eye. His beautiful Cal believed in the brilliant future that only Razal could build. Suddenly, he wanted to see that future again.

A god. Maybe they had never walked the Land, but one did now. One he could shape, one still held back by the limitations of man, limitations he had the knowledge to manipulate.

Dazed, Razal turned to lock eyes with Barus. The man stood haloed in the sun, his face firm and confident, his blond hair coronae around him, posed exactly like the noble heroes of legend.

"A new god walks the Land," Razal said, then licked his lips. It was as if the words came from elsewhere and not himself.

Barus nodded as if it had been his idea the whole time. "A new god walks the land, and we are the mortals called to serve him." Then he stepped from the light and crossed to the door. "Now clean yourself up. You smell like shit and forest. Meet me down in the banquet hall as soon as you are fit." He left, slamming the door behind him, which bounced off the frame settling open.

Razal went to the door. "You!" he snapped at the slave waiting out in the hallway, a terrified Ka'in boy, scrunching down so hard as if he thought he could disappear if he willed it hard enough. "Have hot water brought up immediately," Razal ordered.

He had to compose himself and prepare.

He had a glorious new future to build.

CHAPTER 17

Elaine barely opened her eyes later that night. Maevra pressed a water cup to her lips, but it seemed an absurd thing to drink. She did so only after the older woman urged. Once the wet hit her tongue, she drained the whole thing and craved more. She slept a while longer although it was dreamless. When she awoke a second time, it felt like only moments later. This time though, she sat alone in the mostly dark shelter, completely confused about where she was.

Sitting up turned out to be a mistake as her vision immediately swam. She laid back down and counted her breaths. She was almost asleep again when she felt rather than saw a presence sit down next to her. Forcing her eyes open, she noted Elan's back beside her. He sat on the ground—his elbows propped up on his knees, his hands clasped, his toes tapping a nervous rhythm. She laid her hand on his back, so much broader than her own. Her brother started before turning toward her to brush her mussed-up hair away from her face.

"How are you, sister?" he asked.

"Exhausted. What happened?"

"The demon drained you of your life force," Elan said bitterly.

Elaine sighed, rubbing her face to help her wake up. "What are you talking about? What time is it? How long have I been asleep?"

His mouth worked soundlessly for a second, then he said, "Most of the day."

"I see," she said, surprised but still too weary to show it.

"But Maevra says you are going to be okay," Elan finished hurriedly.

"Of course, I will be," Elaine said, laying her wrist across her eyes, debating whether to ask Elan to get her some water or if she should try to get up herself. "Are *you* alright?"

"Elaine... the demons, the ones that used to be temple guardians... how did you vanquish them like that?"

She double blinked at the question before rubbing her face, buying herself time to consider it. "Well, they were spirits sworn to obey Isa. Since I am a Scion of Isa, they obeyed me as her representative."

"Yeah, but you sang to them. I heard you," Elan pressed.

Elaine sighed. "Our spells, the Ka'in words of power, we hide them in the songs."

Now it was his turn to double blink at her. "What now?"

"Isa's words of power—they're in our songs to keep the Anons from destroying them all. They have already taken so much from the Ka'in; it was a way our ancestors hid what was most important."

"But that's bullcrap. I have sung those songs a million times until I could not stomach them anymore. Nothing ever happened then."

Elaine sighed again. Then she held her wounded palm out to her brother. The marks in her skin were scraped raw with small punctures where gravel had messed them up when she had fallen at some point. She traced a finger over the healing wounds, red that glinted silver.

He looked down at her palm and the marks of her strange blood, his lips drawn into a stiff line. He knew what it meant. Every Ka'in child knew what it meant. "When I sing the words of power, my gift from Isa gives them life."

"And with it you killed a score of demons," Elan said, tracing his own thumb over her scabbed hands.

Elaine pulled her hand back from his grasp. "No, that is not what happened," she said defensively. "I set them free."

"Your demon told me something," Elan said. He paused a moment, considering his words. "He said that if you hurt a demon, like you know, really attack them, even if it were a deadly wound for a mortal, a demon would not die. They would just heal it again. But if you do that enough times, they get to a point where they cannot heal anymore, then they die."

Elaine sat up farther. "That would explain why the warriors often fail more than not to kill the demons that attacked Icathor," she said. "I wonder if we mortals ever knew that or if it was knowledge lost to time."

Elan shrugged. "It is the first I am ever hearing of it, but it explains a lot. Why do you think he told me that?" Elan asked. "It is like he gave me the way to kill him. He must have a secret agenda, right?"

"I have known him as long as you have, brother," Elaine said, pinning her twin with a serious stare. "Elan, can you help me up? I need to go into the woods."

He nodded and helped her stand, but to her disgust, her legs were as wobbly as a newborn calf. What had happened to her?

Outside the shelter, the twins were greeted by a large fire, very nearly a bonfire, burning brightly as the sun had already disappeared behind the trees, leaving painted colors in the sky. Over the fire, large haunches of meat were cooking and smelling glorious. She felt hungry in a way she could never recall before, like she could eat the whole spit and then some. Acies stood in front, outlined in fire, turning the meat so it continued to cook evenly. Maevra sat on a log nearby, and she turned as the twins exited.

"She is awake," Maevra commented. "Hopefully, she can also eat."

"*She* needs to take a moment in the woods first," Elaine said, smiling at the third-person speech.

"Then she'd better hurry," Maevra agreed and turned back to the fire.

Elan helped her hobble over to a suitable tree and waited on the other side.

She felt deeply exhausted when they returned to settle on logs by the fire, but she had no intention of going back to sleep. The heat felt good, toasting her face. She watched Acies slice great hunks of meat from the spit with his bent bronze sword, laying them out on a clean rock. The whole presentation brought water to her mouth. It was only when he offered her a tender hunk on the end of one of Elan's knives that she realized what it was. "Is this venison?" she asked, staring down at the sumptuous offering.

"We found a mangled deer in the woods. Looked and smelled like it had only died a few hours prior, so we brought it back," Elan said instead of Acies, who turned back to his cooking when her twin started talking.

"A gift from the forest," Maevra said and spread her hands up to the darkening sky above. "Great thanks to the Protector of the Forest for this gift, and to the deer, whose flesh nourishes our source," she intoned gravely. Elaine and Elan mimicked her gesture with a brief nod of their heads, though Elaine's hand was still full with her meat on a knife.

She noticed Acies watching them, the underside of his face lit by the fire, casting shadows over his eyes, making them eerie. "<You pray to the Protector of the Forest?>" he asked he asked her in godspeech.

"<When we take from the forest, yes. At least, most Ka'in do, those who still remember the ways,>" Elaine said in his language, taking a small, delicious bite of the venison. "<Many of us are enslaved and in Anon settlements now, so some of the ways and prayers have been lost. My village was one of the last remaining independent Ka'in settlements. Many of the Anon attest that the Protector is a demon now. I do not know if it is true.>" She stared into the fire, watching it dance as she continued to eat.

"<So, he is not a demon?>" Acies asked, pulling her back from her hypnosis as he offered her a cooked root vegetable that he pulled from the edge of the fire. Elaine did not recognize it, but it tasted earthy and complemented her meat.

"<What? No. No, the Protector of the Forest was a god.>" Then Elaine turned to Maevra, switching to Ka'in. "Right? The Protector of the Forest was a mortal god?"

"The Protector of the Forest *is* a mortal god. A minor one, who once served as a companion to the Land God Veres Kai, before he also became a Harvest God and husband to Isa Kai," Maevra stated.

"<I thought the gods were dead?>" Acies asked, directing his question and the surprising amount of acrimony it contained at Maevra.

Maevra lifted her gaze to him coolly. "<The Protector of the Forest is very much alive and well.>" Her godspeech was not as smooth as Elaine's, but she communicated clearly enough.

"I did not know that," Elan said, ignoring all the god-speech he didn't understand, reaching for another slice of meat from the rock with his calloused fingers.

"Know what?" Elaine asked.

"That the Protector was a companion of Veres Kai."

"And now I know who was paying attention during my lessons and who was not," Maevra commented bitterly.

Elaine glanced at Acies, watching the exchange when a thought occurred to her. "Did you know Veres Kai?" she asked.

That stopped whatever old argument Maevra and Elan were about start again as both turned to look at the ancient demon of battle.

Acies turned the spit and sliced another hunk to lay on the rock. "Yes," he replied so low and deep in his chest that Elaine almost didn't catch it.

"Well, I suppose that makes sense. You were there. During the Great War between the Deities of Heaven and the Demons," Elan said, his eyes now shining with interest.

"<What do you know of Veres Kai?>" Acies asked, directing the question to Elaine.

"What did he say?" Elan asked.

"He asked what we know of Veres Kai," Elaine replied.

"Aye. He was a Land and Harvest God, a mortal one, called into being by the people who became known as the Ka'in. See? I did pay attention." Elan directed the last words toward Maevra, sticking his tongue out at her.

She caught it with striking speed. "Do that again, and I keep it," she said with deadly seriousness. That too was an old and unfollowed-through threat, but it had the desired effect all the same.

"Veres ensured the prosperity of the land, which had been an arid place prior to his coming, where very little edible food grew," Elaine continued, ignoring the pair's antics, "and he invented farming, which he taught to the Ka'in people so that they may survive. This was when he also became a harvest god. They honored him as their patron, taking a part of his name in which to call themselves his people."

"Until Isa came," Maevra interjected. "Veres was a successful mortal god, but Isa was a lineage goddess, descended from the Ocean Gods who in turn were born from the God Beyond, the Unknowable Creator of All. Her power greatly outmatched Veres's as she forged her river north in her travels to see the world. Wherever she stepped, flowers and green life flourished. Forests grew and changed the land, bringing with them a variety of new plants and animals for the Ka'in people to eat and use. They no longer needed to work so hard to make so little. But Veres was not jealous of the Goddess Isa. For upon seeing her, he fell instantly in love and begged her to be his wife."

"Which she did after a few weird trials and tasks that he had to complete, which is why Ka'in women make courting men jump through hoops and all that bull," Elan interrupted bitterly. "But anyway, then the war came, and Veres tried to fight, but he was useless at it because none of his powers really worked for a thing like war, and he was killed."

"He was killed?" Acies asked, staring at Elan in such shock it made her brother shift uncomfortably for a moment.

"Aye," Elan said. "He died in battle, along with many of the other deities."

"And when he did, the land became ravaged," Maevra said, picking up the story, "So little could grow without him, and even with Isa's powers, without her union to the land, the Ka'in people barely survived starvation."

"You did not know that?" Elaine asked.

Acies turned away. "<I just remember it differently.>"

CHAPTER 18

Elaine continued to stare at him even as Elan asked, "What did he say?"

"He said that he remembers it differently?"

"What? Really? What is different about it?"

"Have you had your fill?" Acies asked, cutting off Elan's question with his Ka'in words.

"Yes, yes," she said, switching back as well handing back the knife to him. "That was delicious."

"You should continue resting," he said, stabbing the knife into the pile of meat before coming up alongside her to lift her into his arms easily.

"He is right," Maevra agreed when she glanced at her.

Elaine did not protest, letting herself be carried back into the ruined shelter. Her body protested, however, when he laid her down on the ground once again, but there was nothing for it. He wrapped Maevra's shawl about her again as Flicker waddled back in, bearing a new load of wood and rebuilding the small fire.

"Oh Flicker, how are you doing this evening?" she asked as she pillowed her head on her arm.

"I am well, mistress. Thank you for asking!" the little gelic crowed joyfully. Satisfied, it waddled out.

Acies adjusted her makeshift blanket over her before layering on his own cloak, its masculine musk surrounding her. While he labored to make her comfortable, Elaine studied his face, watching the light and shadow play over his objectively handsome features.

"<Did you choose this face?>" she asked, choosing to speak in godspeech since it was easier for him. He paused as she laid her hand on his cheek, tracing his eyebrow gently with her thumb. "<I mean, is this your face, or is this just whatever you got from me?>"

"<I ... do not know,>" he said simply. "<To be honest, I have not looked at my face yet.>"

"<You look like a Ka'in,>" she informed him.

He thought about that a moment. "<I suppose I would,>" he answered.

"<What does that mean? By you 'suppose it would'?>"

"<I think I can answer that best when I actually see what you see. I will check when I pass the next reflective surface,>" he answered, leaning forward to tend the fire some more, making adjustments to Flicker's work. The stoking strengthened the flame, lighting up his visage a moment before plunging back into shadowy dimness. The sight reminded her of the vision she saw of a very different fire playing over his whole body as Isa's fingers traced across his skin.

"<You were her lover,>" Elaine ventured to say. Acies's hands stilled in their work before meeting her gaze with his own, his day-sky eyes nearly night black in the firelight. "<Isa's. Before the Great War,>" she finished.

He sat back, resting his hands on his knees. "<How do you know about that?>" he asked, in a low voice.

"<I saw it ... in a vision,>" she answered, hoping he would not ask more about where she saw the vision.

As it turned out, he didn't.

He settled back to lean against the natural wall, draping his face in shadow that the fire's light didn't touch. He looked so comfortable there that Elaine couldn't ascribe anything sinister to it.

"<Isa had many lovers,>" he said with no bitterness or remorse.

"<That surprises me,>" she said.

"<Why?>"

"<Well, she was married to Veres, was she not?>"

Acies scoffed at that. "<She was one of the great lineage goddesses. She could have as many lovers as she wanted. There would have been nothing Veres could or would have done about it. She was that powerful and that beloved. He was lucky to have the right to call her wife.>"

"<I have a hard time believing that,>" Elaine remarked, then realized what she said. "<Not that she was that powerful, but you are a demon...>"

He went quiet, his gaze far away. Elaine could only imagine what he might be feeling, talking about a being that he had loved and been betrayed by. It also felt strange to be talking about her patron goddess as if she were another person. "<Is it alright that I am asking you about this?>" Elaine asked.

"<When we were in my prison, I swore to you my everything. Everything means everything. Whatever you wish to know, I will tell you,>" he said, opening his hands wide to her.

"<But only if I ask the right questions?>"

He smirked.

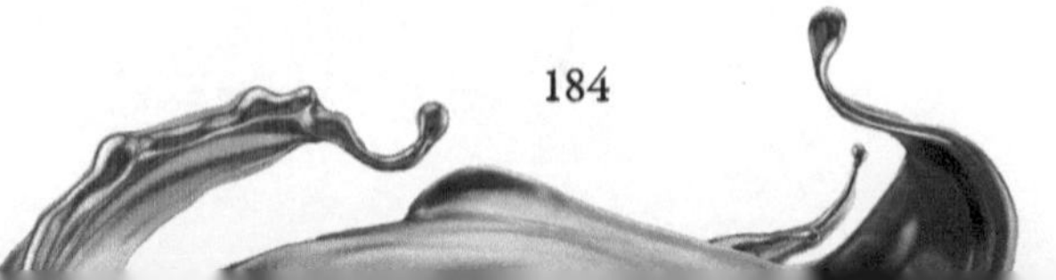

Elaine contemplated a moment. "<Did you love her?>"

"<Yes.>" He said it so simply and so factually that she was taken aback by it. He continued to regard her, his head back in shadow, framed by his long black hair. He rested one wrist on a bent knee and the other on the thigh of his straightened leg. Elaine found the pose—alluring, beautiful, masculine—passively sexual. Those thoughts made her uncomfortable, so she looked away toward the safer fire.

"<And she loved you even though you were a demon?>"

The sound of his voice became thicker. "<That I do not know.>"

Again, Elaine felt a pang of guilt for asking. She considered the other things she saw in her vision of Isa and the demon Acies. Nowhere in any of them had she seen the other principal God of the Kai.

"<Did you know Veres?>"

"<In a manner of speaking.>"

"<That is not really an answer,>" she pointed out.

"<Then, yes,>" he stated, giving her no room for following up easily. The silence between them went on too long.

"<Well, she must have loved you,>" Elaine said, thinking that she was ending the conversation. She settled back to close her eyes. Despite sleeping all day, she still felt so very tired.

"<How do you figure that?>" Acies asked, not letting it go and with enough force that it just felt like a demand for an answer.

Elaine noted that his rising anger didn't make her feel concerned. "<You are still alive,>" Elaine murmured, her eyelids growing heavy. "<She did not want to see you dead.>"

"<You are wrong; she *left* me for dead,>" he argued. "<She left me alone until everyone I knew—mortal, demonic, or

divine—was gone, and this world remade itself into something I no longer recognized.>"

Elaine didn't respond. She had nothing to say to that. Silence continued, punctuated by the crackle and pop of the fire nearby.

Then softly, Acies whispered. "<Thank you for setting me free.>"

Elaine turned her head to look at him, only to encounter the intensity of his gaze, smoldering through his long eyelashes.

He continued, "<I am sorry what it cost you, but I am also truly grateful.>"

His heat transferred into Elaine, burning through her to settle in her chest like potent wine. She felt a wave of continued weariness at having to bear all of these emotions, but she could not disengage.

Elaine licked her lips, her mouth too dry to really wet them. "<Thank you for saving me, my brother, and Maevra.>"

His eyes studied her face. "<Were you afraid?>" he asked. "<When you made your deal with me?>"

A rush of terrifying pressure slipped down Elaine's skin, pressing from throat to groin as the memory of his prison came back to her. "<N-no. I was not afraid,>" she admitted, struggling not to stutter and wondering why it was so hard. "<I felt many things, s-several I still cannot name, but I was not afraid.>"

"<Why?>" he asked, completely heedless of the effect his words were having on her.

She had to maintain her control of herself and her feelings, so she did what she has always done and swallowed them back. "<Well...>" She searched the dark for an answer. "<I suppose after seeing Dakin naked, not much is left to scare one.>"

There was a pause, then Acies barked out a laugh. It was a good laugh, solid and merry.

Relieved, Elaine found herself enjoying it with him, harmonizing her own mirth with his as she privately triumphed at her win against being overwhelmed by negative feelings. The vile tension in the back of her throat dissolved.

"<Goddess, that feels good,>" she exclaimed when it finally petered away. "<I have not laughed in too long.>"

"<Would you like to see me naked?>" her demon offered abruptly.

Elaine felt like string snapped inside her, the strings that held her feelings in their cage. She took a deep breath. What he was asking was not a bad thing. And he was asking, not telling, not forcing.

"<I think it's fairly self-evident that you are superior to him already without that,>" she tried diplomatically, smiling to assure him that there was nothing wrong.

"<Still,>" he continued, his tongue dwelling on the word, "<if you are pleased by me, it would be a better course for our exchange.>"

Elaine could feel her smile breaking. "<How do you mean?>"

"<I offer you protection, but I can also offer you great pleasures,>" he said.

Another figurative string snapped inside. Her hands shook, and an invisible force gripped her heart, stomach, and spine. She buried deeper into the shawl and his cloak, wrapping them over her shoulders so they pulled securely like she was trying to shield herself from what she already felt.

"<No,>" Elaine stated forcefully, the strength of her own voice surprising even herself. The silence between them became awkward and heavy while Elaine's face burned with shame and anger at that shame.

"<I apologize...>" Acies started, but it only snapped another string inside.

"<I will not do that,>" Elaine said, tears burning in her eyes. "<Do not ask it of me again. Ever.>"

"<Yes, mistress,>" he said, which angered her even more.

"<I am not a whore,>" she spat, the real word she heard underneath the term "mistress" or "concubine."

"<I did not mean it like...>" he deflected.

Another string snapped.

"<Yes, you did! That was exactly what you meant. I was not Dakin's concubine by choice!>" She gasped heavily, the breath panting in and out at such speed, the world wavered between light and dark, but she could not calm down. Desperate for air, she uncovered herself, pushing away the shawl and cloak as if they were large snakes strangling her.

"<I know that...>"

"<Then why did you even ask such a thing like that?>" she demanded, sitting up to face him, which did not help the spinning of world. "<How could you?>"

He did not answer; he sat silently, withholding.

"<What do you want from me?!>" she screamed. She knew she was screaming, but she couldn't stop. "<You will never lay a hand on me without my permission ever, do you understand? I do not care if you kill me, but I will never ... ever...>"

Her voice was weakening. She was weakening. She just wanted to die.

He stood up abruptly and left.

The air went out of the room with him.

Elaine collapsed. Exhaustion filled her every limb as the emotions she had held back for so long were finally released. And it was terrible. It was as if knives tore through her soul, and no one could see it. All she could do was lay back down, curling tightly around that pain, pull the blanket and cloak over herself again, and wonder if it was possible to die from this feeling.

It was never my choice.

Unconsciousness came upon her like a tidal wave and pulled her out to sea.

CHAPTER 19

ELAN THOUGHT AND THOUGHT UNTIL THE FLAMES died down into angry, red coals, and the smell of the venison meat had long drifted away on the cooler wind. It was his way, to occasionally sit like that, all through the night, thinking, an activity Maevra would accuse him of not doing enough of.

His thoughts were usually occupied with how to free his people from the clutches of the Anon or what argument he needed to make with Titama on their next move. Now he wished more than anything that he could talk to his old friend now.

"What would you tell me to do?" he asked out loud but quietly.

You got to work with what you have, not what you wish you had, Titama's voice answered in his head.

"I do not have any means that would take on a demon," Elan growled.

But you have an idea.

"Only a god can take on the power of a demon and win," he whispered.

Now he heard Elaine's voice, speaking the prayer of the Forest Protector. *Great thanks to the Protector of the Forest for this gift.*

Grunting to himself, Elan stood up to kick dirt over what remained of the fire, burying the coals safely into the ground. That plunged him entirely into darkness. But in that dark, he knew where to find his bronze sword, picking it up from the ground to buckle back on.

It is a foolish idea, he imagined Titama saying.

"It is the only idea we have left," Elan argued.

There was no time to waste. Dawn would be coming too soon. To execute his plan, he needed to get some distance from their camp so as not to alert the demon, or Elaine for that matter, of what he intended. Especially Elaine... not Maevra; he was sure she would approve of his plan, but Elaine... He knew if she had an inkling, she would try to stop him or undermine him in some misguided desire to keep him safe. Ever since they were little, she did that, always taking the role of elder sister seriously even if she was only moments older.

He didn't want safe. He didn't need it. And it was not what was necessary now. He would not be deterred from his aim. He had already lost too much; he could not lose Elaine as well.

Elan plunged into the pre-dawn forest as quickly as he could before he lost his nerve, his grip white-knuckled on the pommel of his sword.

He had barely gone far when the forest became grayer, warning him of the coming sun. It was enough to see and navigate by.

"Where are you going, brother of the mistress?"

Elan startled but managed to not cry out as Flicker appeared before him, staring up at him with those eerie, solid-black eyes.

"I am..." he started. Then he scoffed. "I do not have to answer to you." He pushed past the creature standing in his path, nudging it aside with his leg as if an errant dog. The move did not seem to deter Flicker.

"Can I help you with anything?" Flicker insisted, following behind at a strangely quick waddle. Elan lengthened his stride to try to outpace the creature. Almost predictably, that did not work. "Are you going to do something to help the mistress?"

That forced Elan to spin back. "What do you mean?"

"You are!" the gelic concluded, crowing it too loudly. Elan shushed with urgency, seizing the bill-like mouth to hold shut, which also didn't stop it from speaking. "I wish to help you, young master."

It took several more shushes to get the temple guardian to calm down. "Hush, hush, be still!" Elan snapped. This time, Flicker grabbed its own bill to hold it closed obediently, looking up at Elan, those eerie, black eyes suddenly the biggest, wettest, cutest eyes he'd ever seen. "Fine, fine, you can come help me," Elan grumbled, unable to resist and frustrated with himself that he was so soft.

Flicker's whole little body shook with excitement, even as it continued to hold its bill to suppress the cawing noise to a muffled state.

Elan stood up, scanning for any signs that someone listened and watched, but he saw only the expanse of tree. "Just keep quiet and walk beside me."

Flicker nodded and waddled after Elan.

Strangely, the Ka'in Prince felt more confident in his plan with the gelic beside him. Once he decided that had to be far enough away from even the demon's hearing, he spoke in a low voice. "Do you know the ritual of spirit summoning?" he asked.

"Yes, brother of the mistress," Flicker responded, matching Elan's lower pitch.

"Then you can help me perform it?"

"Certainly." Flicker nodded its head, the plume dancing with the bob.

"Good," Elan said resolutely.

"Who is it you wish to summon?" Flicker asked, folding its hands into the sleeves of the strange little robe that may or may not have been a part of its body.

Elan thinned his lips as he weighed telling the gelic, but he realized he might as well since he would need to when the time came to do the ritual. "The Protector of the Forest."

"I see," was all the response he got for the declaration.

Annoyed, Elan continued. "I am going to ask... *beseech* him to help me free Elaine from the demon's power."

Flicker nodded gravely. "Only a deity may do so. And he may be willing to help since the Protector was a companion of my Lady Isa."

"So, you think this will work?" Elan asked, a weight lifting off his shoulders at the little gelic's approval.

Flicker waddled silently for a moment. "It is worth a try," it finally said resolutely.

The weight shifted back. "You do not think he will help?"

The crest on Flicker's head bobbed up and down, flicking the little bit of red underneath for a thinking moment. "The Protector is not what he once was. He still guards the forest, but it is like at the temple. The Ka'in no longer come, no longer perform the rituals or honor us. Those that have come have often only taken from the forest and given nothing back. It has made the Protector bitter."

Elan thought about that. "So, the Protector is still alive? He has not turned into a demon?"

"I have been asleep for a long time. I am still not sure how long, but when I last gazed upon him, he was resolute in remaining a god and not walking the path of my kin. It is part of what brought me to shame. But even then, he had forsaken the Ka'in, only maintaining his guardianship of the forest as best he could."

Now Elan was less confident in his plan, but like the little gelic had said, "We have to try."

"Do not give up hope," Flicker said. "She is the Scion of Isa. Such a thing will certainly touch his heart. And I will help you. With your princely spirit, we cannot fail!"

They continued for a way more. The forest had come awake as they walked with the early morning birds making their presence known with bright morning songs. The gray light had shifted to a brighter hue, and there were all the tell-tale signs of a pleasant, sunny day ahead.

And then Flicker stopped abruptly. The crest rose up on its head, flashing red again under the yellow. Elan felt the tension thrum through him as well. The forest had gone silent, almost all at once, the morning birds cutting off their music mid-warble. Elan pulled the sword from its scabbard, the weight doing little to comfort him. Every hair on the back of his neck rose as he crouched down to a knee beside the gelic, but before he could bring the sword up, Flicker laid a hand to bring it back down.

"Lay your weapon on the ground before you," Flicker said calmly as if there were nothing to fear. With a strange dignity not previously displayed, Flicker folded its hands and stood as straight as possible for its little bent body. Every instinct in him screaming against it, Elan did as he was bid, laying his only weapon before him. Then he rested his shaking hands on his higher knee and waited, counting his breaths. An eternity passed and nothing happened. Then the forest seemed to shift.

A form emerged from between the trees, one larger than should have fit through, yet it did not brush against the trunks as it passed.

The Protector of the Forest was the most enormous boar Elan had ever seen, standing taller than a horse with tusks as long as Elan's own arm. It stood proudly, covered in thick fur as dense as a bear's. Elan would not have seen its eyes if not for a pair of lighter patches framing them. Each eye looked down at the kneeling prince like chips of obsidian where the gods had captured a star within each. For a terrifying moment, Elan believed that the boar would rage and charge him. It was clear there was nothing his sword would be able to do against such an epitome of its kind. This was a walking, breathing god, and if the Protector wanted Elan's life, it would be his to take.

As if by some cue that Elan couldn't perceive, Flicker stepped forward and bowed low. The Ka'in Prince only realized what it was doing as it stepped, and he managed to bow his head a half beat behind, setting a fist against his heart to pound twice in respect.

Wind fluttered across the forest floor, blowing leaves and detritus a couple lengths, but it did not affect the leaves or trees above. Elan realized the god had sighed.

"Ka'in," a rumble of thunder came, tumbling forth from the great beast. "Do you remember the old ways, child of the Kai?"

The Ka'in language the god spoke sounded ancient to Elan's ears, reminding him of the way Acies spoke in lilting tones when he attempted Ka'in. Something about that pinged Elan wrong, but it was far too late to do anything about it now.

Flicker spread out its arms in a supplicating motion to the god before them.

"Oh, hear me Great Protector, Lord of the Forest. I have come by the side of this worthy Prince of the Ka'in to offer praise to you—"

"I have no need for your hollow praises. I have not needed the praises or the songs or the offerings of the mortals in thousands and thousands of days or nights. I have no need for intruders in *my* forest."

"My Lord—"

"Your respect for the old ways has earned you a clear passage from my forest. Begone and seek me no more." The god started to retreat, pulling back into the shadows of the trees, and if he went, Elan's plan would fall to tatters.

"My Lord, I beg you!" Elan shouted.

The shadows, as tangible as curtains, stopped their task of cloaking the Protector. The sharp glints in the boar's eyes flared.

Elan kept talking. "My Lord, you are my only hope. My sister... I need your strength to—to—"

"Spit it out, boy. I am losing my temper," the god stated, his voice thrumming with discordant thunder. Flicker moved to stand impotently between the Ka'in Prince and the god, keeping its arms wide, which was not very wide at all.

"My sister has been taken by a demon!" Elan shouted.

"So? This is not a unique occurrence." The god turned his head away, gazing out through the forest but seemingly seeing much, much farther. The darkness hovered over the boar, and the trees wavered as if wishing to wrap their branches around the sacred being but did not yet have permission to do so.

"<What was the Great War for?>" the Protector asked, though it sounded more to himself than the mortal and spirit before him. "<The demon folk have overrun the land anyway, and the mortals have turned their backs on us, lineage and mortal gods alike. None even speak of the God Beyond now. No festivals hallow their gratitude, no offerings, no sacred prayers blessed with majick from the faithful. We are all but forgotten. They call me demon now. Me!>"

Elan did not know what to say to this. He knew it was true; hell, he had said it himself. The Anon had done much to degrade the beliefs of the Ka'in, but such excuses would only anger the forest god more as it proved the Ka'in's faith was weak.

"Please, my Lord. A demon has taken my sister, and only a god can save her," Elan decided to say.

"If a demon has eaten her, there is nothing that can be done now..." the Protector of the Forest said with a heavy dismissiveness as if he were weary and worn despite his magnificence.

"No, my Lord," Elan stood, much to Flicker's dismayed squawking and attempts to bat him back down. "He has not eaten her. Or I mean, he is... he is using her to feed off of slowly. There is still time!"

"You make no sense, boy. No mortal has such majick to sustain a demon for more than one feeding..." But the god's demeanor changed entirely as the answer seemed to come to him. "A Scion. Your sister is a Scion?"

"Yes, yes my Lord. She is Elaine, the last Princess of the Ka'in. My twin."

"And who are you, mortal?"

Elan did not hesitate or point out that he *had* already said. You just didn't do that to a god. "I am Elan, the last Prince of the Ka'in, my Lord. We still follow the old ways and hold them in our hearts, which is why I knew I could come to you to save her from this demon."

"She—she is not *my* Scion," the Protector said regretfully. "It would not be proper... You must go to her deity and ask them for help."

"I cannot, Great Lord. She is the Scion of Isa Kai."

And in that moment, everything changed.

CHAPTER 20

DAKIN HAD NEVER FELT SO ALIVE AND POWERFUL IN his life. As he looked over his gathered warriors, he compared himself to their weakness. They had muscles, yes, but they all moved so slowly like old men waiting to take a shit.

As was appropriate, they straightened up as he approached, Lorab standing in front, looking proud and strong. Dakin hated and loved Lorab, just as he hated and loved Barus. They had what he lacked, but they adored him. Without him, their lives were meaningless.

He stopped before his gathered warriors, casting an iron gaze over the leather-clad men. A handful had bronze, those that could afford it. The stuff was expensive, so only the best fighters were allowed to requisition some, or they had to pay for it themselves.

Lorab was outfitted with a complete set: breastplate, greaves, shin guards, and the like. He looked magnificent except for the leather boots he wore instead of the sandals, which would have been more appropriate to the look. They weren't in the south where the warmer weather made such equipment ideal. Even in the summer, places in the north held their coldness, so boots were what everyone wore.

Except, Dakin realized, he didn't really feel the cold anymore. He had always hated it, but now, he was quite comfortable in the early morning air. His breath didn't even cloud.

He knew compared to these men that he looked downright regal. He had bathed and changed clothes, going so far as to even perfume himself, and the effect had been worth it. His large belly, which was a sign of his prosperity and power, seemed less pronounced that day. He moved easily and lithely as he walked back and forth before the warriors, letting them all get a good look at him.

"Are these the best men you could find?" he finally asked Lorab, stopping in front of the taller man.

"These are the ones I trust to watch my back," Lorab said. It was a good answer.

"Fine, then. Listen up, you lot. Much has changed in the last few days. I do not know what rumors you may have heard or told yourselves, but I think you can all see now what glory is ahead of us." Dakin lowered his voice, gesturing for the half dozen or so warriors to squeeze in. They obeyed, huddling up together like a ball team. "I trust you with a singular task."

All nodded around him, each man with determination in his eyes. Each one an Anon man... except for one. Dakin's eyes focused on the single Ka'in in the group.

"What is he doing here?" Dakin sneered.

Lorab glanced at the Ka'in. "Ka'in are the best trackers. Athorn is one of my better scouts."

"He is a Ka'in. There are no 'better' Ka'in?" Dakin sneered, stepping forward to grab the Ka'in by the throat. The warriors startled back from him like frightened sheep, all except Lorab, who laid a hand on his shoulder.

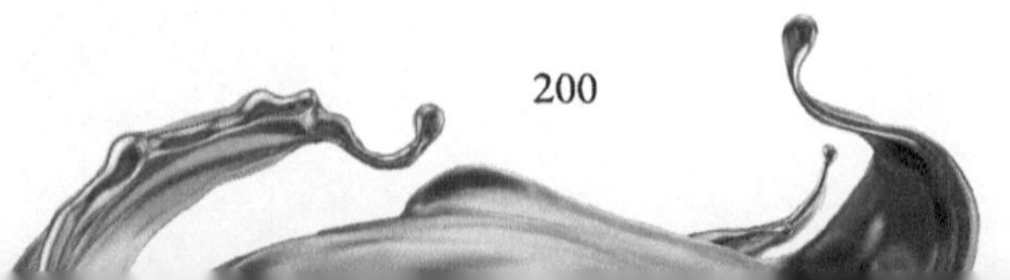

200

"My Lord, please."

Dakin stopped, then turned and slowly looked up the arm to the stoic face. Lorab withdrew his hand. "If you wish to kill him, that is of course at your lordship's pleasure, but then I will be short one warrior, and we have been short too many warriors over the last couple of days."

Dakin huffed. "This is an annoyance," he stated, releasing the Ka'in.

Then Dakin noticed his ears. He snatched one in his hand, moving faster than the eye could see. The group around him gasped. "Fine then. If he wishes to be considered an Anon, then he must at least make himself fit."

Dakin reached for the jeweled dagger he always carried at his waistband only to find and remember too late that he had lost it in the temple. Growling, he opened his hand toward Lorab, who stared at it unsure. "Your dagger, you idiot!" Dakin barked.

Lorab withdrew his finely made weapon and slapped the handle into Dakin's outstretched hand. With a giggle of glee, Dakin brandished the knife toward the Ka'in who began to pant but stood his ground. Maybe there was something worth saving in this creature after all.

Then Dakin began to cut.

It was a rough mess, and the Ka'in started whimpering like a damned child, but soon enough his ears were docked. With delight, Dakin licked his bloody fingers as he stepped away, tossing the knife toward Lorab, who caught it and immediately sheathed it, though unclean.

Dakin had a passing thought to request it back so he could lick the blade but decided that was an unseemly request. Instead, he regarded his new Anon, who painfully straightened.

"Look, he is even a great deal paler than before," Dakin crowed, slapping the man on the shoulder. The Ka'in didn't laugh at his joke, but to be fair, the warrior had just had his ears chopped in half. It didn't diminish Dakin's amusement in the slightest. He turned back to his warriors who were all looking paler themselves.

Then inspiration struck him. Demanding the knife back from Lorab, he pulled it across the pad of his thumb. Strangely, it hurt but did not hurt. As soon as the flash of the blade had cut through, it immediately dulled into nothingness. Simply information.

Dakin then focused on his Sword.

"Open your mouth," he ordered.

Lorab obeyed without question. Dakin inserted his thumb and wiped the blood beading there across Lorab's tongue. The warrior's eyebrows lifted in shock, but he kept his mouth open. Dakin looked down at the too-dark smear he had laid there. "I grant you a drop of my power," he said solemnly. "Let it empower you to do my will."

Slowly, Lorab closed his mouth, swallowing down the blood. Then gently, he tapped his forehead with a closed fist. "I thank you, my Lord."

Satisfied, Dakin turned to do the same to the next warrior. Each opened his mouth reverently, and each swallowed a drop of his blood. The act excited Dakin, and by the time he finished with the last warrior, the cut had healed. He wiped what remained against his side.

"You are all my warriors now, my personal elite, anointed by my own blood. As brothers to me," he added with some poetic inspiration. "Now, that is settled. I have a special mission for all of you," he declared. "I have been betrayed."

He let that sink in a moment. "My concubine Elaine betrayed me at the temple and has run away with other

Ka'in conspirators. This cannot be allowed to stand. While I outwitted her and claimed the greater power for myself, her continued existence is anathema to me. Find her allies and destroy them. Bring me Elaine if you can. Bring me her body if you cannot, but the rewards you garner from completing this great task will be beyond your wild imaginings. And I have always paid my debts." Dakin gave them a knowing smile, and *that* was returned with much elbowing and optimistic chatter.

These men knew what Dakin meant even if he didn't spell it out. This would give him time to figure out what he *would* give the winners who returned with his prize. Maybe he would outfit them all with the finest bronze so they actually looked like his elite force.

"And the spoils, sir?" one bold man asked.

Dakin rubbed his smooth chin, giving that a little thought. Promised riches were one thing, but the immediate spoils of a hunt were a great motivator, whether it was the promise of riches or sex. "Only Elaine remains untouched. Any and all you claim for yourselves is yours to take. The bitch's brother, the Ka'in Prince, was part of her conspiracy, and as I understand it, he has a face as pretty as hers. He should be an entertaining sport."

There were more chuckles and nudges. Dakin met eyes with Lorab and stressed, "If you take Elaine alive, she is to be untouched, do you understand? She is my property alone."

Lorab nodded and Dakin was satisfied. He indicated for his Sword to walk with him a way while the group excited themselves with their prospective slave hunt. "Take what supplies you need. Return quickly in victory."

"Yes, my Lord," Lorab stated, always saying the right thing with as few words as possible. Just then, Razal finally made an appearance.

The slight, older man stood on the edge of the courtyard looking much better than when Dakin saw him last. Like Dakin, he had bathed and dressed in a fresh tunic, laying a sash of green around his shoulders and slashing across his middle to tuck into his belt, a style more favored by the southern regions and befitting his priest.

"Ah, Razal. About damn time. Come forth," Dakin gestured for Razal to join him, and the slight, older man complied, smiling as he bowed once he reached Dakin's arm's reach.

"I am here and ready to serve you, my Lord," Razal said smoothly.

"This here is my man, my high priest," Dakin said to Lorab, patting Razal on the chest while keeping the other hand gripping on his high priest's shoulder. "Come, high priest. All of you kneel!"

The group of warriors complied, including Lorab once Dakin looked at him. "This man is Razal. He was known as the priest of no god, but no longer—he is now my priest. It is like fate knew he needed to wait for his true god to come among you all."

"I do think that is right, my Lord," Razal agreed, nodding.

Dakin slapped him hard on the back, forcing him a step forward. "Well, then priest, bless my warriors before they leave on my mission."

Razal's eyes went wide. He had obviously not prepared for this, but Dakin was interested to see what the old man would do in this situation. The newly appointed high priest raised his hand, then closed it so that his thumb and middle two fingers touched. "Let this be your sign, men of the newly birthed god Dakin. Carry with it his blessing and protection."

In unity, the group of men made the sign with only a couple needing adjustment. When they were confident of it, flashing them at the priest, Razal continued, "This sign is only for the chosen of the Great God Dakin. Guard it well, for it is your divine sword and divine shield."

Lorab barked a "ha" once, and the men followed suit immediately, slapping the symbol against their chests.

Dakin chortled in delight. When their eyes turned to him, he made the sign as well, and they barked in salute again.

Razal raised his hand a final time and spoke something in one of his god tongues then slapped the gesture against his own chest, which the men repeated one final time in benediction.

His newly appointed priest turned to Dakin, and together, they exited the courtyard, the god leading the high priest as was only proper. This gave the men permission to rise and finish preparations for their mission.

"That is well done, Razal," Dakin said once they were out of earshot, clasping his hands behind his back, a feat he had not been able to do in years. It gave him pause.

"Razal," he said, a note of uncertainty in his voice. "Do you think I look less ... prosperous with a lesser belly?" The god looked down at himself. He could definitely see that his belly had shrunk. It no longer hung from him like a ponderous ball but had sunken and hung with more folds of skin than anything.

Razal looked him up and down, his face betraying nothing. "It is not unheard of, my Lord, for the gods to shift shape when it is time for them to take on other tasks. You are preparing for war, so you are shifting to your war form."

Immediately, a weight lifted from Dakin's shoulders. "Of course!" he nodded. "That makes perfect sense. You truly are a divine man of the gods."

"I am the man of one god alone—you, my Lord," Razal said, bowing his head. Dakin patted it like a dog.

"And well you serve me indeed. Soon, I will be the greatest of the gods."

"Absolutely, my Lord," Razal assured. "We have many plans to make."

"That sounds boring," Dakin complained, imagining the planning meetings he had to attend where his appointed scribes discussed minutiae, and he had to approve or dismiss as he willed.

"You are our divine guide now; I will take your will to the people. Grant me your seal and tell me of the world you wish to create, and I will find the means to bring it about."

Dakin rubbed his chin. "Ah yes, my vision for the future. Yes. Come Razal. There is much I have in mind, and it will be glorious."

CHAPTER 21

ELAINE WOKE FROM HER SLEEP, HER WHOLE BODY one big ache. If not for the demands of her bladder, she would have rolled over and tried to dive back into the dream that was not pleasant but not quite a nightmare, yet it was certainly better than waking to reality. *I have been doing that a lot lately,* she chided herself, and she opened her eyes. She could not choose to hide from every day like she had before.

Maevra slept, sitting against the wall beside her, the older woman's head lolling to the side as she uttered a half snore at the crest of her inhale.

Acies was nowhere to be seen.

Neither was Elan for that matter.

That was a worrying thought, so she sat up. The action proved to be easier that morning, and her legs held her once she stood to wander out into the new dawn. The air coolly kissed her skin as a fresh light slanted through the trees. All around her, Elaine could hear the birds chorusing the morning, and below the top of the hill they camped upon, she noted the wisps of fog shifting through the trees, trying to escape the oncoming light.

There was no further sign of Acies or Elan, but there were signs of the fire from the night before. The blackened wood with white along its edges lay dead in the fire-pit. The venison was gone as well, but Elaine noted that someone had packed up their bags and had set them within the shelter. She wondered if the presence of their demon was enough to deter the beasts of the forest from coming close and looking through their new food stores, but she wasn't going to get an answer at that moment. So, she pushed away from the shelter and went to the tree she had used before to relieve herself.

Acies watched her from his safe distance, not particularly interested in what Elaine was doing, only that she was safe, and she didn't seem to notice him. He wasn't ready to confront her about last night or anything else, for that matter.

The demon sat perched on a fallen tree, the branches offering him a natural seat at the bend, letting him prop one leg up comfortably while the other swung. He had been thinking all night, denying the need of his body to sleep, ever since she had finally passed out after their... whatever that was. Not really a fight but not-not a fight either.

They would need to move on today... another reason it had been foolish to not get some rest. For one thing, they all needed water. What they had collected during the rainstorm had been used, and he had not stumbled on a new water source during the night. One had to be close since someone built a house here in the middle of the forest. He idly wondered if Elaine possessed the power of her goddess to dowse for water.

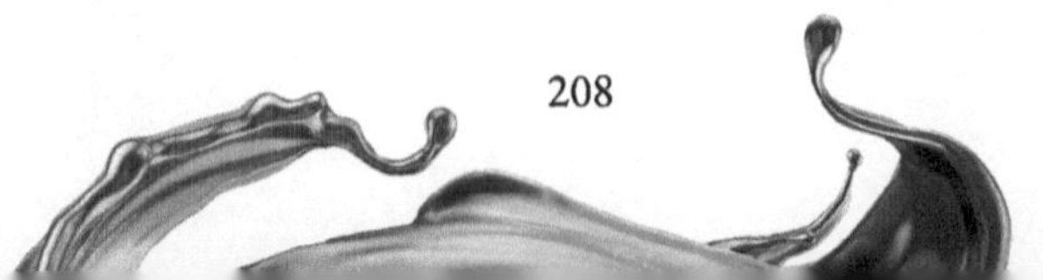

Besides, Isa's river had to emerge from its underground course nearby. Maybe there was a forgotten well? So much had changed that he wasn't quite sure where it would be now, and he used to know every inch of these woods. Maybe his memory had degraded more than he had realized. Could things have changed so much? Even with new saplings, trees grew for centuries.

And Isa's river still flowed.

That, too, was another sign that Isa had to still be alive somewhere. Her river still flowed.

As much as he had intended to hate the goddess all his days, Acies struggled to find his hate. Sitting there, watching Elaine and remembering her words the night before had put him in a different frame of mind. Or maybe it was the sunlight and the warmth of existence.

Harvest time should be soon. A time of festivals and celebrations.

He remembered Isa's face as she laughed, plunging naked and glorious into her river.

He just missed her.

He missed talking to her, listening to her advice and her wisdom as her dark hair rippled around her in the water, her darker skin glistening. That skin had lightened over the years during her time in the north, her nature changing little by little in the cold, dark nights of winter. Or was it because of him that she had changed so much?

In dark moments, in that cell, he imagined doing all sorts of terrible things to that skin, to that hair, to scar her as deeply as she had scarred him. To force her to explain...

Something shifted in the forest, erasing Acies's thoughts as he alerted to it. The song of the birds had died off, raising the hair on the back of his neck. A sensation he had not felt in centuries ran its fingers down his spine. Standing up from where he perched, he slowly drew his sword.

Abruptly, he was slammed onto his back, falling off the log into the ground.

His brain screamed in pain. His eyes registered the arrow fletching sticking out of his chest.

He couldn't breathe, but his body tried, making a terrible sound in his ears. He was drowning in his own blood. His hands scrabbled at the arrow in his chest. Bloodslick hands got around the shaft, but when he pulled, it remained stead-fast. He could feel his life force inside fighting against dying, keeping him alive. If he didn't get it removed, he could burn through his whole supply of arete and die. If he should suc-cumb to passing out, which was threatening to happen as the world wavered in and out, it would be guaranteed.

A figure appeared next to him, drawing his wavering attention. Elan stood there with murder in his eye. Acies forced a burst of power to strengthen and focus his sight because he was not sure what he saw was real.

Yet it was.

In the Ka'in Prince's hands, there was a strange weapon. Shaped like a bow, the thing had a set of wheels at opposing ends. Instead of a single shaft, it was spider webbed with thin shafts of some material Acies would need to be less injured to recognize. A larger handle was secured in the middle of the strange shaft, wrapped with some black leather, peeking through Elan's fingers. The bow string switched back between the wheels three times. In Elan's drawback hand, he held a strange thing that gripped the string and arrow shaft.

It was a Divine Weapon of the Gods.

He'd underestimated the Ka'in Prince. Acies stopped scrabbling at the arrow and closed his eyes, accepting his fate. There was no point once Elan fired his next arrow into

Acies's head. Acies would be truly unconscious then, if not outright dead, and his body would bleed out arete trying to save him until he ceased to exist or something came along to devour what remained. Time was on Elan's side.

"I will not kill you," Elan said. Acies opened his eyes, which were heavier than they had been a moment ago. He met Elan's hard, determined ones. "It will kill Elaine, would it not? If I just let this arrow fly through your head, you die, and she will die too because of your deal. I will not kill you without freeing her first."

Acies wanted to speak to him, but he still couldn't gargle more than the merest breath in. The lung on his left side wasn't inflating. Talking would still be out of the question. His arms still worked, so he used them to pull himself back against the fallen tree, propping himself up so it was at least easier to see his attacker. The pain from the transfer blinded him.

Elan twitched but did not release his arrow, stepping sideways instead to reposition himself directly at Acies. "Do not move!" he ordered.

Acies shot him a dirty look; it was the only attack he had left.

This was ridiculous.

His fingers and toes were numbing, retreating from the non-vital to fortify the vital. He had survived the initial shock thanks to his power. Yet he was helpless.

Elaine.

Elaine would find him and stop Elan. She had to save him. She just had to.

He clung to that flicker of hope. He closed his eyes again and focused on staying alive for her.

She would come for him.

Elaine turned to go back to their camp only to discover she now stood among trees she did not recognize. The shelter should have been a few lengths away, well within sight, but the forest continued unbroken for miles in all directions. Something felt wrong, and a shiver rolled down her spine as she realized that the birds had stopped singing, leaving only silence and the rustle of the ever-present trees.

"A-Acies?" she called out, not truly wishing to call the demon's name for help but recognizing the need.

No one answered her.

"Elan!" she shouted, pressing her back against the tree. "Maevra?"

Still no answers.

Her heart continued to tattoo against her ribs. What was going on?

"Is this a dream?" she asked out loud.

"No, mistress," a little voice answered beside her.

She jumped with a yelp only to find her gelic standing next to her. "Flicker, thank the Goddess. What is going on? Where are we?"

"You have entered the Sanctum of the Protector of the Forest," the gelic said formally. "He wishes to speak to you as a Scion of Isa, and since you are in his forest, it was a simple matter to invite you into his sacred space."

Then before them both, a shadow that was larger than a horse fell over her. The shape took on the brief image of some animal with tusks before condensing down then blowing away like fog. Stepping from the darkness came a tall, muscular man who extended a hand to Elaine.

"Welcome, Scion of Isa, to my domain. I am Vills, Protector of the Forest."

CHAPTER 22

ELAINE STOOD STUNNED AS SHE STARED UNBLINKING at the being before her. He looked as much like a wild creature as a man. Tall, with muscular shoulders and an angular face, he had tattoos covering him. The bridge of his nose up into his forehead was painted in an ochre color with dark whorls angling across his cheeks in black, mimicking a pair of tusks. His chest was bare except for a pelt of soft, brown fur that could have been a bear's, or even a boar's, around his shoulders and fastened with a clasp of bone that matched armbands of bone wrapped around his upper arms. The leggings he wore were of similar make to the cloak. An aura wrapped around the figure, same as his cloak, pulsing with an eerie power, like the hum before a lightning strike.

Elaine had felt a similar sort of presence in the under-temple of Isa. There was no doubt that she was in the presence of a god. And a Ka'in god for that matter as his ears peeked through his brown hair same as Elaine's did.

He waited calmly for her to take him entirely in, smiling gently as her eyes roved. Belatedly, Elaine remembered her manners and dipped low before the Protector of the Forest with her hands spread out, palms to the sky.

"Rise, please," the god insisted in his ancient-sounding Ka'in, moving forward with his open hand to seize one of hers, pulling her to her feet. She rose, but he did not release her, holding her hand within both of his large ones. She realized with him so close that he towered over her, taller than any man she had ever known, even Acies. His eyes were gentle as they gazed down at her, black as obsidian with glinting stars in each.

Now that she gazed directly into his face, he seemed older to her like a youthful grandfather.

She could not help but smile back at him.

His own broadened, making the stars in his eyes twinkle. "Oh, child, you do not know how much the sight of you heals the wounds inside my heart."

"<I am honored that I could do such a service for the Protector of the Forest,>" she said, meaning it. "<I have said your prayer every day of my life.>"

"<You know godspeech!>" He patted her hand still trapped within his own, an expression of amused disbelief on his face. "<Are you truly a Scion of Isa?>"

"<Yes, my Lord,>" she continued in his language since it delighted him so to speak it.

He shook his head. "<I am simply astonished that... Well, Isa's Scions were not known for their deferential behavior,>" he said. "<Where are you from that I do not know of you?>"

"<M-my village was up in the mountains near the Source of Isa's river,>" Elaine said, surprised at her stutter. She silently chided herself. She needed to appear *like* a Scion, and instead, she sounded instead like a milkmaid.

His perfect eyebrows lifted, changing the layout of whorls on his face. "<I see. Indeed, I would not find you there. Although there was a time I was welcome on those paths, my domain has decreased as the passage of time has rendered me lesser and lesser from what I was, and I did not start out as a very powerful god compared to my companions. Yet I am the one that remains.>"

A strange, unsettled look corrupted his smiling face, and it was enough to put Elaine back on her guard.

The second it appeared, it vanished as the Protector turned, gesturing toward the never-ending forest. "<Come, my dear. Come to my Inner Sanctum and tell me your story. I have not heard a tale in a long time, and it would comfort this old god to hear of the Scion of Isa.>"

Elaine agreed, pushing away her feelings of unease to make room for her growing, awe-struck excitement. As he came up beside her to escort her forward, taking her hand in his, she failed to swallow the giggle that escaped her. *The God of the Forest is interested in speaking to me!* she thought.

Even if Vills had been considered a minor god, he was still a figure of legend. She had so much to tell Elan. Her passing thought of her companions was quickly dismissed by the moment.

"<Now, tell me your story child.>"

And so, she did.

Acies continued to slip in and out of consciousness.

Elan watched over him. He had taken up a sitting position against a tree to wait, but Acies wasn't sure for what. The prince had also undrawn the bow but was ready to redraw if need be.

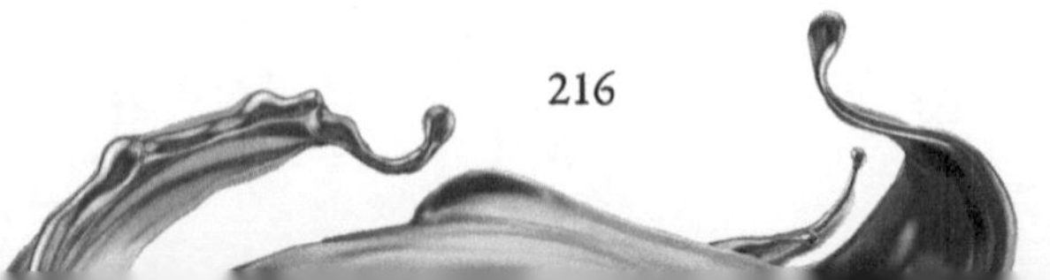

"Bow," Acies finally croaked out, using his precious air to finally speak. The word sounded painful, but it got Elan's attention all the same. "The bow."

Elan looked down at the strange weapon still gripped in his other hand. He held it up, awe painting his features. "A gift. From the Protector of the Forest," Elan declared, proudly.

Acies raised a hand, indicating that he wanted to hold it with a repeated crook of his fingers. Offended, Elan withdrew, glaring at him.

"Dying," Acies growled, thinking, *It is not like I have strength to talk, let alone kill him with it.*

"Forget it," Elan sneered.

Acies opened his hands as much as he could. "What else ... we have ... to do," he managed, before he coughed, wracking pain through his chest, then spit out a clot of blackened blood.

"You would find a way," Elan accused. "You must hate me for killing you."

Acies shook his head. It was the truth; he didn't hate Elan. Hating him didn't matter and took too much energy anyway. They had a contest, and Elan won. Simple as that. Elaine did not seem to be coming, or if she was coming, it may be too late to save him. Still, this awful sitting around waiting for him to die was boring, and he was curious about the bow. Yet it would have been impossible to say all that, so he let it go.

Lacking anything else, he tried to examine the arrow in his chest. Much like the bow, these arrows were strange and unique. Solid black, and the place where the feathers would be were instead fletched with solid pieces of plastic, a god substance, shaped like tears cut in half. It had punched through Acies's body so that the fletched end was only a finger's length from being buried in his flesh. Coated in his own blood, Acies took a renewed grip on it and tried once more to pull it out. His vision blacked out temporarily before it even came a fingernail's breadth.

That was when a howl cried out from somewhere in the trees.

Elan bolted up to his feet, spinning as he brought the bow up to ready. More howls cascaded above, moving all around them. They were surrounded.

"Oh shit," Elan cursed, spinning in place trying to find a target.

The same thought crossed through Acies's mind. "Bogins," he panted, then he held up his hand, displaying his blood at Elan. "Smell ... me. Come for me."

Whipping around in a panic, Elan panted as he continued to scan, but the bogins were keeping to the trees. A simple strategy. Even if they weren't aware that Elan had a god weapon, one arrow was still one arrow. When shot, that arrow would probably go right through a bogin with no problem, maybe even a second or third if they were right behind them, but that was it. There were dozens of bogins up there, and Acies doubted they would be courteous enough to line up for such a shot.

Unaware of where he was in space, Elan backed up until he was within grabbing distance of Acies. From that vantage point, Acies did a quick count and saw a dozen more of the god-blessed arrows. Then Elan jumped, loosing his shot at something that had appeared below the canopy of the trees. A bogin was now pinned there, a good-sized one too, held fast to the tree from the arrow.

One arrow gone. Eleven left.

"M-maybe they'll just go away now," Elan said, resetting another arrow in the bow as he watched the caught bogin fight and twist against the one pinning it.

Several more bogins took the opportunity to skitter down the tree, but they did not go for Elan. Rather, they attacked the pinned bogin, whose cries of pain were drowned out by the howls of his comrades as they cannibalized him. Within several heartbeats, they retreated once more upward, leaving only a dark smear on the tree and the god arrow, still lodged there.

"Oh, Goddess," Elan muttered, his eyes wide as the full moon. He then looked down at Acies, still panting on the ground at his feet. "They are here to devour you," he said, finally putting it together. "The weak devour the weak."

Acies snatched at him then, yanking an arrow out of the quiver. Before Elan could react to stop him, Acies swiveled and stabbed the arrow into a bogin who had attempted to attack from flank over the other side of the dead tree. The thing screeched as the god missile pierced it, but it managed to wiggle away from the point since Acies did not have the leverage or the strength to pin it to the ground like he would have liked. The injury was enough though because as soon as the bogin cleared back over, its comrades fell upon it to add to their own strength.

Acies slapped the top of the tree. "Up. Hold. Position," he coughed.

Elan stared with wide eyes at Acies, clearly unbelieving that the demon had just saved his life, but there was no time for moon cowing.

"Up!" Acies roared, the urgency giving his command strength. Elan moved then, jumping up lightly onto the fallen tree and taking aim with his weapon. He fired and hit something by the answering screech.

"What—" Elan swallowed. "What do we do? I do not have enough arrows for this."

Acies was aware. Nine arrows left, though there was no guarantee the one in his hand wasn't too damaged to fire now. The Demon Lord of the battlefield's mind raced, but he only saw two executable strategies for Elan right then.

He could try to run, leaving Acies and possibly escaping the bogins. Since Acies was the far bigger prize and Elan had the god-weapon, it had a good chance of working, but it would mean that Elan would be risking the life of his sister because the bogins probably would devour him before Elaine was freed from their bond.

The other plan involved getting this damn arrow out of his chest.

He knew which he would choose.

He met Elan's eyes. "Arrow," he said, gesturing to the one in his chest.

Elan shook his head as despair entered his eyes. "No, I will not do that."

"Then ... we ... die," Acies argued. This was not how he wanted to go out, but it was now looking more and more likely.

"Elan!"

Both men turned toward the new voice. The old hag, Maevra, stood a few feet away, clinging to the side of a tree. The bogins' howling dimmed a moment at the intrusion of the new figure but did not entirely cease.

"Maevra! Run! Get away!" Elan shouted, his voice cracking in desperation. It was already too late. Several bogins, who saw only easier prey, leapt down from the trees to come at the old woman.

"No!" Elan cried as he swung around and fired an arrow. The shaft flew true and fast, taking the largest of the attackers straight through its head. It plowed into the ground and was eaten by the horde, yet several bogins pushed past and focused on their prey. "Maevra, no!"

The High Priestess of Isa stepped away from the tree, facing her attackers, her walking stick in both hands. As the first two closed in, she shortened her grip and swung. The walking stick arched and took the first one straight in the face with a resounding crack that Acies felt more than heard. The hit threw the first bogin in the path of the second, tripping it up, and while the bogins were busy, Maevra ran toward Acies and Elan.

"No, get away!" Elan continued to shout after firing another arrow at their flank. Seven arrows left.

To her credit, the old woman bravely ignored his shouts, coming down beside Acies, whose head had dropped back against the log, fighting once more to remain conscious. He had expended too much power saving Elan.

She didn't ask what happened, only took in the arrow in his chest and the demon weapon in Elan's hands, then pursed her lips together in a thin line.

She met Acies's eyes. They asked him if he would fight for them.

He nodded once in agreement.

She gripped the shaft of the arrow.

"Maevra! What are doing?"

The woman didn't answer him. Instead, she roared as she threw her weight back and pulled on the arrow.

Acies passed out.

CHAPTER 23

THE PROTECTOR WALKED SILENTLY ALONGSIDE Elaine, his thoughts obviously far away. She had finished her story, and they had lapsed into this thoughtful silence.

She had never done that before, told anyone her entire story, but there had been such peace in finally letting it all out: about her village, the raid of the Anons, and their subsequent enslavement. She even told him about her violation and being held as Dakin's concubine, all the way to his sacrifice of her at the temple. She never felt shy or ashamed as she spoke of the darkness done to her, though she also didn't shy away from her choices since then, her deal with Acies for a start. And if she could not confess herself to a god, then there was no one.

But as the silence stretched longer, she wondered if she had gone too far or said too much. She rethought every word choice and feared she had disillusioned the Protector. Had she instead proved herself no longer worthy to walk beside him?

It was too late to take any of it back.

"<You have suffered so much, Child of Isa,>" he finally said, his voice thick with regret and sympathy, relieving Elaine's heart. "<I should have been there for you. Had I even known of your existence, I would have come to you and protected you from the Anon slavers.>"

"<It is not your fault for their actions,>" Elaine said, hoping it sounded like a wise thing to say.

"<No, of course not,>" the Protector said as matter-of-fact. "<But there was a responsibility. I should have checked. The prayers I received were so scant, I thought nothing of them. I turned my back on the Ka'in because they had turned their backs on me.>"

"<What do you mean, my Lord?>" Elaine asked, cocking her head at him as they walked. "<My people have always prayed to you. In the village, it was a matter of course to pray to the Protector of the Forest whenever we hunted.>" He still held her hand, and he squeezed it lightly.

"<But how many of them were true prayers and how many of them were simply mouthing the words because everyone else did? Because it was expected?>" the Protector countered.

Elaine had to nod at that point. "<I cannot say for certain what was in anyone else's hearts, but I know for my part, I did mean them.>"

"<I do not doubt it,>" the Protector conceded gently. Then his gaze became wistful and distant once more.

"<Before the Great War, before the coming of Isa, before the Ka'in were the Ka'in, the people of this land would come to the forests in the winter, hunting for food. I took great exception to this. They killed without permission and offered nothing in return. This was before prayers and ceremonies, before the time the people knew how to be grateful. Basically scavengers, hardly a step above animals and unable to do

anything but live for themselves. This was the time when only the greatest of the gods existed, and they were busy creating and making the rules for the world. Mortals and animals were mostly left to themselves.>"

Elaine had heard this story before of course, but it felt different coming from one who had actually lived it. She listened with rapt attention.

"<The forest was my domain, my charge from the God Beyond.>" He smiled at that. "<I am not saying I was equal to any of the greatest of the gods, but it is my charge, and I love it dearly. Otherwise, why would a lowly spirit such as I have grown to such great power? In the summer, the people left *my* forest alone, keeping to the fringes and growing their crops, but they never grew enough to last them through the whole winter. It never occurred to them to ask me for permission or to beseech me to grant them mercy.>"

"<Then the people called a god to help them. He was a land god who made their crops prosper and brought them more food, but as their numbers grew, the crops were still not enough to see them through the winters. So, the god came to me. I found him, in fact, moving through my forest, hunting. He had killed a beast of my forest to feed his people, and I sought revenge from him. We fought for three days.>"

A wistful smile crossed the god's face, and he continued, "<It was not one of my best battles. His neither. A whole lot of jumping around and shouting. We were both so young, and he was a land god, for God Beyond's sake. What did he know of fighting? He was, in fact, more distressed with having killed the deer than he was in having to fight me over it. But I will admit neither could gain supremacy over the other, and we both ended up too exhausted to continue. That was when we talked. He swore to me that he would protect and make

the people honor the forest, and in exchange, I would grant him leave to hunt what his people needed in the winter.>"

"<And that is how you became friends with Veres Kai,>" Elaine finished, marveling at hearing the familiar tale from the source.

He blinked at her in surprise like he had forgotten she was even there. However, his smile never left him. "<Yes,>" he answered, nodding a little.

"<We still tell the tale to our children.>"

"<That gratifies my heart,>" he said softly. "<I wish Veres to never be forgotten.>"

A heaviness fell over both of them, both feeling the loss of the land god for different reasons. "<He died in the Great War,>" Elaine said.

"<Many died in the Great War ... in more ways than one,>" the Protector said, but that strange look passed over him again. It shivered a feeling through Elaine like how the rabbit felt when the eagle's shadow passed overhead.

"<So you knew Isa Kai as well?>" she asked, bringing back the god's attention from where it had gone.

He started again. "<Yes, I did. I knew her very well. I remember the day she came to these mountains.>"

"<Were you there when she met Veres?>" she asked, hoping for more firsthand stories.

"<No, I was not, but I do remember their love. He was smitten with her on first sight. I saw her for what she was.>"

"<Which was what?>"

"<Change. Unnecessary change. Veres and I had a balance. The people respected me and honored me as they should. Veres saw to that, and he had grown in his influence because of their devotion. We had no need for a lineage goddess butting in. What did she bring us that we could not provide the people? Other than heartache. Lineage gods care

nothing for the people. They are only forces wandering the world, too powerful for their own good, and since they do not have any need for devotion or prayers to add to their power, they look down their noses at those of us who do the real work of this world.>"

Elaine furrowed her eyebrows at that. Nothing about it sounded right, but she didn't wish to argue and upset the Protector. He seemed to sense her thoughts all the same.

"<I am not saying that Isa did not care for the people,>" he amended, offering her another, less authentic smile. "<Little Scion of Isa, please do not be offended. I am an old god. It is hard for old gods to forgive the past.>"

"<Not at all. It is fascinating to hear these stories from someone who was there. It somehow makes her seem more real,>" Elaine assured.

He considered her for a pregnant moment. "<It is good to share them, I will admit. It is a pity,>" he said but did not elaborate.

It took Elaine a minute to screw up the courage to ask what he meant, but just as she opened her mouth to speak, he talked over her.

"<You said you made a deal with a demon in order to escape your master.>"

Elaine lowered her head at that. "<Yes. I committed...>" She swallowed. "<I committed the taboo of releasing the demon in order to save my life.>"

A knuckle slipped under her chin, lifting her head back up. "<Please, do not be ashamed, child. Without the guidance of your goddess, what else could you do? Your goddess has abandoned you, and she should have been there when you needed her. There is still a way to make this right.>"

"<What is that?>" Hope bucked like a tethered deer in her heart.

"<Give me what she gave you, willingly and of your own free will, and it will break the bond made between you and the demon,>" he said.

Elaine stood there, stunned. *What does he mean?* she thought.

Reading her confusion, he cocked his head to the side. "<What is wrong, Scion of Isa?>"

"<I just... I do not understand what you mean, my Lord. Isa has not given me anything.>"

"<The majick. Her majick within you, child.>" He pressed a finger into her chest, and she stepped back from its overfamiliarity.

"<You mean my silver blood?>" she asked. "<Isa Kai did not give this to me. I was born with it.>"

He flapped a hand at that, dismissively. "<Your silver blood is of the God Beyond's design, but the majick it contains, that is Isa's. I can smell it in you. It is still a piece of her god power bestowed upon a chosen mortal to wield in her name. Do you have no idea of your purpose, child?>"

"<I...>" Elaine had to rack her brain. She knew what Maevra told her, but it was seeming more and more like Maevra had told her many things, and they were not all objectively true. "<A Scion's purpose ... is to be a bridge between the people and their gods.>"

"<No, no,>" the Protector growled. "<That is what the priesthoods are for. The Scion is meant to be more than that. Do you not know anything, child?>"

Elaine felt stupid and small before this god's questions. He huffed and stamped a foot in irritation. "<A god's influence and power come from the people, especially mortal gods. No, that is an oversimplification.>" He huffed some again, getting visibly more agitated. "<We all have majick

granted to us by the God Beyond. A limited set amount of power, but within mortals, it is different.>"

He looked down at her along his nose, which seemed to grow longer. Two bulges appeared at the corners of his mouth, and as he spoke, she clearly saw two tusks growing longer with every word.

"<Your own power is small, limited. You are small sparks of light, tiny stars next to planets and the sun. Except the stars are not small, are they? While you seem small, your majick is as infinite, each star in truth a blazing sun with so much energy, but you cannot tap it all at once, lest you burn yourselves out. It comes through small doses but renews. You can create it infinitely and give it away and share with each other or hoard it. Gods and spirits cannot do that. Not in the same way. It is not fair!>"

He shook his body, the bristled cloak on his back raising as if the fur was alive. Then he snorted again. "<We of the divine have only limited majick. A set amount given upon our ... creation. Without it, we die. If we need more, you mortals must bestow them upon us. Hence, we must serve you.>"

He looked at Elaine then, his wild eyes roving over her face. "<And then there are beings like you, mortals that straddle both, who can hold greater amounts of majick than most others of your kind and produce it infinitely.>" He snorted. "<I suppose this is why you have come, Scion of Isa. To declare your claim on me in the name of your Lady, that I, a God of the Forest, may serve a mortal such as you.>"

That statement took Elaine aback.

There was violence in his eyes, but then a flicker of understanding returned, and he calmed, reforming as the being he presented himself.

"<I apologize, child.>" He hesitated, then shifted his feet. "<It has been a long time since I have conversed with anybody... I must terrify you.>"

"No, my Lord. I apologize for my ignorance,>" Elaine said, lowering her head to him. It seemed the safest thing to do.

An awkward silence passed between them. Elaine's mind raced for something to say, something compassionate without being condescending. "You must have suffered much as well."

He heaved a sigh that seemed bigger than his body, making the whole forest sigh with him. "Much has been lost after the Great War. Much can never be recovered again. But the fact that you still have a small spark of Isa within you means that not all hope is lost to us." He laid his hands over his heart as though he needed to hold it in place. "No, it could not have been Isa who sent you. I remember now. The God Beyond must have sent you to pass judgment on me."

Elaine didn't know how to respond to that. The Protector shook his head. "Truly, how is it that you can be so ignorant of your role in this world? You say you are a Scion, but you are as knowledgeable as the Anon on things that should be second nature by now."

"<The high priestess taught me...>" But Elaine faltered in Maevra's defense. What had Maevra taught her? Songs and stories and that Elaine was special, touched by Isa to carry what was left of the lost goddess's power. "<Well, the Scions in the stories were heroes. Leaders, peacemakers, guides for the Ka'in in place of the goddess.>"

The Protector nodded. "<So much,>" he grumbled. "<So much has been lost in the war. Years and centuries pass, and what was is forgotten by the generations that come after ... until even I am forgotten.>"

They stopped before a tall wall of bushes and briars, taller than even the great Protector by half the god's height.

Elaine had seen the shaped gardens of Dakin's sister, who used shrubs to divide them in such a fashion, but this seemed far more natural than that, as if the plants had decided to grow that way of their own accord. The Protector gestured again, and the plant life parted, moving by itself and making a path for them to enter. Elaine's eyes bulged widely at the eerie sight.

"<I invite you into my Inner Sanctum,>" the Protector said formally.

"<I am honored.>" Elaine breathed out as she gazed inside.

The space was forest incarnate. A small cascading waterfall tripped and danced over a wall of rocks, filling the air with gentle water drops and spray. The tumbling water itself pooled down into a small stream that wound and snaked through the vibrant trees filled with leaves. Verdant green grew right up to the water's edge, inviting Elaine to sit next to the water, maybe even put her feet in. Flowers cascaded over a rising hill to the right of the waterfall, painted with every color Elaine had ever seen and several she hadn't. It was a slice of immaculate heaven.

"<Come, Child of Isa. Come and I will tell you everything you must know and then you may judge me,>" the Protector declared. He lumbered past Elaine, and she blinked to realize he stood before her now as the largest boar she had ever seen and thought she ever would see.

"<Judge you?>" she repeated, catching the meaning of the words a heartbeat too late.

"<Yes, one of the many duties of a Scion.>" The boar god lumbered over beside the waterfall and stream, dropping down beside it in what appeared to be his usual spot. A few petals from the flowers, whooshed away by the great amount of displaced air he created, danced around him. Elaine felt struck by the poignant beauty of it, wishing she could burn the image in her mind forever.

"<Come, sit beside me,>" he invited.

Before stepping through the bush, Elaine quickly removed her boots since it didn't seem right to wear her footwear in such a sacred place. Leaving her boots at the entrance, she stepped lightly across the soft, thick grass, reveling in the natural feel under her toes. At the water's edge, she sat, but when she moved to plunge her feet in, she hesitated.

"<Go ahead, child. It is only a stream,>" the Protector encouraged.

"<I thought it might be sacred,>" Elaine said shyly, letting her toes touch the surface.

"<It is, of course. It is *my* stream after all, but it is still a stream.>"

Her mind gnawed on that statement, trying to pick out the wisdom in it as she slipped her feet into the water. Warmth washed over her with tiny bubbles that felt like little kisses all over her skin. A small, child-like giggle of delight escaped with the relief that only came from discovering something so beautiful and peaceful after years of harsh darkness and prolonged suffering.

"<Enjoy it while it lasts, for it will not exist for much longer,>" the Forest Protector murmured sleepily. "<I am dying.>"

Elaine scrunched her face. "<You are dying?>"

"<I have only a small portion of my own majick left, yes.>"

"<I thought gods lived forever unless killed,>" Elaine said, shaking her head.

"<Nothing lives forever, but our lives are not determined by the weakness of our bodies as it is with you mortals.>"

She thought back to what he had said about his not needing the prayers of the Ka'in any longer. "<It was not true...

what you told me earlier? You *do* need the prayers of the mortals to sustain you. To refill your life force.>"

"<Settle yourself, child,>" he ordered sternly. "<I have no desire to serve the Ka'in again.>" He shook his head again looking like he was shaking off the Ka'in themselves.

"<But you are dying...>"

"<Do not annoy me with naive hope, Child of Isa. I have no patience for it. Inspiring you mortals has done little to yield what is needed to stop my end from coming. You have all forsaken me and forgotten the old ways. I will not waste what little I possess on the likes of you in the vain hope that I gain a few more prayers from ungrateful mortals that cannot replace what I have lost. Do not waste my time. I protect the forest—I have always done it, and this is all I wish to do.>"

"<I see,>" she said, feeling the pressure to say something.

"<Not yet, Child of Isa," he said. That same strange look she had seen earlier passed over his face, and Elaine realized she knew what that look meant. It was a hungry look. "<But you. You could help save me so that I may continue to protect this forest, maybe even claim it back from the demons who have worn me down and taken too much from me.>"

"<How could *I* do such a thing?>" Elaine asked, starting to believe she would not like the answer but unable to not ask it.

"<Child of Isa, it is your purpose,>" the Protector of the Forest intoned. "<Give me all your majick.>"

CHAPTER 24

ACIES HAD NO IDEA WHAT IT FELT LIKE FOR THE arrow to come out of his chest. He felt only pain, but it was a distant thing. He was also dimly aware there was still shouting and howls, but they seemed so far away. It was like he was in a place within himself, crouched around a small flickering flame that was his life—all he had left of his original being, the arete granted to him by the God Beyond at his birth.

Am I back in that place? My prison? Did you never leave it? Has all that transpired only been an illusion? A madness in what is left of my mind?

Voices, much closer than the howling, penetrate his darkness.

"Maevra, leave him!"

"He is dying."

"Yes, I know. Leave him!"

"How could you do this to your sister?"

"I did this *for* my sister!"

"Acies, wake up. Acies! We need you!"

Someone shakes him. He has a shoulder to shake.

233

Acies cracked his eyes open, seeing the daylit sky above him partially blocked with treetops. The old woman leaned over him, her eyes searching for answers.

"You are too weak to fight," she said.

He knew that. Why was she bothering him? She should leave him to die in peace.

A hand laid on his chest, and pain knifed through flesh as she pressed on his wound now absent of arrow. "If you die, my Lady dies with you. I will not let that happen. Do you have the will to fight?"

Behind her, Elan shot. Two more arrows rattled in his quiver.

He shot the one Acies had used. He saw too clearly the damage on the shaft, the bent plastic of the fletching. They were doomed.

"Take my arete."

He blinked, trying to understand what he had just heard.

The old woman's thin mouth pressed even further. "You are the Demon Lord of the battlefield. Take my arete and win this fight." She meant it. The resolution in her jaw and in the seriousness of her eyes shamed him. To have such conviction in the face of death. The tactical side of him understood her calculation: they were wasted dead soon, but if her death could mean something, mean that her children would live, she was more than prepared.

It echoed another battlefield, another friend, making the same sacrifice.

Tears, honest tears, pricked at Acies's eyes. Tears he had thought himself no longer capable of shedding.

He shuddered a breath in, finally easier and fuller without the arrow. "One drop of Elaine's life equals all of yours," he said. He had to be sure before he did this again.

In response, Maevra offered him her wrist, no flicker of hesitancy in her. "Do it," she commanded.

And he obeyed.

"<Give me all of your majick.>"

Elaine dislodged a rock with her toes at the bottom of the stream bed.

She went still as she stared at it, working out what her eyes saw. The rock was hollow, a broken dome with jagged edges. Carefully, she turned the rock until something appeared on the other side. She wanted to jerk away, pull her feet from the water, and skitter back from the edge, but she didn't dare. She simply stared at the pair of empty eye sockets of the mortal skull staring back at her.

Give me all your majick, she thought, repeating the god's words in her mind as she stared into the dead eyes.

"<Scion of Isa,>" the Protector of the Forest called. Elaine's back stiffened.

As casually as she could, she looked over her shoulder at him and gave him the smile she had perfected for Dakin, soft and demure.

"<What is your judgement?>" the forest god asked impatiently, huffing so hard Elaine could feel the heat from his breath flow over her. It smelled foul.

Elaine thought over everything he had told her so far. "<It does not seem right—a mortal such as I, judging a god,>" she said. She forced herself to withdraw her feet slowly from the water, crisscrossing them.

"<It is not right, but it is the nature of what you are,>" he said with the same contemptuous tone he used when speaking of Isa Kai. "<Do not try my patience, Scion. Am I

worthy or not?>" He pressed himself back up onto his ponderous hooves.

Elaine sprang to her own feet, making sure she stayed facing him, very conscious it would take very little to squish her. "<Worthy of what?>" she asked, even though she knew.

He reared up and slammed his front feet into the turf. "<You are the Scion of Isa. Judge me worthy and give me what is owed. Give me your majick!>" he roared.

Elaine backpedaled, dropping into the water. "<But how?>" she whimpered, imagining that he wished her to willingly put her body in his mouth to bite and tear in half. She couldn't do that.

Yet the question had an effect on the Protector, and he took his own step back, seeming lost in his own world. If a demon was bad, a mad god was even worse.

"<The gods bleed gold, the demons black, and the mortals red for majick they lack,>" he softly sang out, "<but you have both inside you. Metallic and red, not black. Yes. I do believe Tamor would have found that poetic enough.>"

"<Tamor, the god of song,>" Elaine said softly, mirroring his tone as she took a careful step through the water.

"<And mischief. More a trumped-up spirit than a true deity if you ask me. But then who am I to talk? They were a companion of Isa's, ones she picked up from her travels in the South. It was her way to make the lesser deities swear fealty to her and follow her. It was how she turned Veres against me.>" He tossed his head, and she took a step back when he took one forward.

"<Isa was the first to figure out how to bestow a piece of her majick in the Silverblood mortals so that her representatives could act in her name, doing great works such as she would do for the benefit of the mortals who prayed to her, making her even stronger. Near invincible. She had several

Scions, mortals eager to serve her and the people, and those without the silver blood would flock to join her priesthoods. Now, there is only you.>" Elaine continued backpedaling until she was against the hedge, the leaves whispering and scratching against her neck.

"<That power was never yours, and with it, you could save my life, and I can continue to protect this forest.>"

But only if I judge you worthy, Elaine thought. "<What happens to me after I give you Isa's majick?>"

He snorted. "<What does that matter? You are only a mortal.>"

Glancing over at the beautiful stream, Elaine felt sick to her stomach. Then she felt the pressure as his great head loomed over her, the wet snout snuffling.

"<You saw the skulls in the river,>" he stated with deadly quiet. "<Selfish mortal,>" he growled, "<you think your life is more important than mine? I see it in your eyes.>"

She knew better than to speak. Anything she could say would only set him off. Elaine kept her hands behind her back, pressing them into the foliage gently but firmly. She sought to reach past the small branches and leaves, trying to determine how thick it really was and if there was anything more than plant to it.

"<I am not a demon!>" the Protector roared, stamping again. "<I fought back the demons. I bled under their claws, my beautiful hide scarred by their teeth, and they sucked my life away, yet I fought on. I protected the forest!>"

Her eyes darted to the stream; she could not help it.

"<They were violators!>" the Protector insisted.

"<I believe you,>" she assured, taking the opening he was giving her. As long as he kept thinking he could convince her, she had time; however, she wasn't sure what she could do with that time. She couldn't reach back any farther behind herself without being obvious.

A crow cawed loudly, black wings flapping as it soared overhead, clearing the top of the hedge like it was nothing because it was nothing to birds. While the Anon feared the crows as harbingers of ill omen, the Ka'in saw them as messengers and guardians of stories. Both symbolisms seemed to be invoked in that moment as the Protector looked up, startled at the appearance of the creature, the first avian sounds Elaine had heard in his presence.

Elaine didn't waste it. She plunged backward through the hedge.

CHAPTER 25

ELAN STARED DOWN ON MAEVRA, SHAKING HIS head back and forth as if he could erase what was happening if he did it enough. The older woman, his replacement mother in so many ways, lay on the ground. She looked peaceful in her expression, but her skin was pale as death, and she was still. He kept sticking his fingers under her nose to be sure she breathed.

At last, she pushed him away with a weak hand, the one not ripped open by the demon. "I am not dead yet, Elan. Please stop."

"Maevra?" His voice cracked as if he were an adolescent again, the sound he made too thick with tears. She looked up at him with sympathy and resigned love.

"Do not cry for me yet, my boy. This is not your fault."

"It is. It is. If I had not..."

"Focus on your sister now. It is all that matters." Maevra lifted her head a tiny bit, looking to where the demon battled the bogins. In a few short moments, he had cleared them back, moving swiftly in a circle, leaping up and over them at times to intercept every bogin as it moved to attack the pair. Elan had spent his last arrow taking out two in a shot before Acies shoved him toward Maevra, ordering the prince to guard the older woman. The Ka'in Prince didn't need an order.

"I did what I must," Maevra said to him, putting her head back down. "When you tell stories of my ending, tell them I did what I must."

"You will be telling the stories yourself, Maevra," Elan tried to say cheerfully, but she wasn't having it.

"I am dying, Elan."

It hit Elan with that simple statement that she spoke the truth. He had been able to deny it even as he watched Acies bite into Maevra's wrist, and even as he screamed at Acies to stop, he had believed she would recover.

Maevra hooded her eyes as she gazed up at the sky above. For another heart-wrenching moment, Elan thought she had died at last, but then she spoke. "Elan. Where is your sister? Where is my Elaine?"

"She is with the Protector of the Forest, Maevra," he said, his voice croaking through his tears. He plucked her hand to hold in his. "I went to the forest to pray for his help. He said he would break Elaine's bond with the demon and save her. That is why I did all this; do you understand why I did this? It was to save Elaine."

Instead, her eyes went wide. "You did what?" she said, her alarm undercut by her weakness.

"Elaine's bond. He said he could break it, and she will be free of the demon."

"Oh, all the deities above and below," Maevra whispered, closing her eyes, shaking her head. "You fool, Elan. You absolute fool."

"No, it will be alright, Maevra," Elan urged. "I have taken care of it. Elaine is going to be alright; you will see."

"Elaine is in greater danger than we are," Maevra said, opening her eyes again to meet Elan's. "The Protector of the Forest is mad."

Elan furrowed his brows, shaking his head even before he spoke. "What? What? What are you saying?" Elan could not comprehend it.

She tried to grip his hand forcefully, but he could barely feel it, doing more of the holding than she was. "We still prayed to him for the sake of the old ways, but after the Great War, the Protector of the Forest lost his mind in his grief. He turned his back on the Ka'in. He will kill her."

Elan shook his head. "No, no, that cannot be. Maevra, I was in his presence; he did not kill me. The Anon are the ones that make him out to be a demon, but I saw him, Maevra." He tried to assure her despite his own doubt creeping in. "He was magnificent and truly a god."

Maevra gripped his arm with her other ravaged hand. "You must promise me, Elan. Promise me that you will help..." She panted, fighting for each breath. "You will help Acies save your sister."

It was as if she hadn't heard a word he said.

He tried to soothe her. "Maevra! Please be still—"

"Promise me!" She seized his face in her hands, her gaze piercing him with urgency. "Promise me! Elan!"

"I promise" was all he could say. He wrapped his arms around her and held her as if she were the child, pulling the smaller woman to him. He cried. "I promise, Maevra. I am so sorry." He repeated those words like a mantra, rocking the woman back and forth, completely oblivious to anything that happened outside of them.

Crouching down beside them, Acies pulled on Maevra's shoulder, moving her face out of Elan's chest. It was then that Elan realized she was dead. Still, he didn't believe it even though Maevra's hooded gaze did not react to being moved. Her eyes saw nothing. Acies slid an ichor splattered hand down her arm and pressed two fingers against her wrist, but Elan wasn't having it.

"Don't touch her!" he screamed, scrambling back with the body in his arms.

Acies let her go, staying in his kneeling position with his arms at his sides. His expression wasn't full of pity but rather a simple resignation that was far, far worse: the demon understood what Elan felt and was waiting for him to accept it.

Elan kept shaking his head. "No, no, no..."

"She is dead," Acies said aloud.

"No! Maevra, please," Elan pleaded, desperate to do something but having no clue what that could be. "No, Maevra. Maevra, *please*."

He degraded into harsh tears.

But his grief needed a direction, and he found it readily kneeling beside him.

"This is your fault!" he screamed, lunging over Maevra to tackle Acies. The demon seemed prepared though, taking his momentum and tossing him ass over end to land just short of slamming into a tree, his fall cushioned by the corpse of a bogin. The wind knocked out of him, and for a moment he hoped the demon would kill him as well. But no such mercy came.

Elan rolled over back onto all fours, ready to attack. Yet the demon did not even regard him. He knelt beside the body of Maevra, laying her hands over her stomach neatly. The sight of the tender action fueled Elan's rage.

"How dare you touch her!" he screeched and ran for Acies headlong.

Again, Acies stood and intercepted him, this time grasping his arms and using his momentum to slam his back against another tree. He pinned him there while Elan's sight went dark for a moment. He tried to push off the arms pinning him there, but they were as immovable as the tree.

"Listen," Acies hissed, giving him a little shake. "We do not have time for this. We must go and save Elaine."

But Elan wouldn't listen. "You killed her. You killed Maevra," he shouted.

The demon shook him again. "That is enough!" he bellowed in Elan's face.

Elan stopped fighting then, letting his head hang as he wept, bawling pitifully like a child. Acies kept him pinned against the tree, holding him up.

At last, Acies gripped the back of his neck with his hand, pulling Elan's head against the demon's shoulder. "I understand you mourn for her, but if you do not help me, Elaine will be joining her."

Elan wanted to hate the soothing tone of the demon's voice, but he needed it now. He clung to it as his anchor in the sea of his grief. His gaze rested on Maevra's body, lying peacefully on the ground, surrounded by trees and the bodies of bogin.

"But we just cannot leave her like that," Elan wailed. "We cannot..." A hiccupped sob swallowed his words.

"There is no time to do rites," Acies argued. He turned then to gaze on her as well.

"We have to bury her at least," Elan insisted, "or the animals will ... eat her..." which sent him into another fit of sobs. "We cannot leave her to be devoured like that. We cannot."

The demon seized Elan around the shoulders. "This is stupid," Acies grumbled as he led Elan back over to the body, letting him collapse down on his knees beside her. Acies took up the other side, shaking his head.

"This is a waste of arete," he insisted, though Elan didn't think he was speaking to him. Then the demon opened his hands, palms to the sky.

"What... What are you doing?" Elan asked. "We should bury her."

Then there was a cracking sound as the ground displaced itself. She sank underneath the turf as leaves and loam poured in with her, covering her like a blanket. Elan scooted back to prevent himself from falling in, his eyes wide in shock. Then the demon brought his hands together with a grunting effort as if it took all of his strength. The ground rolled back over, sweeping her face from view, covering her in earth until only a small bare mound remained.

With shaking legs, Acies stood and hobbled over to a tree. Grasping one of the lower branches, he tugged at it until a seed, a walnut pod, snapped free.

Reverently, with sweat beading on his forehead, Acies returned and dropped beside the newly covered grave. He leaned forward and set his hand with the pod over the center of the mound. He grunted once and pressed, pushing the seed into the earth as he chanted words that sounded like the language the demon spoke to Elaine with. Elan did not understand them, but there was something familiar about their cadence. When he removed his hand, a small seedling grew from the mound.

"She will be a tree," Acies said between gasping breaths.

Elan reached out and touched the bright green leaves of the seedling in amazement. "How did you do that?"

Acies looked at him with clear annoyance as the demon's chest heaved. He pushed himself up to his feet. "Now we must go."

Flicker was utterly miserable.

Worrying its hands, the creature paced back and forth before the place where the mistress had disappeared. Flicker hadn't expected this. It was improper and irregular to prevent the little temple guardian from accompanying its mistress, even into a god's inner sanctum.

So Flicker worried and paced, shooting glances at the small stone totem of the Protector of the Forest marking the border of the god's domain. The totem had been carved ages ago into the shape of a stylized boar by for those who knew what they were looking at, but it was barely recognizable now after centuries of weathering.

The more time passed, the more Flickered worked itself up. "Oh dear, oh dear, oh dear," it repeated as a mantra until even it could not take it anymore and made a run at the Protector of the Forest's barrier.

Predictably, the small gelic bounced off with a flash pop. Still, Flicker kept trying, making more runs with different angles and going through every ability at its disposal. After trying to blast the barrier with a spark and having it rebounding so badly that it left poor Flicker's feathers smoldering, the small gelic plopped down on its backside and began weeping pitifully.

"Flicker?" a kindly voice asked.

Arresting its tears in mid-wail, Flicker turned toward the voice. "Master Elan!" it cried with utter relief. "You have returned and…" It stopped short at the sight of the demon following the Ka'in Prince.

The demon narrowed his eyes at Flicker, noticing the reaction, and a new flood of guilt washed over the little creature.

"Flicker, quickly, where is Elaine?" her brother asked.

"Within, brother of my mistress, within," Flicker said, gesturing frantically at the stone statue.

"What, within the statue?" Elan asked, his eyes darting from the statue to the surroundings, searching for an obvious explanation.

"No, brother of my mistress," Flicker said, shaking its head, "she has gone *within*."

Elan shook his fists in frustration. "I do not understand what you mean by that!"

"It means she is in the Sanctuary of the Protector of the Forest," the demon said, moving past Flicker to regard the worn-down statue.

"Yes, precisely." Flicker nodded, wondering why it needed to be spelled out so plainly like that.

"Then why did it not say *that*!" Elan cried, staring daggers at Flicker.

"Gelics are used to being intuitively understood on a psychic level with their deity or Scions. Most gelics do not speak to average mortals. It is being clear; it is you who does not understand," the demon said.

Flicker nodded in agreement.

"Fine, fine, then," Elan said, running his hands through his hair. "Why are you not with Elaine? I thought you were—"

"I have been kept out by the Protector," Flicker wailed despairingly. "I tried to follow, but I am not powerful enough to get past a god's barrier. I am only a lowly spirit."

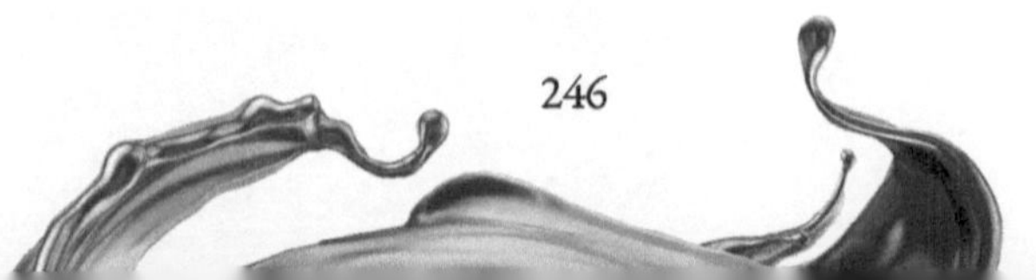

"In a god's sanctum, the god who created it rules supreme even over other gods," Acies added.

"Then how do we get in?" Elan spat at the demon, his fear fueling his anger. "How do we save Elaine?"

"*We* do not. But *I* have a standing invitation," Acies said, setting his hand on top of the statue's head.

CHAPTER 26

Elaine emerged from the other side of the shaped bushes, scraped and terrified, but otherwise unharmed. It had been nothing more than bushes. Relieved, she plummeted forward, running into the woods as fast as she could. Briefly, she saw the path. Running on it would have been easier. Yet the chase would have been just as easy. She tried not to look back, only focused on going forward. Any moment, the Protector of the Forest would be after her.

Then the crow appeared again, landing on a branch nearby. It cawed once and looked at her with a cocked head. She continued in the direction she had been going, so it flitted to another branch a few feet in front of her and cawed poignantly again. This time, she slowed to gaze up at the night-black creature. It bobbed its head at her, then cawed once more before flying to another branch to her left. Again, it bobbed at her and waited.

She furrowed her eyebrows at it. "I do not..."

The crow bobbed its head, this time in a more angular direction as if saying, "This way, this way."

Taking a leap of faith, Elaine went the way it indicated. It flapped its wings and flitted ahead of her, continuing their improvised communication as Elaine ran along. All the while, she continued to scan for any sign of the Protector, but there was nothing. No sound outside of the rustling trees and no sign of the enormous boar, which only made her more apprehensive. From every direction, the trees looked the same, gnarly spikes of wood thrust toward the sky, the ground littered with dead leaves and branches.

Too soon, the crow stopped on a nearby stump, the first difference in the landscape they had encountered since fleeing the bushes. The crow did not look at her, but instead, it cocked its head left and then right. Elaine stopped and held still, struggling to stay quiet as she labored for breath.

Every fiber of her being screamed to keep moving.

Then the crow took off again. "Run! Run!" it cawed.

The cry spurred her feet. Elaine turned and bolted through the trees. The crow flew above her, keeping pace.

She heard it. Crashing trees. The rhythmic tattoo of pounding hooves. Heated breath blowing as wind.

She didn't look back, throwing everything she had into her will to move forward.

"Stop!" the Protector of the Forest bellowed.

She didn't look back. She kept running, her chest tightening and her breath shortening. Still she kept running.

Trees cracked so close behind her. A great trunk fell past. She shrieked, raising her hands in time to protect her face. He hit her from behind. The world spun. She came to a stop on her back. The great boar bounded like a horse over her body. He slid, tearing up great clods of dirt, turning sideways in time to slam into a tree. The tree broke against the force. He turned his ponderous head back toward Elaine.

She scrabbled back onto her knees, clawing at the air for purchase that wasn't there.

He took slow unhurried steps toward her.

The Ka'in Princess came to her feet, gasping for breath, her whole body trembling.

The god's eyes were wild. "<Why do you run from me? What are you hiding?>" He lunged.

She stood frozen, unable to move.

Then the crow dived for the god's eyes, clawing and pecking for all it was worth. "Run! Run! Run!" it cawed.

The spell broken, Elaine bolted again.

"<You traitor!>" the god howled, whipping his tusks until he struck at the valiant crow, throwing it away into the forest.

Elaine thought to go back for it, but she could still hear its cry. "Run! Run! Run!"

Except, Elaine really couldn't run now. She tried, but she was out of breath. Her limbs shook from the lack of air. She ducked around a tree just as the boar galloped past. An involuntary cry alerted him to his miss. She went back the other way toward the mess of felled trees.

"<You are in my Sanctum, Scion of Isa,>" the Protector of the Forest roared. "<There is nowhere you can go and no escaping me in my own domain!>"

Elaine heard his feet pounding as she scrabbled to where the trees had fallen in a haphazard pile, knocked over in the Protector's rage. Beneath one, she saw a divot of earth large enough for a person, a natural bend sloped slightly downward.

Now, she dared a look back over her shoulder.

He came straight for her at a full gallop. There was no way he would be able to stop in time.

She held her breath and pushed her way through the gap under the felled trees. Her back scraped against the rough bark through the material of her shirt. Kicking her legs as if swimming, she tried to leverage herself through. Then more bark gave. She rolled in, flopping onto her back into the soft, stinking earth beneath. Like a grave.

Elaine saw the Protector's shadow leap over her pile of logs. She wriggled to the side of the tight space to peer through, seeing him swing around, throwing his head like a wild horse.

He shifted back to the overly large man.

"<Come out! Demon! You are caught!>" he shouted as grasped the log with both hands and strained to heave it up. For a dying god, he was still plenty strong. The moving log shifted its fellows over Elaine, and she squealed. She crawled, avoiding being crushed by a handsbreadth as a displaced log thumped beside her.

The sudden cascade arrested the Protector's actions, who immediately dropped the log once he saw what he had done. Now Elaine was very trapped with no clear way to unbury herself from beneath the timber. Bugs and dirt fell into her face and mouth.

"<Are you alive?>" the Protector called apprehensively from outside like a little child.

She had no desire to respond to him. Maybe if he thought he'd crushed her, he'd go away. An eye peered down at her through the singular crack in the pile of logs, blocking her light and dislodging more scraps of bark onto her face.

"<You stupid mortal,>" he chided. "<You will die in there a waste.>"

Elaine didn't respond to his jibe. There was no point. Even as she panted, wrestling with her panic against the thought of being buried alive, she started to sing. It was a small song at first, non-sensical with notes of various different tunes, not quite landing on any one song. The eye removed itself, letting in the scrap of light and with it the song coalesced inside her.

> "<Lady of Water, dulcet and fine,
> Protect all your creatures, small and divine.>"

Water, cool and refreshinog, rose from the earth all around Elaine. For a moment, she thought she was drowning, but instead the water seemed to hold her, rushing about her like a circular river, carving away the earth beneath to make room for her body to rest comfortably. The water bubbled up, piercing through the crack of light above her then fountaining down the sides of the pile, filling the in-between places. With buoyancy, the logs lifted up, separating away as they joined the flow of the wall of river, which grew wider with each pass, Elaine at its heart.

Elaine understood what she was doing with no earthly reason as to why she knew. She directed the river around herself, giving the water the intelligence to act, but she did not know why she knew it. With each pass, the water purified and became a part of Isa's river, a torrential flooding that even the Protector—again in his boar form—must give way to before the mightiness of her force.

She also understood that this act was costing her, that the amount of majick needed to maintain such a miracle was draining away. Too soon the ball of river decreased, dropping the logs to the sides as if blown there by an ocean storm, dripping wet and piled haphazardly around her. Gently, her feet touched earth, and she stood there feeling utterly exhausted, her hair dripping wet around her face and her hands hanging heavy at her sides. But her breathing was calm. In fact, when she took a deep breath in, she was breathing clearer and more fully than she had before; the water had renewed her body at the cost of her spirit. The scrapes and cuts on her hands were gone, so she presumed wounds on her face were healed as well. The strained muscles in her legs and back felt normal, but she struggled to find her balance as water drained from her ears and her head still swam. It was a strange feeling.

Just as she thought she might fall to the ground, a strong arm came around her middle, holding her up. A second arm joined it, lifting her legs up, and her head slumped against a shoulder. The world around her spun, and she could not focus on anything, forcing her to close her eyes. A familiar smell wafted over her, inviting her to let down her guard.

"<It is good to see you again, Vills,>" the voice rumbled from the chest she leaned against, and she forced her eyes open to look up into Acies's profile.

The Protector of the Forest trumpeted his rage. "<How dare you invade my sacred—>" Then the pawing stopped. Elaine found she could move her head enough to turn to regard the shocked expression on the Protector's face.

"<No, it cannot... It cannot be you!>"

"<Who else could I be then?>" Acies said, stepping to the side to set Elaine gently on the ground. Their eyes met a moment, and he gave her a reassuring smile, touching her cheek tenderly before swiveling back toward the lumbering beast a few lengths away. "<Could I be the Demon Lord of the Battlefield, Hero of the Southern Lands, or the Winter Hunter, or the Friend of Vills, or...>"

"<Veres,>" Vills, the Protector of the Forest, hissed.

CHAPTER 27

ACIES'S CHEST HURT AT THE SOUND OF HIS TRUE name. Though it had no real power anymore since he'd destroyed it, it still had the power to sting. He could practically feel Elaine bristle in his arms, but why wouldn't she? He was the lost god of her people, after all, not that he had ever intended her to know that. He couldn't imagine what she might be thinking, but it would have to be dealt with another time.

He straightened up, facing Vills. "<You do not look well, my old friend,>" he said.

Vills snorted, blowing his signature windy snort that picked up particles of the churned-up earth to cast over Acies's face. He squinted against the spray but did not look away or turn his head. It was his old friend's go-to when he was irritated. It only made Acies smile.

Yet he also knew he had to keep his attention on Vills. It had been ages since he last battled the old forest god, but

Acies could tell that time had worn away the proud creature into a shadow of what he once was: a dangerous shadow.

But then Acies himself was not what he once was either.

Acies had made the specific choice not to come with the bronze sword in his hand, leaving it sheathed at his side. "<I am not here to fight you, old friend.>"

Vills wheeled about to pace, tracing the ground with his large hooves. "<You should not be here; you should be on the front,>" Vills said. "<Why did you come back?>"

"<The front?>" Acies paused, turning his head at an angle. "<I left the front weeks ago. I miss my wife,>" the demon lied smoothly. Carefully, he set Elaine down next to a tree, flashing her what he hoped was a reassuring smile. Then he turned to face the threat, keeping his hand ready on his pommel.

Vills bristled his back and stood up, his small, star-filled eyes going wide and urgent. "<Veres, you... You came back from the front. You mustn't go to your temple, your lady wife... She will betray you. I mean, she has betrayed you.>" Vills squealed, then he turned and started, grinding his tusks against the trunk of the nearest tree agitatedly. The long shafts of bone gouged long strips of living wood from the side. "<I should have saved you, my friend. I let my friend die. I killed him...>"

"<As you can see, I am fine, Vills. I am right here.>" Acies continued his approach, getting closer and closer until he could lay his free hand on the bristling back.

Predictably, Vills jumped at the touch. "<No! You do not understand! I slay all who violate my woods. I am the Protector of the Forest. It is all I have left. Come with me, Winter Warrior! We will hunt her down together and trumpet our glory so the stars themselves grow envious.>"

"<That indeed sounds glorious, Vills, but I am tired. I have fought many demons this day and have reached my

limit.>" Acies continued to stroke along Vills's back, willing his friend to calm and quiet his broken mind. Acies did not add any arete to it, but it worked all the same. Vills stopped scraping his tusks, which he only did when agitated. Instead, he leaned his body against Acies's side.

"<I have missed you. So much,>" the minor god admitted.

"<I as well,>" Acies agreed, stepping up closer to scratch behind an ear, treating Vills more like a pet than a sentient creature in his own right. The fact that the minor god allowed him to was a clearer sign of any how little time was truly left. "<Speak to me truth, Vills. Are you dying?>"

"<Dying?>" Vills whispered. Then he jolted at a thought. "<The Scion. The Scion of Isa. You must help me. I need to find her. I need… I need the silver blood of Isa from her. With that I would not have to die.>"

"<Ah, but if you take her arete, then I will die. She is mine.>"

"<I am no one's. He is mine,>" Elaine snapped.

Vills pulled away, turning to glare over his shoulder. Elaine had managed to stand, using the tree for support. She was angry. Acies made a point of adjusting his position so he stood between them.

"<You are her demon,>" Vills said, his upper lip snarling. This time Acies did shift his hand to the hilt of his sword.

"<We are each other's,>" Acies said.

Then Vills chuffed, the sound squealing on the inhale. "<You finally abandoned your damn oath to Isa!>" The boar shook his head. "<And now I have to end you, my last living friend. The God Beyond is unjust.>"

"<The God Beyond has nothing to with this,>" Elaine snapped. Gone was the terrified, meek woman who ran, replaced with the god-metal that had always been underneath. And she was pissed.

The Demon of War had to admire her bravery. "<We could leave, Vills. We go our way; you go yours. Nobody has to die today.>"

"<No,>" Elaine countered. She pushed away from the tree. "We cannot allow this to continue."

Alarmed, Acies moved to block as Vills became more restless, shoving him back a few steps like an agitated horse.

"<Elaine, we do not have to do this,>" Acies hissed.

She did not look at him but kept her gaze fixed and resolute on Vills, standing there as solid as ice. "<You brought me here to judge you. Some part of you knows what you have done. And regrets it,>" she said.

"<I must... I have to... There is no other choice! As you said, I am dying. There will be no one to protect the forest if I am gone. I am the only thing holding the demons here at bay.>" Vills bucked, taking Acies up with him.

"<That is demon-talk, and you know it,>" Acies cried, letting his own emotions take his words.

"<I am not a demon!>" Vills trumpeted. He threw Acies off him. Reflexes were all that saved Acies from losing his arm as he skipped back. Elaine caught him from behind, stopping him from falling completely.

"<How dare you! How dare you!>" Vills charged, opening his mouth as the boar god drove his yellowed teeth down.

Acies turned to push Elaine away, but she stepped up brandishing a hand instead. Water erupted from the ground like a geyser, parrying Vills's attack. It shoved them away as well, and only Acies stopped her from cracking her skull on the tree, using one to brace and the other to cup her head against his shoulder.

The water abated as quickly as it rose, melting into the ground.

Vills recovered quickly, snuffing wet air.

"<Vills,>" Acies tried again, turning so he faced the boar, putting space between him and Elaine.

His former friend was having none of it, and he tossed his head to skewer the demon on his tusks. Acies popped back just in time to be missed.

Acies continued to back up but at an angle to take his opponent away from Elaine. He dodged left and right as Vills swung his tusks in a repeating cycle of left and right until Vills's tusk smashed into a tree, bursting a chunk out of it with explosive force.

"<If you go down this path, Vills, you can never unmake the choice. Listen to me...>"

"<I cannot die. She is only mortal! She does not need it!>" Vills cried, his desperation heartbreaking.

"<That is all I am to you gods: a thing!>" Elaine shouted.

Predictably, Vills turned his ponderous head toward Elaine who had taken herself around a large tree for partial cover. Acies pulled his sword then, using the tip to nip at Vills's shoulder, doing little damage but gaining all of his attention.

"<If you are not careful Vills, she could order me to kill you, and I do not want to do that.>"

"<A demon cannot best me in my own Sanctum!>"

"<Do not make me test that theory. If that is what you want, to expend the last of your arete in one last glorious battle, it is up to you.>"

"<I will not die! I cannot!>"

"<Then let's get on with it then!>" Aries shouted back, sweeping his arms wide in invitation. Suddenly, Elaine appeared, stepping between him and Vills boldly and without fear. Vills moved to swipe at her with his tusks, and there would be nothing Acies could do to stop it. Even if he used every last shred of his arete, he simply couldn't get there in time. Yet Vills stopped himself, pulling his own tusks up short. He panted, the streams of his breath blowing the torn-up dirt on either side of Elaine.

"<You can't hurt me, can you?>" Elaine said more than asked.

Vills's sides panted heavily. "<I will fight you demons until my dying breath!>" he shouted, stomping his hoof.

"<No, you won't,>" Elaine stated. She stood there, straight and upright, full of noble bearing. The edges of her clothing blew back with each of the god's breaths, but she seemed not to heed it. "<You will not hurt me, will you? You have done your best to scare me, but you *cannot* harm or kill me and not break your oath to Isa.>"

"<You must give me what I require!>" Vills shouted, but he wasn't attacking. He was listening.

Elaine shook her head. "<I won't do that either. My arete is mine ... to do with as I choose. Not you or any other deity, man, or monster. My choice.>" She cast her gaze at Acies then, clearly dismissing the creature before her. "<We are leaving.>"

Keeping Vills in his periphery, Acies crossed to take Elaine's hand, keeping his sword in his best hand. "<You know that he is not going to let us go.>"

"<There is nothing he can do to keep me here except kill me and then—>" She met Vills's gaze again. "<Then he would be an oathbreaker as well. I do not fear him.>"

The Protector continued to stand there, more like a statue than a living god. Acies kept himself three-quarters turned toward his old friend, with Elaine more or less covered by him. They walked away from the artificial meadow created in the forest by their fight.

To Acies's shock, he did not attack. There was no charge to deflect. No calling or bellowing after. Nothing. Then Acies's ears tingled. *No, that's not quite nothing,* he thought as he heard the sighing sobs from a body too big and unfamiliar with making such noises.

"<In another time, such a scarring of Vills's Sanctuary would end with laughter and much drinking,>" Acies murmured to himself, just to hear anything other than his old friend's wailing.

Elaine said nothing to that; she only kept her eyes focused on the road ahead.

"<How did you know?>" Acies finally asked Elaine. She turned to him, her eyes half-hooded with weariness. "<How did you know he would not attack or chase us?>"

She sighed. "<He told me. I just did not understand at the time. I am Isa's Scion and, therefore, her representative. He brought me here to judge him, just like the temple guardians. I did that.>"

The wailing grew louder.

"<Of all the dark things I have done in this new world, this has been the worst,>" Acies muttered. The light in the sky darkened even more, threatening more rain, but it wasn't there yet. A rumble rolled over the sky.

"<How far until we leave the Sanctuary?>" Elaine asked, eyeing the sky.

"<We have already left it,>" Acies said, gesturing to the trees. "<Hear the birds?>"

A few muted twitters had returned to the forest, the birds possibly discussing the coming storm. Acies did not know if that was true, but he had always enjoyed imagining it was. There was no sound of Vills.

"<A crow,>" Elaine said as if remembering something. "<There was a crow who helped me in the sanctum.>"

"<Really?>" Acies furrowed his brow.

"<Why do you think they helped me?>" Elaine asked softly.

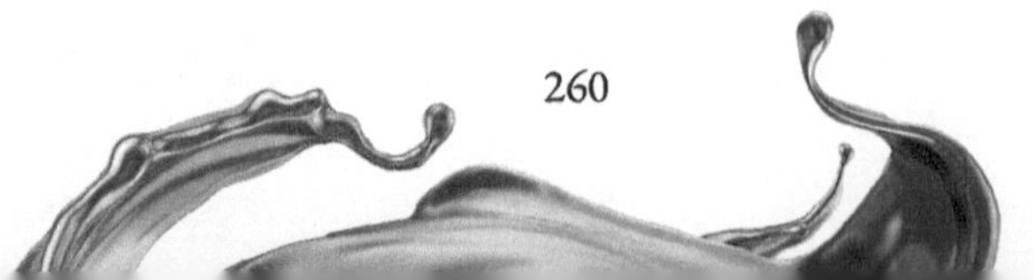

"<Crows are some of the few creatures who can penetrate a Sanctuary without an invitation. I wonder why it would risk it though?>" Acies commented.

"I wish I could find that crow again so I could thank them for their help," Elaine mused, switching back to Ka'in. A small smile graced her face, lifting his heart to see.

Then she stopped, holding still with alerted eyes. Acies turned to see Vills standing in the path before them. The birdsong instantly died. Automatically, Acies raised his sword, but Vills did not notice it. His entire focus was on Elaine. They stood like that, neither moving, the tension as taut as the hind ligament of a rabbit.

At last, Elaine moved first, stepping around Acies. "<What do you want, Vills?>" she asked.

In answer, Vills looked to Acies. "<Take my life, demon.>"

Acies's hand ached, he gripped his sword hilt too hard. "<What?>"

Vills dropped to his knees, then rolled his great body to his side, exposing his long-furred belly to the pair before him. "<Plunge your sword into my heart,>" he declared.

The demon understood.

He wanted to say "no." He wanted to refuse, insist someone else must do it, but he knew there was no one else.

With heavy feet, Acies came up beside Vills.

"<Acies?>" Elaine asked, but he did not answer her.

He laid his empty hand against the great creature's side, feeling the heavy rib bones expand and contract. Deep within, he could tell the breathing was labored and wrong. Now that he could touch him, Acies could tell that he was close to the end of his arete, a few days at best.

"<I am sorry, my friend,>" Acies said as he raised the sword, and he plunged it into the heaving flesh with speed and all his weight.

A squeal escaped Vills, a pitiful squeak of pain; the body stiffened and went still. Yet Acies continued to drive the sword, pushing it deeper and deeper into the body.

"Acies! What are you doing?" Elaine cried, but he did not stop or look away, not until the sword was completely encased in the dying god's body. Inside, Vills was warm and wet as his gold-silver blood washed over Acies's hand. Even as he lay dying, the arete within him sang with the song of the God Beyond, joyful and defiant in a world of darkness.

Then he withdrew, pulling the sword free from the god's side.

The sword had changed. It was glorious.

The blade was carbon steel, the bronze transformed into a metal that did not exist in this world. Wedged and keen, the edge glinted even in the scant light along the much longer blade, a proper long sword. The handle was a crosspiece that glinted gold and filigreed with silver alloy. The grip felt wrapped with fine pig-skin, toughened and durable. Upon the pommel sat a cast image of Vills's boar head, his great mouth open in a scream of triumph at his most glorious. Vills's gold-silver blood continued to drip from the blade, rolling down Acies's arm, but he could not bring himself to wipe it away yet.

"<What did you do?>" Elaine asked, eyes wide as she gazed on the sword as Acies held it aloft.

"<When a god lies dying, instead of disappearing into nothingness, we sometimes turn the last vestiges of our arete into something that will last beyond our passing, so that the world will not forget that we were here. This is now the Sword of Vills, the Protector of the Forest.>"

"<Let me see it, Acies,>" Vills croaked.

The demon came around, brandishing the sword so that Vills could gaze upon his last incarnation. The god's one eye was already clouding, but a warmth of satisfaction filled his voice. "<Ah, yes, it is magnificent,>" he said with great pride. "<Child of Isa, attend me.>"

Elaine came forward and knelt beside the head. "<I am here, Protector of the Forest.>"

"<See what I have done, Scion of Isa. With my last scrap of majick, I have forged a god-weapon from my body. Use this sword, Acies of Elaine, and use me to protect her.>"

"<I will,>" Acies responded, tears burning his eyes.

"<I have fulfilled my oath of service to Isa. Witness this,>" Vills said, his voice fading as his eyes clouded away.

"<I witness it,>" Elaine intoned. "<Vills, Protector of the Forest, it does not have to end this way. I will not give you my arete, but you could bind yourself to me as Acies has and serve...>"

"<No. I will die a god,>" the Protector said finally.

Then she laid her hand on Vills's head, stroking the bristling fire along his nose, up, over between his eyes and back. "<I will never forget, and I will tell your stories.>"

"<Remember, Child of Isa, this world is full of sadness and darkness, there are no true happy endings, but sometimes there are victories, no matter how small.>"

Vills went still, his eye now unseeing. The blood on Acies's hand dissipated, bursting away like puffs of glowing fog, along with the rest of Vills, dissipating into starlight that rose and rose until it disappeared into the clouds above.

The two witnesses stood, watching a long time until only the thunder remained.

"<We must go,>" Elaine finally said. She seemed weary, both from grief and great effort.

"<Yes,>" Acies said, jerking away to put his sword back in the sheath, realizing that the bronze sword sheath would tear apart once the larger sword was placed inside. He would have to carry it naked until he found or made something better. "<Your brother should be waiting this way.>"

He moved off, leading Elaine to follow. He too was weary with grief and great effort. His friend was gone.

"<Thank you, by the way. For coming for me,>" Elaine said, but Acies shook his head.

"<Do not thank me until you have learned the price.>"

PART 2

CHAPTER 28

ELAINE STARED AT THE LIGHTS OFF IN THE DISTANCE.
She stood on the edge of the forest with her shawl folded
around her head to form a hood of darkness. She longed to
walk across the short field between the forest's edge and the
settlement, to join the fire and the people once more, but she
knew it wouldn't be as easy as that.

"Elaine? Are you okay?" Elan asked, coming up beside her.

"So close and yet we may as well be in the forest," Elaine
said. "I did not realize it when I was held in Icathor, but I am
an outsider."

"You are the Scion of Isa. They will be glad to receive you."
Elan tried to assure her.

"I am just glad we found the edge when we did. I was
starting to worry that we were actually lost," he grumbled.
He had Maevra's shawl about his shoulders.

"You are sure we will find help here?" Elaine asked,
studying the flickering lights in the distance.

"There are some of the resistance here, so yes," her brother answered. "We should get some help here before continuing on to Icathor."

"And if there was anywhere else to go, I would," Elaine muttered.

Elan hesitated. "We actually do not have to go to Icathor—"

"Yes, we do," she said with resolution. "We have already discussed it, Elan. It is decided."

Elan thinned his lips and said nothing as they continued to gaze over the sleeping settlement. For a brief moment, Elaine thought he would be like his old self and argue with her. A part of her wished he would because then it would mean he was his old self again.

"As you wish," was all he said, turning away to leave her as he began to walk along the tree line, scanning the field of grasses between them and the settlement. Then he pointed to a section of grass that seemed to be moving all on its own, barely visible in the half-moon light. "Demon signs," he whispered.

Elaine nodded, watching the patch. The demons were very bold to be coming so close to the settlement. If the twins hadn't been upwind, they would probably have been just as in danger of being spotted and attacked.

"Do you wish to cross?" Acies asked, coming up beside Elaine. She stiffened at his presence before forcing herself to relax.

"It would be suicide, would it not? To simply cross this field and join them at the fire?" Elaine said softly. She indicated the swirling grass a quick trot away. Flicker came up to stand in front of Elaine's feet, the little gelic barely glowing in the darkness along its filament feathers. The temple guardian had barely left Elaine's side since she had returned from the Forest Protector's sanctuary.

"If you wish to go there, I will make it happen," Acies said resolutely.

She shook her head. "I do not want anyone else getting hurt."

"We still need supplies," Elan stated. He wasn't really arguing as much as voicing what all four of them knew. "We are not equipped to continuing to live outside like wildlings."

"We are surviving just fine," Elaine said. It was a token argument, and they all knew it.

Acies studied the settlement in the distance. "We can safely go there," Acies concluded. "We can find you warmth and companionship."

Elan pointed to the left of the settlement to another set of smaller and dimmer lights. "That is the slave village. Traders keep some stock there. Most of our people will be there. The settlement has lookouts but not much else. But the rest serve this settlement, working in the fields and households. My contact person is there."

"What prevents the Ka'in from escaping?" Acies asked. "I see no walls or barricades."

"A few do every year. Take the chance to make a run for the wood," Elan said. "Very few survive. Either the demons get them, of which there are always a few hovering about in the darkness, or the roaming bands of warriors will hunt them and return them or kill them if they resist. The threat is often more than enough to keep the slaves close. That is the way of the Anon. The warriors hunt the slaves and fight back the demons, and the merchants support the warriors as needed."

Elaine nodded. "That is who the Anon were before, bands of warriors roving around, making war and taking slaves. But then they got to the point where they decided to keep what they conquered, and the bands roved less and less.

There is a whole economy around it. Most Ka'in do not even take the chance."

"The other question—can you trust your people?" Acies asked, his tongue dwelling on the Ka'in words. He was speaking them better every day, learning more words at an amazingly rapid pace, though Elaine wondered if he wasn't dumbing down his ability to speak and understand Ka'in for some benefit she couldn't put her finger on.

He continued, "The slaves ... may give us away to the Anon for nothing more than extra rations of food or clothing or medicine or some other need that has been denied them."

The Ka'in Prince sneered. "Our people would never do that—"

"Shut up, Elan," Elaine snapped.

Fortunately, he did as he was bid.

He had changed much since losing Maevra. Elaine was not sure if she blamed him or not for what happened; her soul hung too heavy within her to even think about how she felt.

Elaine stared down at the bundles of venison in their makeshift packs. It had taken a lot of work to remake the hide into three serviceable packs to carry things in, including the more useful parts of the deer such as its antlers and a few bones for tool making or trade. Flicker was the only one to remain unencumbered, being too little to bear the pack, but the creature had proven useful in other ways, but not for crossing these dangerous grasses.

"But you are *sure* you can get us in safely?" Elaine asked, directing her question to Acies, who smirked as his response.

"How is he going to do that?" Elan demanded, finding his tongue again.

Acies did not answer him. The demon stepped forward out of the protection of the forest's tree line. After several steps, he stopped and knelt among the tall grasses waving there, practically disappearing all the way up to his neck. Elaine's skin prickled as a sensation washed over her, something similar to what she had felt when she had been in Vills's Sanctum.

She stared at the solid back of the being she barely knew but had trusted her life to. It had been days since learning his secret, but she still did not know how to feel about it. She still hadn't spoken to him about it, not that she would know what to say. He hadn't brought it up either, which also meant that Elan was completely clueless. Some noble part of her wanted to argue with herself that Elan wasn't in a place for another shock right then, and he was better off not knowing that the feared Demon Lord was once the Harvest God for their whole people.

But so much of that was a plain lie. She wasn't ready to think about it. It wasn't like either of them had told her much about Maevra's death either.

Just then, there was a shift in the ground as if it had just exhaled. Fog wafted up from the grass, filling the air with tendrils of cloudy white.

Elan startled back at the eerie sight, but Elaine stood her place as the ground cloud washed over them both, swallowing them in thick, bog-water air. She could barely make out her brother standing next to her and certainly not Acies a few steps away. Flicker glowed softly in the fog between her feet.

"Very clever," she said, as her demon's dark form re-emerged into her now limited view, his towering body a ghostly shadow.

"This will last until morning when the sun burns it away," he said as he knelt down to take up his pack. The other two did the same, and the weight felt good on Elaine's shoulders as if it were grounding her.

"How can he do such a thing?" Elan muttered, but Elaine hushed him.

Elan only huffed once in response then tapped Flicker on the head. "What about Flicker? It's going to give us away."

"I will not!" Flicker declared too loudly. All three taller people hushed it at once.

Then it began to shake. Before Elaine's eyes, the little temple guardian collapsed into itself before dropping to the ground. She bent and plucked up a talisman on a cord. She could barely see it, but the image was warm in her hands.

"If it could do that, why wait until now to do it?" Elan groused.

"Shut up, Elan," Elaine ordered and slipped the cord over her head. The talisman glowed softly like the gelic had, but she tucked it into her clothes. After so many days, a small smile tweaked at the corners of her mouth as she pressed Flicker's warm talisman against her chest.

Elan gripped a back strap of Elaine's pack, but Acies took her hand. With him in the lead, the three of them walked through the dense fog.

The journey seemed to last hours.

Acies moved at a steady pace, walking carefully over the uneven ground, breaking a path through the foliage, which whispered mutely as it slid past. There was nothing to look at but her feet and Acies's dark form ahead of her.

Elaine wished they could stay that way, lost in the fog, walking through the cool night. Danger lay ahead and behind, but in that held space, she felt quiet and wished the feeling could go on forever.

"How much farther?" she heard Elan grumble, and Acies stopped ahead.

He held still without speaking, then dropped down into the grass, pulling Elaine with him. Elan followed a half second later. She still saw nothing in the fog but held her breath as they waited.

They waited and waited. She could feel her brother begin to squirm behind her, and she reached back to tell him to be still, and he seized her hand.

"There," Acies breathed, and she realized he stared off to their right.

A few feet away, just barely within visual sight through the fog, a dark shadow as large as a wolf but too long in the torso moved silently past. Every hair on Elaine's body stood on end as she realized it was a demon. For a moment, it stopped, and she was sure it had sensed them. Then it moved on, sliding past through the fog of the night. She continued to stare long after it disappeared, only registering how hard she squeezed Acies's hand when he pulsed it back.

"It's still out there," she dared to whisper.

"Yes," he whispered back. He did not move. They waited.

A voice screamed, and Elaine startled. Acies pulled her closer, sweeping her under his cloak and against his body.

More shouts came from the settlement. Torches shined orange in the light and accompanied cries of fear, but they did not come any closer to the three, the hallowed lights bouncing past in the fog.

That was when Acies moved. The pair of Ka'in had no choice but to continue to follow him. They rushed over the ground, heedless now of the noise they made in the grass. Elaine wanted to ask why, but there was no time.

To her relief, out of the fog, the shape of a hut manifested, and the trio huddled against the dry grass and mud side. More shouts and calls came from the cluster of orange glows that were scattering and moving away from the Ka'in slave village.

"Do not be afraid," Acies whispered.

"I am not," Elaine answered, and it was the truth.

She felt him nod then turn, leading them along the edge of the building, deeper into the heart of the village.

"Which one?" Elaine whispered back to Elan.

"I... I do not..."

"Elan!" she hissed.

"I cannot see a damn thing in this fog!" Elan said, pushing the definition of a whisper.

"Sshh!" Acies shot back.

Even with the fog and darkness obscuring Elaine's view, her eyes fell upon a stone well situated in the middle of the cluster of huts. It was the one thing there that looked like it had stood long before the village, ringed in stacked stones. Several leather buckets lined the base, all tied to strong woven ropes. The temples of the Ka'in were always meant to be the houses closest to the source of water. Even here, the Ka'in would follow that ancient tradition.

She squeezed Acies's hand three times. He looked back at her with a question in his eyes, waiting for her to direct their next move. She pointed at the well. He crooked an eyebrow at her but followed when she took the lead. Hunching low in the dark, they scurried over to the well.

Elaine prayed she was right as she turned to the closest hut. She faced a blank wall. She peered through the dark at the rest of the huts, but they were just as obscured by fog and night. There were no faint glows of light that would indicate a door's opening, so she wondered if all the doors faced away from the well.

Lacking better options, she continued to the closest hut and ran her hand along the wall slowly, Acies and Elan right behind her. To her relief, a tiny slip of light appeared in the wall on the opposite side from the well. Relieved and apprehensive in equal measure, she scratched the plaited reed covering of the entryway.

Someone inside uttered a small squawk of alarm within.

"<No! Stop!>" a frightened voice said in Anon.

"Oh, no, this was a mistake," Elaine whispered, but it was already too late as the reed door cracked away from the door-jamb so a single eye could peek out.

The eye stared at her intensely.

"We seek the waters of Isa," Elaine whispered, the traditional greeting for those entering a temple of their goddess.

The reeds pulled back farther to show a woman's middle-aged, worn face, backlit by the fire inside. And ears that poked through her hair.

"<Stop. They are demons,>" the fearful voice inside cried in Anon, but the woman stretched out a hand and fingered Elaine's dark, wavy hair between her fingers.

"<Who are you?>" she whispered, also in Anon. "<You aren't from the village, or you would know to speak only Anon.>"

"I am Elaine, the Scion of Isa." She dug into her shirt to pull out Flicker as a talisman and showed it.

The woman eyed the symbol critically.

Then Elan moved up to the door. "<It is me, Sarai. Let us in.>"

Her eyes widened, then crested into smiling eyes before she opened the reed door farther, creating enough of a gap for Elaine to pass through. "<Hurry,>" she whispered.

CHAPTER 29

ELAINE WASTED NO MORE TIME IN COMPLYING, SLIP-
ping through. Acies needed the doorway opened completely
for him to clear it.

The hut was a single small room, roughly circular, that
was already filled with too many bodies for the space. Small
gasps and cries came from the people staring up at the
strangers, many of them very small. It smelled quite ripe with
unwashed bodies tinged with sickness.

Acies could not stand up all the way, so he bent down
and took a knee beside Elaine. She stared at all of the various earth-colored eyes that stared back. She saw calculation
and fear in some of them, and she knew instantly that one
of them would betray her to the Anons. It had been a mistake to come.

"<Why did you let them in here?>" the voice from
before demanded, coming from a balding, reedy man who
looked unwell.

"<Look at her hair,>" a young girl pushing toward womanhood breathed, a sound echoed by several more voices. A small hand reached out to touch Elaine's leg before it was intercepted and redirected.

Then they all saw Elan.

"<Elan!>" the room cooed, speaking his name in the Anon style. Everyone in the hut spoke their master's language. Even in the slave village, the risk of being caught doing otherwise was too great.

"<It is the Ka'in Prince,>" a small child nearly squealed too loudly before the room shushed him.

"<Stay silent, all of you,>" the woman at the door commanded, the one Elan had called Sarai. All held still as more shouts echoed outside. There was another scratch at the door, coming across in a pattern. The woman twitched the reed aside.

"<A warrior was killed and dragged off into the night by a demon,>" a young man said softly to her. "<The others pursued, but this strange fog is too thick. They are returning but taking up posts along the outer edge of the village tonight.>"

"<Understood, Quin,>" Sarai said, then reached out a finger and traced a symbol on the young man's forehead. "<Be safe in the night and watch for the dawn,>" she said, the blessing sounding so strange in Anon.

"<Thank you, Priestess,>" he answered just as softly, then slipped off to go to the next door.

"<He is taking a terrible risk,>" one of the occupants muttered, shaking her head regretfully.

"<So are we,>" the reedy man growled, shooting a dark look at Elan who returned it. "<I thought you left to find your sister.>"

"<I did,>" Elan stated.

All eyes shifted to Elaine.

"<Are you a princess?>" a little one asked, looking up at Elaine with bright eyes.

The sweetness of the child hurt inside, and a small smile creased Elaine's face. She unshouldered her pack, dropping it before the group to open the flap. There were gasps of amazement as she pulled out a package of meat wrapped in the large leaves of the forest. "<There is enough food here for everyone,>" she said, holding it out, slipping into the Anon as easily as if it were her native tongue. She pulled out more packages, which elicited more gasps as the slaves moved in to open everything and look deeper into her bag. Elan's and Acies's own bags joined them.

"But this was for trading," Acies muttered at her ear in Ka'in as everything was divvied out.

"These people have next to nothing," Elaine replied. "There is no point."

Elan knelt beside them, pulling his knife to start carving up more of the meat so that it could be placed on cooking spears and set over the fire in the back of the hut.

"Taun," the priestess said, pulling a youth toward her who was all legs and arms and definitely not a Ka'in. She pressed several packages of meat into his arms. "<Take these to the huts next door. Tell everyone to only take one package and then pass the rest to the next hut and so on. Listen to me...>" She grabbed the boy who almost went out the door like a shot. "<You are to say that these are gifts from Isa, and if anyone is caught hoarding, we will all know.>" The youth nodded and went out the reed door. "<And be quiet,>" she hissed after him. Whether he heard or not mattered little because he was gone.

The priestess turned back to Elaine. She made the sign of Isa before the princess in the exact same way Maevra had, and it almost brought Elaine to tears. "<Thank you,> Blessed

Scion of Isa," she said, this time in Ka'in only because the title didn't exist in Anon.

"<I am sorry it is so little,>" Elaine replied, in Anon, not wanting to invite more risk on the priestess.

But the priestess shook her head at the apology.

"<Why is she here?>" the reedy man demanded, standing up but slouching over as he was too tall for the hut. "<If you are really the Scion of Isa, why are you here now?>"

"<Have you come to free us?>" another woman asked, holding a sleeping child in her lap.

That idea excited the group, and they began chattering animatedly.

"<Hush, all of you! Or the Anon will be on us,>" the priestess chided. Her words had their effect. At least, that or the meat cooking, the smell of it overtaking any other scents in the room and calming the occupants.

"<Come and sit with me, Scion,>" the priestess invited, gesturing for Elaine to a set of mats to the side of the hut.

"Elaine," the Scion countered. "<My name is> Elaine." She couldn't bring herself to pronounce her name in the Anon fashion. Not anymore.

"<I know.> Elan <has spoken of you. I am Sarai,>" the priestess said.

"<It is an honor to meet you,>" Elaine said politely, resetting her shawl around her shoulders.

"It is ... confusing to see you here," Sarai said in Ka'in as her eyes fell on Elan.

Elaine was taken aback by the sudden change in language, after she had been so careful not to bait the woman into it. Yet, she could see that this woman was no fool. Apparently, what she had to say she did not want the others, at least the others who weren't Ka'in, to know. Elaine's gaze washed over the children, especially the Ka'in children, sad to think about how many of them may not even know their people's tongue when they heard it.

"Confusing? Why is that?" she asked, switching to Ka'in herself.

"Because I knew, or I thought I knew, that even if Elan should succeed in his mission, he would not return with you to this place."

"You helped him?" Elaine asked, jumping to the idea.

"I did. And I thought I was foolish to do so. I am glad I was wrong, but why have you returned?" Sarai asked. "It has been days, and we have not heard from Titama or any of the others who went. We feared the worst."

Elaine licked her lips. "We separated from Titama after they rescued me. We all thought it was safer that way."

Sarai nodded, accepting her half-truth readily. "Then, they failed in capturing Dakin?" she asked, her eyebrows furrowing in a confusion Elaine did not understand.

"Dakin was killed," Elaine reported.

Sarai shook her head. "No, no, Dakin is alive."

A shock pulsed through Elaine. "What? No. I saw him. I saw him die."

"All the news we have heard is that Dakin is very much alive and consolidating his forces. Which means," Sarai huffed, worry deepening her eyes, "we still do not know what is going on." She shook her head. "Elan was a fool to bring you here."

"Where would we have gone?" Elaine asked, resigned.

Sarai cocked her head. "Back to your home, I would think?"

"You know of it? You know of Source Temple?" Elaine asked, unexpectedly overjoyed to hear someone mention her village as if it made the place she'd lost became more real because someone else remembered it existed.

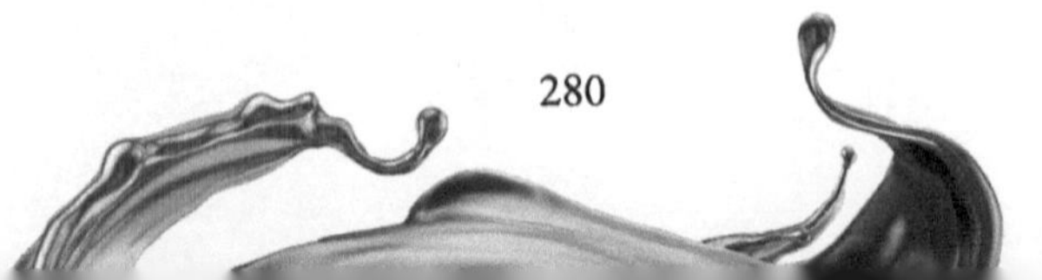

Sarai nodded, blushing at Elaine's delighted reaction. "I visited the Source Temple when you were a bit younger, possibly ten years ago now. I saw you both as children."

Elaine could not keep the surprise from her face. In the dimmer light, she would have judged the priestess to be only a bit older than she and Elan, especially by the heated way she looked at her brother.

"I am sorry. I do not remember you," Elaine said regretfully.

"Much has changed since then," Sarai said with a weighted weariness that Elaine understood all too well. "Including your hair."

Elaine froze at the comment. Near the door where Acies sat, he snapped his eyes to her. She held up a finger with a small shake of her head, he settled back but continued to watch warily.

"If not for Elan, I would not have known you," Sarai continued, her own wary eyes measuring the exchange. "I remember a girl with hair the color of snow and eyes as green and brown as the disturbed earth. Now it is black as midnight, and your eyes…" Her words trailed off. She licked her lips. "I would not worry too much about yours, or his eyes, for that matter. I do not think most will be able to determine the color. I only do because I still retain my godsight. The Anon have not succeeded in beating it out of me. I see things that most others do not."

"You speak of many truths about me, yet I do not know your purpose for doing so," Elaine said levelly, speculating again if this had been a mistake.

"I do not intend to offend you, but these are dangerous times, and as you can see, I have children and the sick here with me and very little ability to defend them. The only reason I can do this is because the Anon see that I solve more troubles for them than I bring. I have broken that unspoken agreement tonight." Her eyes pressed Elaine hard.

"Then why did you?" Elaine asked, biting her lower lip as she looked upon the children around Elan, each being handed a piece of meat by the woman with the baby on her lap as she carved it from a cooked hunk.

"Because this will not last. Something is scaring the Anon, and what scares the Anon scares me even more. Something dangerous is coming. Every household in the settlement has been whispering about things in Icathor."

"You have a String of Whispers?" Elaine said, using the old term from the tales of the Great War, where a string of spies and scouts would bring information on the demons and their forces back to the gods who fought them.

Sarai blinked at that then laughed softly. "I suppose I do. Many households in the settlement have slaves that return here at the end of the day, and they share with me what they have heard. Much of it is upsetting."

"Would you share your information with me?" Elaine asked carefully.

"I will, but I am afraid it is very little, and the accuracy is suspect, at best."

A hunk of meat was brought to Sarai and Elaine, this one on a broken stone platter. Elaine pulled out the bejeweled knife given to her by Elan and sliced away a hunk that she then offered to the priestess. The priestess eyed the piece, hesitant to take it.

"This is not a great hall, and this is not a festival feast," Elaine said.

"Even here, a princess outranks a priestess, if I can even call myself one."

Elaine did not yield, and Sarai solemnly took the meat to set it into her mouth. The princess nodded, satisfied.

"There was a coup to take the fortress almost immediately after Dakin left," Sarai said softly.

That surprised Elaine, pausing her in mid-cut of her own piece of meat. "A coup?"

Sarai took over as she continued to speak softly. "It was all part of a deeper plan. One that I fear is no longer good."

Elaine glanced over at Elan. "Did…?"

"Yes, he knows of it," Sarai said softly.

Elaine let go of the knife, leaving it in the meat, her mind running in all directions at once. "What was the plan?" she asked softly.

"Many of us belong to the Merchant Amira or rather several members of her family. She has been buying up Ka'in whenever she could. It was part of what convinced us she was sincere about delivering us freedom if we delivered her … what she wanted."

"Dakin," Elaine whispered. It didn't surprise her if she was honest with herself. "The wizard-priest's arrival upset many things."

"We have no idea why she needed him, but it was a crucial part of the deal. Our people for Dakin. Alive."

Elaine closed her eyes. "It was me. Elon knew the deal, and he traded all of your lives … to save me."

Sarai's hand closed over Elaine's, but she didn't say anything, not even to exonerate Elan's choice nor her part in it.

"He tries to do the right things, but they always go to shit," Elaine whispered instead.

"It is what makes him noble," Sarai agreed. "Such concepts died out in the Anon. Even reverence for the gods. Without it, every Anon believes they too can become a god in their own right," Sarai said dryly.

"So the merchants moved against Dakin in his absence." Elaine chewed on that thought as she chewed on the meat. "It is chaos then ... in Icathor?"

"I would assume, but we do not know," Sarai said, the weariness sitting on her shoulders. "There are only stories. There have been more demon sightings lately. The world is filling with darkness. If ever there were a time for the gods to re-emerge when we needed them most, this would be it."

Elaine fingered Flicker's amulet around her neck as she glanced over at Acies. She was startled to realize he was still watching her, now with a warning in it. "I ... may be able to help you with that," Elaine said, glancing anxiously away, unable to bear his gaze.

"What do you mean, princess?" Sarai asked, her voice carefully neutral.

Elaine glanced once more in Acies's direction, this time at the sword leaning against the demon's shoulder. He had wrapped it entirely in half of the rawhide of the deer. It was one of two signs that there were still gods in the world. The other was Elan's bow, also wrapped in the other half of the rawhide, stuck under his pack. He had not drawn the bow since Maevra's death. They had only been able to retrieve five useful god-arrows, though they had collected as many of the damaged ones as well. Even one of those arrows could buy supplies for a month if those that beheld it understood what it was. Such a thing would have been prized among the merchants as a new trophy or at a temple as a sacred relic.

"I plan to find Isa Kai," Elaine said softly.

"You are taking the pilgrimage." Sarai nodded. "It may be our only hope now."

She stood then, straightening the smock she wore as if it were priestly robes. "You may stay here, though I would keep the two of them out of sight. The Anon avoid this place

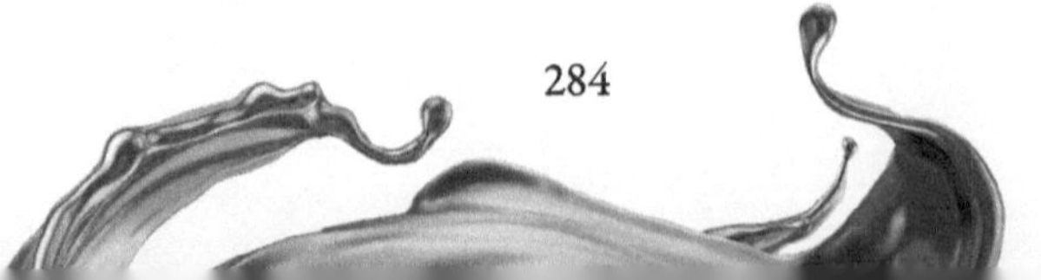

because of the sick, but if they catch sight of your companions, there will be questions. I would also cover your hair."

"Thank you, priestess," Elaine said.

"I am not a priestess," Sarai said softly. "Not anymore, if I ever was. The goddess is gone. We both know that, Scion of Isa."

Elan's hearty laugh cut through the space, and both women looked to him tickling one of the children in his lap.

"Elan has sacrificed too much for me," Elaine said softly.

Sarai's smile was beautiful and pained. "He is a Prince of the Ka'in. What else was he to do?"

She left Elaine then, even though there wasn't very far to go. She went over to the children and Elan to sit with them and started directing the little ones to lie down, signaling for Elan to finish his story.

"It is still possible," Acies said, shifting away from the door to come to sit by her side. "I see enough here to create a fighting force. These people are beaten down, but there are enough that are not broken."

"She told me that there are slaves that go into almost every household in the settlement," Elaine said, jutting her chin in Sarai's direction.

Acies nodded at that information. "In a few days, we could organize. They just need to be told what to do, and we could take this settlement."

"And defend them from the Anon warriors how? How many do you suppose will die in the attempt?" She set her head back against the side of the hut as she looked upon him.

"A few would die," Acies said.

"They all could die," she countered. "These children, they could all be slaughtered."

"Yes, it is possible," her demon admitted.

"They just want their children to grow and be safe."

"You know very little about war," Acies muttered.

"And you know very little about peace," Elaine countered, then switched to godspeech so the others could not understand, even if most of them only spoke Anon. "<So, what makes you think the Demon of War can do a damn thing to make it?>"

"<A Demon Lord of War is all there is,>" he said.

"<You were once a god of the harvest. You must know something of peace,>" she whispered. She had to look at him, force herself to meet the being before her eyes. "<I would think these people would take much hope from knowing that Ver—>"

"<I am a demon. Once you become a demon, there is nothing else.>"

Elaine balled her fingers into fists on her knees, fighting the urge to slap him. "<Get away from me, demon.>"

Acies said nothing to that, only stood and returned to sit by the doorway with the sword he called Vills wrapped in the rawhide across his knees. He left Elaine alone with her own words echoing in her ears.

CHAPTER 30

IT HAS BEEN TOO MANY DAYS, LORAB THOUGHT AS HE sat on the smoothed log staring into the large fire. Much had happened in such a short time, yet his mind had not noted it until he sank onto this log. It had been a week since leaving Dakin's side to go search for his enemies, yet Lorab and his warriors had found nothing.

Well, that wasn't true. They had found countless demons. They seemed to come out from behind every tree and every abandoned hut. The constant fighting had been glorious. Something had changed for warriors of the God Dakin. They were faster, stronger, could see farther, and were more fero- cious than before. Prior to Dakin's blessing, Lorab had been feeling the pressures of age decaying his abilities as a warrior. All he had to hope for was finding a glorious death before his abilities had waned so far as to be noticeable, but now he felt as he had a few seasons ago. As if he could conquer the world. Every battle he fought fed that certainty. They had become so much more than they had before. Divine warriors.

Yet for all their new abilities, they had still failed in their mission.

When he had reached the temple, they found nothing of value, not even the bodies of the men Dakin insisted had been left behind. The temple had been abandoned and spooky, and there had been plenty of demon activity, but nothing they couldn't handle. Simply an abandoned Ka'in temple, waiting to turn into a pile of rubble. There had been nothing that even their Ka'in tracker could follow. There were footprints and signs of the camp, but so many of the footprints went off in so many directions into the woods that there was no clear indication which could be Dakin's prey.

It looked more like the refuse from a temporary market than the sight of a massacre.

Now he stared into the fire, wondering what he would tell Dakin upon his return. While his lord had said "if" he found Elaine, Lorab had not survived so long to become Dakin's Sword by not knowing what his lord meant by "if."

"Is it true what they say?" a young woman asked, pouring a fresh cup of wine for him as she looked at him demurely through her lashes. Her appearance broke Lorab out of his deep, disturbing thoughts.

"And what is it that they say?" he asked, hooding his eyes as he took her in.

The settlement women and a few of the men moved among Lorab's warriors, offering food and drink freely even if it was unwillingly. The settlements never liked supporting Dakin's warriors, but since they could not do anything about it, he didn't care. His warriors did not question his call; they were happy enough to finish the settlement's alcohol and use their beds, even if a few needed to be simply taken. None would truly dare refuse.

For Lorab's part, the dancing boy, a youth just shy of manhood with his lithe frame and talented hips, had caught his eye. It had been a while since he had claimed a paramour. And if war was indeed on the horizon, then maybe the boy would be willing to come with as his page.

The woman in front of him was comely enough as well. Maybe he could claim both.

That certainly seemed to be her intention, the way she pressed her breasts together as she leaned in to whisper in his ear. "Is it true that Lord Dakin has been touched by the gods?" she asked.

He almost blurted out what he actually thought but managed to thrust the lip of his cup into his mouth before something unwise fell out.

She smirked at his stumble, probably concluding that her display was what caused him to fumble on his words like an unblooded youth. Irritated, he set the cup on the ground and yanked the woman off her feet onto his lap.

"Would you like to see for yourself?" he murmured, seizing the back of her head to sniff at her neck. She smelled of sun, warmed fruits, and woman. Her back arched in response, and he liked the reaction so much he took a little nibble.

"Mara, that is enough!" a snappish older woman barked. Probably her mother. When the woman called, Mara jumped to get up, but Lorab put his arm around her and kept her there.

He leveled a look at the older woman. "She is fine where she is," he said, giving as much warning in his voice as in his eye. For a brief moment, he imagined sinking his teeth into the older woman, silencing her shrill voice and drinking in the fear in her eyes as she died.

Whatever the older woman was going to say did die in her throat as she measured the true warrior before her. Her mouth flapped for a second, obviously torn between protecting her daughter and not wanting to upset him further. Wisely, she yielded and turned away sharply, much to the younger woman's delight.

"She cannot be satisfied without an offer for me," Mara suggested, leaning against him as his free hand slipped up her arm to cup a breast under her too thin shirt for the time of year it was. She released a little moan at the touch.

"If I so command, she will give you to me for free and be grateful without a bridal price paid." He took her mouth, and she kissed back with abandon.

"Well, when you put it that way, my Lord," she said when the kiss broke, her eyes drunken as she smiled.

"Ha, Lorab!" a jovial voice called out.

Annoyed, he broke away from where he wanted to keep his attention to lay eyes on a less pleasant but equally welcomed face.

"Rowf!" Lorab declared, spilling Mara off his lap to clasp arms with the head of Wolf Warriors.

"What brings your sorry hide out here?" Rowf asked, his gruff, hairy face beaming with enough red to cover up how much he drank. The two men clasped arms, then he offered his drinking horn to Lorab who politely refused. Shrugging, Rowf took a pull from it, spilling as much as he got into his mouth.

"I am on a mission for Lord Dakin," Lorab explained.

"Still tethered to his leash, eh?" Rowf laughed, slapping Lorab on the chest.

"You mean do I have a full belly and a full bed?" Lorab countered. His men were having a good time; he didn't need to start, or rather continue, this long-standing fight with Rowf. At least not yet.

Lorab reclaimed his seat and his plaything.

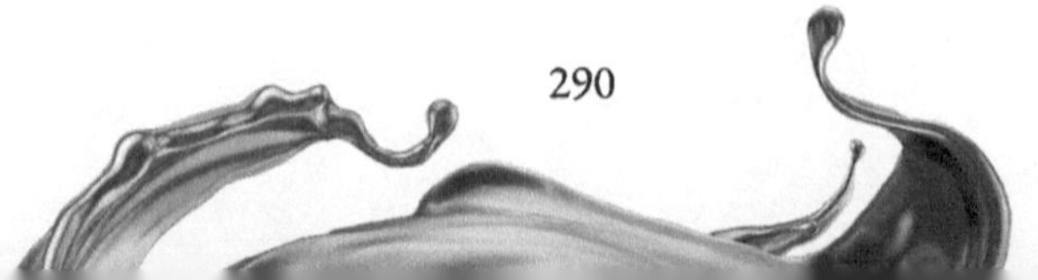

"Now, now, do not take offense. I fight for your master too now," Rowf said waggling his eyebrows as he emptied what was left of his contents.

"Is that so?" Lorab asked carefully. He moved back Mara's hair and tickled his lips along her neck. She gave a tittering giggle.

"No, no, no threat, my friend. We are not replacing you. We are here to gather up slaves for your master's army. As you can imagine, the merchants are not—"

"Are you the Sword?" a voice interrupted.

"Ah, here comes the problem himself," Rowf grumbled, claiming a seat next to Lorab and extending his feet to toast by the fire.

Lorab growled as he turned away from his conquest to stare down the man who had approached him so brazenly.

"Merchant," Lorab stated in way of a cold greeting, looking the man up and down. There was no obvious way he could be anything else, dressed in wool clothing with patterns and little bits of metal and beads sewn along the fringe. The man even had a coil of silver around his wrist in an obvious display of wealth. He was trying to make an impression.

Unfortunately for him, Lorab was not impressed. Merchants were a necessary evil as far as he was concerned, but that didn't mean they were entitled to his respect like they seemed to think they were.

"And who do you think you are to be approaching the Sword of Lord Dakin?" interjected one of Lorab's lieutenants. Every one of Lorab's warriors, who had been nose deep in food, drink, or breasts a moment before, were now all eyes on the merchant. The attention had its proper effect, and the weaker man took a step back from the cadre of warriors.

"I-I only need a moment of your time," the merchant said, looking to Lorab for help. "It is important."

"Make it quick," Lorab said, swallowing the rest of his cup before handing it back to Mara to go refill with a pat on her backside. Mara gave the merchant her own annoyed black look but scurried off to obey. Maybe he would give her family a goat or two for raising such a well-trained woman after all. She was definitely worth at least a goat. "I am waiting!" Lorab snapped.

"Well, sir, honored one, I wish to talk to you about Lord Dakin's most recent decree. As a man by his side, I am hoping you can explain what is going on."

"I have nothing to do with policies or Lord Dakin's business." He nodded at Rowl. "Take it up with him. I sit at his sword hand, and that is all," Lorab said. It was not the first time a merchant had tried to get access to Lord Dakin's ear through his Sword.

"But," the merchant smacked his lips exasperatedly, "he is claiming all of my merchandise, seizing all of my slaves!"

Lorab stared at him. "So what?" he finally asked, making it clear that this conversation was of no interest to him.

"So what... Well... He cannot do that!" the merchant whined. "He is not even paying a fair price for them."

"He is the Lord of the Region," one of Lorab's lieutenants interjected.

"The Lord Dakin has the right to claim what he needs as is his right as the administrator of this region," another lieutenant agreed.

"This is more than a simple tithing!" the merchant insisted, though a companion of his came up beside him and tried to pull him away. The merchant was not dissuaded.

"You do not understand! He is taking *all* of them, not just warriors for his army or a servant or two for his household. He's taking them all! No matter what their talents or abilities or value. Do you think the other merchants are going to stand for this? Do you think the temple will?!" The merchant's voice rose to an unseemly level, and Lorab began weighing the cost-benefit of just outright slaying him to be done with this conversation.

The merchant's companion pulled really hard now, drawing him away, and still the idiot yelled as he went. The antics made Lorab's warriors laugh and the village people uncomfortable, but Lorab let him go.

Lord Dakin is claiming men for warriors, Lorab thought. He knew they had taken heavy losses defending the granaries from the treacherous merchants. The sight of the damn animals set Lorab's teeth on edge now, so Lorab did not care if they were suffering from Dakin's orders. But it gave him an idea. Since he would be returning to Dakin's side without even any sign of the Lord's lost mistress, he *could* bring even more slaves for his army. Surely, such a gift would obliterate any ill feelings. Lorab had used such ploys before, hiding any failure with a larger, grander success.

"Are you sure you can handle an *impressive* man like that?" Lorab sneered as he spoke to Rowl, who was glowering at the man's disappearing back.

"Yes, but he is making it more of a chore than I like," the leader of the Wolf Warriors griped.

Mara returned with a fresh goblet of wine, offering it to him with a demure bow of her head. Lorab took it and downed half as he settled back into his seat by the fire, welcoming her back on to his lap.

"I am sorry," she said. "That should not have happened." Her eyes followed the man as he left.

"And why would you be sorry?" Lorab asked as a serving plate of meat went by, and he stabbed a decent chunk with his knife.

"That was my uncle," she admitted.

"You are a merchant's daughter then?"

"My father works for him," she admitted.

"I see." Lorab dropped her off of his lap onto the ground. She flopped on to her backside with an undignified yelp, drawing the laughter and pointing of his warriors. "So, you were sent over to open his way for me by opening your legs."

"No! Lord! No, I swear by the Goddess Flo—"

"I do not put any stock in oaths sworn to gods," he said. "Get out of my sight before I remove your sight."

"Please, please, great Sword. Do not send me away," she pleaded, shooting a look back over her shoulder at the angry older woman, still staring daggers at the both of them. Seeing the younger woman on the ground brought a cruel twisted smile of satisfaction to the older woman's face, which irritated Lorab more than he would ever admit. It reminded him of someone he would rather forget. Mara began clinging to his leg with her begging, sweet little tears appearing in her eyes. It had to all be an act, he knew, but she did make a very pretty picture like that.

"Very well," he relented, letting her back up onto his lap. He wanted to bed her anyway, and she would be more pliant now.

"Commander," called one of Lorab's warriors sitting nearby, leaning over his own newly chosen woman and shouting too loudly. "Why is Lord Dakin claiming so many slaves?"

"We," Lorab said, catching the attention of all the those around him. "We are about to embark on a great action, something nobody has ever attempted before. Not since the gods walked the earth," he said, proud at his sudden eloquence and taking it for a sign. "We are going to conqueror the known world and make Dakin, our Lord, King Over All. And we need an army to do it."

"So, what he said back at the castle was true—he is going to make us rich beyond our wildest dreams?" another warrior, who had already drunk his weight in alcohol, asked.

"Of course, he is!" Several of his warriors batted at the man, who fell back under their playful blows to a great ugly bellowing.

"What—even the Ka'in?" another voice asked, and the jibs shifted to Athorn sitting on the edge of the group, nursing his drink with a dark look in his eye. He had been staring too long into the fire, and now shifted that dark look at the laughing jeers.

Lorab stood up and cuffed the questioner hard on the ear, cutting off the laughter. "Do not be a horse's ass, Tra," he said, then jabbed a finger at Athorn. "Lord Dakin made him an Anon. Are you saying that Lord Dakin does not have the power to change a man's very nature to be one of his chosen?"

The seriousness of the question killed all the merriment around the fire. The warrior he had just cuffed looked back and forth between Lorab and Athorn, holding his sore ear, a poignant reminder that Athorn had just lost his own. "I apologize, brother," he said at last to the tracker.

The rest of the group echoed the apology, and Lorab held his hand out to Athorn. After a moment, he clasped his forearm over Lorab's, returning the warrior's handshake. Then Lorab made the sign that Dakin had shown them. Each man returned it.

"We are Dakin's chosen," Lorab said.

"We are Dakin's chosen," they agreed.

"Now, I do not know about you all, but I need to fuck," he said to much cheering, his joke returning the celebratory mood to the group. He claimed Mara's hand among the woots and whistles.

"Let us talk more in the morning," Lorab said to Rowl. The warrior's eyes were calculating. One did not become a leader of a band of warriors without having a brain cell or two. He nodded, and that was where the two men left it.

Lorab drew Mara behind him as they left the glowing circle of the fire.

"Which one is yours?" he asked Mara, indicating the ring of buildings.

"That one," she indicated, "I live with my parents."

"Works fine," he declared and moved to head that way. "Go and fetch the dancer and both of you come to that house."

"What?" Mara asked, blinking in surprise.

He pointed at the one he wanted. "Him. Bring him too, or go back to your mother, girl."

He didn't wait to see if she obeyed but turned to march in and claim the house. It was only then, when he was alone in the quiet, that he noted the ache still inside his chest. He had felt that ache ever since he had drunk Lord Dakin's divine blood, and it disturbed him when he could not ignore it. What was it that Dakin had given him? Would the ache ever stop?

Yet the answers did not come.

Maybe he could fuck the feeling away.

CHAPTER 31

ACIES WALKED THROUGH THE QUIET WORLD OF THE settlement, unafraid of the occupants. The fog he had created continued to hang in the air but stayed out over the grasses just beyond the border of the settlement.

He found very little impressive to see anyway.

Although clearly a better living situation than the slave village, it was still a series of wood and grass huts clustered together with access to livestock out their back doors. There were a few permanent stalls for merchanting and a large well for water since this place did not have direct access to Isa's river, but little else of note.

The demon had left once the mortals had all fallen asleep, mostly because he could not himself sleep, so he didn't bother. Instead, he burned a sliver of arete to sustain himself. Casually, he measured defenses and vulnerabilities in the dark. He had told Elaine the truth, that he could take the settlement easily, but without her command to do so, there was no point.

Just as dawn grayed the sky, another presence, almost like a call, caught the edge of his attention. It was sharp and so high that only those with heightened hearing would have even noticed it, judging by the small whines from a nearby dog.

Acies spun in place, searching for the source of that call. It was not quite a shock when his attention landed on the temple at the far end of the settlement. It was built much like the rest of the village buildings with wood and grasses mortared together into its structure that lasted years, not centuries. What marked it as a temple were the runes carved around the door, barely visible in the night but clear to Acies as he enhanced his darkness vision.

The call sounded again, and he hurried to the temple, Vills thumping dully against his back.

Acies's skin crawled as he stopped in the doorway of the temple. Instead of the reed doors of the slave village, this one was made of carved wood, worked by someone with much skill and care. He didn't want to touch it. Here, sacred energy felt alive and potent enough to deter common demons from entering. He could force his way past it but was loathe to lay his skin against its grain.

He didn't have to, for it swung itself open, inviting him inside with that same call.

He growled but entered the obvious trap anyway. He needed to see. He needed to know.

Within the temple was the open space most of them had, especially when they were this small. It was clear that no one had been in there for a while as the space bordered between unkempt and rundown. Rough statues lined the back wall, and he approached them each in turn, looking down on faces he barely recognized anymore. Each was an icon. The one face he picked out immediately from the line was that of Vills in boar form, the stylized bristles of his arching back reminiscent of the bristles of the once-living god.

"<See, my friend, they have not forgotten you as much as you thought,>" Acies said, laying his hand affectionately on the stone head of the icon. As he expected, the quivering energy that should have lived within the stone was gone. All that remained of the Forest Protector's power now lived in Acies's sword alone. He touched the other statues, but they too lacked the buzzing life that he would have expected of them if anyone was there. His own statue, the one when he had been a God of the Land and Harvest, had been shoved to the farthest corner of the temple. That one he did not even attempt to touch. He knew what he would feel, and he had no interest in it.

"<There was a time when my icon would have been in the center,>" Acies said out loud to Vills.

Next to Isa, Acies heard Vills say, though whether it truly was his old friend or just his memory of him, Acies wasn't sure and didn't want to know.

Bitterly, Acies turned to his once wife, her icon standing proud and strong in the very center of the line. This statue he had not yet touched. *Are you afraid to learn the answer?* Vills asked, his voice wheedling in Acies's mind.

Acies didn't answer him, continuing to stare at her face. It was a rough carving and far more fantastical with the representations of spirits and animals and people clustered around her feet, which stood on a cresting wave that represented her river. This likeness did nothing to capture the truth of Isa's face as he remembered it: her beauty, her vulnerability, her heartless cruelty.

But he needed to know.

He lifted his hand slowly as if it was weighted with chains. A shiver ran down his spine upon contact. "<What...>" he breathed as the sensation rolled up the arm and straight to his heart.

It was there. The thrum of arete. It was her. She was alive—except it felt off.

"<I...>" He hesitated and swallowed.

"<Isa,>" he breathed, her name barely forming in his throat. It was like he had swallowed a shard of glass. For long moments, he waited there, holding his breath, expecting her to appear at his calling, yet there was nothing. Not a stir in the energy to indicate that she had heard him or a swelling of that same energy that indicated that she was coming through her icon. Only the odd thrum of her arete. It made no sense.

He let his hand drop to his side just as the statue beside Isa began to glow with power. He took several steps back from it as a being stepped from it.

"<Nymphaea!>" he said, utterly shocked to see the goddess. It had been so long and to see someone he knew, even if it had been someone he had not particularly liked very much, it was a welcome sight.

The goddess stood tall and elegant, her shoulders square to him, much as her statue stood. She wore a shapeless robe of cascading, impossibly white cloth, and around her neck hung row after row of precious jade beads.

She was so stunning.

Acies almost took a step closer to her without noticing the danger. A warning growl arrested him in place as two spirit beasts, great beasts as large as wolves and as fierce as lions, stepped out from behind her. His eyes darted to them both. Her weapons bared their teeth; the rumbling continued. While made entirely of spirit, lacking bodies in the mortal world, these had been given the aspect of teeth and claws that could rend a demon's flesh quite easily. He remembered Nymphaea creating such creatures during the war. Not commenting on them, he raised his eyes to the imperious face level with his own.

Her eyes narrowed with all the haughty contempt and cold fury a goddess could muster.

"<I see it will not be a welcome greeting,>" Acies stated.

Those eyes widened a sliver, but Nymphaea schooled the rest of her face to hold its placid mask. "<Acies, the Demon Lord of War,>" she pronounced, formally calling him by name. He recognized the challenge in those words of god-speech. "<Hear me. If you go into my city, I will destroy you.>"

"<Well, that was quick,>" Acies countered. "<And which city is that, Goddess of Truth?>"

A flare of fire ignited her eyes. "<I am the patron Goddess of Icathor, demon. You will heed me.>"

Acies raised his eyebrows. "<Are you now?>"

"<And I forbid you from entering my city,>" she repeated as one of her spirit beasts renewed their growls.

He unshouldered Vills, still wrapped in his leather covering to set between his feet, maintaining eye contact with his challenger the whole time. "<I do not think you have much authority to forbid me to do anything.>" He pulled on the leather cords binding Vills. The second he cleared the leather over the pommel, Nymphaea gasped. Even in the dull light of the temple—the source seemed to be coming from Nymphaea's icon itself—the worked metal of the sword was clearly that of Vills.

"<The Forest Protector,>" Nymphaea said in an awed tone. Now her eyes were wide as the rest of the sword was revealed, her eyebrows pinching in her beautiful face.

Acies discarded the wrapping, setting Vills's edge into the worn reed mats covering the ground. He let Nymphaea take her time looking over the god-weapon, reading the threat he implied there.

"<Did you kill him?>" she finally asked. It was an expected question yet stung inside all the same.

"<How dare you diminish the Forest Protector's choice?>" he declared softly. Her eyes studied his face for a long moment, knowing the Goddess of Truth worked her aspect over him and he allowed it. "<Vills chose his final path himself. I was only honored to assist him in the role of second to the task. You know I speak the truth, Nymphaea.>"

"<Yes, but you are also one talented in hiding the lie within the truth where I cannot see it,>" she countered. Then she sniffed, having drawn a conclusion, and only by the fact that she wasn't attacking him, led him to believe that she had accepted his truth.

"<You have come seeking revenge.>" It was a statement, not a question, and it was correct. He could not deny it and so did not even try, resting his hands on Vills's crossbar, ready to bring the weapon up to guard. The beasts' hackles rose to needle points, their growls increasing from a low rumble to a louder menacing threat, punctuated by near barks. Acies didn't move or flinch as he stared down the goddess's impassive mask.

"<I had no part in your imprisonment, Demon Lord,>" she stated.

That surprised him, but he believed her. Yet he was not the only being who had learned to hide the lie within the truth. "<Did you know what was planned the day I came back from the front?>"

Her face did not move; it did not have to. The fact that the Goddess of Truth would not speak was confirmation enough.

The spirit beasts came around her, placing themselves in front of the goddess, and Acies shifted his grip, and only his grip, onto the handle of Vills. It would be a fight then. His first battle against the deities that had betrayed him.

Nymphaea gestured. He switched his sword into guard.

One of the beasts dropped to the ground before him, completely relaxed, the fur on its back lying flat and its head brought low to the ground in a submissive pose that belied its fearsome nature.

Acies arrested his momentum, the sword halfway up. The growling ceased from the other beast who stood next to its companion. Nymphaea gestured again, and though the beast on the ground could not possibly see it, his companion moved back to stand next to its mistress. Acies stared down at the beast creature, understanding what was happening.

"<I offer appeasement,>" Nymphaea declared as she rested her hand on top of the other beast's head as it pressed into her.

That disarmed Acies faster than if Vills had been flung from his hands. "<I do not understand,>" he stated.

"<This is yours,>" she gestured to the submitting beast. "<To do with as you choose.>" The implication of what she expected him to do was clear. There was only one thing a demon would do with such a gift. Acies set the tip of Vills back into the ground as he debated what to do. It was an appropriate offering, though some part of him chafed at it.

The spirit beast was merely an extension of the goddess herself. It was an offer of power, of arete. He needed it desperately. A source of arete, freely given. He knew what she expected. Even as she offered it, contempt traced every edge of her features. Closing his eyes, he let out the breath he held.

"<Is this acceptable, demon?>"

Gritting his teeth, Acies snapped his eyes open. Nymphaea flinched. With deliberate steps, he approached the creature at his feet. It did not move or cower as he seized it by the back of the neck.

He also had to give Nymphaea credit; she did not look away even as he sank his teeth in.

CHAPTER 32

ELAN LAY IN THE SEMI-DARK, STARING AT THE roughly made ceiling above. He was wedged with a small toddler under one of his arms, someone's legs over his legs, and a row of feet to his left. Yet it wasn't the close quarters that made it impossible to sleep. This sleeplessness had been going on for days now, ever since Maevra's death.

Every time he tried, he would wake up, but with no dreams or the memory of being asleep at all. He would blink from one thought to the next logical thought, but the night would have passed, and he had not rested.

At first, he told himself that his anxiety was due to fear of further bogin attacks. Yet after the severe massacre of the lesser demons, they did not bother them again, nor did any other demons in the forest. Here in the slave village, there should have been less to fear, yet still he did not truly rest.

He lifted his head to scan the room. Elaine slept against the far-most wall, a bundle underneath her night dark shawl. Beside her, the demon sat. It worried Elan that no one else in the hut seemed to sense anything from the monster sitting among them. At most, the people here had noticed his eerie black hair but said nothing about it. Elan was also convinced after several nights of watching him that the demon also never truly slept. His eyes always seemed to be open, watching everything.

Then there was Sarai. She slept by the door, taking the most dangerous spot in the room for herself. It seemed like the sun and moon had risen and fallen a hundred times since he saw her last. He could not name the feeling in his chest as he watched her sleep, her hand tucked under her chin like the small child she hadn't been in years. When he'd left to save his sister, he had not expected to see her again—that must have been it.

Elan lay his head back down, trying to push away the images of the demon eating Maevra's life. He could see it so clearly—him lying on the ground, her leaning over him holding her wrist out. The desperate way he grabbed it.

Unwinding his own arm, he tried to roll onto his side, only to freeze as he realized someone was moving in the hut. Slitting his eyes, he watched as the reedy man rose from the floor, picking his way silently to the door. Elan did not know him, not even his name. He had not been in the hut when Elan had last been there. Glancing over at Acies, the demon did not move or react to the reedy man's movements.

Maybe he *was* asleep.

Gently, the reedy man pulled aside the door flap, letting in the gray light of pre-dawn. He checked back once, scanning over the room, then slipped out, letting the door fall back into place. Elan's mind raced with questions and settled that if the reedy man was about to tell the Anon about them, this would be the time to do it.

He couldn't let that happen.

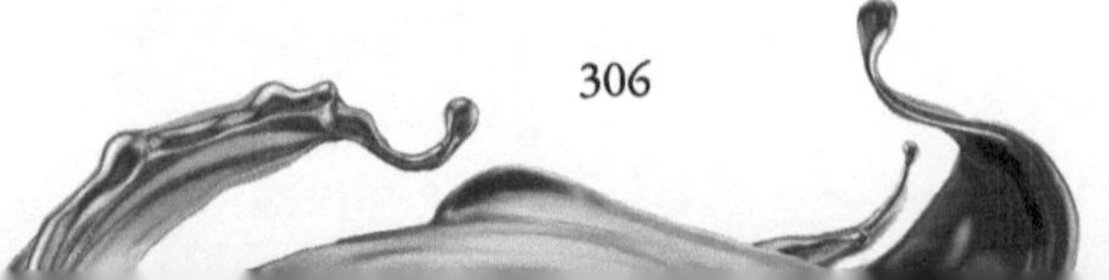

Carefully, Elan extricated himself from the pile, sliding his fur-wrapped bow out from behind his pack. Shouldering his quiver of mundane arrows, he tiptoed through to the door.

The collection of huts sat squat like toads in the grayness. No other soul was about, but after a few steps out from the hut, he saw his target moving.

Carefully, he followed, keeping just out of the reedy man's sight. To Elan's surprise, he did not turn to move toward the settlement, but waded out into the grass, facing the lighter side of the sky. There were no guards in sight, no other people, just a sea of grass ringed by the trees of the forest. When the reedy man stopped, Elan squatted low. The would-be traitor stared out at the gray horizon turning orange as it peeked over the top of the far away trees.

Then the reedy man grasped the hem of his shirt, pulling it up over his head. Against the backdrop of growing warm colors, Elan could see hair slipping down the too skinny back and over the man's shoulders, dark and thick. Then Elan blinked as he realized it was not hair, but feathers.

Long brown feathers, like a hawk, covered his spine and arms, ending at the nape of his neck. He stretched his long arms out to either side of his body, saluting with his whole self just as the disc that was the sun crested over the trees. It was a glorious sight as the body arched back, a single figure against the greatness of the light of the new day.

Then the reedy man bowed side to side, his arms finding new shapes and gestures. He split his legs into a broader stance, and he slapped his chest. Faintly, Elan could hear him sing a guttural chant.

Instinctually, Elan understood that the chant was meant to be shouted, declared loudly to the new day, but that the reedy man was attempting to not be heard by the rest of the village or the settlement. The ceremony ended when the sun was half above the treetops. The reedy man stood in his last pose, fully upright with his arms bent at the elbows and his palms to the sky. Slowly, he let those hands drop to his sides as he continued to stare toward the sun. The lightness of his body melted away as he came back to himself and the weight of reality that bowed his shoulders.

At last, he turned and froze when he spied Elan watching him barely two lengths away. The two men measured each other long enough for the sun to finish clearing the trees.

"You are a Punite," Elan said at last in Anon, since it would be the common language between their peoples.

The reedy man's guard dropped as he ran a hand over his bald pate. "Aye. Our masters require that I pluck out my own feathers to look more like them." He bent down to pick up his shirt to cover the feathers on his back and arms. "Only females are allowed to keep their feathers. It is seen as exotic."

"For us, it is the ears," Elan said touching his own.

"I have seen Ka'in dock their ears in order to fit in or make their masters comfortable," the Punite agreed, crossing to Elan.

The Ka'in Prince offered a gesture of Isa to the Punite. "I am Prince Elan of the Ka'in."

"Ellam Menor ... of the Punite... I guess," he replied, cracking an almost shy smile. "Very similar."

Elan shrugged a single shoulder. "I am used to it; my sister's name is Elaine."

"The strange woman with the night-colored hair? That is your sister?"

Elan nodded. "Aye, we are twins."

"You do not look it," Ellam said with almost impolite directness.

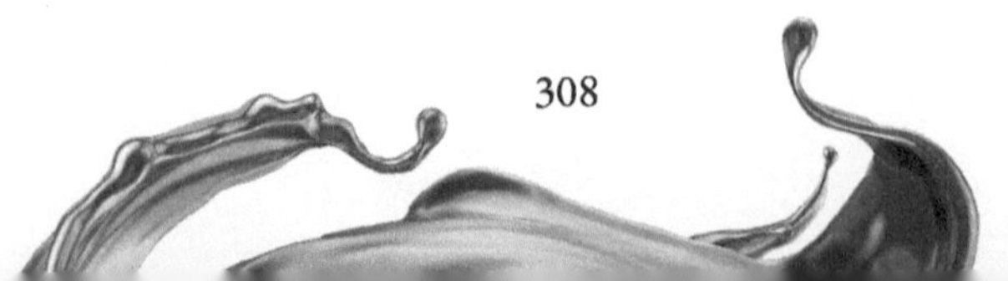

There were several unwise things Elan wanted to say to that, but he couldn't really argue the point. "We never have, but she is still my other half."

"Like the day and the night," Ellam said more poetically. He moved toward the village. "We must return. Others will be stirring soon."

He was right. Even as they approached the first huts of the village, people were rising, leaving the huts to go do their necessary business in the grass. Others walked toward the settlement—except shouts could be heard as Anon warriors stopped those slaves from leaving the village.

"What is going on?" Elan asked, but Ellam simply shook his head.

"I do not know. Something is wrong," he answered. More Anon warriors filed into the village, going to the various huts to throw open the flaps, ordering everyone inside out with short, sharp barks. "We must hurry."

Walking as fast as he dared, Ellam directed his feet to Sarai's hut. Sarai already stood before it, watching with a stiff blank face at what was happening. She made no sign to lift the reed mat or move from her spot.

One of the warriors walked directly up to her, leaning into her face as he shouted in Anon. "Turn out the hut, Ka'in bitch!"

"This is the hut of the sick and—"

"I do not care if it is the hut of ale and open women. Everybody out now!" He seized Sarai's arm to bodily shove her out of the way, but she continued to resist him.

"There is disease within! Do want to catch it and have your dick fall off?" she shouted. Though crude, her choice of words was effective, and the warrior let her go, even backing away a step. By that time, Ellam and Elan had arrived at her side. Elan reached out to support Sarai back onto her feet, but something odd was happening with Ellam. He curled over before the warrior and then with a great shudder of his body, vomited at the man's feet. The warrior uttered a high-pitched squeal and backed even farther away.

"Ellam!" Sarai cried, "What are you doing out here!? Get inside quickly before you spread it to the whole village!" She went to Ellam then, ushering him back inside, just as a small child bolted terrified into the hut ahead of them.

"Hey! Get that child!" another warrior shouted but was stopped by the arm of the other warrior.

"No! Stay away. There is pestilence inside!" the warrior cried, utterly terrified.

The second warrior was not so easily dissuaded. "You are an idiot. They would not allow pestilence inside the slave village; you would lose all of them, and it would spread to the settlement. Let alone let their children near it!" He threw off the first warrior's arm, who continued to stand there unsure and worried.

This time Elan took up the position in front of the door, his bow held in front of him as if it were a staff.

"Get your ass out of my way, you honorless eunuch, or I will kill you right now," the warrior spat in Elan's face.

Elan responded by slamming the end of the bow into the warrior's crotch. The man's eyes bugged out, and all the breath left him as his hands instinctively went to cover the vulnerable area. Elan then swung the other end of the bow up and across his opponent's face. The bow was too light to really do much damage, but it was enough to offset the man's balance, sending him tumbling to the ground.

The second warrior leapt in then, drawing his bronze sword. It glinted golden in the new sunlight, momentarily blinding Elan. He jerked away but still brought the bow up against the bronze sword, sweeping it. Again, the bow was too light to take a direct hit, even if it was a weapon of the gods. Elan feared that too much pressure would break the precious thing.

What he didn't expect was the warrior to spin around as his strike was parried and to throw a hit across Elan's face. It caught him in the ear. Lightning pain shot down his right side and, for a moment he couldn't afford, blacked out his vision. The warrior had targeted the strike purposefully.

Another hit came from the pommel of the sword slamming down on Elan's nose. It broke with another sharp star of pain. Elan fell back hard against the side of the mud and reed hut, a good chunk tearing away with his body weight. The children inside the hut screamed ear-splitting pitches. The prince struggled to get up, to force his hands to let go of his nose and fight. A swift kick to his middle knocked the wind out of him. He dropped to the ground on his back.

The warrior smirked down at the fallen Ka'in with all the knowledge his opponent was beaten. Instead of killing him, the warrior redirected his sword to point straight at Elan's face. Then he bent down and seized an ankle. He dragged Elan away from Sarai's hut.

By that point, the other warrior with the crushed nuts stood up to limp as Elan went by. When they stopped and Elan tried to take his ankle back, he was crushed by the weight of the first warrior landing on his chest. He tried to thrash the man off of him, but two more grabbed his arms and legs, pinning him down.

"Hold him!" the warrior shouted. A fourth seized his head and slammed it painfully to the side. Something creaked in Elan's neck.

"Taking the ears?" the warrior holding his head said.

The warrior with the sword only laughed as he seized the tip and sliced.

Elan screamed.

CHAPTER 33

T HE SOUND OF ANGRY SHOUTS AND DISTRESSED calls jolted Elaine awake, every nerve on alert. Others in the hut were stirring, staring with alarm at each other, then back to Elaine.

She spied Acies standing by the door, his bound-up sword propped against his shoulder. He lifted the reed door the tiniest bit to peek out. "There is something going on outside. We must go," he said in Ka'in with hushed urgency.

"<What is happening?>" Sarai asked in Anon, setting aside a child whose hair she had been braiding so she could stand herself.

"There are warriors in the village. They are herding people out of the huts. Something has gone terribly wrong," Acies said, still in Ka'in, since he hadn't learned much Anon yet. Someone hissed at him to mind his words.

Elaine rose, shouldering the pack she had been using to pillow her head. It was significantly lighter for lack of the venison meat. "<Where is> Elan?" she asked, scanning the faces for her brother.

"<I do not know. He may have gone out,>" Sarai responded, scanning with her. "I will go out to find him, but you must leave now. If they find you in here..."

"<But I have to find my brother,>" Elaine protested.

"They're coming," Acies said calmly, still using Ka'in despite the warnings. He grabbed Elaine's arm. "We have to go now."

She wanted to argue, but it was all happening too quickly. Acies ducked out of the hut, pulling Elaine with him, Sarai right behind. They circled around to the back, away from the oncoming warriors, while Sarai took up a position before her own door.

On the opposite side, they encountered the youth Tuan, who gestured for them to follow him. He led them past the well where a couple of people were drawing water.

"<Their hair!>" one woman breathed practically choking on her Anon words, her eyes bulging out as she stared unabashedly at Elaine and Acies.

"<Get out of here, now! Before the warriors find you,>" Tuan ordered.

The other two people glanced at each other, then seized their already filled waterskins and rushed away.

"<Down here, quickly!>" Tuan said, dropping one of the roped buckets down to splash below. Acies moved first, grasping the rope with one hand.

"<But... how...>" Elaine tried to ask, but more shouts came from the village.

Acies whipped the strap holding his sword around himself to tuck it between his back and his pack. Then he resolutely swung himself over the edge of the well before sliding down into the darkness. The rope creaked scarily from his weight but held until a splash echoed up from deep below.

Elaine swallowed.

She looked to Tuan who nodded at the well. "I will find your brother. I will hide him. May the waters of Isa protect you," the youth prayed, pushing at Elaine's back, then he turned and ran, disappearing from sight.

Lacking any other options, Elaine seized the rope like Acies had done. The rope felt wet in her hands as she gripped it and awkwardly threw a leg over the side of the rough stones. She swung in and lost her grip. Crying out before she could stop herself, she fell forever, only to hit the water too soon. Sinking under, the freezing cold shocked Elaine's system, and she involuntarily inhaled.

I'm going to drown! she thought. Darkness swallowed all around her, and she kicked and thrashed against it. Miraculously, she broke through to the surface. Coughing out as much water as she gasped in air, she tread in utter darkness.

"Acies!" she croaked sorely.

"I am here," he responded somewhere in front of her, and then his hand touched her, pulling her to him. She slipped her arms around his neck, and he tread for both of them. They remained like that, listening. Above them was the single eye of sky too far away, and the fainter echoes of shouts.

"Can you hear what they are saying?" Elaine asked, her voice echoing back the slightest whisper.

"Barely," Acies admitted. "I can hear farther than most mortals, but even that is too distorted for me." Then he went still. "Someone is screaming in pain."

She squeezed him a little tighter. "My legs are going numb," she said. "We are going to f-freeze in this water." Then she remembered. With numbed fingers, she grasped at the amulet around her neck. "Flicker? Are you there?"

The amulet grew warm under her hand, a near burning sensation against her cold skin. The burning sensation slipped through her like liquid fire, warming her down to her toes before settling in her heart. Light accompanied that fire, throwing Acies's wet face into warm relief. Then the amulet was gone, dissipating from her hand, followed by a small splash. Elaine could see a lighted figure under the shimmery surface. Flicker burst out of the water, settling on the top like a duck, wing-like arms tucked against its side.

"I am here, mistress!" Flicker said joyfully before shivering to shake off the water from the warm glowing feathers. Once that was complete, it looked around at the rough carved walls all around them. "Where are we?"

"We had to jump down the well," Elaine said, pitching her voice down, realizing it echoed. "There are Anon warriors above."

Flicker stared up the well, eyes wide. "Oh, dear."

Now that they had light, Elaine could see they floated in a round chamber that narrowed into the shaft leading to the surface. The chamber was wide enough for a village meeting. Flicker swam around, circling the couple in the water as they surveyed the space. "Oh, good, there is a rope," it said, tugging on it.

It hit Elaine that she would have a difficult time climbing out, and that was if they didn't freeze first.

"Oh, look at this," Flicker said suddenly.

Together, Acies and Elaine tread in a circle to follow where the gelic called from. Flicker glanced back at them over its shoulder, then gestured at the wall.

"It is the sign of Isa," Flicker said, jumping from the water and landing on what appeared to be a stone ledge.

"A ledge!" Elaine cried, relieved.

Acies grabbed Elaine's hands, guiding her around so that she clung to his shoulder. It was a struggle to even do that much as the cold leeched her strength. She almost lost her grip when he struck out, swimming them both to safety.

Once they got there, Elaine transferred herself to the ledge, hanging on for dear life. Her pack weighed her down, but she managed to toss it up, and it flopped like an enormous wet fish. Water spilled out of it, backwashing over her face, making her sputter. Then kicking her legs behind her instead of down as Maevra had taught her, she propelled herself out with Acies setting a hand against her numbed backside to help.

She wanted to flop exhausted on the stone, but she willed herself to pivot.

"Gimme your pack," she gasped and helped him struggle out of his straps. He tried to hoist himself out of the water, but to her shock, he failed and dropped back, his head disappearing under the water.

"Acies!" she cried. When his head bobbed back up, she seized the cloth over his shoulders.

He hung there, panting hard for a moment, seeming weaker than she had ever seen him.

"Come on," she insisted, tugging on him to urge him up.

"I... can't..." he gasped.

"But I can't lift you up by myself," she pleaded, but then a wink of light caught her eye. The pommel of Acies's new sword had escaped its wrapping. Intuitively, she grabbed it. "Come on. Get out of the water!" she ordered, trying to pull the sword off him to lighten the weight. Instead, the sword still tied around his chest helped leverage Acies, dragging him up enough for him to roll up and onto his side.

"Acies. Are you all ... right?" Elaine asked, crawling on her hands and knees to where his head lay. Long locks of his black hair covered his otherwise pale face, and she slid a finger along his cheek to wipe it back from his mouth and nose. "Acies."

"I... fine... rest ... a moment," he breathed.

"A-a-acies, what is wrong w-w-with you?" she asked, her teeth chattering in the cold.

He didn't respond, laying there, pale and still.

"I th-thought you w-were a p-p-powerful d-d-demon?" Elaine asked. Frightened, she shook him, then pressed her ear against his chest. Faintly, she heard a small but steady thumping. He *was* alive.

Elaine's own body shivered violently, fighting to warm itself. She clutched at her sopping tunic as she tried to wring some of the water without taking it off.

"What is wrong, mistress?" Flicker asked, waddling over to look down at Acies.

"Why is he not ... h-h-healing h-h-himself?" Elaine asked, wishing she could stop the chattering. "U-u-use his d-d-demon p-powers?"

"Not *all* demons have *all* abilities," Flicker said, reaching out two feathered fingers to open one of Acies's eyes. The demon twitched his head away, but then went still again. "He is the demon of war. His powers are geared toward aspects of war. He can heal wounds but hypothermia? Raising his body temperature must be out of his purview." Flicker gave Acies a little kick with a webbed foot.

Elaine did not know what hypothermia was, but she could take a guess she would die of it too and soon.

"I gota-ta-ta get w-w-warm," she said out loud,

"Ah!" Flicker cried. "Then ... this way, mistress."

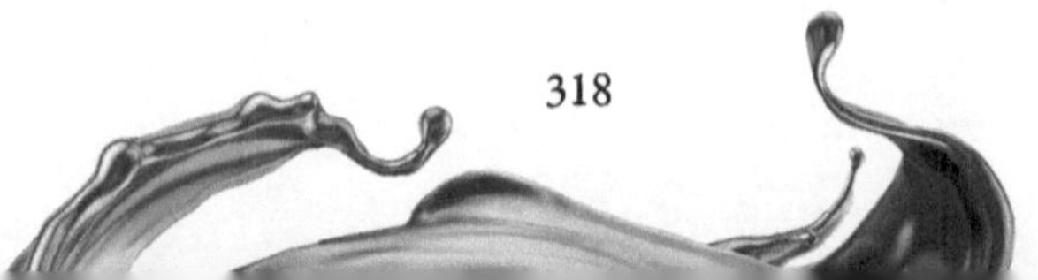

318

Flicker waddled back to the wall to gaze up at the rough carved lines of the sign of Isa.

"Wh-hy w-would there be a s-s-symbol of Isa d-d-down here?" Elaine asked, rubbing hard at her arms.

"I could warm you mistress, but..." Flicker resettled its feathers a second time. "Can you bless me, mistress?"

"W-what?"

Flicker wiggled its little bottom agitatedly. "I am Flicker, mistress. When I was Flame, I could simply burn to warm you, but now ... it is out of my purview, mistress, unless you help me?"

"What..." Elaine's teeth chattered hard, and she had to wait a moment to get control of her mouth again. "W-what do you ... need?"

Gently, Flicker took one of Elaine's hands and brought it to the top of its head. "This is a shrine of Isa, my mistress. Touch the symbol and bless me with the aspect you want me to have."

It sounded absurd, but Elaine swallowed, her throat the only place about her that was dry. "I-I-I b-b-bless y-you, Fl-flicker. W-w-warm."

Flicker and the symbol glowed. Warmth, blessed warmth, flooded into Elaine from Flicker. It was gentle, easing away the involuntary contractions of her muscles. Breathing became easier. Her skin and clothes steamed, the water rising away even as it softly kissed her skin. Elaine pulled her hand from the symbol on the wall, which continued to glow without her touch. Turning back to Acies, she laid her hand on the back of his cold outstretched one.

Nothing happened.

Then Flicker brushed some feathers over the Demon Lord. "Acies," Elaine whispered, "I bless you."

She felt the warmth pass from her into him through Flicker, a sweeping rush of warm water, but that was fine. There was an infinite river within her when she knew how to reach it. Flicker continued to glow, brighter and brighter as the power within the shrine filled all three beings with warmth and safety.

"What is happening?" Elaine asked as her eyesight whited out and a vision replaced it.

A young man comes into view. His hair is bright, a golden brown that waves around his head and dances around his ears. He carries a satchel over a shoulder and whistles a merry tune. He approaches a village and waves a greeting. The people of the village rush out to meet him. They surround him quickly, looking distressed. He pulls an amulet from inside his shirt to show to the people. It is the sign of Isa.

"Help us, great Scion," they cry in a strangely accented version of Ka'in. "We have no water to drink, and our animals and elderly are dying."

The group leads him quickly to the well inside the village. It too is marked with the same sign of Isa.

The people will not approach the well. The young man's face becomes stern, and he approaches alone. Touching the symbol, there is another flash of light.

A vision within a vision.

He sees the village and the Goddess Isa.

She creates the well, bringing forth her waters for the villagers to use.

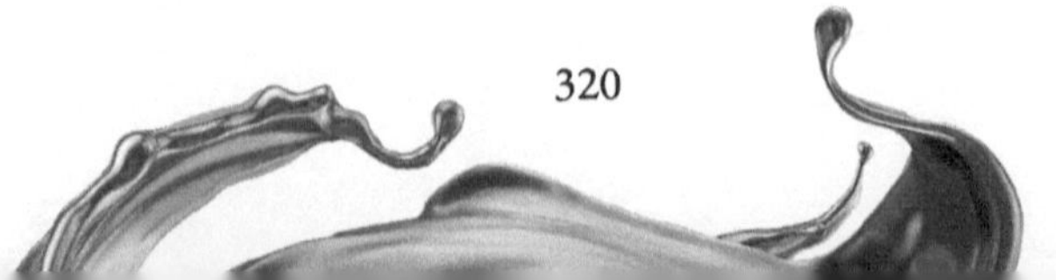

They build a shrine.

*"This will protect the water from disappearing under this sun,"
the goddess explains, speaking a language Elaine and the young
man do not recognize but understand all the same. Isa gestures to
her construction. "Keep the well safe and well-maintained, and it
will serve you abundantly for you children and your children's
children."*

*Isa then places a spirit to watch over the well and shows the
people how to honor the spirit, and the well flows abundantly.*

*The young Ka'in man, the Scion, wakes from the vision, then looks
inside the well.*

"<But you have plenty of water,>" he says.

*The people shake their heads. "<We are terrified to go near the
well, for it is now inhabited by a demon. It has already drowned
two of our beloved children.>"*

*"<Have you not done as the Goddess Isa instructed and kept
faith with the spirit of the well?>" the Scion asks.*

The people insist that they have.

The Scion nods at that and begins to unpack his bag.

He tells the people to go back to their homes, and they obey.

*He lays out ritual gear and begins to perform a ceremony
at the well.*

Once more, alone now, he approaches the well.

*He performs the ceremony. Elaine recognizes it or a version
like it. It brings him into the realm of the spirits.*

*The spirit of the well is revealed to be sitting on the edge of the
well. It looks like Flicker, but with a narrower bill that is more like
a beak and a crest of green feathers with a ring of white around its
neck. The Scion, and Elaine, can also clearly see darkness hovering
around the spirit, leaving a tang of acid in the air.*

"Greetings, Scion of Isa," the spirit says in the accented Ka'in.

"Greetings, Spirit of the Well of Isa," Mory responds. "I am called Mory."

"What may I do for you, esteemed one?" the spirit asks.

"Why have the people come to fear you and to fear coming to the Well of Isa?" Mory asks directly.

The spirit looks down its long nose at Mory. "The people have forgotten the ways of Isa. They come to pray, but their hearts are not in it, and their prayers taste of ash."

"You were charged to guard the well so that the people would not come to harm, yet it is said two children have drowned in your waters?" Mory challenges. "Why would the people owe you prayers and honor you if you have failed to serve them so?"

"I am the spirit of the well, appointed by the great Isa herself!" declares the spirit proudly. "Those two children did not pray properly at my well when they drew the water. I took what was owed me."

Mory's heart seizes as he hears the demon's words, for what else could sit there now but a demon. "You have condemned yourself by your own admission," Mory says.

"You cannot judge me, Mortal. You are not Isa Kai," the demon of the well spits. There is a rumbling sound, and water rises up from the well. It billows out like a living hand and seizes Mory, pulling him down to drown him in the well.

But Mory is a Scion of Isa and clever besides.

He battles the demon in the water, moving like a fish, breathing as if it is air.

The demon does not expect it and fights back ferociously.

Mory is thrown up onto a ledge where he crawls toward the wall, his arm injured and bleeding. He crawls to the wall, and with his silver blood, he etches the symbol of Isa on the wall. It glows brightly, searing itself into the living rock.

The demon raises the water to drown the Scion, but the symbol of Isa freezes it. The symbol purifies the water.

Mory forces the errant creature to submit by seizing it by the neck. Then he commands the water to bring him back out of the well, setting both demon and man once more on the earth.

"But how is this possible? You are merely a mortal!" the demon cries.

"I am the Scion of Isa, whom you have sworn to serve," Mory declares. "As it is with Isa, so it is with me."

Mory begins to sing; it is the same song Elaine sang to the corrupted temple guardians. The demon squirms and fights, but then it breaks apart into shards of light, floating away on the wind.

"<May you be received by the God Beyond,>" Mory says softly, speaking the godspeech reverently.

Then Mory turns to Elaine. He looks her directly in the eyes and he bows his head to her in acknowledgement. She does the same.

The Scion in the past returns to the well. Days pass as he rebuilds the shrine, this time honoring the two children who were lost and setting signs around the well so a demon can never inhabit it again. "As long as you maintain and honor this shrine, the waters will continue to be safe and bountiful for your people," Mory tells them, and the vision fades.

Then all is light.

CHAPTER 34

Elan could barely move. Once the warriors had finished with him, they had left him on the ground, laughing. Elan clutched at his ears, the warm, stinging blood gushing from them through his fingers.

They had docked his ears.

They had *docked* his ears.

Oh, Goddess, they have DOCKED my ears!

It was the only thing he could think, over and over again as he thrashed his head, as if that denial could have any sort of effect.

"Hush. Be still." Sarai's voice cut through the rising, panicked mantra in his head, the Anon words slicing through as sharply as their blades. She peeled back his fingers, pressing a cloth against his throbbing pain.

"Give me another one!" she hissed. There were people standing around him, a wall of the Ka'in and others, creating a sort of body shield. Many were looking down on him with pity in their eyes.

He wanted to scream at them; he wanted to kill them for pitying him.

He wanted to die.

"Hush, that is enough. Hold still!" Sarai ordered.

He obeyed her. He closed his eyes against the tears flooding his eyes, wishing it was enough to hide his humiliation. More cloth wrapped around his head, binding the pads firmly against his head.

"Get him on his feet!" a sharp voice shouted.

"Come on. Help me," Sarai said, and many hands were on him, lifting him up.

Elan wavered, sure he would pass out and fall to the ground again, but those around him would not allow it. He realized then that one of his eyes was swelling, obscuring his sight on the right side.

When had he gotten punched?

"What is this, Ka'in?!" a rough voice demanded. Elan looked up at the warrior, unable to determine if it was one of the ear-dockers. Then he dropped his eyes to his bow. The rawhide had been stripped off, exposing the strange spider lattice of the bow's body to the bright day sun.

"It is mine—" He started to say, and the warrior cuffed him. His ear screamed.

"What is it?"

"I-I do not know. I just found it. I-I use it as a bow," Elan admitted, hanging his head in defeat.

"A bow," the warrior sniffed derisively. He switched his attention back to the weapon, walking away as he assessed its possibilities.

Sarai's arm came around his waist. "Just hold on to me," she said in Anon, not daring to risk being caught speaking Ka'in.

"Where—" He swallowed, his tongue feeling swollen in his mouth. "My sister...?"

"They have gotten away. I saw to it," Sarai whispered harshly, her eyes scanning the situation. "The danger is present here."

"But my sister, she can... She can help ... stop this..." Elan tried to say, but now he did not know how to explain, but still... She could order it. She could tell her demon to murder these warriors. "Elaine will save us," he said with conviction.

More commotion came from across the space. The warriors were straightening everyone up into lines while two others were dividing the group.

"They are taking the healthy men," one woman commented right behind Elan.

"Some of the women too," another noted.

They were right. Healthy, working men and women were being pulled into a group on the other side of the village, families being separated, and any protestations met with violence.

"What do you think you are doing?!" a voice boomed when the warriors were half a dozen people away from Elan and Sarai. All turned to face an Anon merchant, his clothing and the coils of silver around his wrists declaring his status.

"That is Culum," Sarai whispered. "He is one of the more powerful slave merchants."

"What is going on?" the person behind Elan squeaked.

"These are my slaves. Who do you think you are?" Culum demanded as he faced down the warriors, his fists planted on his hips as hard as his feet planted on the ground. The warriors looked to each other, then a large one of their number broke away from where he had been standing next to a distressed scribe making notes on clay tablets.

"Lorab," Elan breathed, squinting hard with his one good eye to be sure.

"You know that Anon?" Sarai asked.

Elan nodded. "He is known as the Sword. He is one of Lord Dakin's most trusted warriors. His champion. What is he doing here?"

Lorab growled as he approached the merchant. It was the same man who had confronted him the night before.

"I have told you—" Lorab started to say, but then the merchant gestured in the air. Several more warriors, not Lorab's own people, these were all from the settlement, moved up behind him, brandishing weapons.

"Do you really think you can take our property without paying for it?" The merchant smirked with satisfaction as he received a stone-tipped spear from one of the men. Lorab measured the wicked looking weapon, respecting its danger. Even if he was armed with bronze, the reach on the weapon was enough of a threat. Still, he could not back down at this point. In doing so, they would never regain this ground—mostly because Dakin would not excuse a second failure.

"We are here under the authority of Lord Dakin."

The merchant spat on the ground at Lorab's feet. "Lord Dakin is not here, and if he were, I would say the same thing to him. He may believe he is the Lord of this area, but we are the masters of these people. If he wishes to take them, he will have to go over my dead body." The merchant took a stance with his weapon extended. The rest followed suit, roaring with pride at their show of force.

The back of Lorab's neck tingled. He felt it every time he prepared to fight. The smell of sweat. The tang of blood in the air. He met the eyes of the merchant, whose expression melted from smirky triumph to somber realization that his show of force would not back Lorab down like he had hoped. Lorab grinned, then roared.

His feet moved before he thought; the action of his sword arm engaged as he stepped in to attack. The merchant's eyes only had time to grow wide as Lorab closed the distance faster than any man ever had. He pushed past the spear. The point glanced away at his bronze plate. His bronze sword hacked into the merchant's neck, stopping when it hit the bone of the spinal column. He pulled it through and free. Blood gushed, pumped out by the dying man's own heart. Movement flurried around Lorab as his warriors engaged the others. He stared into the dying man's eyes as they desperately pleaded, confused as to what went wrong.

A hunger burned inside Lorab. The sight of the blood brought the roaring unease he had felt in his heart to full fury.

He *knew* what he desired.

The shock of it did not blunt the ache in the slightest. He brought the dying man closer. The idiot creature tried to protest but lacked the breath or vocal cords to do it. The blood washed into Lorab's mouth, and he groaned with ecstatic pleasure. His groin stiffened as he sucked it in. He tasted blood for sure, cloying and metallic, but it wasn't the blood he craved. It was the sweet life within it. A spark of power that transferred from the man into himself and eased the pain in chest.

Lorab dropped the body and raised his face to the sky. Blood dripped down his chin, covering the front of his chest, but he did not care. He had never felt so alive before. So strong.

He savored it.

"Lord Dakin is a god indeed," he said out loud, letting the now truly dead body drop to the dust.

Around him, his warriors had followed suit, killing the warriors of the settlement who had dared to oppose them. A few had made the same discovery he did, looking at him with blood down their chins and a glow in their eyes. Athorn's eyes were the most glorious, like a burning landscape.

He turned back to the terrified slaves, all staring at him like petrified deer.

"We march to Icathor. Any who try to escape will meet the same fate."

Oh, Lord Dakin would be very pleased indeed, Lorab thought.

Then the sky split open. A light, brighter than the sun erupted from somewhere in the slave village, cutting a beam into the sky.

"What is it?" one of Lorab's warriors cried out.

Lorab could not say, shaking his head as he stepped back away from it. All he felt was pure terror at the sight of it, going all the way to his bones.

Dakin stared out from the balcony of his apartments at the beam of light cutting into the sky.

"Razal!" he cried, staring at the beam, terror cutting through the Lord God Dakin. What was this phenomenon? A strange wind accompanied the light, whipping back Dakin's hair like the wind of a storm. "Bring me my priest now!"

The slap of Razal's feet could not come soon enough.

"My Lord," Razal called as he came to Dakin's side.

"What is that?!" Dakin screamed, pointing at the beam like a terrified child.

Razal stepped forward, pressing himself against the waist-high wall. "It is... It might be..." he said, fumbling for words.

"What!?" Dakin shouted, grabbing Razal's shoulder and crushing it. The old man cried out in pain, but Dakin did not let go. "Tell me, priest!"

"It is a god sign," Razal cried. Dakin let him go.

Razal cupped his other hand around his wounded arm.

"What god?" Dakin demanded, returning his attention to the beam, already fading from his sight. "What god? Damn you."

"I cannot tell, my Lord. I cannot," Razal said shaking his head back and forth. Then his eyes went wide. "Could it be..."

"Isa," Dakin growled, certain as he had never been certain before.

"We do not know, my Lord. It could be... Nymphaea!" Razal declared, but he sounded like he grasped at straws. "She is the patron Goddess of *your* Icathor, is she not? Or... or... possibly Vills, the Forest Protector..."

"It is Isa. Come to challenge me. To challenge my power," Dakin quavered.

Razal licked his lips. "It is a salutation, my Lord!"

Dakin looked down at his priest. Over the last week the illness in Razal's features had only worsened, turning his sallow skin into something waxy and yellowed as animal fat, with big bruises that should have been his eyes. The skeletal hands reached out to him, but Dakin flinched away. It disgusted the new god to look at him.

Razal was not deterred by Dakin's godly ire. "They are honoring you, my Lord. They are declaring you one of them and wish to make it known to the world."

Dakin blinked dumbly, then reconsidered the beam before him. "Is that so?"

"Of course, my Lord," Razal insisted, bobbing his head. "I must go and make sure that such an important sign is explained to the people. So that they may praise you correctly."

Dakin nodded and dismissed Razal with a wave of his hand. The beam had decayed to a thin string, barely visible now against the sky. Despite his priest's words, Dakin did not feel truly settled.

"Barus! Where is Barus?! Where is my shield?"

"Barus, please. You must help me." Amira wept at the Shield's feet.

The Shield had thought he was safe from intrusion, hiding away in the planning room, located to the side of Dakin's receiving room. He had spent many pleasant hours there, sitting at the large wooden table with its carved map in the surface. He had been preparing his presentation for the meeting he would be having with Razal later that day and had not expected Amira's unwelcome intrusion.

"You need to leave," he snarled at her, seizing her hand to try and dislodge her grip on his pant leg.

"Please, Barus, please. You are my only hope," she continued, seizing his arm with her other hand.

"You brought this upon yourself," he growled. "You would have let your brother slaughter me."

Flashes of the warriors he had called brothers lying dead from Elio's attack ripped through his mind. Even if Amira were to spread her legs for him right there and then, it would do nothing to erase those images.

True, there was once a time when Barus had admired her. The week as Dakin's concubine had not been kind to the merchant's daughter. Her beautiful face and body were a patchwork of bruises. She seemed weaker and more frail as if some force had drained the very life out of her, leaving her a walking, talking corpse. Her once lustrous gold hair now hung in its dressing that should have looked fashionable and beautiful, but again seemed only fit for a corpse late to be burned and buried.

"You did *nothing* to help me," he said coldly, shoving hard to fling her weakly back to the floor.

"There was nothing I could do to stop him!" she insisted.

"That is horse shit, and you know it." He yanked his leg away from her clutching claws as he stepped over her. "You will leave me be, Amira, and go back to your rooms. You are Dakin's concubine now, and I have work to do." He meant it as a dismissal, but Amira scurried to block the door.

"You *have* seen it, have you not? And you are closing your eyes to it," she accused, her eyes fiercely staring at him, the only part of her that seemed remotely alive and like the woman she used to be. "This is not just about the merchants and Dakin or even his great campaign—"

Barus seized her arm and shoved her to the side.

She did not give up. "He has changed, Barus!" The note of desperation in that cry *did* stop him as he opened the door, though he would never admit to himself why.

"You have to believe me," she continued. "We were friends once."

"Were we, Amira? And how much did that friendship matter the minute Dakin left the city?" He let the door shut, not wishing the words he was about to say to echo into the receiving room with its powerful acoustics. "You are a schemer, Amira. Far cleverer than your brother, and you had plans for *him* too, did you not? You had convinced your father and uncle to leave their business to you while keeping your brother the face of it, but you were only doing that until you could find a pliable enough husband to then seize it all for yourself."

"That husband could have been you," she said.

He sneered. "You only say that now. Before, I was not pliable enough. I am not stupid, Amira."

"And I trusted you with that secret," she said. "I am the one that told you of what I planned. I have always been honest with you."

She stood up from where he had knocked her down, affecting the ghost of the grace she used to have. "I have kept your secret, and you have kept mine. Please, we can still be friends, and you need my friendship more than ever."

"I do not think so." Barus turned, not wanting to hear any more. "Every word out of your mouth is poison, and..."

"He is eating people!" Amira shouted, then she pitched her voice down with terrified urgency. "He is a *demon*. I have seen it with my own eyes. Why would I make something like that up? *You* saw it. You saw it too, the night he killed my brother. His face and body covered in blood."

"Blood splatter," Barus tried to dismiss.

"His mouth was filled with blood. He tasted of..." She gestured with her hands over her own chin, her eyes haunted as if she watched it all over again before her.

Barus swallowed the lump in his throat.

"You know I am right. He is not a god. He is a demon. The things he has done to me..." Her face crumpled, and she wrapped her arms around herself as if physically holding herself together. "I do not need much. Just help me get out of here. Please. I will go away."

That pierced his anger the way her other pleading hadn't. "Where would you go?" he asked softly.

Amira's face brightened with hope. "To the south. I would go to my family at the King's city."

"And what could you possibly give me that would make it worth risking my position and trust of Lord Dakin?"

"W-whatever you want," she said, unsure, her hope standing on shaky ground.

He narrowed his eyes. "You have nothing to offer me, and you know it. Dakin has seized everything you once claimed as yours."

Her hands hesitated then slid up her arms to grasp at the straps of her shift on her shoulders.

"You do not even have yourself to bargain with. I would not touch you with the end of my sword," he said, stopping those hands from going any farther. The last thing he needed was to be accused of dipping into his master's concubine.

"Then come with me!" she said. "Come with me to the south and tell the King what is happening here. He will reward you. My family will back you up. You can return with an army and stop this. You will be a hero!"

Her eyes flashed feverish as she continued to ramble about the glory Barus would wash himself in, equal to the Scions of the Deities Above and Below.

"Barus! Lord Barus! Has anyone seen Lord Barus?" a desperate voice echoed out from the receiving room. Quickly, Barus slapped his hand over Amira's mouth. Her eyes were wide with terror over the meat of his hand. He shoved her to the lee side of the door, and it opened. The shouting slave poked his head in, and Barus stepped up to block him from coming farther into his already violated sanctuary.

"Lord Barus, thank the gods. Lord Dakin commands you attend him right away," he reported.

"Where is he?" Barus asked, pushing the slave out the door so he could follow and shut it behind him.

"Up in his chambers, Lord," the slave answered, then scurried away, not checking to see if Barus followed him.

When the slave was out of sight, Barus leaned back to speak through the door. "I will not help you Amira, and I will forget about this incident this once. Do not test me again."

He did not wait for a response. He did not have time to deal with lesser mortals.

CHAPTER 35

ACIES AWOKE LYING ON HIS BACK STARING UP AT A warm darkness. They seemed to be in some sort of cave, dry and safe. A soft glow came from nearby, but it didn't flicker like a fire.

Flicker.

Raising his head, Acies saw the little gelic tucked up into itself, ducky head snug under a winged arm. Flicker glowed a soft orange-yellow down each filament of its feathers in time with its breathing. Between him and the gelic, pressed against his side, was the person who concerned himself the most. Elaine slept in gentle repose.

Careful to not disturb her, he sat up, his long cloak tumbled away from his chest. It had been covering him and Elaine like a blanket. Yet he knew he had not been wearing it when they had escaped the slave hut.

"You are awake, Lord Demon," a sleepy Flicker said, lifting its head up and slow blinking its eyes.

"Where are we?" Acies asked softly, yet his whisper echoed all the same.

"Inside the Well of Isa. Look," Flicker said, brightening the light a little more to reveal the symbol of Isa carved into the rough stone wall. Acies eyed it as he shifted to his knees.

"And where did these come from?" he asked, reaching out to touch the symbol, only to have it snap at him like static.

"The symbol? Elaine says it was set by the Scion Mory—"

"No, the cloak and shawl," Acies interrupted, settling back on his haunches.

"I retrieved them at my mistress's request. You and my mistress were freezing in the water. I was surprised since you seem like a powerful demon."

Acies narrowed his eyes slightly even though the gelic didn't seem to be saying it as a jib.

"I have never been that great in the cold," he said. "It is against my nature. I tend to fall asleep."

"I thought as much. It was either that or the demon warding spell cast on the well," Flicker responded, standing up and giving a good shake.

"Yes. It might be that too," Acies agreed, eyeing the symbol once again.

"It was my mistress that saved you," Flicker informed him.

"How?" Acies asked. He looked around at their surroundings, noting the shape of the well and the distance from the hole above.

"This is a Well of Isa," Flicker said as if it was obvious.

Of course, he thought, chiding himself for asking the obvious. She was a Scion of Isa, so she could simply tap the blessed power in Isa's water. Acies eyed the gelic. "She blessed you, I suppose, and you were able to create the warmth of the fire."

The gelic's chest puffed up.

Acies considered a moment, the strange duck creature with its elemental power the opposite of Isa's purview. "What kind of gelic are you, Flicker? You seem to be of at least three aspects."

"I am of fire, air, and water. I am of perfect design!" Flicker declared proudly.

"Yes, Isa was always one to double or triple up the aspects of her gelics. She always loved to show off," he muttered.

A puff of smoke popped off of Flicker's head as the gelic's heat flared. "How dare you speak of her ladyship that way!"

"I will speak of her however I wish," Acies dismissed as he sat next to Elaine, this time brushing away a lock of her hair from her face. "How long have we been in here?"

Flicker turned away, folding winged arms in front of itself with the billed nose in the air.

"Flicker, do you know what is happening above?" Acies asked.

Again, the gelic stuck its nose in the air, refusing to answer.

"Fine then, *I* will find a way to get Elaine out of this well safely, and when I tell her that I had to do it myself because her gelic refused to do anything to help its mistress—"

Flicker predictably squawked in outrage, then flew out of the well.

Acies smirked because that had been ridiculously easy. Gelics were too simple of creatures to realize such a trick. At least that had not changed.

Yet it also left them in the dark. It was too much like his prison, and as the seconds ticked by, he found it harder to breathe. He could feel it pressing and his brain reached for any scrape of sensory information: the sound of water, the rush of a breeze, the feel of the stone beneath him, anything to tell him he was alive and in the world of form.

Then his hand found Elaine's. He grasped it desperately, lacing his fingers between hers and squeezing tightly. Her natural warmth calmed him immediately. She was there even though he couldn't see her, breathing gently in her sleep.

Unfortunately, a few of those breaths later, she snorted, jerking awake with a startled little cry.

"It is alright. It is just me," Acies soothed, using her more familiar Ka'in to help reassure her.

"Acies?" she finally asked, her voice tiny like a small child's.

"Yes, it is me. We are safe," he repeated.

"Where—" He could hear her swallow. "Where are we?" she asked in a steadier voice.

"In the Well of Isa, remember? We jumped in to escape the Anon. You saved my life from freezing to death." That calmed her even further as her pressure returned against his leg, indicating that she was relaxing.

"Are you alright?" she asked. He felt her fingers reach out, blindly brushing his chest as they searched for him.

He smiled and nodded, though she could not see it as he grasped her fingers. "Yes, thank you."

A long waiting pause while he tried to decide what to say next.

Then she withdrew. "Would you really have died?" she asked, her voice shifting in the dark. He wasn't sure what she was doing, but he imagined it was adjusting her clothing or hair or something as brushes of air whipped past his nose.

"It would have taken a long time, but the cold would have kept me under until I burned out of my arete, or someone found me to wake me," he answered. "And the likelihood of someone finding me down here and knowing what to do to revive me was not great."

"Hmm," she responded noncommittally, then asked, "Where is Flicker?"

"I sent it up to scout for us, to see if it is safe to attempt to leave this place, but it has not returned yet," he said, concerned by that fact.

"I am thirsty," Elaine whispered.

"Well, we are in the right place for that."

"But where is it?" she asked, and her questing fingers bumped his chest again, then retreated. He captured them and pulled her across his own body.

"Here," he said gently, dipping those fingers into the cold water. "There is not really room on this platform to get out of your way, so just lean over me and drink."

There was still that bodily hesitation, but then she slid closer and did just that, resting her belly over his thighs so she could cup both her hands together to drink. He savored her weight; just the solid feeling of her being there in the dark with him felt right.

He was alive. As long as that was true, there was hope.

If he had dared, he would have wrapped his arms around her and squeezed tightly, but he doubted she'd give permission for such an intimate thing.

When she had her fill, she sat back.

"There is no light up there?" she commented. "I see a slightly lighter circle, so it must be the sky, but it is barely there."

"I would suspect it is night."

"So, how *do* we get out of here?" she asked, again touching his chest with her hand and his heart skipped a beat.

He cleared his throat. "We will have to get wet again, but I should be able to climb up the rope if we can find it. Once I am at the top, you will stick your foot in the leather bucket, and I will haul you up. All of that will be easier when your gelic returns. I am growing concerned that it has not."

Just then a light winked at the top of the well.

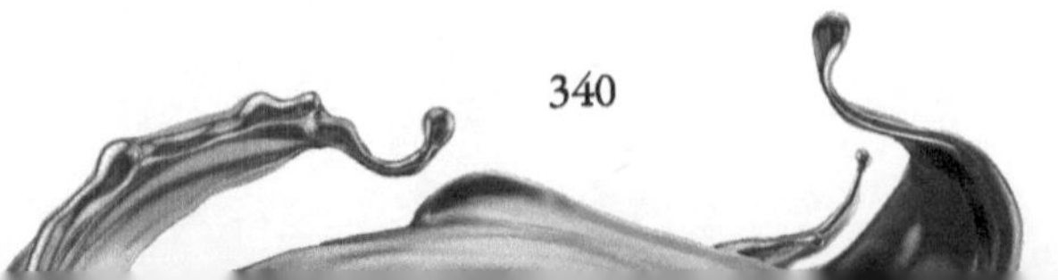

"Hey!" a small voice called down. "What are you doing down there?"

Acies squinted hard at the sudden light, too bright to his night-blind eyes. He held up a hand to block it.

"Hello?" Elaine called up, and she steadied a hand on his shoulder so she could stand up.

"Greetings! What are you doing down there?" the small voice asked again.

"It sounds like a child," Elaine said in a half-whisper.

"You should not be in the Well of Isa," the little voice continued. "It is not a safe place to play."

"Definitely a child," Acies muttered before calling up. "Can you get us some help so we can get out of here?"

"Well, there is nobody around," the child said.

"What about your parents?" Elaine called realizing she must be a Ka'in child, though why she would dare to speak their native language was odd. *But then, she said no one else was around,* Elaine thought.

"Well, I do not know," the child said as if it were a grave matter. "My mother would not be very happy that I wandered off so far, so I cannot really go to her, but I had to come see what that light was. It looked like a god-sign."

"Light?" Elaine asked, her brows knitting in uncertainty.

"Aye, it was amazing! It went all the way to the heavens!" the child cried merrily, her little voice tinkling like bells inside the well.

"Oh crap, what have I done?" Elaine said, covering her mouth with her hand.

"No idea, but too late now," Acies said, then refocused on the light above. "We need to get out of here. Can you run and find *anybody* who can help us?"

"I can help you!" the child declared firmly. "Just give me a second."

Then the light was gone, leaving them in darkness, though at the top of the well, Acies could see the light had moved off only a little. The kid must have had a lantern or oil lamp set on the edge of the well stones.

"What do you think they are going to do?" Elaine whispered.

"I have no idea," Acies admitted. Then something hit the water with a splash.

"Can you grab that?" the child cried, the light reappearing, highlighting the bucket at the end of the rope as it floated in the middle of the well. A second rope also dangled there, the bucket itself submerged, holding the rope straight.

"We will have to swim for it," Elaine said, resigned.

"Can you swing the bucket toward us?" Acies called up, raising himself to a crouch at the water's edge.

"Uh, aye, I think so," said the child. The bucket lifted out of the water, now filled with dripping water. It was slow at first, but the bucket soon rocked back and forth, arcing closer and closer to Acies's outstretched fingers. Elaine stabilized him with her hands holding his waistband so he could lean out. Twice his fingers brushed it but did not catch.

"Can you get it now?" the voice above called.

"Just a little more!" Acies shouted. The bucket swung even farther, and he hooked a finger into the treated leather and its cold-water contents. "I have it!" he called, and immediately, the rope slacked enough for him to dump the water out.

"Excellent! As soon as you're ready, tell me, and I'll pull you out."

"Well, you cannot dismiss their enthusiasm," Elaine said wryly.

Acies chuckled in agreement as he tied Vills once more to his back, then shouldered one of the packs. "I'll still have

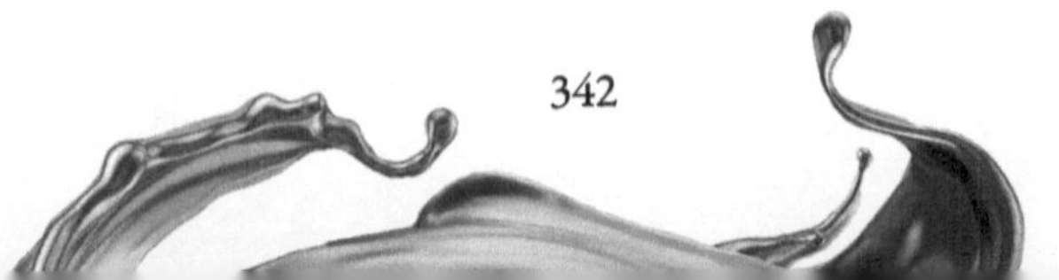

to climb up, if you'll put your foot in the bottom of bucket to hold it taut for me."

Elaine nodded as she settled her own pack on her shoulders.

"Are you ready?" the child called down.

"Just stand back, sweetie, and hold the light for us," Acies called. "I am going to climb out..."

And then they were standing beside the well.

CHAPTER 36

ACIES BLINKED TWICE AS HIS EYES TRIED TO MAKE sense of the sudden change. Elaine gasped next to him, and he turned to her. She stood with one foot in the bucket, both of them holding the rope.

"What... What just happened?" she asked, turning to look down the open hole of the well.

"I have no..." Acies couldn't even finish that thought.

All around them, the slave village was too quiet. The moon had risen in the sky, casting its glow on the world about them but nothing moved. Everything had been decimated; possessions were strewn on the ground. Several huts had been destroyed. Nothing breathed or moved.

And there was no sign of the child.

Acies pulled at the tie at his chest and released his sword, snapping the string on purpose. He pulled out his sword, shaking away the leather covering, all the while his eyes scanned for any whiff of threat.

"Do you think it was a spirit?" Elaine whispered.

"What?" he demanded, the question incongruous to what his mind now focused on.

"That helped us out of the well—do you think it was a Spirit of the Well?" she asked.

"Something to speak about later," he answered, bringing his sword up to a ready position with both hands firmly on the hilt.

"I am not a spirit!"

The pair of them whirled about.

Sitting on a rock beside the well was a beautiful little girl. She couldn't have been more than ten seasons, wearing a child's shift that seemed too small for her frame. It made her look like all legs and arms. She sat with one knee tucked up against her, held in placed with her clasped hands while the other swung freely in the way children moved, completely unconcerned with the display of sword before her.

Instead, she cocked her head to the side. "You should say thank you."

"You are right," Elaine said, coming around Acies, who lowered the point of his sword but did not completely disengage it. Something was not right about this little girl, but he felt no malice emanating from her.

"You are welcome," the little girl said, swinging her leg down before grasping the rock to pop up to her feet with a little bounce. "You can come visit me if you like."

Then she ran off among the huts and disappeared.

"Hey! Wait!" Elaine called after her. She moved as if she meant to follow, but Acies caught her hand.

"Let her go. It could be a trap," he warned.

Elaine shook her head, clearly frightened. "What happened here—"

"It would be better ... we escaped now," Acies countered.

Her fear gave way to resolve. "I am not leaving until we find my brother or Flicker," she stated.

He huffed as she stiffened her jaw. "I did not think we would," he admitted, "but I thought I would try."

Elaine glared at him before casting another worried glance over the settlement. "If no one is here... they must all be at the main settlement. The... the Anons cannot live without their slaves."

"If that were the case ... then where are the campfires?" he asked, pointing in the direction of the darkened settlement that he only could see because of the moonlight overhead.

"Oh gods," Elaine prayed as she realized he was right. "That was the direction the child went."

"Come on," he said, and stepped off to move toward the settlement, his sword raised at the ready.

Just as they crossed the bare space the separated the settlement from the slave village, Elaine stopped as sharply as a nervous deer.

"Do you hear that?" she whispered.

He held his breath. "Weeping?"

Sure enough, just within the first row of huts, they spied a woman sitting on the ground. Her face was buried in her hands. She seemed to be older, but little else was discernible about her as she had her head covered and a shawl wrapped around her shoulders. The hut she sat before was as destroyed as the ones in the slave village, only here among the refuse were unmoving bodies.

While he debated with himself about what to do, Elaine moved past him to approach the weeping woman. He seized her arm, pulling her up short.

"No," he breathed as loud as he dared. "Could be a demon." He had known such that pretended to be weeping women to lure sympathetic prey in.

But Elaine shook her head. "I don't sense that," she said and pulled herself free from his grasp. He let her go but kept his sword at the ready all the same.

Better to trip the trap on purpose than to stumble in it, he justified silently.

"<Are you alright?>" Elaine asked gently in Anon.

The woman startled away from Elaine's outstretched hand and scuttled backward toward the remains of her hut, croaking as if she could not draw breath to scream.

"<We are not here to hurt you!>" Elaine said, holding up her hands in placation.

The woman pointed a shaking finger. "<Demons! Demons!>" A small section of her hut collapsed as she backed into it, and Acies smelled the scent of blood wafting out.

"<Please, we are not demons. We are Ka'in,>" Elaine said, only half-lying he supposed.

The woman hesitated, sending a critical eye over them. Elaine brushed back her hair from her ears, to reveal the points of them. "<Please, just tell us what happened here. Then we will go,>" Elaine promised gently.

The woman licked her lips. "<They... They came. The warriors. They said they were warriors from Icathor, but I do not know. They demanded all our slaves. They did not even pay for them; they just took them all. Then they took other Anon. Free peoples! Men, women, and children. My husband, he objected, and ... now he is dead.>" The Anon woman's voice thickened as her grief threatened to overwhelm her again. "<My children are gone. The warriors took them as well. They destroyed so much.>" The woman lifted her head, staring around at what was left of her home and neighbors. "<I wish I were dead too.>"

She collapsed back into her wailing and allowed Elaine to hold her, rocking her as she mourned.

Acies dipped his head inside the door. Whatever had been for dinner had long burned in the square fire pit with its dying coals. A man's body lay next to the fire pit, a blanket draped over his form as if he were only sleeping. But Acies could pick out the small pool of blood underneath him.

The woman continued to babble, but there wasn't much more to add to her story. She certainly didn't know anything about a specific Ka'in Prince being carted away, but as he went from hut to hut, examining each body as he went, he did not find any dead sign of Elan.

At last, he returned to his Ka'in Princess, who looked up at him as he approached her. "Based on her description, it sounds to me like Dakin's man Lorab. He is known as the Sword," she said in Ka'in.

"Great warrior?" Acies asked, lifting an eyebrow at her.

She shrugged her available shoulder. "Yes. She says they headed toward Icathor." Elaine indicated the direction.

Acies sighed as he regarded the expanse of grass and the bit of forest beyond. "Do you *still* wish to seek your brother?"

Elaine shot him a reproachful, near-angry look. "Why do you keep asking me the same question when you know the answer?"

"Because I keep hoping for a different one," he said.

"Then you are mad," she said.

"That is the most likely possibility," he agreed.

The weeping woman stood up then in a daze. "<I must see to my husband,>" she muttered, her Anon barely intelligible, but Acies understood her well enough. Her language came slower to him than the Ka'in, but the more he heard, the more he learned. He let her go back into her house. There was nothing more they needed from her. For a tense moment, he thought Elaine would follow her in and try to help, but to his surprise, she only stood and watched quietly.

"We should go," she said. "We need to save Elan."

He didn't dare add, *If he's still alive,* but he thought it.

"Do you sense Flicker anywhere?" Acies asked.

Elaine went still as she tried to sense the little gelic before worry lines appeared between her eyebrows. "What could have happened?"

He shook his head, not even wanting to speculate.

"I do not know the way to Icathor from here. Can you track them?" she asked.

"I can track which way the slaves were taken," he acknowledged.

She bit her lower lip, clearly upset by the choice she was being forced to make. "Then ... our course is clear," she finally said, and he couldn't argue with it. Hopefully, the gelic would find them.

Leaving the grieving Anon woman, they foraged among the houses, finding little, but some clean water and abandoned food.

By the time they found what they could, the gray dawn filled the sky.

At last, Elaine resettled her pack and nodded. "I am ready."

He wanted to argue one last time against this plan but held his tongue as he struck out over the uneven ground out of the settlement, pounded by too many feet.

CHAPTER 37

DAKIN WAS ARRAYED IN THE FINEST CLOTHES, A precious white shift trimmed with expensive colored dyes, which made him look like a walking rainbow. He sat on a throne carved from wood with fierce animals crafted out of the back and the armrests. It had been a dying artisan's masterwork, which was never paid for. It was one of Dakin's favorite brags.

Normally, his mistress would be standing by his side, bedecked in jewelry made of coins with his stamp on them and coils of silver wrapped around her arms, and little else, to display his wealth, prestige, and power.

Except Amira was late.

The reception to rebuild relationships with the remaining merchants had started when the sun was a finger above the horizon, and she had not shown up. The slaves kept assuring him she was coming, but their frightened eyes and nervous twitches did not ease his frustration. It was especially galling when merchant after merchant entered to pay homage to

350

him, each with their own concubines, both male and female, beside them, each bedecked in their own show of wealth. It was galling.

"Yes, yes," he finally snapped at a merchant who was flanked by a male and female, each wearing jewels as well as coins. The merchant looked up from their deep bow with a questioning alarm that made his face look like it had been carved from a potato.

Razal jumped in to personally receive the offering of a finely dyed robe from the merchant, nodding while making Dakin's divine gesture with his other hand. "Thank you. You are most blessed," the priest said, much to the merchant's relief. Then Razal lifted the hand so the others waiting in the hallway could see it. "We will be taking a short recess. You will be summoned when the reception resumes."

The doors were shut once the merchant and his retinue escaped, unsure if they were specially blessed or in dire trouble.

Once the receiving room was quiet, Razal scurried back to climb the stairs to just below the dais. "What ails you, my Lord?" he asked, pitching his voice down so it wouldn't carry throughout the chamber.

"Where is Amira?" Dakin growled, spitting the question as a slave refilled his cup of water at the small table beside his chair. The slave trembled so hard water sloshed out.

"She is... she is c-c-coming," the slave sputtered out the same tired line.

"She has been c-c-c-coming for ages. Where is she!?" Dakin roared, rising to his feet to knock over the cup of water to the floor, destroying it in the process.

"My Lord, calm yourself," Razal interceded, holding up his hands in placation.

"You do not tell me what to do!" Dakin roared.

Then the door to Dakin's receiving room opened, and a group of warriors marched a pair of figures in, tied up with ropes. One of the figures was his missing concubine.

"What is it?" Dakin demanded as she was dragged along by a rope bound around her wrists. While the second figure, an Anon warrior by the look of him, was forced to kneel, she was flung down at the bottom of the stairs leading up to Dakin's throne. Tears streaked her face, making tracks in the grim coating it. Her clothing hung torn from her shoulders and a large gap in her skirt showed her bared legs. Beside her, another warrior cast down a pair of packs. Coils of silver fell out to skitter across the floor. The warriors themselves arrayed themselves behind their captives, forming a half-circle to enclose them with nowhere to run.

At last, one warrior stepped forward, making Dakin's sign in salute. "We caught this man trying to escape with your woman," he said, shoving the warrior with a foot. Because of his restraints, he was not able to catch himself on his hands. He landed on his side on the stone floor with an audible grunt behind the gag tied around his mouth.

Razal moved to scurry down the stairs, but Dakin overtook him, moving past to stand over Amira, who looked up at him with tear-filled eyes.

"My Lord, please," she begged. Her teeth flashed with red blood staining the grooves between her teeth.

His hand snapped out as he seized her chin in his hand, stopping her words. She whimpered.

He turned her face side to side, examining it. "Did someone hit my woman?" he demanded, releasing her to stare at the warriors.

Each one shifted, unsure, before the spokesman said, "She attempted to flee when we discovered them. We did what was needful to capture her."

Amira grasped at Dakin's robe with her bound hands. "Please, my Lord, if you will let me explain—"

"Shut up," Dakin hissed coldly. "Animals do not speak."

He returned his gaze to the warriors. "Did any of you fuck her?" he demanded levelly.

There was more shifting. "No, my Lord. She belongs to the great god Dakin. No mortal may touch what belongs to the gods."

"A good and righteous answer," Razal declared, coming around to stand between them once more.

Dakin looked to Razal, who lifted an eyebrow at him.

"Yes, you have been worthy warriors," Dakin added.

The warriors straightened up, clearly feeling more confident now.

"You have the gratitude of a god," Razal announced loudly so the merchants gathered there, peeking through the door could hear.

The priest turned to Dakin and bowed. "What is your will, oh Lord of Justice?"

Dakin stared down at Amira's pleading eyes. "I will punish all who steal what is mine. Return *her* to her rooms," he ordered.

The slaves scurried forward to obey, lifting Amira off the floor as she continued to hiccup piteously.

"Make sure she is cleaned and fed. She has had a terrible fright," he added generously. As she went past, he patted her tenderly on the head.

"Th-thank you. Thank you, my Lord," Amira gushed, seizing his hand to kiss it.

There were murmurs of approval and a few claps as Amira was led away, forced to walk through the people. Many of them reached out to offer comfort and consolation, having known the woman her entire life. She was one of them. It was not a walk of shame for her but an affirmation of that very fact.

"Shall we kill him, my Lord?" the head warrior asked, pulling his sword to lay at the traitor's throat.

Dakin narrowed his eyes at the Anon warrior. The new god approached to stand over the bound and beaten man. Wisely, the prisoner stared hard at the floor, his breath whistling in short pants through his broken nose.

Dakin slipped his finger under the other's chin and forced him to look up.

There was fear in those eyes, naked and trembling terror. It was disgusting.

"You betrayed me. One of my warriors dared to betray me," he said as if he could not believe such a thing. "Is there anyone who will speak in your defense?" Dakin's voice echoed in the chamber.

Razal only smirked. The other warriors stood in stony silence, and the merchants were frozen in the hallway.

"No one?" Dakin asked, playing for his audience. A few unsure glances passed between the warriors, but no one stepped up.

A smile so sly one might call it clever, if all who saw it did not know better, crossed Dakin's face. The self-declared god moved too fast. He grabbed the warrior's head firmly in one hand, tearing his clothing to expose his neck and shoulder with the other.

Then he bit down.

The man screamed, muffled by the gag.

There were other screams, but the god did not register them. His world was the sweet energy pouring into his being, the rich blood in his mouth.

Once filled, he shoved his victim away, dropping the now silent man onto the ground as he lifted his own face in ecstasy to the ceiling. He stretched his arms to either side, his motions sensual and languid as the fresh blood sluiced down his chin.

Drunkenly, he opened his eyes.

From the doorway, eyes stared at him full of abject horror.

"Oh, dear. You all saw that," Dakin said.

CHAPTER 38

"THE FORTRESS IS BUILT LIKE A CONCH-SHELL,"
Elaine said as she squatted beside Acies, looking through
the trees at the monumental landmark. "The wall goes
around three times with the top culminating in a three-story
building."

"Before the Great War, it was a hill fort and trading town,"
Acies commented as he lifted the strip he had torn from his
cloak, tying it around his forehead and over the tips of his
ears. "It still stands. This is..."

"Impressive," Elaine supplied in Ka'in.

"Yes, impressive," Acies agreed.

The two stood side by side, staring across a distance at
Icathor rising up toward the sky on the back of a massive hill.
They had been following the trail left by the marched slaves
for two days, but it became clear that they were not going to
catch up with them before they reached the fortress. As they
got closer, they started encountering more people moving
about the forest, collecting resources into wagons. Since

Elaine would not let Acies slaughter them all, they were forced to move around and sneak away, slowing their pursuit.

"We are probably a day behind them," Acies commented.

She adjusted her shawl, resetting it so it covered her head more completely. "I have never seen Icathor like this before."

"They are gearing up for war." Acies pointed to the black and gray smoke that billowed from within the first wall that ran around the fortress. "Making weapons on a great scale."

Elaine nodded as she watched streams of people with wagons and animals working their way up to the fortress. The first layer of wall was still a good long walk away, surrounded by a patchwork of fields down the gentle slope from the hill and across the lower levels until they bled into the forest. Smaller homes dotted the landscape between the fields to make access to them easier, but all of the grain stores returned to the fortress when it came time to harvest.

"The harvests were completed several days before Dakin left with me to go to the temple," Elaine commented.

"That's coal and peat for fires," Acies noted, pointing at laden wagons trundling up the hill. Shepherds were herding in their flocks. "Food and warriors."

"Warriors?" Elaine questioned.

Acies nodded to a group of people being ushered into the fortress. "Why do you think they are taking all the slaves? Not just for fighters but also for the support..." He struggled for the word a moment, then settled on, "network that goes with it. Food needs to be cooked, tents put up and taken down. He is ... eating his own..."

"Cannibalizing," Elaine supplied.

He nodded. "Cannibalizing everything, it looks like."

The Demon of War walked along the edge of the forest, bringing them closer to the main road through the layout of fields.

"Even the children?" the Ka'in Princess asked, following behind.

He nodded. "Messengers, assistants, pages to the warriors. Lots of jobs for little hands."

Elaine pursed her lips. "And in all of that, there is my brother." Though she knew they couldn't be sure.

"It is not too late to leave him to his fate," Acies said, crossing his arms over his chest.

"No," Elaine stated.

Acies sighed. "You know it is not just your brother. There are the slaves from the settlement and who knows how many others of your people. I can get in, find him, and get out, but if you expect me to rescue everyone, I can tell you right now that is impossible."

"I did not ask you to," she said, focusing on all the work being done before her. *What can someone like me do about all that? It's too big,* she thought. She had no real power in this world. All her majick could not provide her people with a safe place to live, food for their children, and safety for themselves and their flocks. The Anon controlled all that.

Still, she worried at her lip. "It will be winter soon. Is winter not the worst time to make war?"

Acies's eyebrows shot up a little. "Typically, yes." He studied things further, and she could see his mental wheels turning. "Because of that, no one expects an attack in this season. Either your Dakin is a complete idiot or a genius."

"He is not *my* Dakin," Elaine said coldly.

"No, he is not. But you are *my* woman," he said, cracking a smile.

Elaine nodded, remembering the plan they had discussed on the journey. "And you are a warrior for hire."

"A *mercenary*, yes," he agreed.

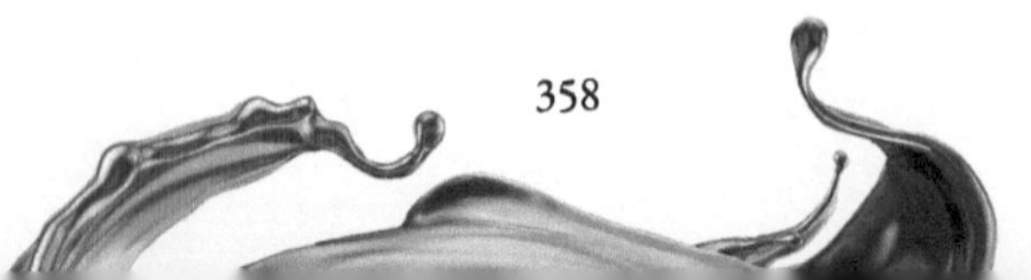

"And how are you going to do that when you cannot even speak Anon?" she challenged.

He opened his mouth to answer her but stopped as he realized the hole in their plan. Then she narrowed her gaze at him as she realized something in turn.

"You were once our God of Land and Harvest."

He narrowed his eyes. "Yes."

"Yet this whole time, I have been teaching you Ka'in. The language of your own people. How is it you do not know how to speak it if you are truly Veres?"

He looked away. "This is not relevant to the plan," he dismissed.

She wasn't going to accept that. "You will tell me—"

"I have forgotten," he snapped.

She shook her head. "How is that—"

"The prison consumed much of me!" he growled, his eyes flaring with anger, only this time Elaine didn't even flinch. She stared him down and he continued, acknowledging he had lost this contest of wills. "The only thing I could control in my prison was what I lost to it. My... our language was one of those things. But through our bond... when you speak the words, I can remember, and what I cannot remember, I can learn quickly with context. The more you speak, the more words I can remember, and the easier it gets," he said entirely in Ka'in.

Elaine stood there, taking all that in. "I understand," she said, relenting.

"My memories were more important to me than words," he added, more truth coming out of him now that the barrier had been broken.

"<Then does it work the same for Anon>?" she asked, speaking those words in Anon.

Acies blinked at her. "<Aye,>" he replied in the same language. "<Aye, these words... I know them too. Because you know them, through our bond, I can know them too.>"

He turned back to the fortress. "It is not likely that the Anon recognize who and what your brother is, outside of a useful slave. If they see him as a warrior, then we should be able to find him in a training yard or camp, some place they should have access to," he said in Ka'in.

"<It will be in the back paddocks,>" Elaine stated, continuing to speak in Anon, gesturing toward the far side of the hill. "<Livestock that is being traded or sold along with slaves are kept there temporarily until they move on. There were plans to convert them into training grounds and bring them within the fortress walls.>"

She realized he was focused on her lips, watching each word as she formed it. After a long pause, he answered. "<How do ... you know?>" Acies asked, his Anon rougher than his Ka'in.

"<A concubine is inconsequential for anything other than fucking. Dakin and his generals talked freely around me,>" she stated as detached as she could from the statement. "<Besides, I was supposed to be dead by now. Sacrificed to you. Much of Dakin's plans hinged on having you at his command.>"

For a second, she thought he hadn't understood her Anon, but then a belated smile crossed his face. "So sorry to disappoint."

"<What I do not understand is, how they are keeping all this safe from demon attacks?>" Elaine asked, more to herself than Acies. "<It is the biggest problem for Icathor.>"

"<Demons are not just... feared by people; they fear each other too,>" he grunted, still assessing what they could see in the distance. "<There is something… here that… frightens them more.>"

That unsettled Elaine's heart further. She wished Maevra was there to assure her this was the right idea, even if she would have said it was decidedly not.

"<Alright then. Are you ready?>" he asked, shifting Vills on his back, the sword once more wrapped in a dry leather covering.

It didn't matter what Maevra would have thought. She had made her decision. "<Aye,>" she said.

They left the safety of the forest, heading across a stripped field toward the main road.

CHAPTER 39

W̲HILE THEY WALKED, E̲LAINE SPOKE AS MANY DIF-ferent Anon words she could think of, and Acies repeated them, picking them up more slowly than the Ka'in, but picking them up all the same. Considering how different the two languages were from each other, it was still a feat in and of itself.

Before too long, they encountered a cart with three workers piled on it, two in the front seat and one hanging off the back. The cart stank of an earthy, heavy smell, but the travelers both fell in behind it. Only the worker hanging off the back looked at them, a youth of some sort, but nothing in their clothes or hair gave away what type.

Soon enough, the wagon came to a near stop as it met the waiting line leading up to the fortress gates. Acies didn't wait but stepped around, threading a path for both of them past with his bulk and presence. Elaine followed in his wake like a duckling behind its matriarch. No one spoke to them;

they were too busy with their immediate conversations and concerns, most of it grumbling about the wait.

It was almost jolting when a friendly voice did call out to them.

"Warrior for hire?" a bright faced man, just barely out of his youth himself judging by the breadth of his shoulders, asked. His Anon nearly squeaked.

Acies redirected over to him, towering over him by at least a head height. The young man held his ground but seemed impressed by the shadow cast over him. "You do not look like a farmer," he quipped, leaning his spear against his shoulder. "You do not have a band? Of Warriors, I mean."

"I do not need a band," Acies responded also in Anon, grinning so wolfishly the young man's friendly expression twitched a second. "I am enough."

The young man gestured to a branching road that peeled off the main one and seemed to loop around the fortress. "All warriors are meeting up on the far side. You will want to speak to Barus the Shield directly. He will want to meet you personally."

Elaine grasped Acies's sleeve at the sound of the general's name, but her demon only nodded a thank you and turned them both to go down the forking road.

"<Barus will recognize me,>" Elaine hissed in godspeech once they were far enough away. She couldn't risk speaking in Ka'in and didn't want to be overheard in Anon.

Acies nodded, thinking. "<He is one of Dakin's warriors?>" he whispered back.

"<One of the closest. He calls himself the Shield. He is in charge of guarding both Dakin and the fortress.>"

"Have you ever heard of the Xiotites?" Acies said suddenly switching back to Anon, straightening as if they were just having a casual conversation. "They are a desert people, and they live with their faces covered, both men and women."

"Why do they do that?" she asked, also in Anon.

"The desert winds carry sands, and it is safer and easier to breathe if they cover their faces. They have done it so often that they cannot feel comfortable showing their faces to people who are not of their kin." He reached around Elaine's shawl and pulled a portion of it over her face, covering her nose and mouth. "They have dark hair as well."

She shook her head. "I have never heard of them before."

"Of course not, I just made them up," he answered, pulling a few strands of her wavy black hair free from the hood made by her shawl. "It will help explain my accent as well," he added.

"Oh!" she said, accepting the adjustment to the plan.

Taking up the end of her shawl, he tucked it back over the lower part of her face. It took some tightening and finagling, but they got it to stay, as long as she didn't move too much or too fast.

At last, they came around the hill. Sure enough, they found the newly created training camp. Most of the warriors walking about freely were men, but not all, with a mix of women and children as well. Several of them were preening up and down the enclosed paddocks, now filled with slaves instead of livestock. What livestock were about had been moved back into paddocks farther away, bleating and mooing at the noise. Shouts and cheers came from one where the ground had been completely torn up to dry, bare dirt. A few pairs were bare-fist fighting to the cheers and jeers of the others. The rest of the slaves stood in silence, watching the world around them warily.

"I did not think I would ever see this place again, and now I am walking into it willingly, not that I saw much of the outside."

"No one will touch you here. I swear it," Acies said behind her.

"I know," she said and meant it.

Another warrior intercepted Acies and Elaine as they approached, standing up from his seat of stone wall to saunter over. He had a bronze sword hanging from his belt at one hip and a long knife with aspirations of being a sword from the other. The mismatched handles made it clear that one had been acquired separate from the other.

"Warrior?" the man asked in a bored tone.

"Mercenary," Acies replied confidently.

The man furrowed his eyebrows at him. "A what?"

"A man who knows how to fight. Will do it for money," Acies replied.

The first man gestured at the collection of people around him. "We all can do that here," he said flippantly.

"Not like I can," Acies assured, crossing his arms over his chest.

Elaine only paid half her attention to this exchange. She scanned the myriad faces all about, trying to pick out one in particular. It proved to be impossible as there were many narrow-faced, bright blondes among the sea of sunny browns, dark earth browns, and fire reds. And the people kept moving, shuffling slaves in and out of the paddocks as they were sized up and assessed for their new life as warriors, or for support, as Acies called them.

"I am to see Barus the Shield," the Demon of War continued.

"Hmm-mm," the warrior said, picking at his teeth with his tongue, not at all impressed by Acies's claim. Elaine could have seen the bruised ego from a field away. Nothing had changed in Icathor.

"If you want to see the general, you are going to have to go through me first," the warrior declared.

"I find your terms acceptable," Acies replied, followed by his fist popping out to sock the man in the nose.

The warrior screeched at the burst of pain and blood coming from his face.

Without missing a beat, Acies stepped forward and kneed him in the groin.

The warrior flopped hard to the ground in a pile of moans, whimpers, and blood.

Acies stepped forward and undid the warrior's belt quickly, sliding the leather sheath holding the long knife off the one end. He then stood over the man, squinting up and cursing at him as he held the knife out for the fallen warrior to see.

"This is mine now. You want it back, you come take it back. Next time, I take your life," Acies warned with a brutal smile, then stepped away to where Elaine waited.

No one stopped him. At most, the fallen warrior got a few glances from those nearby, but once Acies disengaged with his trophy, they all turned back to other points of interest.

Acies handed the blade to Elaine. "We need to get you a belt for that," he said softly, still speaking Anon. "Just keep it with you for now."

"If you give it to me, he will think he can take it back from me a lot easier than from you," Elaine whispered.

"I do not want to be here long enough for him to get the courage back up to try," Acies said. "Just keep it and use it if you have to."

"I suppose it is less flashy than the jeweled one," Elaine conceded and secured it under her shawl. "I want to go by the paddocks to see if we can see Elan."

Acies nodded. "Now that I have established my credentials, we should not be too bothered by everyone else."

"Hey," someone said, immediately bothering them.

Elaine and Acies turned to another warrior who had been standing near the paddocks. This man had a bronze sword at his side as well but was in no hurry to use it. "If you are looking for the Shield, he is over there where they are keeping the Ka'in."

Acies acknowledged the man's help and started off in the direction indicated.

Elaine gripped the new knife under her shawl tightly in apprehension, but she did not let any of it show on what little of her face could be seen. There had been several curious glances over in her direction, but none of them had a flicker of recognition about them. As they wove through the crowd, she found herself separated from Acies enough so that a cadre of warriors stepped in front of her, blocking her path.

"What are you doing over here, little one?" a rough warrior with stinking breath asked in barely comprehensible Anon.

Elaine raised her eyes to the men, and one of his comrades hissed appreciatively under his breath. "She has eyes the color of the sky."

So much for no one noticing her.

"The color of the Ocean," the third warrior said, a taller man with curly blonde hair and a round face.

"Like you have ever seen the Ocean," the second warrior scoffed, but the first warrior did not lose his focus as the two men smacked each other behind him.

"Why do you cover your face? Are you trying to hide something?" He reached out to pull her impromptu veil back when Acies's larger hand seized his wrist.

"She is mine," he said, wrenching the man's wrist up, "And if you touch her, then this is mine as well."

The warrior tried to reclaim his wrist, but Acies simply didn't let him go. A flash of panic crossed his features, then he glanced back at Elaine.

"I am sorry for touching your woman. She was flirting with me—" Acies's other hand came down on the back of the man's neck, forcing him to kneel on the ground.

"Kiss her feet," Acies ordered.

"What!?" the captured man bucked, but Acies kept him in place, the man's compatriots backing away a few steps.

"If she blessed you as you say with her attention, then you should thank all the gods in all the heavens at your great fortune to have been graced by one such as her. Kiss her feet and show her how grateful you are at her favor," Acies stated. The man continued to buck and weave but could not break free. This interaction had the attention of all around, many watching with amusement or confusion at the display.

"I said kiss her feet!" Acies shouted. Whatever sliver of pride the man still possessed kept him from screaming out, but the grunts of rage and shame were damn near pig-like.

"Acies, we do not..." she started at the same time as the warrior relented. He grasped at the leather of her shoe and slapped his lips on them as if he had tried to headbutt her feet. Once the deed was done, Acies relented. The man scrambled back to standing, squaring up to Acies.

"I am going to make you pay for that," he growled, red-faced, at Acies. "Draw your sword!"

Acies stood there, calm and waiting, his hands empty, which he spread wide with a clear dare.

The goading was enough for the man. He seized his friend's sword and rushed at Acies. The Demon of War side-stepped and tripped him in one move. The other man's sword was then in Acies hand as he spun. Riding the momentum, he slashed down as his opponent sprawled. His back split open.

The man screamed. Blood went everywhere.

Acies did not look back at him; instead he walked over to Elaine as if they were at a market. He held out the blood covered blade toward her as he examined it in the sunshine.

"This needs reforging. The balance is all off," he commented casually to her.

Elaine felt nothing but rage. "We were supposed to be discreet," she hissed.

"You are right. It did not work out that way," he said, matching her softness. "Do not turn around." He then stepped past her. "Are you in charge of this mess?"

"I am," the hefty voice of Lorab answered. Elaine felt her pulse stop, and she lowered her eyes. Slowly, she turned, keeping herself in profile. Acies had set himself between her and the man she feared. With a shaking hand, she tucked her face covering a little tighter.

"You owe me a warrior," Lorab stated.

Elaine could practically hear him crossing his arms.

"I would say so. All you have are children ... playing with their father's weapons."

There was a long, heavy pause, and then Lorab barked out a laugh. On that rare cue, the other warriors around laughed along, and the tension drained out around them.

"Aye, yes, you have the right of it," Lorab said, and the other warriors began to fade back to what they were doing, the show officially over. "Half of what we got here are barely off their mother's teat, and the rest are reluctant slaves who are only going to be best used as front-line shields for the real warriors.

Lorab strutted closer, and Elaine turned around, folding her hands before her while keeping her gaze down. He paused as he noticed her. "Ah, is this your woman?" he asked, amused, leaning over to try to look under her hood.

"Yes, she is mine, and I am hers," Acies responded, putting an arm around her while Elaine continued to avoid his eyes.

"Why is her face covered up? She scarred or something?" Lorab asked, slipping into talking about her as if she was not a person. Under her shawl, Elaine gripped the knife handle tighter. The urge to plunge it into Lorab's condescending throat was unexpectedly overwhelming. Hate seized the back of her throat like bile.

"Are you asking her or asking me?" Acies said instead of answering.

Lorab double blinked at that. Then he quirked his eyebrows, caught off guard by the question. "Asking you, of course."

"We are from the desert," Elaine said, affecting Acies's accent as best she could. It sounded terrible to her ears. "It is the tradition of our people to cover our faces."

Lorab did not respond to her but continued to talk to Acies. "From the desert?"

"I have come to sell my sword."

The Sword nodded, then clapped a hand on Acies's shoulder. "Aye, then. Come with me. You shall share my fire tonight."

Elaine growled in the back of her throat as they followed, but it was lost in the noise of the warriors cheering for the bare-fist fight in the nearest paddock.

Lorab led them through the crowd to a small collection of tents set up by themselves in their own empty paddock.

This space had fresh grass still growing, and the walls were of newer stone construction. Warriors sat around a fire in the middle of the circle of tents, which had a spit over it, turned by a haggard-looking woman. The warriors greeted Lorab warmly. Many of them had familiar faces. Elaine even knew several of their names. They passed curious eyes over them but looked to Lorab for signals on what to do.

Their fearless leader spun about and gestured to the food and the fire. "Have a seat and tell me about yourself. Your woman can go with the others in that tent. They are preparing food."

"My woman stays with me," Acies said.

Lorab eyed him but didn't drop the welcoming demeanor. "I give you my word she will be safe, and no one here will touch her now that we know she belongs to you," he declared, lifting his voice so anyone in earshot would get the message and spread it to the others. "But men's talk is not a place for a woman."

Acies narrowed his eyes. "Interesting," he said. Elaine gripped his arm but said nothing. He looked down at it and took her silent message.

Lorab read the body language as well. "Mara," he called.

A woman emerged from one of the tents, young and fresh and pretty. She came over to the group of men and slid her arm around Lorab's waist. Elaine did not recognize her.

"Mara, please show our new guest's woman to the tent. Get her something to eat and keep her company."

"Oh, I think I can manage that," Mara said saucily as if there was an innuendo in it.

Elaine did not want to get the joke.

Lorab chuckled then grabbed her face in his hand and kissed it roughly. The woman winced but covered it up, smiling at him when he broke away. He then patted her butt. "Go, get to it. And send Coro out with some fresh wine."

At that name, her smile dropped a little. She then looked at Elaine. "Come on then."

Elaine squeezed Acies's arm one more time and turned to follow Mara over to the large tent. The woman waited for her, holding the flap open with an insincere smile. Just before Elaine entered, she spotted one of the warriors sitting around the fire. He eyed her when the others were more focused on Acies.

"Oh, do not mind him. That is Athorn. He is a Ka'in," Mara said dismissively. "Do not let the ears fool you. They are docked as if that would hide what he really is." Mara pressed on Elaine's back to encourage her to go in the tent, all while shooting Athorn warning eyes. He narrowed his and looked away.

CHAPTER 40

Inside the tent was spacious enough for five women and one man to be kneeling around a low table working away to prepare food while chatting companionably. They all looked up with that same curious stare at Elaine as Mara escorted her in.

"Scoot over, all of you. make room for our guest," Mara insisted, pushing Elaine to a spot at the table while the women shifted over, one of them smoothly dropping a pillow down for their guest to kneel upon. "Coro, Lorab wants more wine."

The single man exchanged a hostile stare off with Mara, then stood up with sharp movements, shaking the table as he did so. He snatched a bottle of wine from one of the crates along with a bottle knife to cut the wax seal and left.

A huge sigh of relief came from all the women, who then giggled at each other's reactions. They began chatting to each other companionably again, ignoring Elaine completely. Mara plunked a plate of food and a cup of wine before Elaine, then sat down in what had been Coro's spot.

"Damned whore does not know his place," she muttered, then glanced over at Elaine. "He is my cousin. Cannot fight worth anything but insists that he outranks us."

Elaine nodded noncommittally then looked down at the food, contemplating how she was going to eat any of it with her shawl over her face.

"So why is your face covered?" a familiar voice asked, but Elaine couldn't figure out who asked it. The other women around the table all turned to her, waiting for the answer.

With a bit of hesitation, Elaine reached up and pulled her shawl away from her face. "It is the way of our people," she said slowly, affecting Acies's accent. "To protect our face from harm."

"What kind of harm can you find here?" a woman next to Mara asked, scoffingly.

"In my home, sand," Elaine said, picking up the wine cup. "It can scour the skin from your flesh in moments. Here? Rain, wind, the eyes of men." She took a sip to wet her dry mouth.

"Huh, my mother would have loved that," Mara commented, just as her cousin returned through the tent. "She was always intent on keeping me at home to be her personal slave, even though we had three in the house. She was furious when I left with Lorab."

"I *did* think we were going to be inside the castle, not in a damned drafty tent," Coro murmured as he re-entered the tent, killing the lighter mood immediately with his presence. "The Sword would like some more food, Mara."

"Then get him some more food," she challenged, staring him down. Jutting out his lower lip, he stomped over to the table to seize a plate of prepared food, casting dirty looks at his cousin the whole time.

"You do not want to go into the castle anyway," a familiar voice said to Elaine, but she couldn't tell who had spoken.

"It is not a castle; it is a fortress," Mara corrected.

"Do you know why?" Coro snapped, ignoring Mara. "Any of you? Have you actually seen the people inside the fortress?"

The other women glanced among themselves, and Elaine realized they hadn't. That was odd.

"What is wrong with the people inside the fortress?" one of them asked softly.

Coro propped the platter against his hip, obviously enjoying the undivided attention he had acquired. "Have you also noticed how slaves go in, but none come out? They say that the Lord Dakin eats—"

"Curse you, Coro. Get out of here!" Mara picked up a walnut from a bowl and lobbed it at him. He smacked it away violently, his nostrils flaring. The young man took two steps forward like he was going to hit her, but she stood up. Mara was clearly taller and more imposing than he was.

To his credit, he did not back down. "Maybe you should be sleeping with the dogs when he chooses me tonight," Coro barked.

She grabbed a hank of his hair, pulling his head to the side. "I said, get out!" And she threw him from the tent. The flaps blocking the outside billowed wide, and Elaine could see Acies sitting by Lorab at the fire. Both men turned as the rest of the warriors hooted at the show. The platter of prepared food went flying.

"You stay out here!" Mara barked. "You do not even make a decent woman to be allowed to sit among us."

The warriors outside howled with more laughter. Mara flounced around and came back into the tent, replacing the flap. She set herself back in her spot at the table, a proud queen having just flexed her muscles. The other women praised her and agreed that they were all fed up with Coro, and the chat continued into more inane things.

Every second of sitting there after that was agony for Elaine. She forced herself to eat the meal provided and helped grind up spices in a pestle and mortar to flavor the dishes the other women were preparing, but none of them spoke directly to her, and what they were talking about was so boring and frivolous, Elaine couldn't bring herself to try to join them. Finally, needing something more to do with her hands, she took up a roll of dough and began dividing it into pieces.

"Whatcha doing?" the familiar voice asked, wiggling around the table to watch Elaine as she rolled the pieces out. Elaine didn't look up, wrestling with one of the strands of dough as it thinned too much and threatened to break. From what she could tell from glancing in her periphery, it was a little girl.

"I am going to make a braided bread. It was my favorite when I was a girl," Elaine said as she finished the braid, tucking and pinching the ends under. "And then you brush it with a little honey." She claimed the honey pot and used the small coarse brush inside to paint a gold layer over it. "Then bake it."

"Wow," the little girl breathed, and she stuck her finger in the honeypot to scoop a globule out into her mouth.

"Oh, you should not do that," Elaine said, moving the honeypot back. "We have to use that for everybody." Then she stopped as she finally looked the little girl full in the face. "It... it's you..."

The little girl smiled, unworried. "You should cover up now."

Before Elaine could ask her what she meant by that, the flap to the tent came open again. This time Lorab came in with Acies right behind him. Elaine turned her head and quickly tucked the shawl over her nose, but she couldn't get it to hold in place, so she had to leave her hand up to hold it. By the time she looked back, the little mysterious girl was gone again.

"Alright, ladies. You, come," the Sword ordered, pointing at Elaine.

She glanced at Acies, whose face remained passive but steady as he met her eyes. She stood up, and her demon offered her his arm, which she blinked at only for a second before taking.

Lorab noted it too, but only sniffed as his comment and walked out, marching over to one of the tents at the far end. Just as they approached, Athorn emerged, carrying his stuff.

"Hurry up. Get a moving," Lorab snapped at the Ka'in tracker. It did not inspire him to actually move any faster.

Again, his angry glance met Elaine's, and she had no doubt he knew who she was. She swallowed bile down her throat and looked back at the newly cleared tent. It was like the others, not nearly as grand as Dakin's had been but about par to any other tent: tall enough to stand up and wide enough for a camp desk, double cot, and a chest for anything else. There were even rugs on the ground.

Lorab marched in and swept his hands around the space. "This is yours. Do with it what you will. We are not moving for a while yet, but when we do, it will also be yours."

Acies glanced at it, not nearly impressed enough in Elaine's opinion to appease an ego like Lorab's, but the Sword didn't actually seem to mind. Instead, Acies grunted, then crossed his arms. "I want to choose my own band now," he said.

"Take a second to settle in," Lorab said with a dismissive wave. "There is no rush. I will come get you soon."

After that, he left. Elaine waited several breaths then came closer to Acies. "<What happened?>" she whispered in godspeech, pulling her shawl down.

"<I made a good impression,>" Acies said loudly in Anon, apparently not at all afraid of eavesdroppers. "<When he comes back, I will go look over the slaves, find Elan.>"

Elaine could not be as relaxed. "<Acies, the man we took this tent from. He was a Ka'in,>" Elaine said urgently, continuing in godspeech. "<He recognized me.>"

Acies's eyes widened, slightly. "<He saw your face?>" he asked, now switching to godspeech as well.

She shook her head. "<No, but...>" Drawing in a deep breath, she forced herself to calm down. "<I knew there was a risk coming in here. I am just saying we need to hurry before they find us out.>"

Acies nodded. "<We will hurry,>" he assured her. "<You will stay here?>"

"<Yes,>" she said definitively. "<Find Elan. I will be alright.>"

Her demon hesitated too, clearly reluctant to leave her alone but knowing this was what they had come here for.

"<We can do this,>" she assured him.

"<I did not doubt it,>" he agreed, which helped her feel more solid.

She reached up and pulled gently on his hair, adjusting the band over his forehead so his ears remained covered. "<Do not let them see this,>" she warned.

He nodded, then he was gone.

Elaine sank on the edge of the bed, taking a deep breath in as she listened to the sounds outside. No one was looking for her. They were all pre-occupied with the chaos and preparations for Dakin's war.

So close.

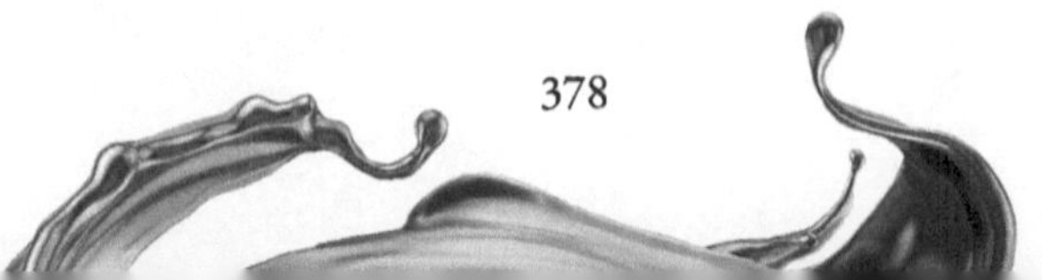

She was so close to the fortress she swore she could hear his voice out there. And all she wanted to do was run.

After a few fortifying breaths, she became aware of the single eye peeking in at her through the tent flaps.

I forgot to tell Acies about the little girl! she realized.

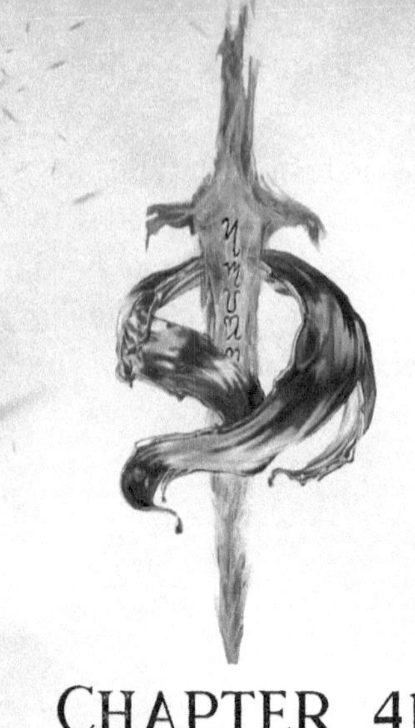

CHAPTER 41

"I SEE YOU THERE," ELAINE SAID, AND THE LITTLE girl came the rest of the way into the tent.

"I am so glad you came," the little girl said, skipping over to plop next to Elaine on the cot. "Are you going to stay here awhile?"

Elaine smiled. "Not too long," she said, noticing the pendant bouncing at the end of a cord.

Could it be...? she thought.

"Why are you here?" the little girl asked without any preamble, kicking her legs out freely, her physical shaking of the cot verifying for Elaine that she was very much a real little girl and not a ghost. She wasn't ready to rule a spirit out, though. "Hey, I asked you a question."

"That was going to be my question," Elaine countered, crossing her arms in front of her at the rude little visitor. It wasn't that the child wasn't a ball of sunshine delight, but with so much at stake, Elaine feared for the child's safety as well as her own.

"Yeah, but answer mine first. Why are you here?" she repeated, giggling.

Elaine dropped her arms and sighed, unable to keep the smile from her face. "I am here to get my brother back and find a shrine of Isa," she said, then brought her hand up to her mouth in shock. "I had not meant to say that."

"<Find a shrine of Isa?>" the little girl repeated this time in flawless Ka'in. "<Who is Isa?>"

"<A powerful Goddess of the River that passes by here,>" Elaine said, again speaking the truth without really meaning to, even answering in Ka'in despite herself. "<I am looking for her." It was compulsive>.

The little girl's face went very serious, like she was trying to understand a deep problem. "<Why would you want to find her?>" the little girl asked.

"<Because I am her Scion, and I need to know what my purpose in life really is,>" Elaine said, even as she actually tried not to even speak.

"<Hmm, okay,>" replied the little girl, as if what Elaine had said wasn't profound or amazing, but she supposed it wasn't to a little girl.

To Elaine, however, it was profound.

Unfortunately, her guest wasn't giving her any time to contemplate.

"Tents are amazing, but do you want to see where I live?" the little girl asked, switching back to Anon as she sidled up beside Elaine.

"Well—" Elaine started also able to speak as she wished again but kept her focus on the familiar pendant that continued to bob and weave as she moved. "Where did you get that?"

Elaine attempted to grasp the familiar symbol of Isa, confirming in that moment that it *was* Flicker's amulet, but the little girl bolted away.

"Hey!" Elaine called, chasing after her.

The little girl was quick, rushing between the tents to leap up onto the stone wall of the paddock. She apparently didn't expect Elaine to continue to chase so far because she had almost caught the brat at the wall.

With a yip, the little girl jumped off the other side and took off, her bare feet crunching the grass.

"Hey, wait!" Elaine called after her, though still pitching it down so she didn't catch unwanted attention as she climbed up and over the mid-waist stone wall. The little girl did not heed her but took off up the hill toward the wall of Icathor, Flicker's amulet bouncing wildly from side to side of her little body as she ran.

Elaine couldn't let her get away. She knew she could catch her as the hill grew steeper, forcing the little thief to slow down. Yet the closest Elaine got was within an extra arm's length, and still, the little girl eluded her. And then Elaine slipped. Her whole body slapped against the turf before sliding back down the hill a little. It might have been a league because the little girl made it the rest of the way to the wall of the fortress, stopping once she reached it.

From where she lay, Elaine could see a small portal in the wall just to their left. She was certain that the little girl would head to the gateway and escape her.

Except, instead, the little girl went to the right, skittering not as quickly as before along the rounded wall. For the life of her, Elaine could not figure out why she would go that way since there was nothing to the right except the even steeper side that led down to Isa's river. She would be cornered.

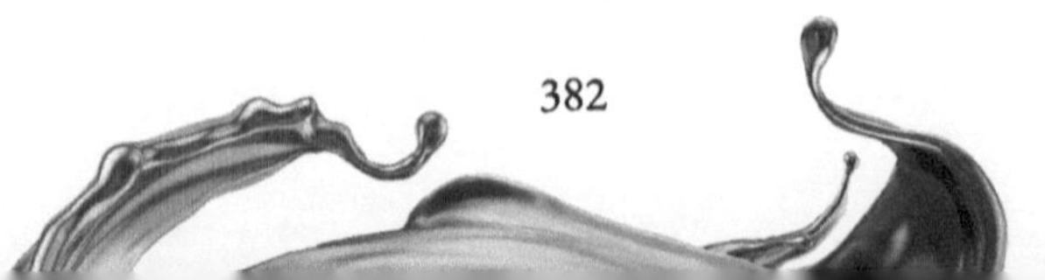

Realizing she still had a chance to recover Flicker, Elaine pulled herself back up to her feet.

Following along the wall was easier, and soon enough, Elaine found herself out of sight of the training camp. To her surprise, she spotted the little girl bending down beside a blank section of wall before disappearing.

"What in the world...?" Elaine asked as she huffed up to the spot where the little girl vanished. "Ah ha!"

A grate covered a small tunnel through the wall built of dry, flat stones. Lacing her fingers through the bronze metal rods, greened from exposure to the elements, Elaine pulled. The cover attached to the rods popped free easily. Sticking her head in, Elaine was greeted by a rank smell, like fetid water and all the wastes the human body was capable of creating bound together as one epic scent. She could also hear rustling echoing down the tunnel and the labored breathing of a child.

"Dammit," Elaine muttered, realizing what she was preparing to do. She fit just exactly through the grate entrance with no room to turn around and replace the cover. Hopefully there would be an opportunity soon, but for now, she focused on crawling forward into the tunnel.

When she thought before that the stones were dry, she was sad to realize she was wrong as her hands encountered pockets of slime trapped in the places where the stones were no longer flush with each other. It was also incredibly dark as her backside blocked most of the light. She had gone two lengths of her own height into the tunnel and was considering giving up and crawling back out when a light did appear only a person's span ahead of her. The little girl's legs were in bright relief as she stood, pushing another grate up and out. Then the legs disappeared.

Elaine hurried, crawling as fast as she could before the light disappeared. She arrived beneath it just as the cover above dropped back into place. Not letting it stop her, Elaine pushed up on to her knees and lifted her hands. To her relief, it shifted away immediately, and the little girl yelped in surprise, her toes dancing away from the edge as Elaine popped her head out.

"Give me back my pendant," Elaine hissed, but the little girl took off running again.

The tunnel had led out between two mudbrick houses just wide enough for a person to walk through and not scrape their elbows.

Elaine hauled herself out of the hole and tried not to think about how badly she smelled. She scraped the muck from her hands along the stone ground. She wanted to take off in pursuit again, but she needed to be cautious.

She was inside Icathor.

Then a small face peaked around a corner, smiling brightly. "Come on. This way."

"Oh, come on," Elaine sighed, but she couldn't forsake Flicker.

The little girl continued to be only a few steps ahead of her, but Elaine simply could not catch up. As winded as she was, the little girl seemed fresh as she scurried between the permanent buildings.

The fortress was all very organized with the buildings themselves lining a main road winding up. The inner ring of buildings were built against or carved from the stone in the hill, right out of the living rock. Each building paralleled the one butted against the outer wall.

For some reason Elaine couldn't fathom, she didn't see a single person moving on the main thoroughfare.

All was quiet as the pair of fugitives ran through their streets. Even though she had never walked among the people of Icathor, Elaine had seen them go about their business from the window of the concubine's room. But this was midday, and there wasn't a soul about. And there was a scent on the air.

Elaine had thought it was simply the smell from the sewer tunnel, but it was stronger and thicker inside the fortress. She paused at a door that stood open, the smell emanating so strongly from within it made her gag.

"Death," she whispered, recognizing it. She pressed her shawl against her nose and mouth.

"What is wrong with you? This way," the little girl called too loudly, practically out of thin air, her fists pressed into her hips like a mother scolding her dawdling child.

Elaine only glanced back at the open door before she turned away to continue her pursuit.

Abruptly, she found herself standing before an entrance formed in the rock and earth wall. Or at least, it did not look like a natural cave, but rather one that had been shaped by skilled hands. Signs and markings were etched into the surface, and while plant growth had worked its way in between a few of the stones, it did not lessen the care someone had once taken in it. Garbage and plant matter decorated the ground just within the opening, which reflected its change of status to the people it once served. Elaine hesitated as she took in the elegance of it.

The little girl laughed as she darted in. "Come on, Elaine!" she called. "Come see!"

Surprised the girl knew her name, the Ka'in Princess followed her, slipping through the narrow entry into a tight corridor, plunging once more into the dark. As her eyes adjusted though, they were greeted at the end by a warm space filled with soft light from countless oil lamps. A spicy scent tickled at her nose, reminding her of the temple back in her home village.

The space was furnished with wooden chairs and a lounger, covered in furs and even more precious woven clothes draped over everything including the floor. It was a whole different world from the one Elaine expected. A small table held a platter filled with wooden bowls of fruit, cheeses, meats, and loaves of scented bread. Elaine's stomach growled impolitely at the smells.

The little girl bounced up onto the lounger, kicking her feet some more with a joyful grin. "Come on! Come eat!" she cried, gesturing at the food. "You are welcome."

"<Indeed, you are welcome, Scion of Isa,>" a mature, womanly voice echoed.

Lorab did not stop talking to Acies the whole time they toured the slave paddocks, mostly about the strengths and potential of what they saw. Lorab seemed to appreciate Acies's own assessments and had decided that the demon was his new best friend. Easy comradery had always been a simple thing for Acies. He understood it and slid right in as if he had been a part of this growing army for months instead of hours.

"No, Ka'ins?" Acies finally asked after they had made their final pass at the paddock.

"No, all the Ka'ins have been chased inside," Lorab said jovially.

"Then what are all these?" Acies asked, pointing a finger at a pair wrestling in the dirt with no shirts and plenty of sweat.

"I think half of them used to be farmers or something," Lorab commented. "Quite a few came out of Icathor, but I do not know. That is a scribe's job anyway."

Lorab directed their steps back toward the camp paddock, and Acies rested his eyes on the fortress.

"Seen anything like it?" Lorab asked.

Acies shrugged a shoulder.

"Your Anon is quite good. Where are you from?"

"The desert lands," Acies lied easily.

An eyebrow quirked. "You are a long way from home then?"

"I have come farther than I ever thought I would," Acies agreed.

"So, we have proved your prowess in a fight, and such, but do you mind me asking," Lorab continued, "why do you travel with a woman?"

"You travel with a woman," Acies commented, nodding at Mara who had appeared beside the firepit with the other women.

"Yes, but she is new, and I did not have to travel very far with her. Or her cousin." Lorab laughed, slapping his chest with a fist. "A powerful man has powerful appetites. If you wish to take a taste of her, you are more than welcome," Lorab offered, chuckling with a sidelong look.

Acies could see the test with his eyes closed. "I only take the spoils owed me. I do not indebt myself to another man," he said, quoting the old battlefield wisdom.

Lorab nodded at that, the germination of intelligence hinting in his eyes. "That is a clever saying."

"I cannot take credit for it, but it has proven true more often than not."

A faint scent wafted through the air, stopping Acies in his tracks. It came from another group of warriors in a paddock farthest away from any other activity. Several of the warriors were kneeling before a man holding a chalice.

A very familiar man.

As he turned, Acies recognized him as one of the priests that had been at the temple to sacrifice Elaine. He had slaughtered so many of them that night, he had not realized this one had escaped.

The priest held the chalice out before him, saying words that were carried off by the wind. Then he went before each one, sticking a finger in the chalice. Obediently, each man opened their mouth to receive a drop of some black substance before making a symbol with their fingers.

His guide slapped him on the back. "Well, what do you think, Acies? Are you in with us?"

Acies glanced at the man who smiled the satisfied smile of someone who believed he knew the answer already. He sensed the other warriors encircling them but did nothing to stop them when they seized his upper arms. He found himself "dragged" into the paddock and unnecessarily forced to kneel before the priest. The old man came up to him, studying his face. Acies met the gaze unwavering, waiting to see what would happen. The old man's expression didn't change, and he held up the chalice with a deep reverence that almost made Acies laugh.

Now that he was closer, the demon could smell exactly what it was.

Demon blood.

"Show him the sign of our God Dakin," the priest declared, and every one of the warriors around him flashed the sign. "Do you accept the sign of our new, true god?"

All around him waited expectantly, and he formed the signal with his fingers. The priest then dipped his finger into the chalice. "Open your mouth," he commanded.

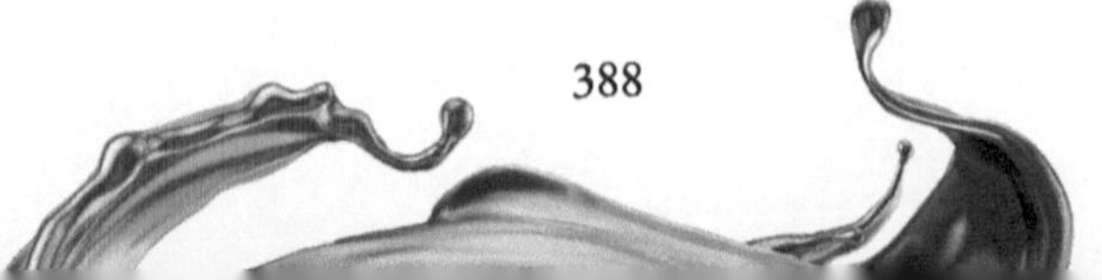

388

Acies glanced at Lorab who smirked, then nodded. "You want to be one of us? Do what he says. It is this or death, and no matter how good of a fighter you are, we outnumber you."

He took long enough to make a show of measuring the strength of those surrounding him before Acies opened his mouth and let the priest drip the demon blood into his mouth. It burned and stabbed at the back of his throat, forcing him to swallow several times to keep from coughing.

It did nothing to him, of course. He was already a demon in his own right, and the traces of arete in this blood were nothing compared to his own.

"Rise, my son," the priest said with an imperious gesture. "You are now a child of the one living god, Dakin. May you fight for his glory!"

Lorab, again, companionably slapped Acies on the shoulder. "Come on. Now that that is out of the way, we can drink and feast 'til our dicks need wetting!"

The demon stood up and followed his host out of the paddock without a backward glance. While he had been expecting an initiation ritual of some sort, this one forced him to change his calculation of the fledgling army.

"You could have warned me," Acies commented.

"It is a test for a reason. We do not need any weak shits around here," Lorab answered. "I knew you would have no problem with it, a warrior like you. But it was a privilege, remember. Only those worth anything will be initiated."

"Meaning the slaves do not get this blessing?" Acies asked.

Lorab shrugged. "Maybe if they survive a few battles, they might be worth it. But enough of this. Let us go."

Yet Lorab didn't turn toward the camp but, instead, directed Acies to the road leading up to back entryway into the fortress.

"To the fortress?" Acies questioned.

"Yes, there is a feast tonight, and you are my guest," Lorab said proudly. "I wish to introduce you to our Lord."

Acies looked to the tents where Elaine was waiting for him to report, then back to the fortress where he knew he would not be welcome should its appointed patron goddess catch him there. He wanted to tell himself that he did not care about that, but it would be a stupid lie, even if it was just to himself. He was walking into danger, and a true warrior noted it.

Lorab noticed. "This feast is for warriors only. No ... paramours," he warned.

The demon turned back to the other demon, then slapped him hard on the shoulder. That set Lorab off to laughing, and the pair headed up into the fortress.

Elaine would have to be alright for a few hours.

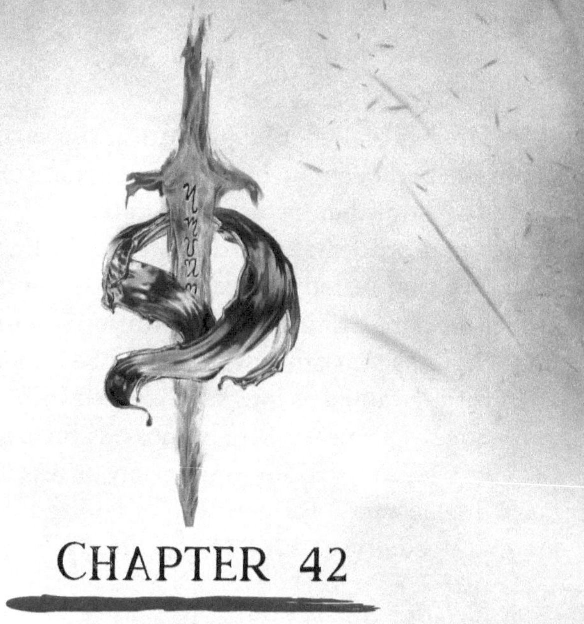

CHAPTER 42

DAKIN STARED OUT WITH LONGING OVER HIS WAR-
riors and their feast. It had barely started, but the screams of
the dying already echoed off the walls as each presentation
was set upon by five or six warriors apiece, drinking down
the blood and power within that blood as gleefully as if they
had ripped into a roast beast.

Yet he alone seemed to be suffering in agony. The slow
sort that did not seem like anything until the pain went on
for hours, then days, until it ate him alive. He wanted something he could not put a name to—the hunger inside simply
could not be satiated.

He shoved one of the dead slaves with his foot, knocking
the limp, lifeless body bonelessly away from his chair. He had
tried everything. He ate the blood of animals, of the slaves,
then just the Ka'in slaves. Their small bits of life fed his body,
but it did not satisfy. It seemed like nothing could. And it
brought him no joy. Certainly not the ecstasy he saw on his
warrior's faces.

"Amira," he called. She jumped in the seat next to him where she had been pushing around a plate of the food he used to consume before his ascension.

"Yes, my Lord?" she asked demurely, adjusting the Coronet of Icathor that rested on her head, its bejeweled and gold surface winking at him. She had turned out to be as much of a delight as that other woman had been, letting him do whatever he wanted as long as it pleased him. The Coronet had seemed a fitting token of his possession to place on such a woman. He enjoyed her immensely. It was amazing how easily she accepted his new way of taking sustenance. All she had needed was a little breaking. "What do you wish, my Lord?"

But Dakin pursed his lips, unsure of what to ask for. He had everything he ever wanted, at least in the material realm.

"Is there anything I could help you with, my Lord? Could I ease your burden?" she pressed. She stood up to let the fine linen robe she wore fall open slightly.

He eyed the pretty picture. She was so wonderfully thin now. Her ribs showed along with her collar bones, and the lines of her face were sharp and clear. He relished it. She was exactly how he truly desired women, beautiful and thin. Just the sight of her made him harden with anticipation, but he waved her away dismissively. If he indulged now, she would think that she had a way to control him, and he couldn't have that.

"Send for Razal," he ordered. "I wish to consult with my priest."

She dipped and hurried away. He enjoyed watching his concubine go. For a moment, he thought about bestowing his blessing on her as well, then she would enjoy these feasts more, but he decided he did not need her getting stronger or more powerful. She was fulfilling the only thing she needed to. If he had only known that the merchant's daughter just needed some straightening out, he may have taken her sooner as a second mistress and avoided the whole mess with the insurrection. She was a wonderful possession.

Yet even in that he was unsatisfied. She was all too ... Anon. Too human. He had not tasted her blood, but he knew it would be like ashes in his mouth. What he longed for was so much richer than that. He closed his eyes, and he was there again. His Ka'in woman lying in beautiful repose, the scent of her more intoxicating than wine. It was *her* he wanted—to control, to possess, to consume. If he had her, then he would feel complete.

A growl rose in his throat. "How dare she," he muttered. The ache for her was painful. "How dare she cause me to suffer!"

"Who, my Lord?" Razal asked, making his presence known.

Dakin turned, pinning his priest with an angry stare. "How long have you been listening?"

"The Lady Amira bid me see you, and I came instantly," the old man explained.

"The *Lady* Amira?" Dakin questioned.

"Why yes. All who lay with a god are blessed ladies, are they not?" Razal asked smoothly.

"Of course, of course. That makes perfect sense." Dakin nodded, waving the concern away. There were more pressing issues. "Razal, I am ... troubled."

"Commune with me, my Lord, and I will find a way to ease your burdens," Razal assured him.

Dakin eyed the feasting room. Smoothly, Razal gestured for a slave to bring a goblet of thick redness to Dakin. "Our Lord desires to take a walk and survey our glorious future."

The room cheered as Dakin rose, taking the offered goblet. He saluted the room, then followed Razal out the back set of doors to the garden beyond.

"Now, my Lord. Tell me what troubles you?"

"I am not pleased with Amira," Dakin said, taking a long but disappointing draft from his goblet.

"What displeases you, my Lord?" Razal asked with the grave concern the statement warranted.

"She is insufficient. Isn't that enough? I am displeased."

"I see. Well, that is easily remedied," Razal said, relaxing his shoulders as he folded his hands into his sleeves. "Give me a few days, and I will bring you a selection of females for you to choose from for your harem. In fact, have you considered blessing Amira—"

"No," Dakin snapped. "Why would I do that? She is just a concubine."

"She is your last thread to the merchants."

Dakin narrowed his eyes at the wizard-priest. "Which ones? They are all dead now," he scoffed.

"The ones to the south," Razal said simply.

That gave Dakin pause, so Razal continued.

"We may have seized everything from the merchants here, but if we are to succeed with your grander plans to conquer the south and make you High King, we will need allies. Amira's family is one of the most powerful, and Amira is now the only heir. If she is bound to you as an equal... a queen..."

That gave the god Dakin pause as he considered it. "I accomplish that if I keep her as a concubine."

"Aye, my Lord," Razal agreed, bowing his head.

A cheer went up back in the feasting room, piquing Dakin's curiosity. "See to the harem, Razal. Personally."

"Of course, my Lord. It will be worthy of a great god such as yourself."

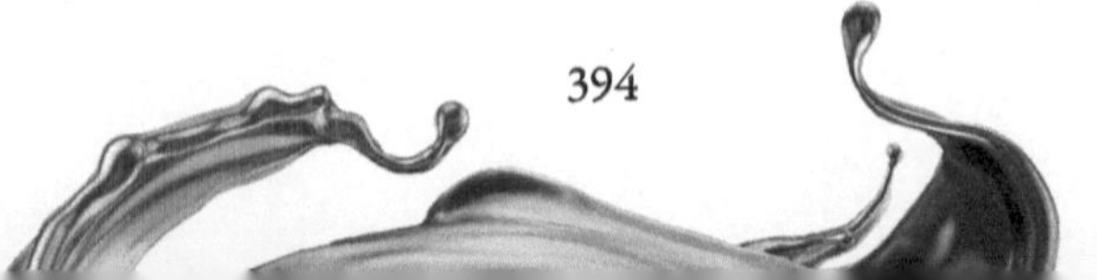

"Very good, good, great," Dakin muttered and returned to his celebrations. Razal was right. A harem was a perfect solution.

Amira waited, breathing shallowly beside the banquet room's inner door. She should have returned to the feast, but she simply could not stand it there one more minute.

Her only other option was to retreat to the concubine's room; she still couldn't bring herself to think of it as her room. This couldn't be her life. She wouldn't accept that this was her fate.

She was a free woman of the Anon. A respected woman. A leader.

She had to escape. It had failed once, but she had been spared, so there was still another chance if only she could find a better way to do it.

Twice she had sent messages to her father through two of the slaves she could trust, both Anons, that had been placed by her brother to spy on Dakin. Yet they had not received a single reply. Very little news was coming from outside the fortress.

Another person screamed.

Amira bit her lower lip, refusing to let her eyes water into tears. Weeping would only signal defeat to these monsters, but the pressure of them came anyway.

"Get a move on, hurry," a harsh voice barked down the hall. Amira froze, then scurried back into an alcove out of sight.

A string of Ka'in were brought on a line of rope up the stairs from below. Another round for the feast. Amira could barely look at them. For the first time in her life, she did not see Ka'in or Anon, she only saw people who would soon die in a horrible way.

Then she stared hard at a young man third from the front. She knew him.

She was sure of it.

"You there," she said to the lead Anon who was barking at the line to sidle up along the wall.

He turned, his ugly expression shifting to uncertainty at the sight of Amira. "Yes?" he asked.

She adjusted the Coronet of Icathor and struck a pose, standing in soft torchlight of the building as regally and full of authority she could muster. Then she pointed at the third Ka'in in the line. "I want him," she stated.

The guard pursed his eyebrows together. He looked at the line and then looked back at her. She didn't flinch away, only waited serenely as if she fully expected her order to be obeyed. There was another scream from the feasting room, and they all flinched, including the Anon, at the sound, which was followed by the roar of laughter and cheers from the warriors.

Amira did not flinch; she only smiled at the Anon.

"Yes, my Lady," he said, cowed. He didn't bother untying the man. He simply cut him from the line, leaving his hands bound in front of him. He handed her the length of rope, which she received serenely.

Now she was faced with the next problem. While the Anon's eyes were on her, she couldn't exactly lead the Ka'in up to a safe place without arousing suspicion. Moving with him through the feast room was the same as guaranteeing his death.

She let her gaze wash over the rest of the line. "You may take the rest away," she said, in a sudden burst of inspiration. "They are not needed for tonight."

A cry of relief rose up with some of the offering as they turned to move down the stairs. Before the Anon could do much of anything, the Ka'in were already in full retreat. There was little he could really do but follow along, only glancing back toward the feasting room with uncertainty.

Once they were gone, Amira breathed a small sigh of relief before turning to the Ka'in beside her.

He looked at her with sharp eyes, or rather eye as the other was swollen shut. There was still defiance in that gaze. That was good. Defiance was what she needed right then.

"Come with me," she whispered urgently, tugging his bound hands. He blinked once at her but resisted. "Unless you would like to go in there?" She gestured at the feast.

Understandable fear washed over his face, and he yielded to her next tug. As they went past the doorway, she prayed to the Goddess of the City that no one saw them.

"Hurry," she whispered, and this time he did so. They ran up the stairs all the way to the third floor where the lord's rooms were, as well as the concubine's. But she knew she couldn't hide her prize in her chamber.

Improvising, she turned to the left to the final room on that floor—one that housed the private shrine to the patron goddess of the city, the Goddess Nymphaea.

"This way, quickly," Amira said.

The room was being used for storage, all reverence for the city's goddess forgotten as prayers went unanswered. This neglect, however, allowed Amira to tuck herself and the Ka'in among the stacked crates, out of anyone's sight.

The statue of the city's goddess stood in the same place it had for centuries. It had been a beautiful statue carved from rock to resemble a graceful woman, proud and strong, holding a stone hammer in one hand against her chest and a shield against her legs, emblemed with a rose. At another time, Amira would have marveled at her personal chosen god's likeness wrought in the polish quartz stone.

Maybe if the goddess had answered her prayers.

"Why are you helping me?" the Ka'in asked as she squatted down beside him so she could keep an eye on the doorway.

"I am helping myself, Ka'in," she said sharply. "You are only lucky that I recognize someone who can help me make that happen. You are one of Titama's men, correct? I know you."

The Ka'in arched the eyebrow over his unswollen eye, the blonde-white hair ghostly in the dim light. "I am," he said guardedly.

"What is your name?" Amira pressed.

"Why would I give you that?" he challenged, his Anon accented but fluent enough. He bit each word like the taste of them in his mouth was foul.

"I can simply call you Ka'in if you like, but—"

"It is <Elan,>" he said, turning his attention to the rope still binding his hands together.

"Elan," she repeated, or thought she had.

"No, <Elan>. His eyes flashed hostile.

"Fine. My name is Amira," she offered in exchange as she moved to help him unbind himself.

"I know," he responded. "I know who you are, Anon."

"Oh" was all she could think to say back as she worked her fingers into the overly tightened knot and managed to pry it loose.

Once he was free, Elan rubbed at his wrists, which had been clearly abraded. "I do not know where Titama is at this time," he said.

"I do. He is dead," Amira responded grimly.

Elan went still before searching her eyes to verify the truth. "How?" he finally asked.

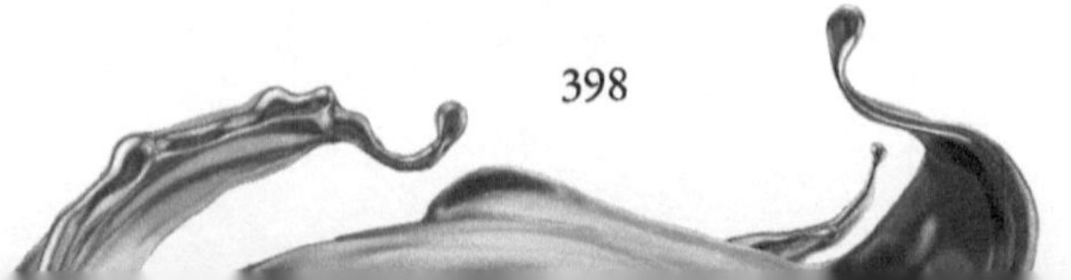

"He was killed when I was captured. He... He died saving me," she half-lied. His saving her was more a coincidental side effect of saving himself, but she needed some sympathy if she was going to get this Ka'in to help her.

"Then he died stupidly," Elan dismissed with an unexpected hardness that sent Amira back into her calculations again.

"You were not friends?" she asked warily.

"We were rivals mostly, but we fought side by side," he said, giving a warrior's answer.

She moved to brush his hair back from his damaged face and revealed the bindings at his ears from being docked. She hissed a surprised intake of breath at the horrendous sight. He flinched and pulled his hair back over the mutilation, glaring at the floor.

"I am sorry," she said softly, her own compassion burning.

He only continued to glare, obviously more humiliated than hurt by the act. She pulled away the sleeve of her fine tunic from her shoulder, revealing bruises down her side and along her back. Her hands shook as she did it, holding the cloth against her chest as she did so. Yet the Ka'in's eyes softened at the sight of his own pain reflected at him. Very gently, he took up the cloth and pulled the sleeve back over her shoulder, hiding away her own suffering and restoring her dignity.

She gently brushed away the water at the edges of her eyes. "You see you are not the only one to have suffered, Ka'in." She had to clear her throat.

"What do you want of me, Anon?" Elan asked.

"I want to be free of this nightmare. I want to go home to the south," she said, her voice returning to its normal control.

"You want to run away."

She shot him a dark, offended look. "I want to survive, and I will call you a liar or fool if you do not want the same thing."

"You have no idea what I want," he said bitterly.

She took it for the opportunity it was. "Then tell me what you want, and I will do everything in my power to fulfill it in exchange for your help getting me out of here," she stated, knowing the gambling game she played.

He chuffed a dry, mirthless laugh. "You are as powerless as I, princess," he muttered, glancing pointedly at her Coronet.

At first, she was insulted, but then she turned that word over in her mind. It was not one that any used, but the Ka'in... "You are the Prince of the Ka'in, tell me true?" she asked softly.

He flinched, confirming it.

She nodded. "Yes, you are the one that eluded the Anon all those years. Titama's secret throwing bone."

He stared at her, keeping his own counsel. Unfortunately, Amira could not see a way to use that to her advantage. He was right, such a fact was irrelevant now; his title had no power behind it just as her status had been despoiled by the same force that had docked his ears.

So where did that leave either of them? She needed to think. She had already risked so much without a plan.

"Stay here," she said, standing to leave. "Do not move until I come for you. I will be back soon."

"Blessings from the gods are difficult to bear, are they not?" a voice said, making her jump out of her skin. She spun to the voice, even as Elan tucked himself farther back into the line of crates he hid behind.

Razal stepped into the shrine, folding his hands once more into his sleeves as he continued to smile that eerie, mocking smile at her. Pulling at her robe, Amira forced herself to stand, keeping a hand on the goddess's leg for balance and to fortify herself.

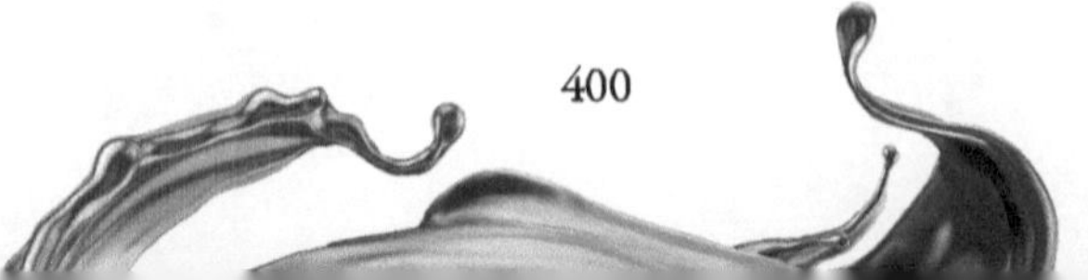

"I apologize for disturbing your prayers," Razal continued, bowing his head politely. "You seem to be in need of some counsel. May I be of some help?"

"There is nothing I need from you," Amira said, gathering herself to try to walk straight past the wizard-priest and lead him away from her secrets. She folded her hands to hide their shaking and hopefully make an innocent picture.

"Oh, I think there is much you need," Razal said. "I think you have not fully grasped the situation you now find yourself and are struggling to find your place in it. Our god has asked a lot of us mortals. That *is* why there are priests."

"He is not a god," Amira said, spitting the word with force. It was a mistake, and she knew it the moment she said it, but it had been a truth too hard to hold back. Her negotiating skills were all that were left to her, and never before had she felt more inadequate to the task. *I need to find serenity if I do not wish to lose my head,* she thought.

Amused by her obvious struggles, Razal's smile deepened into something closer to madness than mirth. "Oh, he is. I have worked very hard to make him so." Razal stepped away from the crates, encroaching farther on Amira's space. Two more steps, and he would see the hidden Ka'in easily. "And I will give my last breath to make sure he remains so."

It took every ounce of willpower not to look at Elan at her feet for help, to keep her eyes on Razal, like a ferret staring down a snake. Then the priest looked away from her to contemplate the statue of the patron goddess behind her with pitying, amused eyes.

"There is no comfort to be found here, child. She is just empty stone. An illusion for gullible creatures to bow to in place of the real thing. But I suppose I do not need to tell you that." He looked at her knowingly.

As if he had called them forth, visions of her pleas to the goddess going unanswered to save her from Lorab and the other warrior dogs that had violated her went unanswered. Water filled her eyes, blurring Razal's features. Desperately trying to blink them away only launched them like ships down a river from her eyes.

"Yes, yes," Razal cooed. "It has been very hard to live in a world where the gods are a lie. But do not despair, child. I am here to help you."

"Please," she whispered, "Please just let me leave."

Razal stretched out his thin fingers and stroked her hair. She endured it.

"Do not be so fearful; I am a friend to you, Amira of the Anon. You are in a unique position and are not easily replaced. It is to both of our benefits that we ally." He seemed to mean the statement as a compliment.

"What do you mean?"

"Oh, come woman, you are smarter than that. Think about it. You are a respected daughter of the merchant class, and you are now the concubine to a new god who will usher us into a new world."

Amira's mind raced as he stated these obvious things. She had already realized that was the reason she was still alive. Her family connections to the south were valuable. "You wish me to help you negotiate with the south."

"See, you are a smart female," Razal assured her, as if such a thing was unique.

"Dakin will not listen to me," she said, shaking her head. "The merchants to the south will see no profit in dealing with a... a..." Any of the words she would use to describe what Dakin was now—murderer, oath-breaker, tyrant...

"Conqueror," Razal said, finishing her phrase for her. "With my support, Dakin will listen to you. He intends to claim

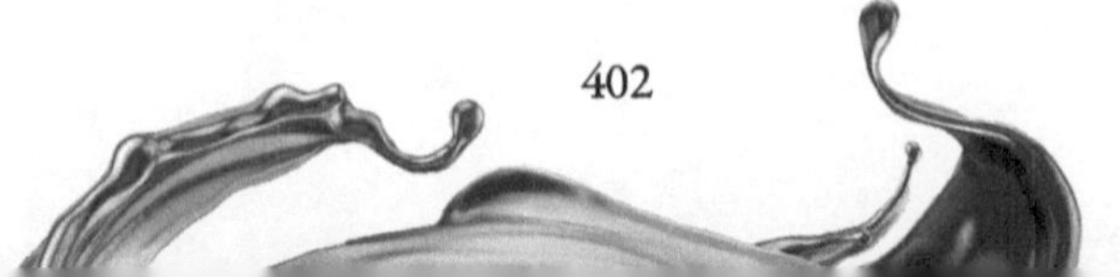

all these lands under his holy rule, and he has the power to do it. You can still have everything you wanted, Amira, everything you dreamed of. With a little time, I can arrange to have you marry Dakin, to make you his consort and first among his women. You will bring the Anon into a better position under him, increasing his power and therefore your own. You would be the treasured mother of a new nation."

Amira's fingers curled against the statue. "Mother of a nation?"

Razal's voice lowered as he leaned closer, practically whispering in her ear. "Maybe even a consort goddess." He reached up a hand and laid it against the stone statue. "Maybe this is you, the patron goddess of this, the first city, divinely chosen to consort with the greatest god this world has ever seen."

Amira's heart thundered in her chest, horrified and tantalized by what she was hearing as she stared over Razal's shoulder.

Then she saw him, the Ka'in. He rose up from the other side of the crates, moving stealthily, a length of wood in his hand raised and poised to strike. Her eyes widened as she realized what he intended, and he stopped, meeting them with his own.

"Yes," she said. "Do it."

CHAPTER 43

Elaine stood dumbfounded.

On the other side of the opulent chamber stood a woman draped in a robe the color of amber. Elaine was struck by the richness of the cloth as the elegant woman moved to set a carafe of wine on the small table next to two glass-fired goblets. Her hair hung in long elaborate braids, each tipped with shining clasps of gold. Around her neck hung a necklace of black jet strung in five rows, the majickal beads tapping lightly as she moved. Her eyes were the same eerie blue color as Acies's, and she seemed nearly as tall.

Once she had deposited her wine, she came toward Elaine with arms outstretched, moving to cup her face. Elaine did not resist as the gentle woman leaned closer and set her forehead against the Scion's, closing her eyes in a trusting repose. It felt natural to respond in kind, and Elaine felt warmth burn in her chest. Unbidden, tears pricked her eyes as the woman leaned back to regard Elaine's face.

"You are most welcome here," she assured her tenderly in beautiful Ka'in.

Even though Elaine had no idea who this woman was, a sense of peace and belonging washed through her as if she had just come home from a long, treacherous journey.

"Thank you," she said, unsure of what else to say and again, feeling compelled to speak in Ka'in, but not resisting it this time. She allowed herself to be led to one of the chairs, sinking onto the furred softness draped over it. She accepted a goblet of wine, downing half of it before taking a breath. The burn from the alcohol slid easily into her stomach and chest, dancing sweetness on her tongue. She looked down at the goblet itself, marveling at the greenish-black glass, smooth and perfect under her fingers. It was a marvelously rare treasure that not even Dakin had.

"You must eat. This is all mortal food, I assure you," the woman said.

At the choice of the word "mortal," Elaine hesitated. "I am sorry. I am accepting your hospitality, and I do not even know whom I should thank."

The woman's smile faltered a little, and Elaine felt terrible, like she had broken her host's heart.

"Of course, of course," the woman said before straightening up. "I am Nymphaea, patron Goddess of Icathor and guardian of its people." She then gently laid a hand on the little smiling girl nibbling on a piece of cheese beside her. "And this is my daughter Rosamund. I welcome you to my Inner Sanctum, Scion of Isa." She bowed her head, and Elaine mirrored her, now appropriately awestruck.

She had known of the patron Goddess of the City but had never been allowed to venture out of Dakin's home within the fortress. She knew of the shrine at the top of the fortress, but it had been nothing more than a repurposed storeroom and Nymphaea was not her goddess anyway. Still, like with Vills, and possibly in spite of Vills, her spirit felt lighter to be in the goddess's presence.

"I thank you for your hospitality and heartfelt greetings," Elaine said formally. "I apologize, too, that I did not recognize you."

Nymphaea shook her head. "It is not your fault, child. You are not of Icathor, and I have not given you much reason to know me. The world has moved on from the deities that once served them. What little remains of us are mere ghosts."

Rosamund began to bounce, kicking obnoxiously until her mother laid a hand over the child's legs, helping them to still with a gentle shush. "Please, eat and be filled at my table. There is much I wish to speak to you about, Scion of Isa."

"Elaine," the Scion said, offering her name as was only polite. "I am called Elaine." She spied a small bowl of clean water with bits of flower petals floating within it. Recognizing it as a finger bowl, Elaine proceeded to wash her hands, clearing the embarrassing amounts of grim, dried slime, and blood from them. If she could, she would bathe her whole self. She couldn't imagine how she must smell, but the goddess did not even seem to notice.

Nymphaea cocked her head to the side while she washed. "Elaine. As in the Princess of the Ka'in?"

She could only offer a half-shrug. "Princess, more or less, but I am Elaine. My brother is Elan. He is ... a prisoner, I hope, of the Anon at this time."

"You hope? That is a strange desire," Nymphaea said.

"The alternative is he is dead, and so yes, it is a hope."

Nymphaea nodded and selected one of the plates of meat to hold out for Elaine. The Scion obliged and took a bite in a show of good faith, only to wolf it down on the next bite,

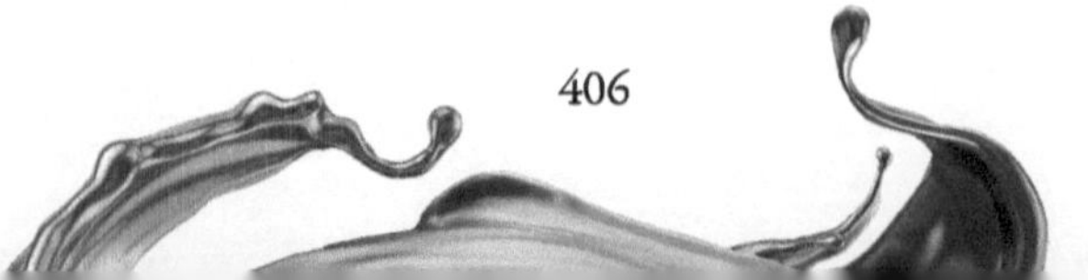

her stomach demanding it. Soon, she was eating from all of the dishes.

"My, it has been a long time since I have witnessed such ravenous feasting," Nymphaea mused as she cleared away a couple of the empty plates that Elaine finished. "It has been just as long since I have had a feast day."

Elaine took her wine goblet, thinking about that. She could not, in all of her time in Icathor, remember the Anon celebrating the patron goddess in any feast or ceremony.

"The people do not think you exist anymore," Elaine said, marveling at the being sitting across from her. "Yet you are. You are very much alive. Like Vills."

The goddess's eyebrows popped up at the mention of the Protector of the Forest. "You have seen him?" she asked, genuinely curious.

"Yes, we did, but he has passed now," the Scion said.

"I see," Nymphaea said softly.

"Mama, who is Vills?" Rosamund asked with all the sweet innocence of any mortal child.

A sad smile spread across Nymphaea's face. "He was a mortal god who protected the forests before the Great War." The goddess gestured over an incense burner sitting on a side table, wafting her fingers through the smoke. The smoke expanded and gathered around her elegant digits, then she gestured, painting forms from the smoke. "He looked like a giant boar that stood taller than any horse or cow. He also had tusks the length of one of Mama's arms."

"Wow!" the little goddess breathed as the smoke took on the likeness while her mother told her story. As she finished her drawing, the smoke Vills came to life, throwing his large head and stamping his feet on the smoke ground. Then the smoke creature took off, charging around the room, and Rosamund took off chasing it with a cascade of giggles.

"Yes, he was a great god, in his forest at least," Nymphaea said with a sad wistfulness.

"He died a hero," Elaine agreed.

"It is the fate of all of us in the end," Nymphaea said, casting her gaze back to Elaine. "Even to patron Goddesses of Cities."

"But why?" Elaine asked, shaking her head. "Your people are right here. They could sustain you, but you do nothing for them. I do not understand why?"

"You know of the old ways. You are a Scion," Nymphaea noted. "I do not blame you for the question, even if it is impertinent to question a deity in her own sanctum. In fact, I believe it is truly a blessing of Fate that you have arrived when you have. Do you know anything about how children of the gods are made?" she asked.

Elaine shook her head. "No. No, I do not."

Nymphaea picked up the decanter of wine and filled their goblets again, this time pouring out a clear, aromatic liquid. "It is alright. There really is no reason you should know. Such knowledges were kept... well, not secret among the divine, but it is not something we talked about openly, even with each other. It is not like with you mortals where any two couplings can produce a child whether you mean to or not. When gods make a child, it is very much a choice, and it has a very high cost." Nymphaea's gaze grew long as she spoke, sipping her wine absently. "The war took many of us, including my beloved husband. When I lost him..." The long gaze turned haunted. "He died so that I would survive. All that remained of him was within his Scion. For a while, his Scion was my only comfort."

"You were lovers?" Elaine asked, shocked as she understood the goddess's meaning.

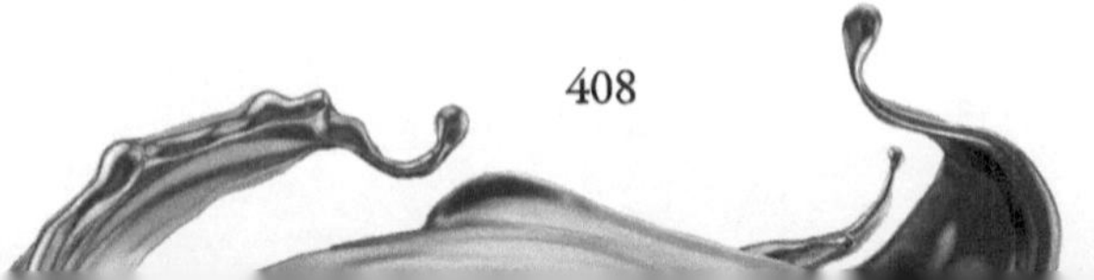

The goddess stood up to stroll across her space to a stone shelf against one wall. Carefully, she pulled down a torque of copper worked over with concave dents. It shined so that each concave facet caught the light as she turned it. She brought the torque back to Elaine. "Not at first. We were friends first. He guarded and served me as I mourned what we had both lost. Then friendship turned to love, then it turned to something else." The haunted look returned. "Do you know what happens to a Scion that gives up their majick?"

"They become fully mortal," Elaine said, though she felt like that answer wasn't quite right anymore.

"The majick of a god lengthens a Scion's life expectancy. Something changes within them as the two powers merge. They are no longer entirely mortals anymore and not quite gods. The majick binds to the Scion's life force, and when that majick is removed, either given to a god or consumed by a demon, it takes the mortal's life with it. They can no longer be separated. You are right, they become entirely mortal, but they waste away within days. My Trystin died in my arms. If I had known what would happen..."

"Why would you do that?" Elaine breathed, shocked by this revelation. "Why did you not give it back to him?"

"It was already too late by that time. We had created our Rosamund," Nymphaea said, her voice a sweet whisper full of the love she had for her daughter. "The goddess with two fathers. That is the price to create a new deity; it took the combined majick of enormous power to bring her into existence. And I must nurture her until she is grown in her power as a lineage goddess. Only mortal gods can survive on their own from creation, but it takes a whole community of mortal's belief in them to sustain them for very long. Belief in me had already begun to wane when we concocted this idea of a new goddess. With both her earthly and heavenly fathers gone, it falls to me to sustain her until she is grown. All of my remaining majick goes to keeping her alive and safe until she chooses her first aspect. When you say I have abandoned my people, you are correct—I have. I cannot answer their prayers, so they have stopped praying. If I used what power I had left to help them now, we both could perish."

Elaine sat there struck by what she was hearing. "Why... Why are you telling me all this?" she asked softly.

The goddess blinked, as if she had forgotten she was speaking to anyone at all. "You... You are a Scion of Isa."

"I was a Scion of Isa before," Elaine said, her eyebrows puckering together.

The goddess stood up, moving gracefully about her room, but to what purpose Elaine couldn't figure out. She seemed agitated and that put Elaine on her guard again.

"I... I can see what an impossible situation that is for you," Elaine said.

Nymphaea's shoulders stiffened.

The Scion continued, "I mean it. I am sincere. There is not a child I have seen lost that their mother wouldn't give her last heartbeat to save."

"When we are in deep grief, we close ourselves off to the world because we cannot handle anything else," Nymphaea said, a defensive edge to her voice.

Elaine couldn't help thinking of all the times she had begged for help from some higher power and it had not arrived. "So you were ... aware ... this whole time ... what Dakin was doing to me..." She hesitated, aware that her next words were an accusation, and holding a goddess accountable was a dangerous thing to do.

Nymphaea's hands clenched. "Men like Dakin... it was just easier to let them do as they will. To leave you mortals to sort yourselves out by yourselves. It has only been in the last few days that I have reckoned how foolish that truly was." She turned to eye Elaine, her haughty anger flashing. "All you mortals think we gods can simply do whatever we want when we want, that it doesn't cost us something. He has no belief in me, and therefore, it would take a *great* show of force to bend him."

She pressed her fingers to her temples as if she suffered a headache. "What little prayers I still receive are a few token words of praise from the merchants to bless their dealings. There is hardly any majick in them. And even they are losing their faith in me. Half the time they don't even speak my name correctly and so their prayers never reach me."

Elaine furrowed her brow. "But where are your priests to protect your name?"

"As prayers failed, so too did their influence until there are none left. And these Anon do not even take responsibility for their mistakes. The Ka'in do not pray to me either, but cling fervently to their dead goddess as if she still exists to help them."

"But what should that matter?" Elaine pressed. "You are a goddess of the Ka'in."

Nymphaea dismissed the idea with a wave. "I am the goddess of the city, not the Ka'in. I protect the residents of my *city*. *That* is my purview, be they Ka'in, Anon, or anyone else. They have only to invoke my true name. But they have forsaken us and if they forsake us completely, I will lose even this temple. I am in a precarious position."

Then why don't you do something about it? Elaine thought but dared not say.

Nymphaea stared off into the middle distance. "This city is lost, and I will not let it take my daughter with it. That is why I need you, Scion."

"You want me to give up my majick to you," Elaine said flatly.

The goddess's eyes went wide. Clearly, that statement stunned her.

Elaine stood up from the table. "I have had enough. Thank you so much for your hospitality, but the answer is no." She turned to leave, knowing that she may not make it three steps, but if this goddess wanted to take her majick, she would have to do it herself.

"I was not going to ask you to!"

That stopped Elaine in her tracks on the third step. "What?"

Nymphaea crossed to Elaine, holding out her hands bearing the torque. "I would never ask that of you. I am so sorry if you thought that I would. No, Scion, please. You will instead take me and my daughter to the south, to a place I may finish raising her in safety."

Unsure now, Elaine rubbed her hands together in a soothing motion. "Why do you need me to take you from this city? You are a goddess; can you not leave yourself?"

"I am bound by my aspect as the patron deity of Icathor. In order for me to leave, my icon must be removed by mortal hands. In exchange for this, I will expend what power I can to help save your brother," she said—as if it were a done deal and Elaine had agreed to it.

On the other hand, who argues with a goddess?

CHAPTER 44

"BUT I DO NOT WANT TO LEAVE," ROSAMUND WHINED.

The little goddess sat in the main sanctuary of her mother's temple sulking terribly. It just was not fair.

"I mean, it's not like Icathor is a great place to be right now. In fact, it's become pretty awful. For one thing, there are no other children to play with anymore, no one to talk to except Mother, and... and if I tell the truth, no amount of toys or treats make up for it!" Rosamund declared to the empty room. "And it's strange. All the children disappearing, not just from Icathor, but I couldn't find any out in the other settlements either! I looked everywhere."

She flopped back on the stones with the biggest sigh. "Maybe this is like the time Car and Yor's parents moved them to the South City? Maybe... maybe everyone went there. But..." She sat up. "But if we leave too, how will my friends know where we've gone? It's not fair!"

Driven to tears, she plucked up her most recent prize from the cord around her neck and looked once more at the foreign symbol wrought in some strange black material that seemed to be both stone and glass. It was warm to the touch as she rubbed it all over with her little fingers.

"<Will you come out to talk to me?> We can be friends?" she asked the symbol, first in Anon, then in Ka'in. When it didn't respond at first, she pushed a little of her majick into it to wake it up. Like nudging a sleeping dog with a foot, the symbol began to move, unfolding itself and growing. The cord dissipated from around her neck, and the symbol was engulfed in a bright bit of fire. Then a small duck-like creature burst out of it, bright yellow as a baby chick. It landed gracefully onto its webbed feet, then shook itself out, fluffing up all of its feathers.

"Play with me," she said to the little duck-thing just as it finished shaking.

The duck-thing flared out its feathers. "Absolutely not, you horrid little girl!" it shrieked, stamping its duck-like foot with clear agitation.

"How dare you speak to me that way!?" Rosamund shrieked back, completely shocked. None of the other kids had ever talked to her like that. At least as long as they weren't playing tyrants and demons or something. "You are just a little spirit, and I am goddess!"

"I am not a spirit," the duck-thing declared, straightening the little cloak draped over its back. "I am a gelic, a temple guardian, and I must return to my mistress forthwith!"

"No! You cannot leave until I tell you to, spirit. Those are the rules," Rosamund declared, crossing her arms in the way Mother often did when she was laying down her divine law.

The spirit did not even have the manners to look impressed. "I am not your spirit, whoever you are! I only obey my Lady or my Mistress. I have a name granted to me by my goddess. My name is Flicker, and you will address me as such!"

"Flicker? That is a strange name. Mine is Rosamund, named after one of Mama's favorite priestesses. She says it means 'Rose of Protection.'"

"Well, it has *not* been nice to meet you," Flicker said, though it still gave a little bow of respect to the little goddess now that she had introduced herself.

Rosamund returned the bow as was proper.

That seemed to settle the little spirit down somewhat. "Even so," Flicker continued, "I wish you had not stolen me."

"Well, you were pretty," Rosamund conceded. "I wanted to play with you."

That seemed to mollify the temple guardian even further, and its feathers settled down.

"I suppose you are right. I am rather impressive," Flicker conceded.

"Hey, if you are a temple guardian, why are you not in a temple?" Rosamund asked.

The creature shivered its feathers again with indignation. "My temple was ... destroyed," it said.

"Oh, I am sorry," Rosamund said, truly meaning it. "That must be terrible. I cannot imagine what losing your temple must be like. You must not have been a very good guardian."

Flicker narrowed its eyes at Rosamund to the tiniest of black slits. "If I may ask, what are you the goddess of?"

"Nothing." Rosamund shrugged.

The gelic's beakish face wrinkled in a surprising show of emotion that shouldn't have been possible for someone with a beak for a face. "You cannot be the goddess of nothing. That makes no sense."

"I have not chosen an aspect yet."

"Oh, then you are not any better than a spirit yourself."

"Why would you say that?" Rosamund was getting mad again.

"I at least know my purpose. Even if my temple is gone, I am still a temple guardian serving the last Scion of my lady goddess. And now I must find her."

"She is here," Rosamund said because it was true. The gelic's feathers flared again, this time flashing a bright light that rolled down the filaments of each feather.

Flicker pivoted its head around the sanctuary space as if they would see her any moment. "Where is she?! My mistress?"

"She is not right here. She is in Sanctum," Rosamund explained, getting tired of how little this temple guardian seemed to know. "Can you do that thing again with your feathers?"

"No!" it shouted, its feathers doing it again despite the protest. "I must find Mistress Elaine at once. Take her to me!"

"I cannot," Rosamund whined. "Like I *said*, Mother is with her, and I am supposed to go somewhere to play, but there is *nobody* around."

"Who is your mother? I would speak to her at once!"

"Nymphaea, the patron Goddess of Icathor."

That paused the gelic's antics. "Oh. I see. The Goddess of Truth," it said contemplatively.

"What? No," Rosamund said, confused. "She is the Goddess of Icathor. Why does everyone care about what kind of goddess they are? Why should it matter?"

Shouts echoed down the hall into the sanctuary, stopping whatever response Flicker would have given her. Both gelic and goddess looked up as several little bodies rushed into the room.

Other children!

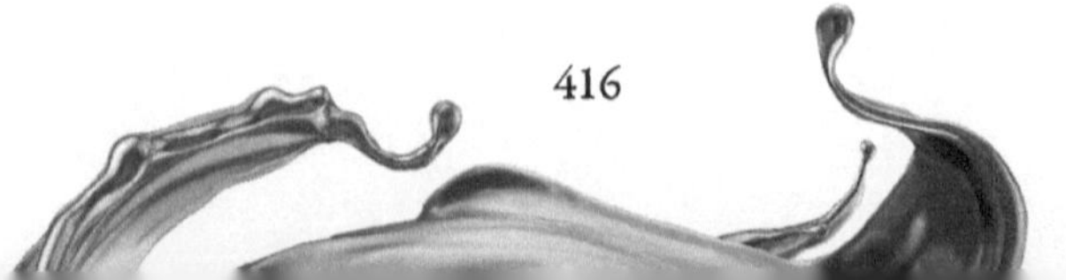

Several were crying, and all of them seemed very scared as a woman followed the little ones inside.

"It is alright; it is alright everyone. We are going to be fine," she repeated, proving herself to be a Ka'in woman, though it was odd since the Ka'in rarely spoke their language in the city. Also the woman was lying about "we are going to be fine."

The woman herded the children to the farthest side of Rosamund's mother's statue that sat in the middle of the space in her shrine, but there were too many of them to hide behind her very effectively.

"What is going on?" Rosamund asked, coming up to the children and the woman as they clung to each other.

Her Ka'in words caught the woman's attention. "Come on, sweetie. It is going to be fine. We are all just going to sit together and play at being really quiet," she continued to lie even as she smiled at her and spoke with soft words. The lying frightened Rosamund more than anything else in her existence ever had.

"Sarai, I am scared," a little girl cried.

The woman wrapped the girl in a quick hug. "I know. I know. But we are going to pray for help, okay? If we pray really, really hard, surely help is going to come, right?" The woman thought that was a lie too, but Rosamund knew that praying to the gods was a good thing. Why was that a lie?

Rosamund sat down among the children and was immediately hugged by two boys about her size from either side, clinging onto her and each other for dear life.

This all seemed wrong. Why were they all so afraid, especially inside her mother's temple?

More shouts came from the entrance. Big shouts from men with angry voices. All the children's faces jumped toward the entrance, and the woman released the little girl to go stand in hallway.

"Be quiet, children," she urged as she moved to block the hallway. More shouts, then shadows overcame her as the woman turned to face down the hallway. She cried out in pain as she was grabbed. "<No, please, these are children, please! Please!>" she begged in Anon.

Two men pushed in, seizing the screaming woman as she fought, trying to scratch and slap and hit. They ignored her thrashing. One punched her across the face. She fell to the ground. More warriors entered. They kicked her. They hit her. They spat on her. All around Rosamund, the children screamed and cried as the woman was beaten. All Rosamund could do was stare in shock.

A few more men came in, these bearing cudgels. It stopped the attack. The warriors handed the cudgels to each other, then turned to the cluster of small faces staring up at them in terror.

"<This is going to be fun,>" one of them chuckled.

Rosamund gasped at the men. Because they were not men.

Men's eyes were kind and their hands were clever with strength used to make wonderful things.

These men's eyes were dead. They were not men. They were monsters.

They raised their cudgels.

"<No! Please!!>" the woman screamed, still alive. And the children screamed, their small voices shrill and cutting.

"<Stop!>" Rosamund shouted. Power infused her little body as she stood up. She held out her hand. "<Stop!>" she commanded again.

But the cudgels didn't stop. They arced down.

There was a flash of light, and the cudgel cracked. Flung from the warrior's hand, it clanged dully against the wall. Two more cudgels followed.

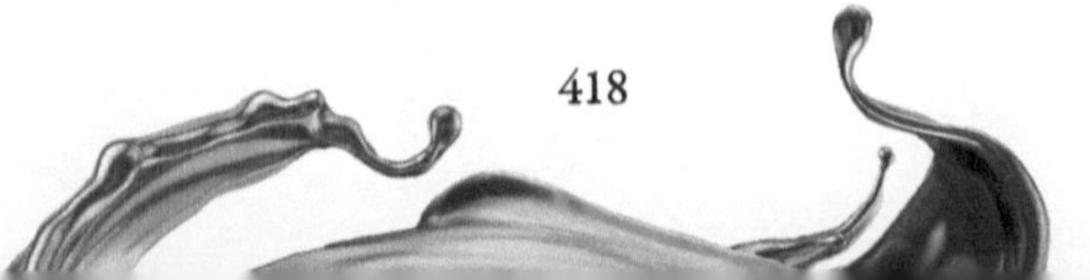

All eyes turned to Rosamund, who did not realize she glowed with ethereal divine light.

"<Who are you?>" the first monster sneered, its black-colored teeth grinning at her.

"<I...>" Rosamund held her head up high like her mother would. "<I am the Goddess of Children,>" she declared, her voice ringing with power.

Something had changed. She had never done that before. She felt so different.

"<You will not harm them,>" she said defiantly. "<They are under my protection.>"

"<Goddess of Children,>" the first monster scoffed. The other monsters shifted on their feet. "<There is no such thing. Sit down and die quietly.>"

"<No! *You* leave!>" she shouted, pointing an imperious finger at them. "<You all leave right now!>"

She stepped forward through the crowd of children, placing herself between them and the monsters. The monsters backed up as she approached, eyeing her uncertainly.

"<Or you will what, little one?>" the lead monster asked, sneering at her.

"<Or I will... I will...>" Rosamund's uncertainty was her undoing.

The monster grabbed her by the hair, and she screamed. The children behind her also screamed. The screaming stopped when she slammed against the wall of the temple.

"<Let me go!>" Rosamund struggled, but the monster licked its tongue along her face and neck.

"<You are going to taste wonderful,>" it laughed.

"<Mother! Mother! Please help me!>" Rosamund screamed.

But her mother didn't come. The monster tore at Rosamund's shirt front, rending the fabric away from her small body. What was happening? Why were they doing this to her?

"<Mother! Help me!>" she screamed again, not knowing what else to do. Why didn't her mother come?

The monster pressed into her and bit down.

She screamed.

Fire erupted everywhere. The monster jerked away, drips of Rosamund's gold blood dribbling from his mouth. The other monsters shouted and turned to run, exiting the shrine quickly, terrified of the fire.

"<Leave her and come on!>" one of them shouted, pulling on Rosamund's attacker's arm. But the monster didn't let go. Instead, he tucked Rosamund under his arm and ran off with the shocked, limp goddess in tow.

CHAPTER 45

"THIS IS STUPID," AMIRA HISSED, BUT ELAN ignored her as he pushed the door inward to Dakin's chambers. "We should be escaping. We have to hurry."

He stared into the room. He wasn't sure what he had expected, but it was a normal bedroom complete with bed, side tables, and a couple of woven chests lined along the wall. Everything was clean, neat, and ordinary. It was in this room that Dakin had nightly assaulted his sister. He wanted it to reflect that level of evil. He wanted it to be dark and forbidding with chains and ropes and blood on the linens and furs.

Evil shouldn't look this ordinary, he thought.

Elan pushed into the room and went straight to the woven chests. Each one was given structure by a wooden frame and so opened easily when he pulled on the leather strap. Within, there were only clothes neatly folded, which Elan undid as he dug through, looking for anything with an edge. He growled when he found nothing and did the same with the other chest.

Amira stood by the door unhelpfully, rubbing her arms and avoiding looking at the bed. He didn't blame her, but she was still an Anon, one of the elites that had traded in his people. It almost cancelled out any sympathy he would otherwise have for her.

Almost.

"Instead of standing there, help me look for a weapon."

"They are going to catch us," she growled, but she did as he bid, turning to go into the adjoining room that served as a place where Dakin could relax, play games, or socialize in private with his closest people. "He would keep his swords and such in here."

Elan stopped his fruitless search and followed her into the adjoining room but found she had stopped in the doorway. "Oh my," she breathed, and he looked over her shoulder.

The room had been overtaken and converted into a rough armory. Bronze weaponry and armament were laid out on the chairs, tables, and every inch of floor, only leaving a small path through it. They were all different kinds and designs.

"Oh, my Goddess," Amira said, pressing the back of her hand to her mouth as she entered to lay her fingers across a beautiful bronze breastplate. "This was... This is..."

"What?" Elan asked, her reaction muting his urgent harshness.

"These belonged to friends of my family," Amira finished, already looking to the next piece. "And these. And those. Oh, Goddess."

She spun in place and stared at a sword that had been set up in a place of honor over the rest, waiting in a stand and shining as if just freshly polished. "That was my brother's." She went to it, touching the leather grip hesitantly before running her finger down some masterfully worked filigree. "He was so proud of it. His gift from our father when he became a man."

Elan came up beside her, reaching to touch the other side of the handle, his larger fingers covering her smaller ones. "How would he feel about me using it to avenge him?" he asked softly. He could feel her fingers tense under his.

"I think..." she said, enunciating her words carefully, "he would be an ass about it." Then she turned to look up at him, both magnetically and repulsively too close. "But I would be delighted," she whispered huskily, and a shiver rolled through him.

He pulled the sword from her hand, and she found a scabbard to sheath it in. While he fixed the belt around himself, something hung sloppily on the wall caught his eye.

"<Oh, my Goddess, there it is,>" he said in Ka'in, absolutely amazed.

Amira turned to follow his line of sight. "What is that?"

Elan went to the wall and pulled down his stolen bow. "It is a weapon of the gods, given to me by the Protector of the Forest," he said, switching back to Anon since she didn't speak Ka'in. He ran his fingers over the shaft, checking it over for damage.

"It looks like it was made from a spider-web," she commented, touching one of the wheels at the end, but it didn't move under the string's tension. "This thing is bizarre."

"Find me some arrows," he said as he checked the string, only guessing at what he needed to be looking for. It took a second to realize that the Anon hadn't moved. He glanced up and saw her standing there, staring at him with her arms folded, an imperious look on her face. His own jaw stiffened in reaction. Despite their circumstances, it was obvious she still thought herself superior to him, and he began to rethink doing anything more to help her.

A noise snapped them both out of their indignant positions. The door to Dakin's bedroom opened. It blocked the view into the side room, which gave the two fugitives time to duck back out of sight. Elan held the bow out before him as he stood straight. In these close quarters, it might not be the most effective weapon. He sensed, rather than saw, Amira pull her brother's sword back out of the sheath from his side. Whether she knew how to use it or not was irrelevant; it was better than nothing.

The sounds in the next room were muffled but distressing. Sharp squeals were the loudest thing, full of distress and terror.

Elan took a cautious step forward when he felt pressure against his open hand. He glanced down and found Amira pressing a quiver full of arrows into it. He didn't acknowledge the act, but he pulled the strap quickly over his head and pulled with practice smoothness to arm his bow. The wheels pulled then clicked as he held the arrow ready.

There were more noises as a man's grunting accompanied the squeals. Elan edged around the doorway to see a man's back as he forced a small form onto the bed. Elan felt sick. It was a child.

"That is enough," the man growled as he slapped the child across the temple, his other hand covering her mouth so she couldn't scream or move. She cried and cried pitifully. Then he went back to tearing away her clothes.

Elan didn't wait or hesitate. He nailed the arrow into the man's back. The bow worked powerfully, forcing the arrow through the figure. The man jerked, uttering a strangled cry. If it had been an ordinary man, that shot alone should have killed him. Elan knew with the certainty of a master archer that he had nailed him through the heart.

Instead, the attacker bucked back, swiveling drunkenly around, even as his arms tried to reach around to pull out whatever had stabbed him.

"Lorab!" Amira gasped, recognizing him.

All Elan saw was a demon.

The Ka'in Prince pulled another arrow, but the god-weapon was not as fast to load as his short bow, but it made up for that in power. The demon dashed at an insane speed, coming straight for his attacker.

Elan released the arrow, and it shot true. It nailed Lorab through the eye, punching out the back of the monster's head.

Even then, the demon didn't go down, only to his... its knees as it clawed at black fletching in the hole in its face.

To Elan's horror, he realized the thing was trying to pull the arrow out!

It came with a slurpy pop. Black blood oozed from socket. Dropping it with fingers that didn't seem to work very well anymore, the demon called Lorab drunkenly wavered as it looked up.

"I am ... invincible," it crowed weakly, smiling with teeth coated in blackness.

Elan pulled another arrow. He fired it into the other eye.

He pulled a fourth.

He pulled a fifth.

He pulled a sixth.

"He is not dying!" Amira cried in horror beside him.

Lorab the Sword roared in rage, even as he forced himself to stand, blindly swinging his arms even as his body betrayed him. Yet even without eyes, the demon managed to stumble toward Elan, closing the distance. The Ka'in Prince had no time to fire another arrow. Instead, he managed to block the demon's flailing with the bow's body. As he struggled, he sensed Amira move away to the side.

The Sword pushed in, spitting his demonic blood over Elan's face. He gained ground, pushing Elan back, both their faces straining. They stumbled against the wall. A clay something knocked over and smashed to the floor.

"I will devour you!" Lorab snarled, snapping its mouth closer and closer to Elan's face, completely heedless of the bow sinking into its neck. There was a give on the bow string and the tension snapped. A line of black appeared on Lorab's face, bleeding horribly. Still, it kept the pressure on, the teeth clacking inches from Elan's nose.

Then Lorab jerked sideways, falling to the ground. The pressure on the bow released and Elan gasped a deep breath in he hadn't even realized he needed. Lorab's leg had been chopped in half, spewing more blackness all over the floor as the demon fell to its side.

In front of him, Amira brought her brother's sword up over her head. With a mighty roar, she slashed the blade down onto Lorab's neck. The blade wasn't made like Acies's. It didn't cut all the way through. The blade stopped on the spinal column.

It didn't stop Amira. With a fierceness that Elan had not seen from her yet, she pulled the sword out and brought it down again, hacking another chunk. On the third time, the head came free.

All Elan could do was stand there wide-eyed and stare as Amira labored for air.

Lorab's body lay on the floor, still twitching and flailing, but the head rolled away.

Amira stood over it, the sword still in her hands as the tip dragged on the floor as if her arms were turning to jelly.

The head on the floor continued to move, though now it made no sound, since it had been detached from the parts of it that made sound.

Amira cried out when she realized the mouth was also still moving. Whimpering, she tried to bring the sword back up to continue attacking, but Elan caught it from her. He put his other arm around her shoulder to hold her up. "It's alright. I got you."

"Why... Why won't it die?" Amira cried.

"He is a demon. You cannot kill them like a mortal. You have to drain out their majick until they cannot continue."

Amira spat at Lorab's moving corpse. "Dark majick," she cursed.

He couldn't argue. Stepping over the corpse, he raised the sword and slammed it through the torso, pinning it to the floor. Still it flailed. Amira seized the head by the hair.

"No! Wait!" he tried to call, then she flung it, sending it out the window. Below there was a moist splat sound. The body at their feet finally went still.

"Is it dead?" Amira asked as the stared at the corpse warily.

"If not, it should be soon. It cannot replace its majick now without a head," Elan said, brushing the back of his hand against his lips.

"No! Stop!" Amira cried, surging forward to seize his hand. "That thing's blood is all over you!"

She pulled him across the room to the sideboard where she seized the clay pitcher that sat there. With no ceremony, she splashed a good half of the pitcher into Elan's face, then she rubbed hard with a towel like a mother quick washing their child. "That is how he makes more monsters like him. They drink the blood." As she washed his hands, Elan blinked hard, trying to clear his eyes without them.

"Did any get into your mouth?" she asked, rubbing his eyes for him.

"No, I do not... I do not know," he admitted.

She pursed her lips together into a worried line, handing him the remains of the pitcher. "Wash out your mouth," she ordered. This command he obeyed, swishing then spitting onto the floor.

Having done what they could, he turned back to the bed, finally remembering other victim in this land of demons. "The child," he said as he went to the side of the bed.

"Is it an Anon child?" Amira asked.

"What does that matter?" Elan sneered. "A child is a child."

He saw no sign of the little being, just the pile of furs on the bed. Gently, he knelt on the edge. "Child?"

The pile of furs pulled in tighter.

"It is safe now, <it is safe now>," Elan said softly speaking in both Anon and Ka'in. His fingers picked at the edge, and he pulled back on the fur. "I won't let anyone else hurt you."

Under the fur, the most beautiful child he had ever seen poked her face out. Her golden eyes were tearstained and red.

Elan smiled at her. "It is okay." He set his hand against his chest. "I am a prince; I can protect you." Little girls loved princes.

"You are a prince?" the child asked in a sweet little voice.

He nodded.

She came out farther. Her skin was scored with welts and dried... He leaned in, focusing on the marks on her shoulder. It looked like someone had bitten her, but the wounds reflected light back to him. Amira's hand appeared, touching the marks lightly. Her fingers came away glittering.

"It is gold," she said, amazed. The two adults met eyes. "Elan... she has golden blood."

"Who are you, child?" he asked as he turned back to her.

"I am ... Rosamund, the-the Goddess of Children," she said, then broke down crying as she scooted into Elan's arms to hide. Though he was unsure, the Ka'in Prince held her

close. Amira pulled the furs back up and over the little half-naked form of the child. He couldn't read her eyes or expression, but then, he couldn't really parse his own feelings either.

"Do not fear anymore," he said. "We will protect you."

CHAPTER 46

ACIES SAT AT DAKIN'S FEAST, WATCHING THE ROOM.
Lorab had disappeared fairly shortly after arriving with him.
The room was full of carnage, but the Demon Lord did not
feel any eagerness to participate.

Frankly, it was disgusting to watch.

The creatures in the room, to call them demons would
be generous, fell on the corpses, sucking and guzzling their
fluids, but he doubted they were getting any arete from them
at all. Still, it seemed what slivers they managed to imbue
sent the drinkers into a sort of grotesque ecstasy, like alco-
holics trying to hydrate by drinking more.

He found it very easy to not partake, and no one even
noticed him to pressure him into it. He took up a position by
the main doors, leaning against the wall with his arms crossed.

"<Oh, Vills, this is a dark world without you,>" he said
softly in godspeech.

<It has been a dark world for a long time,> the sword answered, though Acies felt he heard it more in his mind than actually heard it.

Acies chuckled. "<So enough of you passed to the sword to gain sentience?>"

<Enough to have an opinion or two if you want them.>

The Demon Lord snorted, continuing his scan of the room.

<What is it you seek, old friend?>

"<Answers, but they do not seem to be here,>" Acies admitted. "<What did we fight the Great War for if this is what we earned for it? Mortals turned to demons anyway.>"

<So why are you standing here? Are you not searching for the Scion's brother?>

"<If he is not in this room, I may not be able to ever find him.>"

<Veres was not the kind of god to simply give up.>

Acies worked his jaw.

<Or are you still only interested in revenge?>

Acies didn't respond. Across the space, a corpulent figure appeared, entering from the garden beyond. At his appearance, the room turned and cheered, which the walking dead man drank in as gluttonously as the monsters on the corpses before them. The cheers turned to a chant. "Dakin the God! Dakin the God! Dakin the God!"

All the hairs on the back of Acies's arms rose, shifting him from his bored, observant stance to a wary one.

"<Something is coming,>" he muttered. The electric shift he felt rippled through the room, silencing the cheers. A burst of power erupted in the middle of the room. Displaced air flung back forgotten cups and some knives, startling the feasters. In the center of the ring of tables, a figure appeared.

"<Nymphaea,>" Acies breathed. "<At last, she reappears.>"

The goddess stood tall and regal in the center of the demon warriors, each one staring shocked and seeming more mortal than they had been for hours. Nymphaea turned in place, casting her eyes coldly over the assembly until she made the full circuit, ending with her facing Dakin. The demon who claimed to be a god stared round-eyed at the real one before him.

The tension built as she stared him down. Sweat beaded down Dakin's face as he looked right and left at the assembly, anywhere but at the fierce gaze of the goddess. "Wh-who is this woman?" he asked stupidly. Everyone in that place knew who she was. Her likeness still marked everything in Icathor, even if no one heeded them.

Nymphaea straightened even more if that was possible. "I am Nymphaea, patron Goddess of Icathor," she declared in a commanding voice full of power that Anon words were never meant to hold.

Dakin's jaw went slack for a moment as her voice continued to ring out in the room.

Acies smirked. Nymphaea certainly still liked her trappings of power.

"As leader of the city of Icathor," Dakin started, licking his lips, "a-and as the newest god to this world, I-let me welcome you to my feast—"

"Where is my daughter!?" she demanded, cutting him off with words that thundered. The demons around her shrank away in terror, hiding on the other side of their tables. A few even fell to their knees.

Again, Dakin looked stunned like a student who had been surprised by a question that he hadn't prepared for. "Your what?" he asked.

Nymphaea's eyes flared in rage. She pointed her finger directly at Dakin. "My daughter! What have you done with my daughter, the goddess Rosamund? Your monsters attacked my temple, shed blood on my sacred stones, and stole my most precious treasure. Produce her this instant, or I will bring this city down around your ears, you foul beast!"

The insults seemed to sputter Dakin out of his stunned stupor. "H-how dare you…" He looked around for someone to speak up for him, but all he got were the frightened faces of his sheep-like followers facing the first real challenge of their short existence.

"You!" Dakin shouted, pointing to the nearest warrior. "Get up. Get off your knees. What are you doing? All of you. Get up. What are you kneeling for? A goddess? This woman is not Nympha; look at her."

His words didn't seem to have the effect he wanted even as Dakin smacked the nearest kneeler on the back of the head to bully him back up.

"You think you can just come in here and order me in *my* hall—"

At last, Nymphaea's eyes landed on Acies. Within seconds, they narrowed to slits, widened to coins, then narrowed even sharper. "You!" she growled, her beautiful voice grinding against the mortar of her rage.

The room swung its attention to the Demon Lord standing by the door. Even as he had been ready for the possibility of her spotting him and doing exactly this, the hairs all over his body stood up on end at the intense force of it. In response, he cocked a smirking half-grin at her.

It stoked her rage. "You are responsible for all this. I warned you not to enter my city! The unrest, the forges burning everything to create more weapons, the crops being devoured as if by locusts, death and subjugation are all servants to one such as you, Demon Lord of War! Dishonorable wretch. I should have known. You take appeasement and seek your revenge anyway!"

"You!" Dakin squealed, his rage child-like and weak compared to that of Nymphaea. Acies cast his gaze over, bored and lazy, toward Dakin. The fat demon pointed at him. "It was you who killed me! You stole my woman. You— You—" His words degraded to sputtering incoherence.

"<Where is my daughter, Demon Lord!?>" Nymphaea demanded as if Dakin had not spoken, returning to godspeech.

Acies returned his gaze to Nymphaea. "<I have no idea,>" he said casually as if it was a thing of little consequence. With his hands, however, he pulled on the cord binding the rawhide around Vills, freeing the pommel so he could pull out the sword. It wouldn't be a clean pull, but that wasn't important.

Nymphaea's eyes flared at his remarks. "<I will kill you!>" she screamed and gestured.

Instantly, the walls came alive. The solid stone began to undulate, expanding and reforming until both entryways were blocked. He could feel the world shift around them as she pulled this mortal room, and its occupants into her Sanctum, reshaping it into an arena.

The stone beasts formed out of the walls, lining the room. As soon as they cleared, they began to shake and unfold, the sharp stone hackles becoming soft fur. They were creatures shaped like great wolves, but with leonine faces and claws far more wicked and sharp. A clear and definitive growl hummed through the air.

As soon as Nymphaea's spirit beasts were free from their confines, they lunged and pounced on the crowd of man-shaped demons.

The goddess herself had disappeared, nowhere to be seen, but Acies didn't trust that. He pulled Vills from the rawhide, bringing it before him as he pivoted toward the closest beast who had made the unwise choice to focus on him.

"<Well, then,>" the demonic warrior said, squaring his shoulders and shifting along the wall of what now was a completed arena. "<Shall we get on with it?>"

CHAPTER 47

"OH DEAR, OH DEAR, OH DEAR!" FLICKER REPEATED as Elaine stared down into the arena. She pressed against a surface that felt like glass, but it was no kind of glass she had ever seen before. It was like a sheet covering a window and clear as water. It had appeared suddenly along the wall of Nymphaea's Sanctum where the goddess had left Elaine after they had discovered the attack within the temple.

It had been a surreal thing. The goddess had stopped mid-sentence and gestured. The room they had been in shifted, becoming dream-like as it revealed the reality of the stone sanctuary within and the children cowering there.

It had taken Elaine's reassurance to get Flicker to stand down, the little gelic guarding them fervently from any attack.

Now, those same children were sleeping soundly in a pile within the safety of Nymphaea's sanctum, exhausted from the terror.

"I cannot believe any of this," said Sarai. She sat next to Elaine, propped up on a beautiful chair made of wood, wrapped in a blanket. She looked terrible with one eye swollen and cuts all over her face; it was a wonder that she was conscious at all. Sarai had several injuries covered under the blanket and was pressing another miracle against her middle, a cloth filled with shards of real ice. "The goddess is real."

Elaine understood how she felt. "So are the demons," she muttered.

Below the two women, it was carnage. The beasts and Dakin's forces were in a full-on fight with each other, teeth against blade. It was difficult for Elaine to figure out who was winning, but it did not matter. It was all awful.

Acies roared with laughter after he slammed hard into the wall.

The beast backed away as well, having taken a nice cut across its snout, pawing at it as if it burned.

Acies brought up the sword once more, brandishing it so that it almost sang as it moved through the air. This was nothing like the few skirmishes he'd had so far. This was a proper fight with his beautiful new god-weapon. He couldn't help but feel Vills would have been proud of the sword he had become. It had bitten and snapped at the beast, driving it back and withstanding its attacks in a way bronze never could have.

Acies was thoroughly enjoying himself.

"<Hypocrisy is still your vice, eh, Nymphaea?>" the Demon Lord said out loud, his godspeech ringing out.

The beast growled in response so acutely Acies wondered if the lineage god had gotten talented enough to take on an animal avatar and was fighting him herself. It would explain its use of tactics and strategy far above that of a normal beast or spirit.

The Demon Lord chuckled as he reset his sword, bringing it parallel to his ear, the point directed at the beast.

"<I know what you are, demon. I know what you have done. I know what you would do,>" *Nymphaea finally answered him*, confirming his suspicion as the words echoed from the spirit beast.

"<I broke no agreement between us,>" Acies countered.

"<Liar!>"

She lunged, and he deflected, turning away with quick feet enhanced with arete.

She spun to face him. He took slow measured steps to the side, beginning the counter circle with the creature that slunk through shadow to moonlight to shadow in equal pace with Acies's steps.

"<You know nothing of me,>" he growled in return. "<I had no intention to bring harm to you…>" The beast lunged, cutting off his words. He scored a slash across the other side of the beast's muzzle.

All things considered, Acies felt like he was doing fairly well.

Around him the other warriors fared even worse. Many of them had fallen under claw and fang, taking not nearly as many spirit beasts as they could. He had lost sight of the true villain in all this, but frankly, he couldn't care about the walking corpse as the remaining beasts began to circle him, the remaining threat in the room.

"<Is this how you rose, Great Nymphaea, the patron Goddess of Icathor? All the stronger better gods fell, and you simply took their place, sat on your ass, and did nothing?>" he shouted, panting between his words before blocking a set of jaws from taking a bite from his thigh. The sound of teeth against steel was horrible. The beasts backed off, returning to their circling with him the fawn in the center. "<This was supposed to be your city, and it is dying!>"

The largest of the beasts leapt at him just as two others went for his legs. He had to burn a little arete to pull off an impossible sideways leap, spinning himself and his too-heavy sword out of the way. While it probably looked amazing, it was very costly as he beat it to the other side of the arena.

"<If we get through this, my old friend,>" he said to his sword, "<I swear, I am going to polish you with the finest oils until you out-gleam the sun.>"

Vills did not gleam in that moment, covered all over with blood and beast slime. But the sword had not failed him yet.

"<You are a liar. You are a failure as a god. Only fit to waste away into oblivion!>" Nymphaea screamed.

Anger flared heat at the back of Acies's neck. *She knew! She knew I had been dying in my prison and had done nothing to help,* he realized. He also was aware she was baiting him, and that it was working. He moved faster than he should, burning arete in the flame of his temper.

The great beast charged again, all teeth and claws.

He managed to block the teeth against the blade, but the claws sank into his body before tearing away as the beast lost its balance and grip on the warrior.

"<Mama!>" A tiny voice rang out, the godspeech being projected into the space for all that remained to hear. A calling.

"<My daughter!>"

While the spirit beast was distracted, his god-weapon plunged into the side of the beast.

Vills cut deep. Vills cut true.

Somewhere, he heard Elaine's voice scream, "No!"

He completed his strike, breathing hard, almost doubled over with the effort. He closed his eyes, understanding what he had done.

The great beast thumped to the ground, and the other spirit beasts yielded, falling back into their stone forms, becoming statues. The ones that had fallen crumbled into rubble.

Above them, there was a crash. Glass tinkled down in front of him, and Acies stared perplexed, unable to process the sight of Elaine dropping to the ground from out of thin air. She landed lightly on the stone, then took off past him.

"Elaine…" he said, but it was ineffectual for both of them.

Elaine slid to a stop next to the fallen goddess on the ground. Nymphaea had returned to her original form, dressed now as a warrior, pressing herself back up to sitting. "I am alright. I am alright, Scion," she assured, though she did not look alright at all. Across both cheeks were cuts that bled golden drops. She pressed her hands into the deity's side, the crimson robe darkening rapidly. Elaine's hand came back golden. Nymphaea was bleeding out majick, weakening quickly.

Elaine turned to Acies. "<What did you do?!>" she shouted, the godspeech slapping him with power.

He stood there unrepentant, Vills still in his hand. "<I did what I always set out to do,>" he answered simply. "<The gods betrayed me, and I will have my revenge.>"

"<I cannot heal it,>" Nymphaea said desperately, her breathing terribly labored. "<I cannot heal it, oh God Beyond.>" She gripped Elaine's shoulder spasmodically.

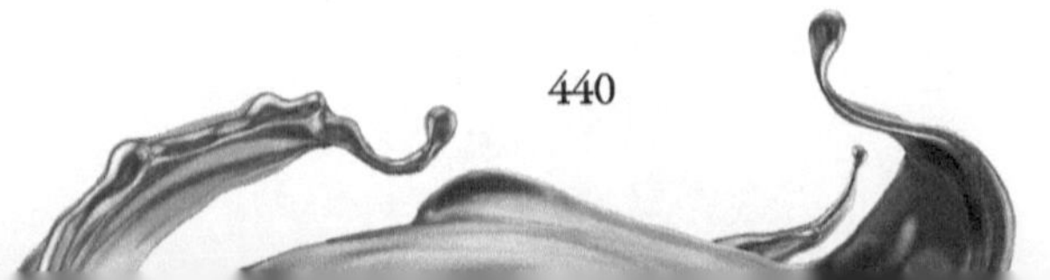

440

"<You have been slain by a god-weapon, Nymphaea,>" Acies said, holding Vills out, the weapon shining brightly even in the dim light. "<You will not heal easily.>"

Nymphaea grasped at Elaine's fingers, pulling her attention back. "<My daughter, please. You must find her. She is all that matters. She is the future, our only chance,>" she begged, gold blood bubbling from her mouth. "<You must find her... You must...>"

"<No, it is going to be alright; I won't let you die,>" Elaine assured, the tears slipping from her eyes even as she smiled.

"<Elaine?>" Acies stated in a questioning tone, but she ignored him as she leaned in to set her forehead against the goddess's.

"<You may take my majick. I give it to you freely,>" she said. In her heart, Elaine whispered. *I am sorry, Elan. I am sorry, Maevra. I am sorry... Isa.*

"<Elaine!>" Acies shouted.

"<I cannot let a daughter lose her mother when she needs her most!>" Elaine shouted back.

"<You cannot. Maevra...>"

She wheeled on him. "<It was the same choice Maevra made! She sacrificed herself for another...>"

"<She sacrificed herself for *you!*>" He pointed at her. "<For *you.*>"

"<And you want me to live with that!>" She turned back to the goddess. "<And maybe it was for this. To bring back the gods for the world's sake.>"

"<Thank you, thank you, thank you,>" Nymphaea wept. She embraced Elaine's face, laying her hands firmly against each side.

"<Elaine, stop!>" Acies shouted. She could see him bolting toward her now, his hand reaching out to snatch her away.

The Scion of Isa raised a hand, summoning a stream of water from the ichor and blood all around. Acies was repelled and slammed against the wall where he dropped. Dazed, he tried to stand up, only to fumble, his arms and legs not working properly.

They didn't have much time.

"<Do it quickly,>" Elaine said, replacing Nymphaea's hands. The Scion closed her eyes. "<Will it hurt?>"

"<No, not when given freely.>"

The Ka'in Princess took one final breath in, then blew it out gently. She could feel the goddess pulling on her soul, taking the energy from her.

I do not want this! Elaine thought, the sudden truth overwhelming her intention. *I truly do not want to die!*

Nymphaea spasmed. "<I cannot,>" the goddess said, shocked. Elaine snapped her eyes open. Nymphaea's eyes searched her face. "<You are not giving it to me freely.>"

Elaine knew it was true. In her heart of hearts... "I do not want to die," she whispered out loud, Ka'in words carrying her truth.

Then the goddess was ripped away from her.

"Acies, no!" Elaine screamed, reaching out for the goddess's fingers.

But it wasn't Acies.

Dakin dragged the goddess back by her hair and robe. She fought him, but he wrapped an arm around her head to lock it in place while opening the space of her neck wide for him. He sank his teeth in as she screamed. Gold blood burst from the wound, shooting out rays of light with it. Nymphaea struggled, but she was so weak. He was eating her life away.

Elaine moved before she realized it. Water blasted up like a slicing wave, hitting Dakin squarely. He stumbled back but

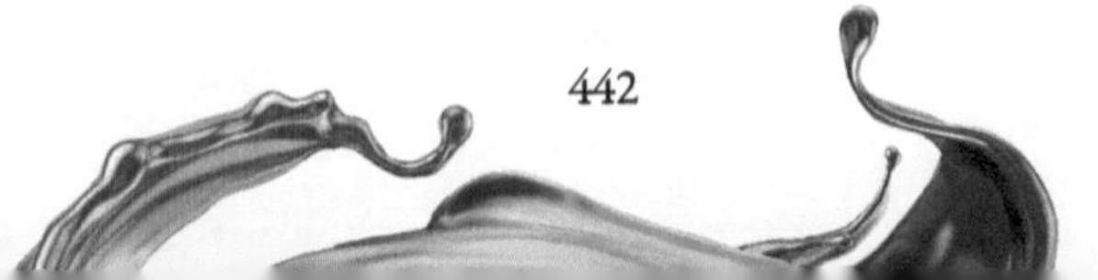

only a few steps, sputtering as his body reacted to drowning even though he in truth couldn't anymore.

Nymphaea dropped to the floor, and Elaine stepped over her, placing herself squarely between them. She pulled the bejeweled knife from inside her shawl, holding it out before her in a defensive stance.

The fat demon stared at her, huffing air, looking like a half-drowned badger. But there was light in his eyes, the unnatural glow as the majick from Nymphaea infused him.

"<Elaine,>" he croaked. "<You are alive.>" He seemed surprised, trying to comprehend what was going on, but he had none of his advisors to tell him. All around, the bodies of the dead were piled, but he looked about as if expecting them to stand up.

"<Why are you here?>" he finally asked, returning back to Elaine. "<Have you returned to me?>"

"<No,>" Elaine said, wrinkling her face, truly disgusted. "<I will never return to you. Ever.>"

"<You know, you did not follow the plan,>" he stated, grabbing at Elaine's knife hand to wrench the blade out of her hand. "<You were supposed to make me a god, and you did not follow through.>"

Out of the corner of her eye, Elaine saw Acies, who had finally gained his feet, do nothing as he stood there leaning against the wall watching.

Dakin held up her knife to examine it, only to then notice his own hands covered in gold blood. He turned them over as they glittered brightly. "<This will make me a god, won't it? The blood of the city itself.>"

He chuckled, his laughter ringing against the dead walls. They were no longer in the arena. The room had reformed into the feasting hall at the fortress.

Dakin licked the gold from his hand and ecstatically shuddered. "<I feel so powerful!>" he continued, oblivious to anything outside of himself.

"<Mama!>"

Everyone turned to the doorway to see the little goddess, Rosamund, standing there with Elan and an Anon woman... Amira. Elaine was surprised to see the merchant's daughter, but could not think any more about it in that moment.

Her brother stood straight and proud, his god-weapon notched with an arrow that he sighted straight at Dakin.

Yet the little goddess immediately took off running toward her fallen mother.

"<No, Rosamund, stop!>" Elaine screamed, but it was too late. Even as Amira reached to stop the little goddess, she moved with god-like speed, too fast to be caught.

Time seemed too slow to Elaine as she watched with perfect clarity.

Dakin lunged at the vulnerable child goddess, the jeweled dagger held high, also moving faster than Elaine could.

"No!" Elaine screamed.

There was a clang.

In the next blink, she saw Acies standing between Dakin and the little goddess. Vills blocked the jeweled dagger just inches above the nose of the shocked child goddess. Dakin shifted his hateful gaze up from the little creature along the length of Vills up to Acies's face.

"<You.>"

"<Me,>" Acies said and punched the fat demon in the face with his off hand.

Dakin spun away, and an arrow bloomed out of his back. He bellowed as the jeweled dagger went skittering across the stone floor.

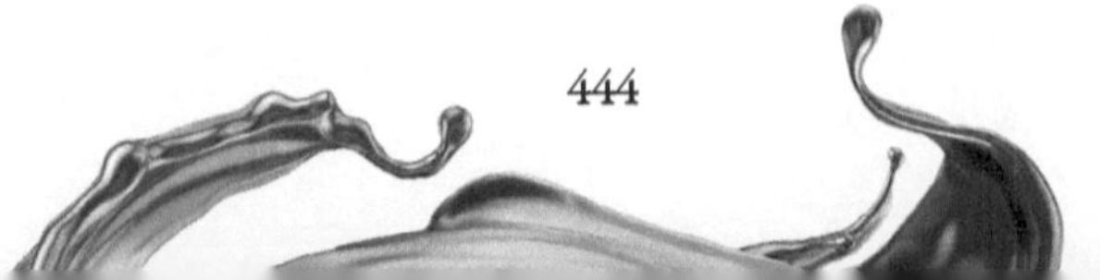

444

"Ka'in! Catch!" Acies grabbed the little goddess with one arm and bodily flung her back toward Elan. Her brother barely managed to drop his bow in time to catch her.

Acies barely had time to react before Dakin was on his back, sinking his teeth into the Demon Lord's neck. This time black blood flowed, mixing with Nymphaea's gold. Acies struggled, but Dakin only chewed, the blood gushing. Together, they stumbled, gaining momentum so that Acies managed to slam his attacker hard into the wall. Dakin released. Acies shoved off and spun around, bringing Vills back up, slouching over in a warrior's stance.

"<I am the Lord over Gods and Demons!>" Dakin crowed laughter, slurping the black and gold blood up off his chin, his few wounds and injuries disappearing in a flash of power.

Elaine could tell Acies had spent too much of his own majick as well on his fight with Nymphaea. He was weakened. Suddenly, her demon stumbled, dropping Vills's point but refusing to let go of the handle as he flopped against one of the upset tables from the feast. He slid down the flat side, Vills slanting across his body.

"<You,>" Dakin sneered, and he stalked over toward Acies. "<You killed me. And now I am going to kill you in return!>"

Acies tried to defend, but Dakin was too fast. The demon swung, backhanding across Acies's face. The Demon Lord's head snapped, slamming into the wood behind and cracking the table in two under the force.

"<Dakin, stop it!>" Elaine shouted, but her words had never stopped Dakin before.

"<Did you fuck my woman, demon?>" Dakin spat and continued to swing his fists, hitting Acies back and forth.

"<Dakin, leave him alone. It is me that you want!>" Elaine crossed the space, grabbing her former master's shoulder. He stopped, but not before spitting on Acies at his feet. Black blood spilled down the Demon Lord's face as he flopped to his side at last, Vills falling over him so that it leaned over his body, as if the sword intended to continue guarding him as best it could.

Dakin studied Elaine's face, his eyes asking questions of her. Gently, he stroked the back of his hand along her cheek in the tender way he did sometimes when he was in one of his better moods.

Elaine let him, unflinching.

"<I have missed you, my Ka'in Princess,>" he said with so much feeling it made Elaine sick. "<I do not think I can live without you. But I cannot let you live either, not after how you betrayed me.>"

"<Do not worry, Dakin,>" Elaine said, giving him her smile, the one she had trained that pleased him the most. "<I know a way I can be by your side forever.>"

His eyes twinkled, excited as a child. "<How?>"

She plunged the other knife, the one Acies had won for her, into his chest.

"<I bind you, demon,>" Elaine said, her godspoken words echoing, remembered from a deeper memory, igniting from the deeper power within herself.

She could feel her will battling with his.

Dakin blinked at her, the stars still flickering in his eyes before he looked down to stare at the handle coming out of his chest.

With a huge grunt, Elaine pushed harder, forcing the knife in, inch by painful inch. He stumbled backward and fell against the wall.

Still she kept pushing, forcing the handle in. "<Demon, I bind you!>

Her hands disappeared into Dakin's chest.

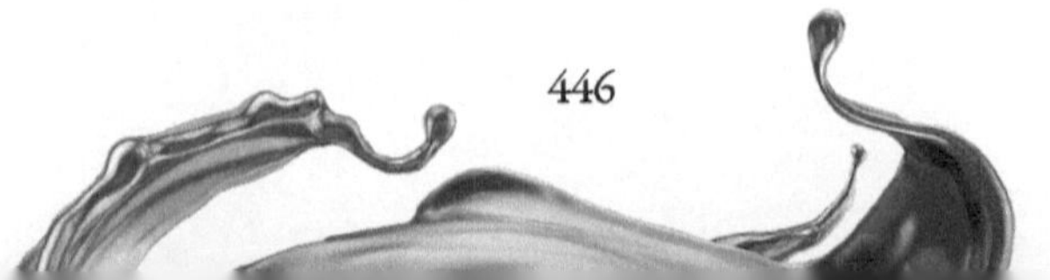

"<No!>" Dakin whimpered as he tried to grab her arm to stop her.

"<Demon!>"

His eyes met hers, full of fear. "<Elaine, please,>" he begged.

Her own glowed fiercely. "<I bind you.>"

Darkness erupted from the wound as the end disappeared into him.

The heat blazed over her skin. She knew her hands were burning away as the knife tore through into the heart of his raw majick. Still Elaine held on. She howled from the intensity. Dakin howled with her. The world shook.

And then the darkness faded.

For an eternal second, all was still.

She felt she could barely move, but Elaine forced herself to pull the knife out of Dakin's body.

It had changed, just like Vills's sword had. It was now covered in jewels larger and darker, worked into a handle of sweeping silver and gold.

Dakin slumped against the wall. He was still aware, his glassing eyes staring at the knife in Elaine's hand.

"<What... What is happening?>" he asked, his voice small as a child's.

"<Look, Dakin, you are now a god,>" Elaine lied, kneeling down in front of him, holding out the knife. "<Look.>"

His eyes were filled with wonder at the sight of the beautiful weapon. "<Thank you,>" he breathed. "<Thank you,> Elaine." Then Dakin the Would-Be God broke apart, his body dissolving into particles of darkness, melting away into the ground.

Elaine stood up, still holding the demon-weapon in her hand.

It was over. It was truly over, but...

She turned back to Nymphaea, lying in repose on the ground. Gently, Elaine shook her, searching all over the deity's body for signs of life.

"<Mama,>" the little goddess said as she approached the side of her mother, her godspeech sounding so small.

At the sound of her child's voice, Nymphaea fluttered her eyes open, seeking and finding the small, beautiful face. "My daughter," she whispered hoarsely. "My treasure." She lifted her hand to press against the little girl's face, and Rosamund held it to her cheek with both hands desperately.

"<Mama, I do not want you to die,>" the little girl moaned.

"<Yes, dear, I know. I do not want to leave you either, but all things die in the end. Only the God Beyond is eternal,>" Nymphaea whispered.

"<No, Mama, no!>"

Elan set his hand on Elaine's shoulder. She didn't have to look at him to know it was her twin. She clasped the hand back.

Amira came up behind Rosamund, setting her hands gently on the small goddess's shoulders as she wept in the unreserved way of small children. Nymphaea's hand left her daughter's to reach out toward the Anon woman.

"<Please, Amira, daughter of my city. I know I have failed you in so many ways, but will you forgive me by taking my daughter and keeping her safe as your own?>" she asked in Amira's language.

A complicated look passed over Amira's face, one that Elaine understood all too well, before she nodded.

Nymphaea then pressed a finger into Amira's forehead. "<I ... bless ... you as ... godmother,>" Nymphaea said the power echoing through the godspeech. Her breathing becoming jagged as she struggled. Then Nymphaea stretched up and pulled from Amira's forehead the beautiful Coronet of Icathor from her brow.

This she held out to Elaine. "<Time is almost … up. Please.>"

Elaine took the coronet, meeting the goddess's eyes, understanding passing between them. Then she glanced at Amira, who also understood. She pulled Rosamund away.

Elaine pressed the coronet into the wound at Nymphaea's side. The goddess moaned and Rosamund screamed, but that was all the sounds that were made as the metal disappeared into the wound. Again, Elaine felt the burning sensation in her fingers as the remaining power within churned the metal. Once the light faded, she pulled out the goddess-crown. The coronet had been transformed into a proper crown. The tiers around the crown were squared like the buildings of Icathor, wrought with jewels all around.

"<It is beautiful,>" Nymphaea breathed, looking at the creation. "<Thank you.>" She took the crown from Elaine's fingers and brought it toward her daughter. "<Rosamund,>" she called. The little goddess rushed to her once more, and her mother nestled the crown atop her child's golden curls. "<You are now the patron Goddess of Icathor. And now, I will always be with you.>"

The goddess burst into a million fragments of light. The lights swirled around, touching everyone in the room with light whispers of love and peace and gratitude. Rosamund stood among them, her eyes closed in peace, each light making the jewels of her crown shine. Then they swept up and away, passing through every stone of the room. For a moment, the building came alight. For no reason Elaine could understand, she could see without the walls of the room to the whole city around the hill of Icathor, every building touched and purified by the goddess's light.

Then all returned to normal. The bodies were still there, strewn about the room. The damage was still done, but there was no trace of demonic darkness cursing the city for all time.

Elaine felt exhausted.

She turned to face her brother. He couldn't smile for her, but he pulled her close and hugged her hard.

"It is over," he whispered in Ka'in, but she knew it was not.

It never could be.

CHAPTER 48

Elaine stood over Acies, still unconscious on the bed.

"You should just leave him to die," Elan said.

"You know I cannot. My life is bound to his," she said simply.

She fingered the pommel of the knife, shaped into an unfamiliar symbol to her, an eye above a crescent moon. She could never bring herself to take it off or leave it alone for a moment. He would always be with her now, but now as a weapon instead of a wound.

"We have had no sign of Barus," Elan said after a moment. "We're now sure that many of Dakin's other warriors are missing as well. If I was him, I would have taken them with to form a band."

Elan turned to walk out onto the balcony of what had once been Dakin's room overlooking what had once been Dakin's fortress. It was no one's fortress now.

Elaine joined her brother on the balcony to gaze down at the streets. All the remaining people were working busily, building, repairing, and purging out the bodies, Anon and Ka'in, as well as the other slaves who were all now free.

"The leaders of the Anon are all dead," Elaine muttered, watching two Anon with a cart distributing food from the granaries.

"What's that?" Elan asked.

"I am just amazed at how willing they all are to work side by side with those they thought of as slaves. I suppose it is because all of their leaders are dead."

"Except Amira," Elan muttered.

"Yes, except her."

"They are all following *her* lead," Elan continued. "They lost as many lives, if not more, to Dakin. It has broken a lot of spirits, and no one has any idea how to mend them." He sighed. "But for now, they are accepting all this."

"Because we hold the granaries," Elaine said.

"Because we hold the life-giving granaries, even if they resent us for it," Elan agreed. "The Prince and Princess of the Ka'in. Titama would be shitting himself right now if he knew how things turned out."

Elaine nodded but did not dwell on her fallen old beau for a moment. She thought instead of the actions they had taken quickly after entrapping Dakin. They had freed the Ka'in people, especially the warriors, as fast as possible. Amira had left almost immediately, going to merchant houses and not coming out since. There was no stirring or hint of armed animosity coming from there, and all offers of food and supplies were accepted with polite thank yous.

A knock at the door disturbed the twins' reverie.

"Excuse me, lady and lord," a Ka'in woman said, opening the door to lean in. "The messenger from the Lady Amira has just arrived."

The twins exchanged a mirrored pair of looks then Elaine said, "Thank you. We will be right there."

Elan nodded agreement and went to the side room to fetch his god-weapon. It had broken in the fight with Dakin, the string unhooked from the pair of flywheels so it would not fire again, but Elan was determined to figure out how to fix it. For now, it made a very clear symbol of authority to those around them. The Ka'in Prince had the favor of the gods.

For Elaine, it was Flicker, back in its symbol of Isa pendant which hung around her throat.

Elaine exited first and started down the hallway. Other people, the former slaves of the house who continued on in their same jobs, all stopped and bowed to Elaine as she passed, heralding her with "Scion" in respect. It felt odd, but there was no taking it back now. All the Ka'in knew her to be the Scion of Isa, and after everything that happened, she needed every shred of political power that status could muster.

It was also why she received honors before her brother, but he did not seem to mind. He even chose to walk two steps behind her for that reason.

They made their way down to the receiving room. Ka'in guards were in position on either side of the door and at the foot of the stairs leading up to the throne. Bile coated the back of Elaine's throat as she mounted those steps to sit upon it. Elan followed and took a position over her shoulder. While it all felt disingenuous, she had no idea what they faced.

"Bid them enter," Elaine declared once she was settled and held her breath.

The messenger was Anon, a scribe if she read his dress correctly. He entered and bowed before them, so that was a good start.

"I hail the Princess and Prince of the Ka'in," he declared in a strong cultured voice, speaking Ka'in himself surprisingly well.

Elaine couldn't help her eyebrows as they bobbed up toward her hairline.

The messenger continued. "I bring a message from the Lady Amira of Anon." He held up an official clay tablet.

Not knowing what else to do, Elaine gestured with her hand. "You may read it."

That seemed to be the right answer because he held it before him with practiced ease and began.

After some flowery language, he translated the letter from Anon to Ka'in, "I, Lady Amira, so appointed by my people the Anon, and the godmother of the patron Goddess of the City of Icathor, do reach out to ask for terms from the new rulers of Icathor in the hopes that peaceful settlement may be reached between our peoples. We understand that we have shared in the suffering with the Ka'in people and would seek to find a path forward into the future of Icathor. We request a time and place to meet and discuss this proposal at your earliest convenience."

Elaine and Elan looked at each other for a long time as the scribe waited patiently for an answer.

"We will discuss and respond," Elaine finally said. "If you will please wait without."

As if he expected this, the scribe bowed and turned to leave. The guards shut the door after him.

"Well, this was more than I expected," Elaine said, leaning forward to rest her elbows on her knees.

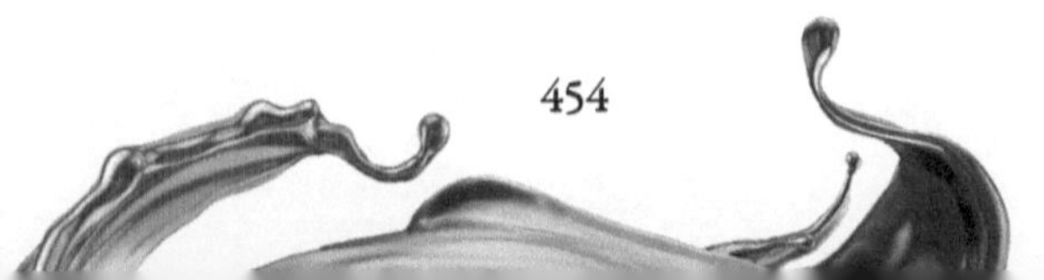

Elan took a few steps down the stairs and sat himself to face his sister. "Did you hear that? The godmother of the patron goddess."

"Well, she is," Elaine said, tapping her fingers against her lips.

"She is going to make a bid for the throne of Icathor, and we are all going to be right back where we were before," Elan grumbled.

"We do not know that," Elaine countered.

"No, which is why we are going to meet with her, are we not?" Elan sighed.

"Aye, I agree, brother."

"<Marriage,>" Elan stated flatly, spitting out the Anon word as if it tasted foul. Of all the things he thought he was going to hear, that was not one of them.

He stared at her across the table of the council room beside the receiving room. It had seemed the logical place for the meeting after Amira agreed to come with an armed guard in tow and assurances that neither she nor her people would be harmed.

"<Yes, marriage,>" Amira said as if it were the only logical and reasonable course of action.

"<Between us?>" Elan continued, still wrapping his head around it. He gestured between them. "<Between you and me?>"

"<Between the godmother of the patron Goddess of Icathor and the Prince of the Ka'in who has conquered and slayed the tyrant Dakin and so can claim the city as his by conquering rights,>" Amira stated, holding her head up regally. "<You are a liberator, and I can convince my people to follow you if I am by your side.>"

Elan stood there flabbergasted. "<Marriage between a Ka'in and an Anon?>"

"<There are already plenty of people in Icathor who can claim parentage from both—>"

"<Through force,>" he sneered.

"<And the plain and simple fact is there are not enough people to save Icathor unless we come together,>" Amira continued undeterred.

The two sides stared each other down hard. Elan wanted to fling the Anon out of that place and never look back. Judging from her wrinkled nose and the way she did not touch anything the Ka'in had touched, she must have felt the same way.

It was Elaine who started laughing. "<Agreed,>" she said.

Elan jumped out of his skin and wheeled on his sister. "What?!"

Amira's own eyes swiveled to the princess in confusion.

Elaine smiled at her. "<Among our people, it is the senior-most woman of the household who decides the marriages for our families. So, yes, I agree. Elan will take you as his wife.>"

Elan felt his jaw moving up and down, but no sound would come out. His brain just did not seem to be able to form a coherent argument as everything in his upbringing obeyed. Elaine *was* the senior-most woman of his house.

"<It is the right decision, but don't think for a moment I make this offer out of anything but necessity,>" Amira said to Elan. She stood then, her face very grave. Elaine's joviality faded, and the grip on Elan's heart renewed.

Amira continued, "<We are in more danger now than ever before. A danger more serious than finding food and restoring trade, and both of those are of the utmost importance. For all

his evil, Dakin's presence here protected us from one thing, and now that thing will come for us.>"

"<What one thing?>" Elan asked, furrowing his brow.

"<You wanted Dakin captured alive,>" Elaine said as if she already knew.

The Anon sighed and shook her head. "<Not wanted—needed. We needed Dakin alive because of the High King to the south. When Dakin first arrived here in Icathor, he came with a sealed promise from the High King that should he ever be killed by the merchants up here, then the High King would come and wipe us all off the face of the world. It was a way to keep us in line and assure that we would not overthrow the bastard immediately. He was not liked at all in the south, but he was a part of a very powerful and loyal family to the High King. As long as Dakin lived, I believed that we could negotiate an alternate outcome.>"

Elan felt his knees go, and he sat back on his chair. This was the secret that Titama had kept from him and the rest of the Ka'in. Elan could not fault him for it either. The Ka'in Prince leaned forward in his chair, setting his elbows on his knees as he dropped his head into his hands. "Oh, Goddess. Oh, Goddess," he murmured back and forth. It was just like with Maevra. He had condemned all their people when he thought he had been doing the right thing.

Amira resumed her seat again, assured that the gravity of what she had come to tell them had been properly conveyed.

"<I see,>" Elaine said.

At her tone, he lifted his head. She did not seem to feel the same despair he did. Instead, his sister's gaze was far away and contemplative. Slowly, she reached for her belt and pulled out the dagger she now called "Dakin," and she set it carefully on the table. "<Then I must take him south,>" she said.

"No!" Elan barked out as if someone had punched the word out of his stomach. The two women looked at him.

"<I do not believe a knife will appease the High King,>" Amira countered, her eyebrows pursing together as if Elaine was crazy.

"<Dakin became a demon, and I cast that demon into this knife. I will bring this knife and our story to the High King and petition him for his mercy,>" Elaine responded patiently. "<I am not saying that I know it will work, but it is a chance, and it may buy you time to prepare.>"

Now she looked at Elan, her eyes willing him to understand. "<You will wed Amira and do the hard work of uniting the people here. A common enemy is the only reason this union is even possible.>" She gestured between Amira and himself, and the fist around his heart clenched tighter.

He knew she was right.

"<Elaine, this is not your burden,>" Elan tried to say, but she laid her hand over his. They were the same age, she only minutes older, and yet her hand seemed small against his larger one. And she was expected to carry the world.

"<Do we have an agreement?>" Elaine said, turning her head with all the confidence and gravity of a queen to Amira, who matched her.

Amira nodded, then said in Ka'in. "We do."

Elaine stepped into the sanctuary of the little temple. The place already felt so different in the absence of the former goddess, but she approached the statue that stood in the middle of the space with all the reverence it deserved. She looked up at the woman carved in stone.

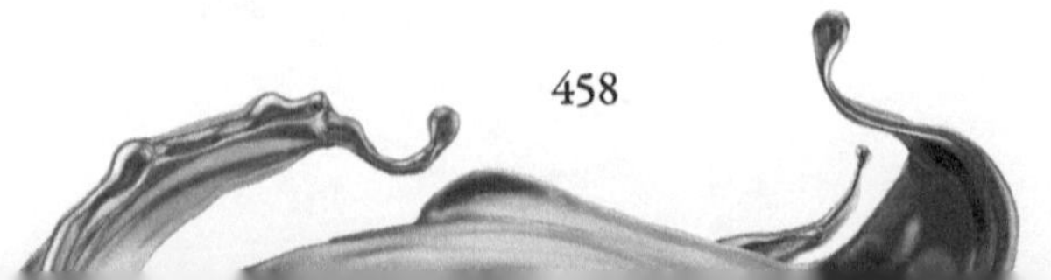

"Her face has changed, has it not?" Sarai's voice asked, the Ka'in words echoing slightly as she came to stand next to the Ka'in Scion. The older woman limped a little; she was far from recovered, but she did not seem any less diminished.

"Aye, I would say so," Elaine agreed. "I do not think she had a crown before."

"I believe this is what our little goddess will look like when she is fully grown." Sarai reached out to adjust a flower that was threatening to fall off the plinth. "The children have been bringing these to her every day. They often play in here, though even they are more somber than children should ever have to be."

"And I am leaving when all of you need me most," Elaine said bitterly.

"No, daughter of Isa. You have your work to do, and we have ours. And I bless you for it." Sarai squeezed Elaine's shoulder. "And you will not be alone." She turned her to look back toward the entryway.

The reedy man from Sarai's hut stood there, and he looked so different from when she had first met him. The sour bitterness was muted on his face, showing an otherwise fine man underneath. More interestingly, buds were growing across the pate of his bald head the same color of the feathers that covered the backs of his now bare arms. "This is Ellam. He is a Punite from the south. He wishes to go with you, to guide you through."

Elaine's instinct was to object, but she knew it would be pointless. "<Thank you, Ellam,>" she said, switching to Anon since they both spoke it, nodding her head toward the Punite.

He nodded in return and, with a voiceless request from Sarai, went back outside to wait.

"There is something else," the once-priestess added. "I want to thank you for leading me back to my path."

"You are a priestess again?"

"Yes my lady, but not just of Isa." Sarai raised her eyes. "I will always hold her in reverence, but now my call is to be a priestess to the goddess who needs me."

Now knowing if it was wrong or right, Elaine laid a hand on Sarai's head. The older woman closed her eyes in serenity at the touch and something, some energy, passed between them. A tear escaped Sarai's eyes. "Thank you," she whispered. "Thank you."

Tears threatened Elaine's own eyes.

Then Sarai straightened, capturing Elaine's hand in her two of her own. "There is something I need to show you before you leave."

Taking Elaine's hand, Sarai led her to the back of the sanctuary. There in the surface of the living stone were some faint carvings, almost impossible to make out in the dim light. But Sarai pressed them with her spare fingers.

"The wind will dance when the lady comes, the trees that bow before her, may songs of heaven all be sung, the day the Goddess of the River wanders," the priestess sang.

Letters ignited, filling the carved words, casting them into sharp relief. Elaine gasped as a section of the back wall shifted back and slid aside, revealing a set of steps leading down. Warm, wet air kissed all over Elaine's face. She grasped Flicker's icon, now hanging around her neck, the little spirit within buzzing under her fingers with excitement.

"Thank you," Elaine whispered, and then descended the steps into the hidden shrine to Isa.

Acies floats in a void, lost and alone.

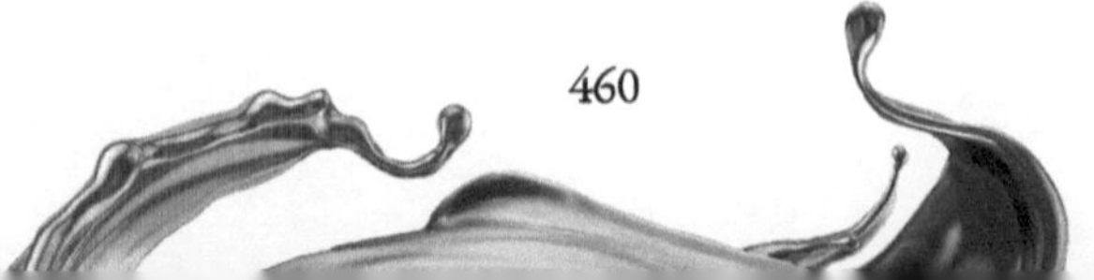

He wants to scream, but he can't. No sounds escape him. Is this what I deserve? He had taken Nymphaea's appeasement yet exacted his revenge all the same.

No. Nymphaea had violated the appeasement, attacking him first. His honor is clear. Besides, he saved her precious daughter...

There is no point to these arguments anyway.

Maybe this is what he deserves.

"*<What do I do?>*"

He hears her voice, her godspeech roughly accented, but he cannot see her. "*<Elaine?>*"

"*<How do I wake you up again?>*"

He is asleep. He is not back in that place. The relief of that revelation washes through him as he floats in the nothingness.

Then he isn't imprisoned.

He is dying.

Their promise.

"*<In exchange for your mind, body, or soul, I will give you my everything,>*" *he whispers.*

He feels her now. She touches his forehead, running her fingers through his hair. He focuses on that touch. "*<Where are you?>*" *he asks. He feels her now, beside him. He senses water. He tastes it, smells it, feels it over his skin. He floats in it beside her.*

"*<Why did you save Rosamund?>*"

The tension in that question is a sword over his heart. He knows if he answers wrong... But what is wrong? Does he tell the truth, or does he say what he thinks she wants to hear? What she thinks is right?

"*<You killed Nymphaea.>*"

"*<I got my revenge on Nymphaea,>*" *he answers. He will not apologize for that.*

"*<Was she one of those that betrayed you?>*"

"*<She condemned me before and did again now. You heard it yourself, did you not?>*"

"<I did.>"

"<I will not be dissuaded from my revenge.>"

"<Then why did you save her daughter?>"

He gathers himself. He knows what he must answer. "<Because she did nothing to me.>"

"<That is your reason?>"

"<I could not let Dakin empower himself more with her arete.>"

A pause. "<Is that really the reason?>"

What is she asking? What is she looking for? he wonders. "<I do not know,>" he finally says. "<I do not know why I saved her.>"

She takes his hand. He squeezes it. Her arete fills him as she merges with him. "<Come, Acies. It is time to wake up. We have much to do.>"

CHAPTER 49

EPILOGUE

BARUS PULLED UP THE HORSE AT THE SOUND OF THE rumbling thunder. Off in the distance, darker clouds were consuming the lighter ones, flashing angry in their forward march. The storm would be on them soon, and if it wasn't a guaranteed death behind him, Barus would not be venturing into the storm god's own wrath. Next to him, his companion pulled up, his own stolen horse whickering in protest at the rough treatment.

"What is wrong?" Athorn demanded, the Ka'in tracker's eyes darting about fearfully.

"Nothing," Barus, once called the Shield, lied. He turned back to look back over the grasses at Icathor, now barely a hill in the distance.

"We are almost to the river," Athorn stated as he nudged his horse forward, parting the grasses before him.

Barus caught sight of a snake slithering away, which sent a shiver down his spine. It was not merely snakes that hid themselves in the grasses. He stared at the Ka'in's back, thinking on the strange circumstances that had brought the two unlikely companions together.

"How is your head?" Barus asked.

"Concerned for my well-being, Anon?" Athorn said derisively.

"It matters not if you die on me, only that you find me the route to the south," he replied. The Ka'in curled a lip, but that suited Barus just fine. They were companions of convenience, and he hadn't decided if he should not kill the Ka'in before he reached Lady Eveline, Lady of the Fortress of Morna and older sister to the Lord Dakin.

Barus's only hope now.

"How much farther, Ka'in?" the former general demanded, urging his horse after.

"Many days," Athorn muttered. "Once we are in sight of the fortress, we part ways."

Barus shook the coil of silver just out of the sleeve of his shirt, letting it gleam dully in the gray light. "As promised," he agreed.

The Ka'in nodded and set the horse to a trot. Barus laid a hand on the skull of Razal, tied into a bloody bag to his saddle. It stank, but he could not let it go. He clicked at the horse. They had to hurry.

The sky rumbled again as the demons watched from the grass, tasting the scent of trailing demon majick on the wind.

END OF BOOK

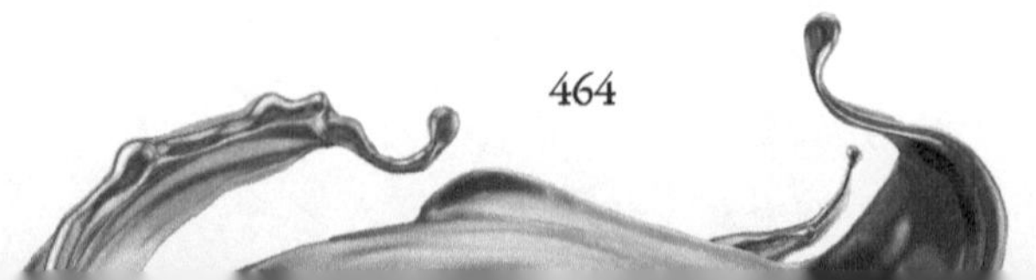

STUDY QUESTIONS

1. What does it mean to sacrifice? Is it a sacrifice if another person is made to do it?

2. Would you have taken Acies's deal?

3. Should Elan have made a deal with the Protector of the Forest? What could he have done instead?

4. Does Acies have a choice taking the life force of other beings?

5. What made Acies a demon and Vills not?

6. Why do you think so many of the Anons are allowing Dakin and his demons to destroy their lives? Why aren't they resisting?

7. What do you think actually happened to Isa Kai?

8. Do you think Elan and Amira can rebuild a better Icathor? What challenges do they face?

9. Whose side is Acies really on?

10. Where do you think the story is going from here?

AUTHOR BIO

Beyond the smashing success of her inaugural, Amazon bestseller, *The Finder of the Lucky Devil*, Megan Mackie is the author of The Lucky Devil Series (urban fantasy/cyberpunk), the Dead World Series (Post Post Zombie Apocalypse), *The Adventures of Pavlov's Dog and Schrodinger's Cat* (Mid-grade science fiction) and the Working Mask series (wannabe superhero).

Her other work can be found on the Yonder app, where she has published three web novels, *Cookbooks and Demons* (paranormal demon romance), *Star Courier* (speculative Firefly-like fiction), and *Novantis* (steampunk political intrigue with sky pirates—think *Bridgerton* meets *Black Sails*). Outside of her own series, she is a contributing writer for the RPGs Legendlore and Legendlore: Legacies by Onyx Path Publishing and Sirens: Battle of the Bards through Apotheosis Studios.

When she isn't writing, she likes to play games—board games, puzzle boxes, RPGs, and video games. She lives in Chicago with her husband and children, two dogs, two cats, and her mother in the apartment upstairs. She also has a thing for iconic leather hats.

Whats the news, Barman?

Sign Up for Megan's Newsletter!

https://www.meganmackieauthor.com/newsletter

Also check out her free Wattpad novel!

https://www.wattpad.com/1423396171-i-can%27t-get-the-vampire-rogue-to-romance-me

**It was all fun, until she got
sucked into the game.**

Other Books By Megan Mackie

Urban Fantasy/Cyberpunk

The Lucky Devil Series
The Finder of the Lucky Devil
The Saint of Liars
The Devil's Day
The Digital Mage
Demonic Inc. – Coming Soon

The Saint Code Series
The Lost
Constable – Coming Soon

Mid-Grade Science Fiction

The Adventures of Pavlov's Dog and Schrodinger's Cat
Maxwell's Demon

The Ship of Theseus - Coming Soon
Sniffy the Virtual Rat – Coming Soon

Post Post-Zombie Apocalypse

Dead World
The Prisoner of the Dead
The Journey to Naraka – Coming Soon
The Damned Road – Coming Soon

Superhero

Working Masks
The Vilification of Aqua Marine
The Indemnification of Black Heart - Coming Soon

Epic Fantasy

Silverblood Series
Silverblood Scion

www.ingramcontent.com/pod-product-compliance
Lightning Source LLC
Chambersburg PA
CBHW061037310726

48969CB00004B/993